ALSO BY DARRYL BOLLINGER

The Cure
Satan Shoal
The Care Card
The Pill Game
A Case of Revenge
The Medicine Game

THE HEALING TREE

A MEDICAL THRILLER

Darryl Bollinger

JNB
PRESS

JNB Press
Waynesville, NC

www.jnbpress.com

Printed in the United States of America

First Trade Edition: February 2021

ISBN 978-0-9989975-2-0

In memory of Nina Childs

THE
HEALING
TREE

Oh, what a tangled web we weave, when first we practice to deceive!

—Sir Walter Scott

1

Life wasn't fair, Justin Reeve thought, hiking in the same woods where he and his sister Karen had rambled so often. It was a beautiful fall day in the Great Smoky Mountains National Park beneath a Carolina-blue sky. Three hours east, she lay in a sterile hospital room, fighting for her life.

The leaves were just beginning to turn, portending the approaching winter. Senescence, the botanists called it. Karen was also changing, but unlike the trees, she would not awake in spring. For her, winter signaled death, not hibernation.

Red berries caught his eye as he walked the steep, narrow trail. They belonged to a small tree that looked like an *Ilex collina,* some distance below. Botany had long been Justin's hobby, and he wanted to get a closer look.

Focusing on the tree, Justin didn't see the half-buried chunk of granite poking up in the shadows. He tripped, and with arms flailing, somehow managed to keep from falling. Without his hiking stick, he'd have done a face plant or, worse, tumbled down the drop-off.

He heard a girlish laugh and turned to look at the petite brunette a few steps behind him. Alice, his fiancée, was shaking her head.

"One day, you're going to fall off the mountain, looking at plants instead of where you're walking," she said.

"I know. Still thinking about Karen, I guess." He pointed in the direction of the plant responsible for his misstep and said, "I'm pretty sure it's a longstalk holly. You don't see those often."

The ten-foot-tall shrub grew only at higher elevations and was on the IUCN Red List. The list, compiled by the International Union for Conservation of Nature, was an inventory of threatened species.

Spread out over half a million acres, the Park contained more than 19,000 species and was one of the most diverse plant-rich areas in the world. Although more than eleven million visitors a year came to GSMNP, most saw only a fraction of it. Access to much of it was difficult and only for hardcore hikers. To Justin, who grew up in the area, it was his backyard. And his therapy.

Late yesterday afternoon, Dr. Stewart—Karen's oncologist—had called to tell him that he may have to delay next week's treatment. He said they'd discuss it further Sunday when Justin went over to see her. When he got home yesterday evening, he and Alice had stayed up late talking about Karen's condition.

"I know you're worried about her," Alice said. "You didn't sleep well last night." She stepped over and put her arms around his neck, holding him close.

He buried his head on her shoulder, tears sliding down his cheeks. They'd met their freshman year at the University of North Carolina at Chapel Hill. Justin was pre-med, and Alice wanted to be an investment banker. Though on different tracks, their paths continued to cross throughout undergraduate school.

After graduation, his friend's dad offered him a job as a pharmaceutical scientist at Nuran, a small lab in Western North Carolina. It was a safe choice. Home. He accepted the offer, never explaining to Alice why he'd changed his mind about medical school. He was ashamed to tell her about how he'd made a mistake at the reference lab where he worked, an error that could've caused a patient's death.

Soon after he settled in to his new job, he asked Alice to move in with him.

Justin stepped back, wiping his eyes. "I keep thinking there's something else I can do for her."

He knew Karen's treatment wasn't working. He'd tried to get her enrolled in a clinical trial for Tramorix, a new breast cancer drug Nuran was bringing to market, but she didn't meet the criteria. Now, he was trying to figure out other ways to get her the medicine.

Expanded access was a possibility. Sometimes called compassionate use, expanded access was a legal way to obtain an unapproved drug outside of clinical trials for patients that had run out of options. Karen certainly qualified.

Alice shook her head, her sad eyes conveying empathy. "You're doing all you can. Quit beating yourself up."

He took a swallow of water and offered some to her. She took a swig and handed it back.

"I'm glad we came hiking," he said, putting the bottle back in his pack. "I needed this."

He nodded downhill. "Let's bushwhack our way down there. I want to get a closer look at that tree."

She peered over the edge of the sharp drop-off, then looked back at him. "Are you crazy? We're supposed to meet Tsula and Atohi in town at six." The Cherokee couple were close friends of theirs.

Justin still struggled with some of the Cherokee names, including Tsula, pronounced "JOO-lah." He had known Atohi since they were kids, so "ah-TOH-hee" had never been a problem.

Justin surveyed the terrain and looked at his watch. "We've got time. I think we can circle down below it and come up from the other side." He pointed out where he'd last seen the plant. "C'mon. Let's go."

The going proved more challenging than he'd thought. Although his orienteering skills were above average, they still hadn't found the holly after twenty minutes of rock scrambling and fighting the thick vegetation. He was reluctant to use the machete attached to his belt, trying to preserve the native plants as much as possible.

They stopped for water and a break. "We have got to leave," Alice said. "We're going to be late."

Justin consulted his map and compass. From their location, there appeared to be a shorter way back to the trail and his 4Runner. He took another drink and shook his head.

"Okay, I give," he said, sticking the map and compass in his pack.

He started in the new direction, parting the thick undergrowth blocking their path. After a few yards, he stopped, transfixed by the sight in front of him.

With delicate blue-tinted flowers and narrow, waxy green leaves, a lone tree stood in the small clearing. It was as if he'd stumbled upon an ancient forest shrine with the tree as the altar. The towering trees around it created a natural cathedral.

"What is it?" Alice said, almost running into him.

"Look." He pointed to the tree.

Her eyes followed his outstretched hand. "Wow. What is that?" She stared at it for a few moments, then said, "Is it some kind of rhododendron?"

Shaking his head, he said, "No, it's not a rhododendron, at least not like any I've ever seen."

Rhododendron maximum, commonly called rosebay rhododendron, was native to this area and one of the most common shrubs. While the plant he was looking at shared some of its characteristics, there were distinct differences.

This plant was blooming late in the year, unusual, but he knew of other plants in this area that bloomed this late and some even twice a year. The leaves were also smaller and opposite instead of alternating as on the rhododendron.

Puzzled, he stepped closer to examine the tree, reaching out to touch the leaves and bark. He took out his phone and snapped some pictures before cutting off a small branch, which he carefully placed in his backpack. After zipping the compartment, he slung the pack over his shoulders and looked at Alice.

"I've never seen anything like this. I don't have a clue as to what it is."

2

Justin opened the door to Frog Level Brewing for Alice. Located in the historic area by the same name, the microbrewery was the first in Waynesville.

"It would've been nice if we'd had a chance to shower and change," she said with a tight smile. They had come straight from the trailhead to meet their friends.

Justin didn't spot Tsula and Atohi inside and figured they were out back by the creek. They stopped at the bar where Justin ordered a Nutty Brunette for himself and Alice's glass of water.

When they stepped through the door to the deck, he saw their friends sitting at a creekside table. On the stage, a young guy with a ponytail sat on a stool, playing guitar, a tip jar at his feet. Justin recognized the tune as John Prine's *Please Don't Bury Me.*

"Sorry we're late," Justin said as they sat. "My fault," he added, trying to appease Alice.

"We're used to it," Atohi said. "We just got here ourselves." He held up an almost full glass of beer. "Just don't be late for the big day," he added, laughing.

Alice shot Justin a look, then said, "If he is, then it'll be a funeral instead of a wedding."

Everyone, including Justin, chuckled. Tsula took a sip of her beer and said, "Looks like you came straight from the woods."

Alice nodded toward Justin. "We did. Thanks to you-know-who, we didn't have time to change."

"Where did you go?" Atohi asked.

"Enloe Creek, below Hyatt Ridge," Justin said.

Justin and Atohi had hiked nearly all of the 800 miles of trails in the Park and camped in most of the backcountry sites. The familiar footpaths were metaphorical streets in their neighborhood.

"Any wildlife? Deer?" Atohi asked.

Justin shook his head. His friend was an avid hunter, always scouting the area for game. Deer season was approaching, and he knew that Atohi would be in the woods opening day.

"I saw fresh tracks but no deer. But, I did see this." He took his phone out of his pocket, pulled up the tree's pictures, then passed it over to Atohi.

"Look at this," Justin said. "I've never seen anything like it."

Atohi flipped through the pictures, then shook his head. "That's odd. I've never seen anything like that." He passed it over to his wife. "What is it?"

Tsula studied it and zoomed in on one of the pictures. She looked up at Justin. "Where'd you find this?"

He shrugged. "We were on our way back to the Hyatt Ridge trailhead. I thought I spotted a longstalk holly and wanted to take a closer look, so we went off the trail to find it. That's why we were late. We ran across this tree on our way back to the trail."

Tsula looked at it again, then handed the phone back to Justin. "Can you send that to me?"

"Sure." He pulled up Tsula's number and sent it to her, hearing the telltale *whoosh* on his phone.

"We saw only one tree like it," Justin said. "Do you know what—?"

Tsula's phone beeped before he finished his question, confirming receipt of the picture.

Atohi snorted and nodded at Justin. "This is a first. I've never seen the plant man stumped."

Tsula pulled up the photo on her phone and then shook her head. "I'm not sure, but something about it looks vaguely familiar. I'm sending the pic to Mom. She's a walking encyclopedia on the plants in the Qualla Boundary."

Qualla Boundary was the term for the area mistakenly called the Cherokee reservation by white people. It was the home of the Eastern Band of Cherokee Indians, unique in that it was not a reservation like others created by the U.S. government. The 57,000 acres are all that remains of a vast territory where the Cherokee lived long before the first European settlers arrived.

"I've got a small branch in my pack if you want to take it to her," Justin said.

As they were finishing their drinks, Tsula's phone beeped. She picked it up and read the message, then looked up at Justin.

Her stunned expression prompted Alice to ask, "Is everything okay?"

"Mom thinks she knows what it is."

"Why the surprised look?" Justin asked.

"She says the tree has been extinct for a hundred years."

"What?" Justin said.

Tsula nodded. "She wants us to meet her at the house."

"Now?" Atohi said. "Tell her we'll be home as soon as we finish here."

Tsula nodded and texted her mom, getting an immediate reply. "She said we could have snacks with her at the house."

Atohi looked at Justin and Alice.

"We haven't ordered food yet. Fine with me," Alice said.

They finished their drinks and drove to Atohi and Tsula's house in the Qualla Boundary, where only the Cherokee tribe members could own property. When they got to the modest house, sitting on two acres of land in the hills outside the town of Cherokee, Tsula's mother was waiting.

Mary Richardson was sitting on the porch, a small woven bag beside her. Justin always thought she'd aged gracefully, looking younger than her years. He'd questioned Tsula once about her name—Mary. Tsula had told him that many Cherokee had an English-sounding given name as well as a tribal name. Mary wanted her daughter to have a more traditional name, hence Tsula, Cherokee for "fox."

Mary stood to greet them. She was tall and thin, with the same dark hair and high cheekbones Tsula had inherited.

"Thanks for coming over on such short notice," she said.

"Good to see you." Justin held his upturned palms out in apology. "We're pretty grungy. We didn't have time to shower before we met them in town," he said, nodding toward Atohi and Tsula.

"I don't care," Mary said to him and Alice, hugging each of them. "Always good to see you both."

"We can sit out here," Atohi said, gesturing toward the chairs on the front porch.

"Something to drink?" Tsula asked the group.

After getting their guests' requests, she and Atohi disappeared into the house.

"What can you tell me about the tree we found?" Justin asked.

Mary shifted in her seat. "It looks similar to a tree I thought was long gone."

"Fascinating," he said. "What was it called?"

Mary hesitated. "I'm not sure."

"As much as I've hiked in the park, I've never seen anything like it. Tsula says you're a walking encyclopedia on plants in this area. I have a branch and flower in my backpack if you'd like to see it."

"I'd love to." Embarrassed, she continued. "Growing up in the Boundary, I'm familiar with many of them, but by no means an expert. I'd like to see it if you don't mind."

Tsula and Atohi reappeared with drinks and snacks as Justin went out to retrieve his pack.

"Sorry, I didn't have a chance to prepare anything more substantial," Tsula said as she placed the tray on the table. "Report took longer than usual, and I was late getting off work. I figured we'd eat at Frog Level." She shot her mother a look.

"I'm sorry, dear," Mary said. Tsula, a nurse at the Cherokee Indian Hospital, was still wearing her scrubs. "I hadn't eaten yet, but you could've eaten first, and I could've snacked. I feel bad. I just got excited when I saw the pictures."

Munching on a carrot, Alice said, "No worries. A lot of times during the week, all we do is snack for dinner. No problem."

Tsula smiled at her mom, lightening the mood, and said, "That's okay. You owe me dinner."

Atohi set a beer down at Justin's place, a glass of wine for Tsula, and waters for Mary and Alice. With the other beer, he stood, watching Justin return with his backpack.

On the porch, Justin opened it. He removed the branch, with flowers and leaves still attached, and handed it to Mary. No one spoke while she examined the specimen and set it on the table, nodding.

Mary reached into her bag and pulled out a small framed drawing. She studied it, then looked over at the branch. Then, she placed the picture on the table next to the small limb and sat back in her chair, inviting them to compare the two. The resemblance was indisputable.

"Oh my gosh, Mother," said Tsula, looking up at her. "That's why it looked familiar. This is the picture you have hanging in your bedroom."

Mary nodded. "Your Elisi drew this," she said, using the Cherokee term for a maternal grandmother.

She turned to Justin and Alice. "Was this the only tree?"

Justin nodded. "We didn't have much time to search, but I didn't notice any others nearby."

Mary picked up the branch, her voice cracking with emotion. "I never saw the actual tree. The Cherokee thought it extinct. When I was seventeen or eighteen, she told me that she was not much older than me the last time anyone had seen the tree. She gave me this drawing before she passed."

Justin picked up the drawing and examined it. The detail was extraordinary. It reminded him of the famous Harvard Glass Flowers, commissioned by the first director of Harvard's Botanical Museum, George Lincoln Goodale. Justin flipped it over and recognized Cherokee writing on the back.

"I recognize it as Tsalagi, but can you please translate?" he asked, handing it to Mary. He knew a few Cherokee words but was unable to decipher this.

Without looking at it, Mary glanced at Tsula then back at Justin. "She wrote a brief description of the plants she drew," she said, not volunteering to translate further.

Justin nodded. "Was there anything special about this one?"

Once again, Mary shot Tsula a look, indicating an unspoken communication between mother and daughter.

Justin continued. "I don't mean to be rude. It's just that you asked us to meet you here, so I figured it must be important."

Resigned, Mary responded. "In Cherokee lore, it's considered sacred."

"Sacred? How so?"

Mary shrugged off the question. "Like most Native Americans, the Cherokee thought many plants had medicinal properties, including this one. We thought it no longer existed. Where did you find it?"

Tsula interjected. "You said you were on the Enloe Creek Trail, right?"

"Yes," Alice said, nodding.

"In the Park," Justin added.

Tsula said, "Maybe you weren't actually in the Park. At certain points, that trail is close to the Boundary. If you were off-trail, you could've been in the Qualla without knowing it."

Justin shrugged. "It's possible. What difference would it make?"

Mary spoke to Tsula in Tsalagi, but Justin didn't understand what she said. Tsula nodded, then responded to her before turning to Justin.

"It's an important part of our culture," Tsula said. "Before you mention it to anyone, first give us a chance to determine if it's on Cherokee land."

"Sure. How do we do that?"

"Sam Bear," Mary said, this time in English, "is a close friend of mine here in the Qualla. He's a surveyor. If you show him where you found it, he could tell us."

Justin wondered why this particular tree was so important to the Cherokee. As Mary stated, the Cherokee thought many plants had medicinal value. Why was this one sacred? He wanted to ask more but felt that he was intruding.

"If you have him get in touch, I'll take him to the tree. And I won't tell anyone where it is."

3

The next morning, the soft glow of the hospital sign materialized in the dense fog, reminding Justin to exit the busy interstate. Karen was a patient at Wake Forest Baptist Medical Center, located in Winston-Salem, North Carolina. In another place, and in another life, a faulty lab test led her caregivers down the wrong path. When she finally arrived here, they discovered she had advanced breast cancer. It had metastasized and was now Stage IV.

Karen was an outlier at age thirty-four. For women in their thirties, the risk of breast cancer was less than one-half of one percent. Good odds, unless you happened to be in that group. He wondered if this were karma, payback for a mistake he'd once made as a lab tech when he was in school.

Justin exited I-40 and made his way to the nearest parking garage. He parked the tired 4Runner and took the walkway over to the Cancer Center.

Karen's treatment team had tried everything in their arsenal, but so far, the cancer was winning. The latest and last-ditch effort had been high-dosage methotrexate. HDMTX required giving lethal doses of methotrexate to kill the cancer cells, then administering Leucovorin to rescue the healthy cells. HDMTX was walking a tightrope, which required careful inpatient administration and monitoring as the body had to clear the toxic methotrexate before the next treatment.

He took the elevator up to the oncology floor. The doors opened, greeting him with the smells of sickness and death. He felt nauseous. It reminded him of his mother's last year of life, a revolving door of hospital visits as cancer cells ravaged her body.

When he got to Karen's room, he paused to confirm that her name was still outside the door. He took a deep breath and tapped lightly on the partially open door.

"Come in."

He smiled, recognizing his younger sister's voice. The only siblings in their family, they'd been close growing up. Karen had loved the mountains as much as he did, and they'd spent many hours hiking the numerous trails in Western North Carolina. He used to call her a mountain goat, the way she'd scamper up the steepest trails with him struggling to keep up.

Justin frowned when he realized how long it had been since they'd been able to do that. Shaking his head, he replaced the frown with a smile and entered the room.

Karen was reclining in bed, wearing her stocking cap with the covers pulled up around her neck. She had always been cold-natured, but the treatment had exaggerated that. Thanks to the methotrexate, she'd lost her hair several weeks ago.

Clear plastic tubes—connected to an infusion pump next to her bed—snaked under the covers, delivering various fluids to her weakened body. A monitor at her head softly beeped, displaying vital information.

"Hey, sis." Justin walked over to her bed and squeezed her arm.

"Brat," she said softly, managing a slight smile.

He had to grin. Karen had called him that since they were children, and the nickname had stuck.

He laid a couple of magazines on her bed. "Compliments of Jo. Great article in *Travel + Leisure* on Greece." Jo was one of the owners of the bookstore where Justin regularly shopped.

Karen scowled. "Do you read all of my magazines first?"

"Of course. Might as well."

"I'm going to call her and tell her to put them into a sealed box next time." A thin smile replaced the frown as she shook her head. "You're hopeless. How's Alice?"

"She's good and sends her love. She had to finish a report for her boss this afternoon. The bank auditors are coming in the morning."

Karen loved Alice, his fiancée, and the feelings were mutual. Alice was one of the few people Justin had dated who merited Karen's complete approval. A big plus in his book.

"How are you feeling?" he asked, a tone of seriousness creeping into his voice. Monday would be a week since her last treatment. The first few days after her weekly treatment were rough, but she usually began to feel human again by the end of the week. Today was Saturday, and she still looked frail.

Karen never complained, at least not to him. Justin wondered if the oncologist was going overboard with the methotrexate dosing, realizing this was his last chance at arresting the cancer. Although science formed the basis for dosage calculations, Justin knew there was a certain amount of alchemy involved.

She shook her head. "Tired. Every week it seems to take longer to recover. I can't believe it's almost time for the next one."

Every time he visited, she seemed weaker. Justin couldn't tell whether it was the treatment or the cancer or both.

He asked her what she wanted for lunch. The chemo had played cruel tricks on her taste buds. Foods she used to like, she could no longer tolerate. And, she wanted things she once shunned, like anything fried. Lately, she craved fried chicken from Sweet Potatoes, a favorite downtown Winston-Salem restaurant.

After she gave him her order, he left her room to get lunch. While waiting for the elevator, the doors opened, and Tina stepped out. Tina was the Nurse Practitioner assigned to Karen's case.

"Hi, Justin," she said, moving to one side of the opening to stop and chat. Like her boss, Dr. Stewart, Tina was direct and didn't sugar-coat things—traits Justin admired.

"I was just coming to see you. Dr. Stewart is tied up this afternoon, and he wanted me to update you," she said.

Tilting his head back toward Karen's room, he asked, "How's she doing?"

Her long pause spoke volumes. "Not as good as we would've hoped at this point. I just got her latest blood work. If her MTX levels haven't dropped significantly by in the morning, we're not going to be able to give her the next treatment."

This was not good news. Dr. Stewart had said he expected signs of improvement four to six weeks after treatments began. This week was her eighth.

"Have you rerun the tests?" he asked.

Before she could answer, Tina's pager went off. She immediately unclipped it from her pocket and read the small screen. "Sorry, I've got to run. I'll ask Dr. Stewart to call you when he can," she said as she hurried away.

The whole way to the restaurant, Justin couldn't stop thinking about what Tina had told him. Karen's treatment regimen was almost complete, and it wasn't working. Would they delay the next treatment, or worse, discontinue the MTX? If it had been early on, Stewart would probably wait. But this far along? Justin knew the answer.

He had to find a way to get Tramorix to Karen. What if he couldn't get enhanced access approved?

By the time he'd picked up two lunches and returned to the hospital, he'd resolved that they were going to have a pleasant lunch together and enjoy the remaining afternoon. He wasn't going to spoil it by mentioning his conversation with Tina.

The fragrance of the fried chicken dinners Justin carried filled the elevator, overcoming the hospital smell. Several passengers commented that some lucky person was getting something good for lunch.

Once in Karen's room, he sat on the bed with her as they enjoyed the still-warm fried chicken. Karen ate more than he thought she would, which pleased him, yet she didn't come close to finishing the lunch. Setting her fork down, she asked him about the wedding plans.

Alice wanted a simple ceremony on Waterrock Knob, a popular spot on the Blue Ridge Parkway. Hiking was what brought them together in the beginning, and a hike to Waterrock Knob had been their first date. Alice had asked Karen to be her maid of honor. Justin told her what little he knew of the plans.

"I hope I'm able to make it," Karen said. The sadness in her voice was depressing.

"You better be. I'm not carrying you up there."

That comment prompted a slight smile, and Karen said, "I'd hate to have to beat you up before your wedding." When they were younger, she would regularly thump him and never let him forget that she was the boss.

"Those days are long gone, sis." As soon as he said it, he regretted his choice of words. "I mean—"

"Stop. I know what you meant. You've been bigger and stronger than me for years, long before I got sick."

Tears welled up in his eyes. He tried to smile but couldn't. "Dammit," he said.

"I know." She squeezed his hand. "It sucks. Have you been hiking lately?"

Relieved to change the subject, he nodded. "We went yesterday. Enloe Creek."

She smiled. "That was always one of our favorite trails, near the Qualla. Not many hikers used it."

"We didn't see anyone else the entire time we were out. Perfect hiking weather. I wish you could've been with us."

"Me, too. No bears?"

Justin laughed. One of the few times he'd seen a bear in the Park had been on the Enloe Creek trail. With Karen.

"No bears. But, I saw a tree there I've never seen before." He pulled his phone out and showed her the picture.

She looked at it and shook her head. "What is it?"

He thought about his conversation with Tsula and her mother last night. "Some sort of sacred tree that the Cherokee thought was extinct. Tsula's mother recognized it but then got kind of cagey about telling me exactly why it was so important."

"Mom would've known what kind of tree it was."

Justin chuckled at the mention of their mother. With a musician husband, the family had needed a reliable source of income and benefits, so she'd taken a post office job. His father was always on the road, playing gigs wherever he could find them. While he was away, she would load Justin and Karen into the car and drive Western North Carolina's rural roads. She narrated the journey, pointing out the various plant life, and telling stories about how they fit into the native culture. Justin had inherited her love of plants.

"She probably would've," Justin said.

"Do you remember the last time we hiked?" Karen asked.

He nodded. "Last August. Mount Sterling." He wished that he'd known then that it would probably be their last hike together. It's a shame life didn't give you those kinds of warnings.

"I miss hiking with you," she said.

"I miss it, too." They were silent for a moment, then he asked, "You up for a movie?"

She nodded, and he cleared the bed. He noticed that she'd eaten less than half of her lunch. He pulled his chair up next to her. "I picked last time. It's your choice."

"*Serendipity*," she said.

He rolled his eyes. The movie, starring John Cusack and Kate Beckinsale, was one of her favorites. "I should've known. A chick flick," he said, teasing her.

When the movie was over, he looked up at the clock on the wall. It was time to head back home.

"Anything I can bring you when I come back?" he asked as he got ready to leave.

She shrugged. "A cure would be nice. Other than that, just you."

She flashed a glimmer of the mischievous smile that he hadn't seen in a while and added, "And quit reading my magazines."

Back in his SUV, Justin headed west on I-40, his thoughts returning to Karen. Time was running out.

His phone buzzed. He picked it up and looked at the screen. Dr. Stewart.

"Thanks for getting back to me," Justin said, putting the phone up to his ear, not bothering to put it on speaker. Besides, his aging vehicle didn't have that capability.

"Sorry, I didn't catch you before you left. I've only got a few minutes."

"Tina said it wasn't looking good for Karen's next treatment."

"Unfortunately, not." There was a pause, then Stewart continued. "We'll see where her methotrexate levels are tomorrow and reassess it then."

"What about applying for enhanced access? For Tramorix?"

Before Stewart could answer, the horn blasting in Justin's left ear startled him. Justin jerked the steering wheel to the right, narrowly missing the car beside him. The driver gave Justin the finger as he veered past on the shoulder to avoid a collision.

"You okay?" Stewart asked.

"Sorry. I almost ran someone off the road. I was asking about enhanced access for Tramorix?"

"Why don't you concentrate on driving and get home safely? I have someone waiting. I'll call you tomorrow, and we can discuss it then."

Leaving him little choice, Justin said, "Sure." He disconnected and put the phone back in the console.

Justin was disappointed. Stewart was stonewalling, not a good sign.

4

Nuran Labs occupied a nondescript two-story building in an industrial park east of Waynesville, North Carolina. Robert Kendall, Jr. had chosen this location when he moved from the expensive Research Triangle area four years ago. Waynesville was inexpensive but close enough to Asheville to benefit from that city's rapid growth.

He sat at the head of the table in the cramped conference room, tapping his pen. Only one other person was in the room, a portly, ferret-faced man standing at the credenza pouring coffee.

Robert watched as Carter Knox added cream and sugar to his cup and then tasted the concoction. *Disgusting,* Robert thought as he sipped his espresso. He didn't understand why people claimed to like coffee and then add all sorts of artificial flavors. Decent coffee didn't need anything else.

"Good coffee," Carter said as he walked over to the table and sat, taking yet another swallow of the vile mixture. He was an old friend and the head of Junaluska Investment Partners, a New York-based investment firm. Carter had flown into Asheville late yesterday evening and wanted to meet with Robert first thing this morning.

"Always a pleasure to see you, Carter. But I am curious. What was so important for you to fly down here just to see me? You know, we do have the internet here in the mountains, along with video conferencing capability."

Carter chuckled. "I wanted to see your reaction in person. One of the advantages of owning a jet. Since I've got to be back in New York for a lunch meeting, I'll cut to the chase." He paused for effect, then delivered the punch line. "Bearant wants to buy you out."

Robert wrinkled his brow as he stared at his friend. Bearant was one of the largest pharmaceutical firms in the world. Why would they be interested in buying Nuran?

Enjoying the bewilderment in his friend's expression, Carter continued. "One word. Tramorix."

Tramorix was Nuran's only drug. After Robert's wife died of breast cancer, he'd dedicated his life and fortune to finding a cure. He started Nuran Labs for that purpose and hired Dr. Gareth Hadley, a renowned cancer expert, to lead the effort.

Tramorix was the result. Both Phase III clinical trials had been successful, and Nuran had filed the New Drug Application, the final step. Approval of the NDA, required before being allowed to market the drug, was expected to be forthcoming within the next few months.

Robert was confused. Bearant also had a cancer drug close to release.

"Why would they be interested in Tramorix? I thought they were releasing their new breast cancer drug this month?"

Carter grinned. "They thought so, too. But the FDA is going to deny their application."

"What? Where'd you hear that?"

Robert didn't believe it. The word on the street was that Bearant's drug was going to be the new oncology blockbuster. He didn't expect Carter to name names. Still, Carter Knox had never been averse to using inside information to his advantage.

"A reliable source. Apparently, there were some issues with the Phase III trials that have not been made public.

The point is Bearant's drug is DOA. My source tells me that Tramorix has a green light for approval, and Bearant knows it. They're willing to buy Nuran to get it. That's why I'm here."

Robert sat back in his chair. "You've got my attention."

"It gets better."

Robert waited as long as he could, then held out his upturned hands. "And . . ."

"Their offer is the reason I flew down." He paused, took a sip of coffee, then said, "We're talking five *billion* dollars, Robert. Cash."

"Jesus Christ. You're kidding?"

Robert quickly did the math. He and his son Bobby owned seventy-five percent of Nuran, which meant almost four billion dollars. Carter Knox owned twenty percent, and Gareth Hadley owned the other five percent. Four billion dollars in cold, hard cash.

Carter shook his head. "I don't kid about that kind of money. They're doing their due diligence to make sure there's nothing in anyone else's pipeline that would be a threat. Right now, there's not. But, we both know that could change any day, so we have to move fast."

Robert considered the news. "With their drug off the table, Tramorix will be the only one of its kind on the market. Nobody else is within years of having anything close. Bearant will earn that back in a few years. Why wouldn't we bring it to market ourselves?"

Carter shook his head. "You know how fickle the pharmaceutical business can be. Who knows what could happen down the road? Negative side effects could surface. You say that nobody else is close, but what if some discovery surfaces overnight? It's happened before. Plus, Bearant has the clout to drive this to the top. This is a chance to see your dream come to fruition. We'd be crazy not to cash out for that kind of money."

Robert nodded. "Valid points, I suppose. When do you think we can close?"

"As long as no glitches surface, within a month or two. I'm assuming there are no issues with Nuran."

"None. You know we run a tight ship here. They won't find any surprises."

"You said there's nothing else out there close to Tramorix. How certain are you? There's no whiz kid out there in some university working on a competitor?"

"Positive. Lots of people are trying. A cure for breast cancer is worth billions, as you've seen. I'm not aware of anything substantive, but I'll double-check with Hadley."

Carter shifted in his seat, wearing an uneasy look. "Make no mistake, Robert. Bearant, or any other pharmaceutical firm, doesn't want a cure. They all want a treatment. Big difference. Bearant's paying five billion dollars for a cash cow, not a cure. Tramorix is a cash pipeline. Patients have to take it for the rest of their lives. At $25,000 a dose, it's a pharmaceutical firm's wet dream."

"You're pretty cynical."

Carter shook his head and stood. "Just pragmatic. Keep this close. I'll be in touch."

Robert looked out the window at the north wing of the lab and spread his arms. "And what happens to this place?"

Carter grinned and leaned forward. "Who cares?"

5

On the far side of the Nuran building, Justin pulled out the branch he'd found Saturday and set it on his desk. He studied it, making a note of identifying characteristics. After a few minutes, he took one of his well-worn plant taxonomy books off the shelf.

Convinced it belonged in the genus *Rhododendron,* he started there. He flipped to that section and rifled through pictures. Nothing matched. Turning to his computer screen, he went on the internet to a plant classification site. He found several plants that resembled the specimen he had on his desk but no match.

Frustrated, he sat back in his chair. Thinking back to the conversation Saturday evening, he leaned forward and Googled "Cherokee sacred plants." With over a million hits, he started perusing links that caught his attention.

"Cherokee sacred plants? What the hell?"

Justin hadn't heard the owner of the voice, Bobby Kendall, walk up behind him. The two had forged an unlikely friendship at UNC when they sat next to one another in freshman biology.

At the time, Justin had worked at a reference lab to put himself through school, majoring in biology, hoping to be a doctor one day.

While Justin was working as a lab tech, Bobby was partying with his fraternity brothers. They shared a dry sense of humor, a love for animals, and a taste for good beer. Thanks to Justin, Bobby managed to make good enough grades in math and science to graduate.

Robert Kendall, Jr., Bobby's father, was the owner of Nuran Labs, a small firm he'd started in the Research Triangle area of North Carolina. Due to the high costs there, Robert had moved the company to Waynesville, just west of Asheville. After they graduated, Bobby convinced him to offer Justin a job as an entry-level pharmaceutical scientist.

The timing was perfect. Justin had made a grave mistake in the lab where he was working, an error that had shaken his confidence. He'd passed on a tissue sample, not recognizing anything remarkable. Fortunately, the supervising pathologist caught it in time. Coupled with the prospect of going deeper into debt for medical school, Justin changed direction and accepted the position at Nuran.

Justin held up the branch. "I found this Saturday. I've never seen this tree before, and I'm trying to figure out what it is."

Bobby took the branch and studied it. "What do the Cherokee have to do with it?"

"This entire area used to be Cherokee territory." Remembering his promise to Mary Richardson, Justin hesitated before continuing. "Alice and I were hiking in the Park and spotted it. I was just curious."

"Interesting." Bobby handed the branch back to him. "You want to grab a beer after work?"

Justin started to say "no," then changed his mind. It might do him good. "Sure. What time?"

"Six?"

"See you there."

Bobby turned and walked away. Neither of them had to ask where. Frog Level Brewing had been their watering hole of choice from day one.

Justin turned his attention back to the computer screen. On the first page of his query, there were numerous references to Cherokee sacred and medicinal plants. That reminded him of Taxol, one of the most successful cancer drugs on the market. Taxol was a derivative from tree bark.

The vibrating cell phone on the desk interrupted his train of thought, and he looked over at the screen. Dr. Stewart.

"Hello, Doc," he said.

"Hello, Justin. You have a few minutes?"

Dr. Stewart told him that Karen's methotrexate levels were not low enough to give her another treatment this week.

Justin recovered and asked, "Where does that leave us? What about next week?"

"Right now, I'm not optimistic we'll be able to resume treatments."

"What are you saying?"

"The high dose methotrexate was our last option, Justin." He paused, then continued, "At this point, I think we're talking about hospice."

Justin had feared this and was ready. "Okay, then what about Tramorix? We can file for expanded access."

There was a pause before Dr. Stewart continued. "After our conversation yesterday, I reviewed Karen's records and also spoke with the lead investigator for Tramorix. The bottom line is Karen's methotrexate levels are too high even to consider giving her Tramorix. It—"

"She's dying. You've said yourself that methotrexate was her last option. She didn't qualify for the trial. What does she have to lose?" Justin knew what the requirements were for expanded access, and Karen qualified.

"With her methotrexate levels, Tramorix will most assuredly kill her. That is my professional judgment, as well as that of the lead investigator. You're welcome to get another opinion."

Justin also knew that one of the criteria was that the benefit had to justify the risks. If the consequences were almost certain death, that was going to be a hard sell.

"Are you sure her test results are accurate?" Justin asked, desperate, reaching for something, anything.

With a trace of annoyance in his voice, Stewart said, "I reran the tests—same results—and spoke directly with our chief of pathology—Nora Sanders. She is excellent, tops in her field. I'm sorry, but the results are right."

Nora Sanders? Justin shook his head, surprised to hear a name from his past. It had to be the same person. Dr. Nora Sanders had been his boss at the reference lab. She was the one who caught his nearly tragic mistake.

Justin's hand shook as he disconnected the call. Hospice was the end of the road, one he knew well. It was the last resort, reserved for the transition from living to the afterlife. He'd pinned his hopes on Tramorix, but that no longer appeared to be an option.

What now? He felt powerless and angry that he couldn't do anything for his little sister. He was all she had left, and he was able to do nothing.

His mind drifted back to Nora Sanders. He'd lost track of her after he quit the reference lab while in school. Until just then, he didn't realize she was at Wake Forest hospital.

He recalled the last time he'd seen her. It was the end of his shift, and he was tired. He didn't recognize anything abnormal on a tissue sample and passed on it.

Sanders was the supervising pathologist. On a whim, she decided to check behind him for a change. She spotted the anomaly immediately.

"Reeve," she said, looking up from the microscope. "You said this was negative." She pointed to the microscope.

He rubbed his eyes and peered into the eyepiece. The abnormal cells stood out like a billboard. He blinked, but they were still there. He'd missed them.

He stammered, fumbling for the words. "I guess I must have been referring to the previous slide," he said.

She glared at him, not believing his lame excuse any more than he did. She looked down at the paperwork accompanying the sample, then back up at him.

"People's lives depend on you not making a mistake. This patient could've died because of your error. This is unacceptable."

He'd quit that day.

He couldn't quit this. Karen was dying. He'd said the words, and there was no denying it. How was he going to tell her? As soon as he mentioned the word hospice, she'd know. There had to be another way.

Struggling with the realization, he turned his thoughts back to Taxol. Justin recalled that Dr. Gareth Hadley, the lead scientist at Nuran Labs and also his boss, had been involved in Taxol development.

He had to talk with Hadley. Justin logged off his computer and went to his boss's office.

As usual, Hadley's door was open. Justin stopped and rapped on the door.

The gruff, gray-bearded man looked up from his desk. "The door is open. Do you require a formal invitation?"

Justin smiled and walked in. Gareth didn't suffer fools gladly. But, for some reason, he'd taken a liking to Justin and had become a mentor to him. Still, Justin knew to get to the point and dispense with idle chatter.

"Taxol," Justin said as he sat.

"Brand name for paclitaxel, one of the most successful cancer drugs ever. Developed from the bark of *Taxus brevifolia*, otherwise known as the Pacific yew tree. The active ingredient was isolated in the mid-60s by my colleagues at Research Triangle Institute—RTI. What about it?"

"How was it discovered? I mean, what possessed them to consider that specific plant?"

Gareth shrugged. "Serendipity. In 1962, Dr. Arthur Barclay, a Harvard-educated botanist, roamed the West Coast collecting plant samples as part of a federal program to find natural cures for cancer. That summer, he was in the Gifford Pinchot National Forest near Mount St. Helens in Washington. One of the over 600 specimens he collected that year was from the Pacific yew tree. Why he chose such an unremarkable conifer is a mystery. It had no known medicinal properties and no commercial value."

"How did your colleagues find out it had cancer-killing properties?"

"That particular plant sample was assigned to RTI. Drs. Wall and Wani, medical chemists there, did the initial testing. The crude extract exhibited cytotoxicity against human cancer cells, so they pursued it. After much testing and refinement, the FDA approved Taxol in 1992."

Justin shook his head. "Thirty years. Isn't there a faster—" He stopped, realizing he was about to ask a stupid question.

Hadley raised one bushy eyebrow and stared at Justin over his glasses. "Why all the questions about Taxol?"

"Just interested in plant derivatives."

Not convinced, Hadley continued staring. "Why do I think there is more to this line of questioning, Mr. Reeve?"

Justin took a deep breath. "My sister has metastatic breast cancer. Her oncologist had her on a HDMTX regimen. It's not working, and he's suspended treatments. He just told me we need to consider hospice."

Anticipating Hadley's next questions, Justin continued. "She's at Wake Forest Baptist Medical Center. She's completed eight treatments. Elliott Stewart is her oncologist."

Hadley nodded. "I'm sorry." After a few seconds, he added, "I know Elliott. She's in good hands. He's one of the best."

"I tried to get her in the clinical trial for Tramorix, but she didn't meet the inclusion criteria. Yesterday, when he told me he was suspending treatment and suggested hospice, I asked him to request expanded access for Tramorix."

"And?"

Justin lowered his head. "He suspended treatment because her methotrexate levels were still too high. And giving her Tramorix—"

"Will kill her," Hadley completed Justin's sentence.

Justin nodded. "That's what Dr. Stewart said."

"Elliott's right. So why the questions on Taxol? It's not appropriate, either."

Justin hesitated before saying more, remembering his vow to Tsula's mother. But, he trusted his mentor and knew the secret would be safe with him.

"Saturday, Alice and I were hiking in the Park. I found an unusual tree. One I'd never seen before." He pulled out his phone and showed the pictures to Hadley.

"Hmmm," the professor said. "Doesn't look familiar."

Justin thought again about his promise to Mary Richardson, but that was before Karen had received her death sentence. Besides, he wasn't sharing the exact location, so technically, he wasn't breaking his word.

"I showed the pictures and a small specimen to Cherokee friends of mine. They said nobody had seen one for a century. Evidently, the Cherokee consider it sacred."

Hadley stroked his beard and leaned back in his chair. "Interesting. And you think this may be another Taxol?"

Justin shook his head. "I don't know. But I know my sister is running out of time, and she doesn't have thirty years. What if this tree has cancer-killing properties?"

"Why would you think that?"

"My Cherokee friends said that it had medicinal properties. Maybe—"

"Did they say it specifically had anti-cancer capability?"

"No, but nobody thought the Pacific yew did either."

"What kind of medicinal properties?"

"They didn't say. But, I intend to find out."

Back in his cubicle, Justin picked up the branch on his desk and studied it. He remembered Karen's comment about bringing her a cure.

What if this tree had cancer-killing properties?

He knew this was a stretch and the desperate wish of a sibling. He needed to learn more about the plant. Why did the Cherokee consider it sacred? And, what were the medicinal properties?

Justin picked up his cell phone and texted Atohi.

Need to talk ASAP about tree

6

Across town, Alice Miller sat at her desk at Carolina Community Bank, where she was the assistant branch manager.

Alice had graduated from UNC with a degree in finance at the same time Justin graduated. She applied for a job in Charlotte, the banking capital of the southeast. Weighing offers from three different banks, she'd called Justin for advice. He invited her to come to Western North Carolina for the weekend and go hiking.

She did, and before the weekend was over, he'd asked her to move in with him.

There hadn't been many job opportunities in Waynesville. She'd taken a job as a teller with CCB, thinking she'd find something more suitable later in Asheville.

The small bank turned out to be challenging and rewarding. Alice had rapidly moved up the ladder, and what started as a temporary job turned into a career.

She had a clear view of the lobby through the glass wall in her corner office. Just before noon, a tall, thin woman with short blonde hair walked in the front door. She appeared to be about Alice's age, and something about her stride seemed familiar. The blonde, focused on the lone teller, didn't notice Alice staring at her.

Alice started to get up and walk over behind the teller window to get a closer look, but something made her hesitate. Then it came to her. Debra Hunt. Debra had attended high school with Alice in Indianapolis.

Alice picked up her desk phone handset and turned toward the credenza as if she were looking for something. *What the hell was Debra Hunt doing in Waynesville, North Carolina?*

She had not seen Debra since she left Indianapolis. She didn't think Debra would recognize her but didn't want to take the chance. After what seemed an eternity, Alice turned and risked a glance. There was no one at the teller line. She looked at the lobby, and it was empty.

She waited a few minutes and dialed the extension for the teller. "Glenn. The tall blonde who was just at your window. What was her name? She looked familiar."

"Uh, Foster. Debra Foster. She wanted to talk to someone about a loan for a vacation home here in the area. I saw you were on the phone and asked her to wait. She said she was late for an appointment and would stop by right after lunch."

"Okay, thanks. Not who I thought it was." She hung up the phone, her hand shaking. Foster must be a married name, but Alice knew it was Debra Hunt. Someone from Alice's past, someone she couldn't afford to see. And Debra was coming back later.

Alice grabbed her purse and walked over to Walter's office. "Hey," she said, sticking her head in the manager's office. Walter was the one who had hired her.

He looked up from his desk. "How's it going?"

"Good. Listen, I need a favor. A woman named Debra Foster stopped by this morning. She told Glenn she wanted to talk to someone about a home loan. I was on a call, and he told her I'd help her as soon as I got off the phone. She had somewhere to be and said that she'd just stop by after lunch. I'm late for a lunch appointment. If she comes back before I do, would you mind talking to her?"

Walter nodded. "Sure, no problem."

On her way out, she told Glenn the same story and that Walter had agreed to handle it.

Outside the bank, Alice sat in her car, trying to decide what to do. She was too nervous to eat and, besides, didn't want to risk running into Debra. She needed to go someplace where she could be alone and think.

Two hours later, Alice walked back into the bank and went straight to Walter's office.

"Hey," he said, looking up to see her standing in his doorway.

"Sorry, it took longer than I expected."

"No problem. Ms. Foster came by, and I took her application for a loan. She and her husband want to buy a second home in the area. I put the paperwork on your desk."

"Great. Thanks for taking care of it. I'll go through it and get back to her."

Alice went to her office and rifled through the stack in her inbox to find Debra's application. She pulled it out and scanned the handwritten form.

Debra H. and Brad P. Foster had applied to pre-qualify for a $300,000 loan for a vacation home in the area. The Fosters lived in Carmel, Indiana, a suburb of Indianapolis. Debra listed Brad's occupation as V.P. Sales with an Indianapolis equipment firm while she showed hers as an interior designer. They claimed no dependents.

Their income and debt appeared to qualify them for a loan without difficulty. Walter had already pulled their credit scores, which supported her assessment.

Alice set the paperwork aside and pondered the situation. Debra Hunt Foster would be back, and Alice would have to deal with her. As much as she would've like to, Alice couldn't avoid it.

The dilemma was that Debra knew too much about Alice's past, a past that Justin knew nothing about.

She considered confronting Debra head-on and risk Justin finding out. The odds were low. The house here would be a second home, and the chances of running into her socially were minimal. Alice could keep the interaction professional and distant.

The other option was to act is if she didn't recognize Debra and hope that Debra wouldn't recognize her. Debra hadn't seen her in ten years, but could she pull it off?

Alice retrieved her purse and went to the restroom. She pulled out the high school picture she had in her wallet, a photo she'd told Justin was her cousin, now deceased.

She looked in the mirror, comparing the image to the picture. The high school Alice was chunky, with long, stringy blonde hair and glasses. The current Alice was slim, in shape from hiking and exercising. She was now a brunette with short hair and had been since she'd met Justin. Thanks to Lasik eye surgery, she no longer wore glasses. And living in the south had given her midwest accent a slight drawl.

Alice went back to her office and sat at her desk. She decided to go with the second option. If it failed, she could always claim she didn't recognize her friend from high school.

Confronting Debra was too risky. Waynesville was a small town, and while the odds of encountering her were remote, it wasn't out of the question. The possibility that they'd meet in front of Justin was a chance she couldn't afford to take.

7

On his way to meet Bobby at Frog Level that afternoon, Justin stopped by Blue Ridge Books.

Jo greeted him when he walked in. "Well, well," she said as he walked over to the counter. "I was beginning to think you'd forgotten how to get here."

"You know me, I've been going over to that bookstore in Asheville," he said, forcing a laugh. "They don't harass me like you do." That was their running joke. Justin was probably their best customer at Blue Ridge Books, stopping in weekly.

Jo gave him a thoughtful once-over and asked, "You okay?"

Justin shook his head. "I went over to see Karen Saturday. I took her the magazines you gave me. She told me to say hello." He looked down and added, "She's not doing well. I'm afraid the chemo's not working."

"I'm sorry, Justin. Anything I can do?"

"No, thanks. She appreciates the magazines you send her. That means more than you know." Changing the subject, he said, "Hey, do you happen to have any books on Cherokee sacred or medicinal plants?"

"That's an interesting subject. Maybe. Where'd that come from?"

He started to tell her about finding the tree but then recalled his promise to Mary.

"Just doing a little research on ancient remedies."

She came out from behind the counter and walked over to a bookcase against the wall. Turning her head sideways, she scanned a shelf, pulled a slim green book out, and handed it to Justin.

"Written in the 50s by William Banks," she said. "It's a classic reference book on the subject. It's seventy years old, so it might be helpful for old-fashioned treatments."

The bell at the door rang, indicating a shopper had entered. "Let me help this customer. I'll be right back," Jo said.

"Go ahead. I'll check it out."

Justin flipped it over to the back copy. *Perfect,* he thought as he read. Fascinated, he opened the book to the foreword and continued reading.

In 1953, Banks wrote the original manuscript as a master's thesis titled "Ethnobotany of the Cherokee Indians" while at the University of Tennessee. Discovered fifty years later, it was published as *Plants of the Cherokee* by the Great Smoky Mountains Association—the book he now held.

A few minutes later, Jo returned. "Well? What do you think?"

Justin glanced at his watch and handed her the book. "I think it'll be useful. I'll take it," he said. "Can you ring me up? I've got to run."

Jo rang up his purchase. "I should have a few new editions of Karen's favorite magazines next week. Tell her hi."

"Will do. Thanks."

On his way to Frog Level, his phone buzzed. Tsula. "Hey," he answered.

"Atohi forwarded your message to me. You wanted to talk about the tree?"

"Yeah, I need to know more about it. Your mother said it had medicinal purposes, and I'd like to know what kinds. Why was it considered sacred?"

There was a pause on the line, and Justin thought he'd lost her. "You still there?"

"Why would you ask that?"

"Why? Several reasons. It's my job for one. Plants are also my hobby."

"Sorry, I don't know anything about it, other than what Mother told us last night."

"Maybe I should give her a call."

Another silence.

Finally, Tsula said, "Why don't you and Alice come over tonight? I'll see if Mother can join us."

"Okay, that'd be great. I'm on my way to meet Bobby for a beer, but I won't be long."

"I'll call Alice. Oh, and please don't mention the tree to anyone. Especially Bobby."

Justin thought about his recent conversations with Bobby and Dr. Hadley. He probably told Bobby more than he should've, but Bobby had caught him researching Cherokee sacred plants, so he had to tell him something.

He'd disclosed more information to Hadley, but he was confident Hadley would keep it to himself. Besides, no one knew where the tree was other than Alice and him.

"Okay," he said and then disconnected. *No harm,* he thought, trying to convince himself. As he parked in front of Frog Level Brewing, he wondered what the big deal was over an unidentified tree. Lots of plants supposedly had medicinal purposes. Why would the Cherokee want this kept secret? Maybe it had extraordinary healing capabilities? That would explain why they wanted to know if it was on the Qualla. If the tree was on the Qualla and had a similar value as the Pacific yew, it could be worth billions to the tribe. He knew he was jumping to conclusions, desperate for something to help Karen. He was determined to get answers from Tsula and her mother.

Inside, he walked over to Mary Ann, who was tending the bar. "Missed you Saturday," he said.

The cute blonde smiled and poured him a Nutty without even asking. "I don't work all of the time, you know," she said as she slid the beer across the bar to him. She nodded toward the patio door. "Bobby's out back."

When Justin stepped through the door, he spotted Bobby sitting at a table next to the creek and walked over to join him.

Bobby held up his half-empty glass. "After sitting in meetings all day long, I was ready for a beer. How was your weekend, besides hiking Saturday?"

Justin held up his glass to Bobby's, then took a drink. He shook his head. "Busy. Yesterday, Alice had to work, so I drove over to see Karen."

"How's she doing?"

Justin shook his head. "Not good. I talked to her doctor this morning." He took another sip and composed himself before continuing. "The chemo isn't working. She's getting weaker, and he's stopped treatments. Dr. Stewart said we need to be thinking about hospice."

"Hospice. Damn, Justin. That sucks. Isn't there something else they can try?"

Justin shook his head. "He says they're out of options. The methotrexate was the last resort." He took another drink, then said, "Can we talk about something else right now? What's going on with you?"

Bobby took a swallow and leaned over. "Big news. But you can't say anything."

Justin nodded. *What the hell, is this National Secrets Day?*

"I'm serious. We could go to jail for what I'm about to tell you," Bobby said, keeping his voice low, even though the nearest patrons were on the opposite side of the patio area.

"What'd you do, rob a bank?"

"Close." Bobby took another drink, then stared at Justin. "Somebody wants to buy the company from the old man."

"Really? Who?" Justin's interest was piqued.

"It's a whale." Bobby looked around, then whispered, "Bearant."

"Bearant?" Justin repeated. Bearant Pharmaceutical was huge, one of the largest drug companies in the world.

Bobby nodded. "They want Tramorix, bad. And they're willing to buy the whole damn company to get it. Dad didn't mention a number, but he said it was 'fuck you money.'"

Justin bridled at the mention of Tramorix, thinking about his failure to get Karen enrolled in the clinical trials. It was an anti-cancer drug, the first product developed by Nuran. All roads kept leading back to Karen. Maybe if he'd succeeded, she wouldn't be dying. Now, it was too late.

"What happened to Bearant's new drug?" Justin asked. Rumor on the street was that Bearant was coming out with a competitive drug.

Bobby shook his head and lowered his voice. "We've heard that the FDA is not going to approve it. Tramorix has a clear field, and Bearant has nada."

"Wow, that is news."

Nuran was at the end of the Phase III trials with Tramorix. Justin knew the results were encouraging, and the company expected FDA approval soon. It required expensive monthly treatments for the life of the patient. Justin had heard numbers of as much as twenty to twenty-five thousand dollars per dose. With Bearant's drug off the table, Tramorix could be the next blockbuster cancer drug.

Justin frowned. "I just wish we could've gotten Tramorix to Karen."

Bobby exhaled, then shook his head. "Justin . . . we tried, remember? We did everything we could, but she didn't meet the inclusion criteria."

Bobby took a drink, then raised his hand. "Hey, what about filing for expanded access? Her doctor could—"

Justin silenced him with a shake of his head. "I asked Dr. Stewart. Her methotrexate levels are too high."

"Yeah, but—"

"Giving her Tramorix would . . . with the methotrexate . . . " He couldn't finish the sentence, but Bobby nodded, seeming to understand.

At last, Justin said, "I verified it with Hadley. He concurred."

They sat in silence for a few minutes before Bobby spoke.

"I'm sorry, Justin. I wish I could do something."

"So do I."

8

When Justin got home, Alice met him at the door with her jacket in hand.

"Tsula called and said she had talked to you about going over to their house," she said.

Justin nodded. "Let's go."

On the way, he filled Alice in on his meeting with Bobby and worked backward to his meeting with Hadley. He showed her the book he'd bought.

"The Cherokee used dozens of plants for all sorts of medicinal reasons," he said. "I didn't see the one we found, but it makes sense that they could've used it that way."

Alice studied him and put her hand on his arm.

"You think it might help Karen, don't you?"

He started to dismiss that as ridiculous but knew she wouldn't buy it.

"I honestly don't know. I do know that we're running out of time. At this point, I'm willing to try anything."

As they pulled into Atohi's drive, Alice noticed Mary Richardson's car parked out front. "Mary's here?"

"Tsula said she would try to get her to come."

"What's going on? All Tsula said was that she'd talked to you about us coming over."

"I texted Atohi and told him that I wanted to talk about the tree. I think there's more to it than what Mary told us Saturday night. He passed it along to Tsula, who called and invited us over. She said that she'd try to get Mary to come."

Justin looked over and saw Alice's skeptical look. "I know it's a long shot."

With sad eyes, she nodded. "I know you're upset and want to do something. I don't want you to get your hopes up."

He switched the engine off and opened the door. "Let's see what they have to say."

Atohi met them at the door as they got to the top of the steps. "Come in."

Mary and Tsula stood inside, chatting.

"Hey guys," Tsula said. "Thanks for coming over on such short notice. Mother just got here. Can we get anyone something to drink?"

"Water for me," Alice said.

"Same here," Mary said.

Justin looked at Atohi, who said, "I'm having a beer." Justin nodded in agreement.

"Why don't we have a seat?" Tsula said, gesturing to the dining room table. Atohi went to the kitchen to get drinks.

Once they were seated and had drinks, Mary turned to Justin.

"Tsula said you wanted to know more about the tree you found?"

"I do. I'm curious about several things. You said it was sacred and had medicinal properties. Why was it sacred? And what kind of medicinal uses? Why the big secret about where it is?"

Mary cocked her head. "Why are you asking these questions?"

Justin held up the copy of *Plants of the Cherokee* that he'd brought in.

"According to this, the Cherokee believed many plants had medicinal value. Taxol, one of the most successful cancer drugs ever, was developed from the bark of a tree that grows wild in the Pacific Northwest."

Tsula said, "So, you think the tree has value to your company, commercial value? That maybe it could be the next Taxol?"

Justin narrowed his eyes. "You think *that's* the reason for my interest? That it might be a new product for Nuran?"

He shook his head and continued. "I don't know if it has value to Nuran or not, and frankly, I don't care. What I do know is that my sister is dying. I talked to her doctor this morning, and he's suspended chemo. It's not working, and he suggested that we consider hospice. *That's* what I care about."

"I'm sorry, Justin," Tsula began. "I didn't know . . ."

Mary held up her hand and shot Tsula a glance. "I'm sorry to hear that, Justin. I knew she was sick, but I didn't realize it was that serious. Is there anything we can do?"

"That's why I'm here. Karen's out of options, and I'm willing to try anything. Maybe you could introduce me to a Cherokee medicine man . . . or woman? Someone who knows anything about that tree."

Tsula folded her arms. "Spiritual subjects are sensitive topics for the Cherokee and not discussed outside of—"

"Others have," Justin said, holding up the book.

Mary stared at Tsula and then Atohi. She turned to Justin and Alice.

"Could you please give us a few minutes?" she asked.

He laid the book on the table in front of Mary, nodded, and stood. He and Alice walked out on the porch.

"I don't see what the big deal is," he said to Alice after she closed the door. "I'm not asking for any tribal secrets."

Alice shrugged. "Maybe you are."

"That's ridiculous. I'm just trying to help Karen."

"I know that. And you know that. But the Cherokee have suffered greatly from greed and exploitation. I can empathize with Tsula's point."

Alice was right. White settlers, supported by the United States government, destroyed villages, forcibly took Cherokee lands, and undertook the task of "civilizing" the Cherokee. Acculturation meant relinquishing their language and culture in favor of becoming like whites. President Andrew Jackson signed the Indian Removal Act, even refusing to enforce *Worcester v. Georgia*, a Supreme Court ruling acknowledging the Cherokee Nation's sovereignty. President Martin Van Buren then ordered federal troops to round up over ten thousand Cherokees. The soldiers then forced them to walk westward to their new home in present-day Oklahoma, a journey sadly known as the Trail of Tears. Less than a thousand remained in North Carolina, where they had established the Eastern Band of Cherokee Indians.

"But we're not like that," he said in his defense.

"Their lack of trust isn't personal, Justin. Surely, you can understand their reluctance? Any secrets would eventually be leaked to other whites who would then find ways to exploit them."

Justin lowered his head as he considered what Alice had said. She was right. This wasn't personal but understandable, given the Cherokee's experience. He lifted his head when he heard raised voices inside but couldn't make out what was said. Thirty minutes later, the door opened, and Mary asked them to come back in.

Atohi and Tsula were seated. Mary stood, looking at Justin and Alice, indicating for them to sit. "I apologize. We needed to clarify some things amongst us."

Mary paused a minute to allow the group to take a breath. Still looking at Justin and Alice, she said, "As Tsula stated earlier, spiritual subjects are sensitive topics for the Cherokee and not discussed outside of the tribe."

Justin started to speak, but Alice stopped him with her hand on his arm.

Mary continued. "What she neglected to add was that you are family."

She looked over at Atohi and then back at Justin.

"You are brothers. You grew up together. You *are* family. Our concern is those who are not Cherokee. Those who are not family. Those who do not respect our culture and traditions. That is not you." She paused to let her words sink in.

Justin glanced at Atohi, who was nodding. Mary was right. He and Atohi were brothers—the only brother either of them had. Remembering his childhood, Justin thought about all they had shared. Atohi had always been welcome in Justin's house, and he had always been welcome in Atohi's.

Justin's eyes watered as he remembered Atohi comforting him at his mother's funeral. He allowed himself a thin smile as he recalled the unfamiliar customs at the Cherokee funeral for Atohi's mom, where he could provide comfort to his grieving brother.

"Thank you," he said to Mary in a barely audible voice, not trusting himself to speak out loud.

"All I request is the same thing I ask of Tsula and Atohi. Please keep what I tell you in the family."

Justin looked across the table at Atohi and Tsula, who were nodding. He realized that this was a solemn promise they were all making here, and he had to be careful to observe this, regardless. He owed that much to his Cherokee family. But, what about Karen? What if it came down to keeping this commitment or helping his sister? He looked up at Mary, who seemed to be reading his mind.

She gave him a slight nod and smiled as if to say, *I'll do everything I can to help your sister. Just talk to me if that time comes.*

"I understand," he said, his eyes locked onto Mary's.

"Certainly," he heard Alice say next to him.

"Agitsi called it the healing tree," Mary began, using the Cherokee term for mother. "I remember the stories she told about it. She was a good artist as well as a healer, and she made detailed drawings of many useful plants."

Over the thirty minutes, Mary shared with them the legend of the sacred healing tree. She vividly recalled her mother telling her about it. As soon as she had seen the pictures Tsula sent her, Mary knew it must be the same tree.

"Tsula's Elisi was a healer. A Cherokee medicine woman, if you will. When Elisi passed, I became a healer."

Mary looked at her daughter. "And Tsula will be the next healer."

Justin looked at Tsula. He was both surprised and not, knowing Tsula was a nurse at the Cherokee Indian Hospital. She was always suggesting remedies for various ailments.

Mary continued. "Agitsi claimed that the tree produced a rare and potent medicine, reserved for only the sickest people. She brewed a strong tea from the leaves and bark, adding flowers when they were available."

The tea had a powerful, almost magical healing property. The trees were not numerous, found only in the vicinity of where Justin and Alice had been hiking. Their identity and location were a closely guarded secret in the tribe, shared only amongst healers. Not even the chief had that knowledge.

"I'm not sure what illnesses it cured. You must remember that many modern illnesses were unknown back then. People referred to the symptoms, such as fever, convulsions, or dysentery. I do know that Agitsi thought it was the most powerful medicine, one of last resort, and able to heal people that were dying."

Tsula, her voice soft, looked at Justin and said, "I'm sorry. I know you are just looking out for Karen. I'm not worried about you, but others. Like the company you work for."

Justin nodded. "I understand. I haven't told anyone where it is, and I won't, not without your permission."

He turned to Mary. "Do you know how to make the tea?"

"The recipe is written on the back of the drawing. I'll need more leaves, several flowers, and a small piece of bark. Again, I never saw her make it, but the instructions are explicit. As soon as you get me more material, I'll make it. I can't promise it will work."

"What if it makes her worse?" Alice asked.

"Worse? She's wasting away in the hospital. Her doctor, who I understand is excellent, has suspended treatments. What's the harm in giving her a natural potion? It worked for the Cherokee."

"With all due respect, Mother, we only have anecdotal evidence about this," Tsula said. "What if Karen dies from this tea?"

"She has no other chance," Justin said. "She is dying, even as we speak."

"The difference is that if the tea kills her, then my mother will be guilty of murder."

"I won't let that happen. I take full responsibility. I'll give it to her."

Atohi said, "Okay, assume she gets better. What then? Won't the doctors want to know how it happened?"

Justin shrugged. "Then, the world will have a new medicine, and the Cherokee will own the rights to it."

Tsula shook her head. "It's never that simple when white people are involved. Even if we find out it's on

Cherokee land, who says they won't just steal the land as they did before."

Mary interrupted. "Justin is family. His sister is family. We have to try to help." She looked at Justin. "Get me the material, and I'll make the tea. The rest is up to you."

9

It was still dark the next morning when Justin pulled up to Atohi and Tsula's house. Alice was right behind him in her car. She had driven so she could get to work before lunch when they got back from the Park.

Justin had offered to go alone to get the additional material from the tree. Still, they had insisted on going with him. Since today was a workday, they decided to leave as early as possible to get to the trailhead by daybreak.

Atohi and Tsula met them outside before Justin could switch off his SUV as Alice climbed into the passenger seat next to him.

Atohi opened the tailgate to load their packs and hiking sticks as Tsula got in.

Justin turned around and said, "Everyone doesn't have to go, you know. I can get the material for Mary. That way, none of you will be late for work."

After tossing their gear in, Atohi shut the rear door and got in back next to Tsula.

"You said that last night. We're here, and we're going," Atohi said as he passed a thermal mug up to Justin. "Drink your coffee and drive."

"Okay, I tried. Thanks," he said, taking the coffee.

"Where are we going?" Tsula asked.

"Straight Fork Road."

It was barely daylight when Justin parked at the Hyatt Ridge trailhead. They put on their packs and started up the steep trail. An hour and a half later, they arrived at the junction of the Enloe Creek Trail. They had worked up a sweat and stopped for a minute to rest. That section of the Hyatt Ridge was uphill, with a 1,500-foot elevation gain over less than two miles.

"At least Enloe Creek's downhill from here," Atohi said, wiping his brow and chugging water. "I'd forgotten how tough this part was."

"Tough? You're getting soft, my friend," Justin said with a laugh.

Atohi had served three tours in the Middle East as an elite Army Ranger. Justin remembered him talking about Ranger school and how physically and mentally challenging it was. The first week ended with a twelve-mile march carrying fifty pounds of gear. Less than fifty percent of candidates, already in top physical shape, made it through the first three weeks.

Atohi looked at him, grinning. "I am. In my Army days, I was younger and in better shape. Besides, these mountains are higher than the ones in North Georgia."

Justin nodded, remembering that Ranger school's mountain phase was near Dahlonega, Georgia. Georgia's highest point was less than 5,000 feet. Haywood County, where they were, had thirteen peaks higher than 6,000 feet.

"Hey," Justin said, "I'm just giving you shit. I'm proud of you, brother, and I'm sure you could still kick my ass," Justin said. He noticed that Tsula had pulled a small notebook out of her pack.

He moved closer and saw that she was writing down the time and location. "Afraid we're going to get lost?" Justin asked.

She shook her head and laughed. "Not with you and Atohi. But since Sam Bear couldn't come today, he asked me to record the tree's location as best I could. Then, he can come out and determine whether or not it's on Cherokee land."

If it is, she explained, the Cherokee could claim ownership and control access. If it were in the Great Smoky Mountains National Park, then the federal government would have possession, and access would be impossible to enforce.

After resting for a few more minutes, they started their descent into Raven Fork Gorge. As they got closer to the Fork, they could hear the distant roar of the water. Justin stopped and surveyed the area. He pointed to the right, over the steep edge. "I think it's down there."

Alice looked where he was pointing, then shook her head. "No, this isn't it."

Justin started to argue, but he wasn't confident enough in his choice to challenge her.

"I think it's a little further down the trail," she added.

"Okay, lead the way," Justin said, yielding the point position to Alice.

She slowly made her way another fifteen yards or so before stopping. Studying the terrain, she nodded. "Right here is where we came out," she said.

"Are you sure?" Justin asked.

"Positive," she said. She pointed down the trail. "If you go twenty more yards, you'll find your rock—the one you tripped over when you were looking at the holly."

Justin felt his face go red as he remembered. He stared over the edge of the trail. Looking closer, he was able to see faint evidence of the path he'd bushwhacked last week. Alice was right.

Now that he was sure of their location, he led the way and slowly picked his way through the underbrush trail. Thirty minutes later, he spotted the clearing off to their left. "Over there," he pointed.

They made their way over to the opening and stopped at the base of the healing tree. It still had quite a few flowers on it. Justin remembered the effect it had on him when he first saw it. He glanced at the others as each of them stared at the tree, mouths agape.

"Impressive," Atohi said.

"It's beautiful," Tsula said as she got her phone out to take pictures. "Damn, no service," she said, looking at the device. "I was going to mark the location for Sam Bear. Now, all I can do is take pictures."

"No problem," Justin said. No cell service in the mountains was typical, particularly out in the Park, but he had another idea.

He took his phone out of his backpack and opened a trail app. He zoomed in, pressed the screen a couple of times, and showed it to Tsula. "Here's our latitude and longitude."

She looked down at the screen, then back up at Justin. "We don't have cell service. How—"

Atohi and Justin both laughed.

"GPS doesn't need cell service," Atohi said. "Independent functions."

Alice looked at Justin. "I didn't know that. Why didn't you mark the location before when we were here?"

"To use the map without cell service, you have to download it first," Justin said. "I did that this morning before we left the house. Most of the time—like the other day—I don't bother. Besides, I don't like being dependent on technology. Dumbs you up."

Atohi patted the side of his backpack. "Justin and I know most of the trails well enough without a map, but I still keep one in my pack along with a compass. Habit. And, no batteries required."

"How accurate is it?" Alice asked, nodding toward Justin's phone.

"Within thirty feet or so," he said.

Tsula took a few photos, then asked, "How far is campsite 47?"

"From where we left the trail, maybe half a mile," Justin said. "From here?" He looked around, shaking his head. "Not a clue."

Alice and Tsula took pictures of the tree from different angles. Meanwhile, Atohi looked for other trees like it in the immediate vicinity and came up empty-handed. Justin cut off a small branch containing a dozen or so leaves and several flowers. He put it in a plastic bag and stuck it in a pocket.

As he pulled out a drawknife, Tsula cried out. "What are you going to do with that?"

"Just taking off a small piece of bark for Mary." He held up the gleaming knife. "I cleaned it before putting it in my pack. It won't harm the tree, I promise."

He pointed out an old scar on the trunk. "This one is probably from an elk." He pointed to another. "Looks like a bear sharpened his claws here. Just like us, trees get scratches along the way. They heal quickly."

Carefully he cut a piece of bark off the trunk and put it in the same plastic bag as the sprig. He zipped it shut and placed it into a compartment in his backpack.

Satisfied he had everything he needed, Justin said, "Anything else?"

"You still haven't found your holly," Alice said, snickering.

With the excitement over the healing tree, Justin had forgotten about the longstalk holly that had started him on this adventure.

"That'll have to wait for another trip," he said with a wink.

* * *

When they got back to Atohi and Tsula's house, Mary was already there. In route, Tsula had called to let her know they had the material from the tree.

Inside the house, Justin removed the material from his backpack and gave it to Mary. While she started preparing the tea, Justin described what he intended to do. "First, I want to run some simple tests in the lab with the tea to see if it is toxic to cancer cells."

As a nurse, Tsula was quick to understand. "Makes sense. Then what?"

"That's the easy part. Assuming it exhibits toxicity, then comes the hard part. The normal protocol would be to isolate the effective agent. Next, you'd increase the complexity of the cancer cells and adjust the strength to gauge dosing. Eventually, you'd do animal trials and gradually move to human trials."

By trying to summarize the process for the non-scientists in the room, Justin realized he was grossly oversimplifying it. The sheer enormity of the task was indescribable. He was going to have to take innumerable shortcuts to get results in time to help Karen.

Tsula seemed to read his mind. "But wouldn't that take years?"

All eyes were on him, waiting for the obvious answer. Tramorix had taken ten years and hundreds of thousands of hours of research and testing, all with meticulous documentation at every step. And it still hadn't been approved for general use, a billion dollars later. No wonder Taxol took thirty years. No one said a word as he looked at each of them.

"The standard protocol would. Obviously, we don't have the luxury of time on our side. We'll have to accelerate the process."

They all looked at Tsula, who was leading the questions. "Won't that compromise the safety of the potion?"

He took a deep breath. "There are always risks with a new medicine. And, yes, speeding up the process may increase the risks."

He looked over at Alice. "If the tea proves toxic to the cancer cells, I will ingest it first. Provided it doesn't cause any severe reaction, I plan on giving Karen the tea as soon as possible afterward."

Bedlam erupted, with everyone speaking at the same time. "But—what if—how do you know—is it safe—for her?"

He held up his hand. "I don't know. But, it doesn't matter. She has *nothing*, repeat, *nothing* to lose. We're out of time and out of options."

"And you've explained all of this to Karen?" Tsula asked.

"Not yet. But I will."

10

At home that evening, Justin held up the small jar of tea that Mary Richardson had brewed and stared at it. The liquid was clear but with a pronounced greenish-brown tint.

"What are you thinking?" Alice asked.

He shrugged. "Wondering if this could be the next Taxol. And not because of Nuran, but for Karen. Wondering if it does have medicinal properties."

He thought back to Arthur Barclay. Barclay, the botanist who discovered the Taxol tree, collected over 600 specimens. Only one produced anything of value.

Alice walked over, put her arms around him, and pulled him close. "Maybe it does. And you're the one to find out."

Justin put his arms around Alice, holding her tight. They stood there, embracing, not saying a word. The grandfather clock chimed, breaking the silence.

"I want to believe in miracles, but the scientist in me doesn't want to get his hopes up. It's a one-in-a-million chance. He exhaled, shaking his head. "I should take this over to the lab while it's fresh."

"I understand." She kissed him and stepped back. "Give me a call when you're leaving, and I'll start dinner."

"I won't be long."

There were few cars in the parking lot when Justin arrived at the lab. *Good,* he thought. He was counting on the lab being empty. He parked near the front door and grabbed the tea jar. As he got out and walked toward the door, he saw Kyle, the night security guard, sitting at the front desk.

Damn, he hadn't considered that. Kyle would be curious as to why he was carrying an unlabeled jar of liquid into the lab. He swiped his badge at the front door and entered. Behind the desk, Kyle looked up and smiled when he saw Justin.

"Mr. Reeve. Working late again, huh?" Noticing the jar, Kyle asked, "What's that?"

Justin slowed his pace but didn't stop walking. "Uh, just some soup that Alice made. A midnight snack."

"Great. I know where to come if I get hungry."

Over his shoulder, Justin said, "If I'd known you were going to be working, I would've brought you some." He heard Kyle laugh.

One of the advantages of working in a pharmaceutical lab was access to equipment and materials. Justin planned to prepare a 6-well culture plate to leave in the incubator when he left. He would insert breast cancer cells in all of the wells. Four would be treated with various tea amounts, leaving two untreated as a control. At the lab door, he peeked inside. A light was on in the far corner, but he didn't see anybody.

Justin opened the door, stepped inside, and looked around. No sign of anyone. Probably just a light that someone left on. It dawned on him that he needed a story in case he ran into someone else. Although he was on his own time, he wasn't working on official business.

He went over to one of the Class II hoods to prepare the culture medium, the first step in the process. Ten minutes later, immersed in his work, he didn't hear the person come up behind him.

"Hey, I didn't—"

"Jesus," he said, almost dropping the flask in his hand. He turned around to see Simone, one of the junior scientists standing there holding a cup. "What the hell? You scared the shit out of me."

"Sorry. I thought you heard me."

"Hell, no. There was no one here when I came in."

"I'm in the far corner. I just went down to get a cup of coffee," she said, holding up the cup. "When I came back in, I saw you over here. What are you working on?"

Justin shook his head. "I just wanted to run some cultures tonight. Still working on streamlining the production protocol for Tramorix."

He glanced at the tea jar ten feet away and hoped Simone didn't notice it. He didn't ask her what she was working on and didn't care.

"Cool. I'll let you get back to it. Just wanted to say hi." She turned the other way and walked toward her corner.

Shook by the interruption, Justin had to read his notes to see exactly where he was. He still had a lot of work to do before he left.

Five hours later, Justin returned home. Alice was curled up in her favorite chair, reading. He'd called her three hours ago and told her to go ahead and eat without him.

"Hey. Are you hungry? I saved you some dinner," she said.

"Starving. Thank you."

He walked into the kitchen, expecting to see pots. The stove was empty.

"I prepared you a plate and put it in the fridge so I could clean up. I'll warm it for you," she said, joining him in the kitchen. "Sit." She pointed to the bar.

He complied, and she pulled out a beer, opened it, and set it in front of him.

"Thank you," he said, taking a drink.

"I was beginning to think you were going to stay the night," she said as she put the plate in the microwave. On more than one occasion, Justin had spent the night at the lab engrossed in a project.

"I just wanted to finish up what I started. Put a bunch of different samples in the incubator so I could check them tomorrow."

"Did you find out what's in the tea?"

He laughed. "Hardly. It's not like in the movies, where you put it in a super-duper analyzer, and it spits out the results in minutes. If only it were that simple. I'm just doing some crude toxicity tests."

He looked over to her book on the counter. "What are you reading?"

"*The Overstory,* by Richard Powers. You'd like it."

Justin cocked his head. "That's the book about trees? Won the Pulitzer Prize, right?"

Alice nodded. "The trees communicate and work together. They have feelings."

He grinned. "Yeah, I'd like that. Let me read it when you finish."

The microwave dinged. She removed the food and set the plate in front of him. She brought her glass of water over and sat next to him.

He attacked the baked chicken and fresh vegetables as she told him about the book. Halfway through eating, he paused long enough to say, "Delicious. Thank you."

Alice laughed. "You'd think day-old pizza was delicious right now."

He finished the beer and food at the same time. She started to take his plate, and he waved her off.

"I've got it. You go back to your chair. I'll put this in the dishwasher and come join you."

Ten minutes later, he sat on the couch next to her chair. Five minutes after that, he was asleep.

* * *

The next day at the lab, Justin checked on the samples he'd put in the incubator last night. He put the 6-well plate into the digital colony counter. Ten minutes later, he got the results. The two untreated samples had shown a significant increase in colony size, indicating the cancer cells were multiplying. No surprise there.

He shifted his focus to the four treated samples. He blinked and looked away. *Impossible,* Justin thought as he sat back.

All of the treated samples showed a substantial reduction in colony size. The degree of reduction varied between them, but it was by a sizeable amount in all four. Justin turned back to the computer screen, re-evaluating each of the four. The results were unmistakable.

Unbelievable, he thought as he shook his head and looked out the window. Could it be true that the tea had killed off cancer cells? He'd been hoping for a modest reduction, but this exceeded his wildest expectations. He massaged his temple, refusing to believe it. There had to be another explanation. Maybe the colony counter was faulty?

He looked around the lab, spotting Raul, another scientist. "Raul," Justin yelled across the lab. Raul looked up, and Justin motioned him over.

"What's up?" Raul asked.

"When's the last time this thing's been checked?" Justin said, pointing to the colony counter in front of him.

"Last Monday. I ran ten plates on it Friday. It was perfect. Why?"

Justin shook his head. "Last Monday? What about the day before yesterday? It's supposed to be calibrated *every* Monday morning. I ran a plate on it overnight, and something's not right."

Raul shrugged. "Are you sure? Do you have another plate?"

"No, I don't have another. I expected the thing to be checked and operating properly, so I just prepped one plate."

"I'll check it when I finish—"

"No, check it now. That way, if necessary, you can submit a maintenance ticket on it—before someone else ruins their samples. I just wasted a whole damn day."

Justin shook his head as Raul walked off toward the machine. Running new cultures would take another twenty-four hours of precious time.

He went to the refrigerator and pulled out the jar of tea that Mary had brewed. He had no way of knowing if the container was sterile and what other compounds may have been in it. Other substances could've been on the plant samples. This was the problem when taking shortcuts and skipping steps—too many variables.

He wondered what the half-life of the tea was and whether the potency had been affected. He jotted the question down on his notebook, adding it to his list of things to check.

Back at his desk, he sat, tapping his pencil against the edge. He'd have to accept the toxicity results as-is. The tea killed abnormal cells—cancer cells. That was the first test. But was it toxic to healthy human cells? He went back over his notes and calculated the dose's strength in the culture sample that showed the highest efficacy.

Careful not to attract any attention, he mixed a solution in a small, sterile beaker. He held it up to the light. It almost looked like a weak combination of green and black tea. Putting his nose inside the mouth of the container, he tried to identify the scent. Not much to go on. Vegetal, earthy, maybe grassy.

Still holding the beaker, he set it down and stared at it. He'd considered trying it on one of the lab mice first, but that would take too long and attract uninvited attention. And, it wouldn't demonstrate the impact on normal human cells. Another step skipped.

After the date and time, he wrote *initial human trial* in his notebook along with his initials. After looking around to ensure no one was watching, he drank the contents. It was bitter, and he took a sip of coffee to erase the aftertaste.

When he told them last night that he planned to give Karen the tea, they assumed he was talking about a drinkable form. He knew better. Testing the tea himself for human toxicity was the first step. But oral administration would be too slow to be effective for Karen.

He would have to compound the tea into a concentrated injectable form. While he would like to isolate the active agent, that would take too much time. He intended to eliminate most of the water and other known, inert ingredients. That would leave behind the active agent or agents.

Justin was also relying on Mary Richardson's identification of the plant. It too closely resembled a *Rhododendron maximum* to suit him. The rosebay rhododendron was highly poisonous, with the entire plant containing neurotoxins. He'd have to do some quick tests to confirm their absence, but what he just drank would probably show that.

Dosing would be tricky. Yesterday, he'd picked Mary and Tsula's brains about the strength of the tea. Neither of them had used the tea or seen it in action. All they had to go by was the recipe Mary's mother had written on the back of the drawing. Dosing would be a pure SWAG—scientific wild-ass guess.

Then there were other considerations. Thinking back to his conversation with Tina, he wondered how the tea would interact with methotrexate. The methotrexate had already stressed Karen's kidneys to the max. Adding another unknown agent could push them over the edge and lead to kidney failure.

He put the pencil down and massaged his chin. Things were moving faster than he preferred, and he worried that he was skipping too many steps. He thought about what his friend, a retired Marine first sergeant, always said.

Improvise, adapt, and overcome.

It was as simple as that.

11

Thursday morning, as Justin and Alice were having breakfast at home before leaving for work, Justin's phone buzzed. It was Tina, Dr. Stewart's NP.

He answered and listened as Tina gave him an update on Karen. Her latest blood tests showed elevated liver enzymes. She was more fatigued and complaining of back pain. Her lack of appetite was getting worse. They did a PET scan, and it showed that the cancer had further metastasized to her spine and liver. The treatments had not been successful. Dr. Stewart would have to move Karen to hospice this week.

Justin disconnected. He turned to Alice and, in a subdued voice, filled her in on Karen's condition.

"I'm going over there." He paused and added, "I'm going to give her the tea."

He'd told Alice when he'd drank the tea. Other than an upset stomach and a slightly elevated blood pressure, he'd seemed to tolerate it well. He attributed the increase in blood pressure to stress. While unpleasant, he decided the gastro side effects were acceptable. He'd not told Alice that he was planning on injecting it.

"Are you sure it's safe for her? Don't you need to do more testing?"

He raised his voice, frustrated. "Yes, I'd love to do more testing. I'd love to have a few more months—years would be even better. There are a million other things I'd like to do first. But we're out of time."

"Have you told Karen?"

He shook his head. "Not yet. But I will when I get there."

"Maybe you should tell Dr. Stewart?" she said gently.

He slammed his fist on the counter, rattling the dishes. "You don't understand. I can't. If I tell him I'm about to give his patient an unauthorized substance that I cooked up at work, he'll have me escorted out of the hospital. And rightfully so. And when Hadley finds out, I'll be fired and most likely my career ruined."

"I'm sorry. I'm just worried about Karen. And you. This seems risky."

"It is. But time's wasting." He finished his coffee, rose, and said, "I've got to go. I need to stop by the lab on my way."

At the lab, Justin went in and collected a small bottle that he slipped into his pocket. As he walked to his vehicle, he fingered the vial. It contained the concentrated solution from Mary's tea that he'd compounded at work yesterday. After seeing the initial toxicity results yesterday morning, he spent the rest of the day trying to refine the dosage. He had reviewed his calculations numerous times, but in the end, it was pure guesswork. The odds weren't good, but it was still Karen's only chance.

He knew that she had an IV site on the back of her hand. That would allow injecting the extract directly into her bloodstream. He would have preferred to do an infusion instead of a bolus or push, so there would be more time to monitor the effects. Another luxury he didn't have. He'd be lucky to get the few minutes he needed to inject the contents of the vial into the IV without getting caught.

He got on I-40 and drove east. His speed kept creeping up, and he wished the cruise control worked. He was in a hurry to get to the hospital but slowed slightly to nudge the speedometer back under eighty. The last thing he needed was to get stopped by the highway patrol.

When he arrived at Baptist Hospital, he parked in the garage away from other cars. He glanced around to make sure no one was near. He didn't want to risk filling the syringe in the lab and attracting attention but needed to pre-load the one he brought before going inside.

After filling the syringe, he capped it and stuck it in his pocket. He locked the SUV and headed across the familiar walkway to the Cancer Center.

Concentrating on the positives, he tried to convince himself that the extract would work. It definitely killed breast cancer cells in the lab. He'd re-run the cultures and saw similar results. He'd drunk the tea—twice—and suffered only mild side effects. Mary had anecdotal support for its healing powers and the written formula from her mother. Even if it didn't work, it was worth a try. From Karen's perspective, there was nothing to lose. If he were in her place, he'd do it.

The magnitude of what he was about to do cast a long shadow over him. Just the act of giving an unauthorized, untested substance intravenously to a patient in the hospital would mean the end of his career. Criminal charges were likely, prison a distinct possibility. He had thought about these things earlier, but then they were abstract. He felt the syringe in his pocket. This was real.

Worse outcomes reared their ugly head. There was more than a remote possibility that the extract could kill his sister or cause her more suffering. How could he live with that? Would he want to?

On her floor, he walked down the hall to her room and tapped on the door. A female voice, not his sister's, said, "Come in."

"Hey," he said, walking in as Karen's roommate Nicole rose to greet him. She walked over and hugged him.

"How is she?" he asked, looking over her shoulder at his sister. Her eyes were closed, and her breathing shallow. Several IV bags were hanging at her bedside, the clear tubing snaking its way through the pump, piping the liquids into Karen's veins.

"Not good. The times where she's alert and lucid are shorter and farther apart. Right now, she's taking a little nap."

He walked over to Karen's side, reached down, and put his hand over hers.

She stirred, blinked, and opened her eyes. She turned her head slightly to see who was there and saw him. A weak smile crossed her lips. "Brat," she said in a low whisper.

He chuckled and squeezed her hand lightly. "Good to see you, too, sis. How are you feeling?"

Justin saw a faint shrug, then a slight shake of her head. "Tired."

He'd always planned on discussing his intentions with Karen to get her consent. Now, seeing her weakened condition, he worried that any such conversation would be too exhausting.

He turned to Nicole. "I'm sure you could use a break. Why don't you go down and get something to eat?"

Nicole seemed to sense that he wanted some time alone with Karen and nodded.

"I am kind of hungry. Breakfast was a long time ago. Besides, it'll give you two a chance to talk." She rose, patted Karen's hand, and walked out, closing the door behind her.

Karen squeezed his hand with no more strength than a small child. "Dr. Stewart came by."

Justin leaned forward to hear her better.

"A good talk." Karen paused to catch her breath. "Direct." Another pause. "I like that . . . about . . . him."

Justin nodded, tearing up. "Me, too."

"I'm tired," she said.

"I know. But we need to talk."

She squeezed his hand in acknowledgment.

Where to start? he thought, regretting not telling her earlier.

"I know you're tired, so I'll try to keep it concise. Remember the tree I found? I showed you the picture. The Cherokee called it the healing tree, and they believed it had healing powers."

Her eyes narrowed slightly, which indicated she was listening.

"Tsula's mother is a Cherokee healer, and she knew about it. She had the recipe for the extract—" He stopped mid-sentence when he realized Karen's eyes were closed.

Justin held his breath until he saw her chest move up and down. Her breathing was peaceful, and he glanced at the monitor above her head. Her heart rate was slow but steady. She was asleep.

He looked down at his sister, his only sibling. She looked so peaceful. Maybe he should let nature take its course. Who was he to choose for her? He cursed under his breath as he realized that they would not be able to have this conversation. Justin was going to have to decide. On his own. Without her knowledge or consent.

After a few minutes, he leaned over and kissed her forehead. "I love you, sis."

Justin reached into his pocket and slipped out the syringe. He stared at it, saying a prayer as he prepared to inject it into her IV line.

He almost dropped it when he heard a faint knock on the door. A nurse in blue scrubs walked in as he barely managed to palm the syringe. She was a bit thick, with short blonde hair. She appeared to be older and wore a pleasant smile.

"Hi," she said. "I'm Olivia, Karen's nurse this shift."

"Hello. I'm Justin, her brother."

The syringe felt as though it were burning his hand. He stole a glance and saw the tip of the orange cap he'd hastily put back over the needle. *Damn.* He adjusted his grip to hide it, hoping Olivia hadn't seen anything.

"I just need to check her vitals," she said. She stood next to him, waiting.

Momentarily confused, he realized she needed him to move.

"Oh, I'm sorry," he said, getting up and stepping aside.

Olivia moved to Karen's side, checking the monitor and IV pump. She checked the IV site on Karen's hand.

"Has she been asleep the whole time you've been here?"

"In and out. We were talking, and she kinda dozed off."

"That's pretty common," Olivia said, nodding. Satisfied that everything was okay, she entered a brief note on the computer.

"Nice meeting you. Let me know if you need anything," Olivia said, turning to leave.

"Thank you. Nice meeting you, too."

Fuck, he thought, taking a deep breath as he waited for Olivia to close the door on her way out. *That was close.*

He moved back over to Karen's side and sat, waiting a minute for his nerves to calm. He still had the syringe in his hand, thankful he hadn't dropped it. Good thing. He hadn't thought to bring an extra.

When his hands stopped shaking, he injected the contents into the IV on Karen's hand as slowly as he dared, carefully watching the monitor. He withdrew the syringe, capped it, and put it back in his pocket.

He leaned over and kissed his sister on the forehead.

"Forgive me, sis. I'm not ready to let you go, not yet."

12

Monday morning, Justin was driving back over to see Karen for the fifth consecutive day. Hospice did not have an opening until today, so Dr. Stewart had kept her in the hospital. Justin had injected the extract into her veins every day, staying as long as possible to monitor the effects.

He had told Alice and Dr. Hadley that he wanted to spend as much time with Karen as possible since she didn't have much longer. Justin was exhausted, and Alice had urged him to get a room in Winston-Salem. He told her that he couldn't, that he had urgent things to do at the lab. The real reason was that he was compounding more healing tree extract and tweaking the dosage as he went.

The first day, Karen's blood pressure had spiked after the injection, setting off alarms that sent Olivia rushing back into the room. He'd held his breath while Olivia worked to stabilize Karen, fearful he'd done more harm than good. She eventually got Karen's pressure back to normal.

That night, in the lab, he had diluted the compound slightly for the second dose.

He was flying blind. He figured that it would take multiple doses to see any noticeable improvement, and he would've preferred to wait a few days between each dose.

Not convinced that she'd make it that long, he decided to give her successive daily doses.

Yesterday was the fourth day. The first four doses hadn't produced any noticeable change. Discouraged, he'd come today prepared to transfer her to hospice. He'd brought a fifth dose with him but wasn't convinced to give it to her.

As before, Nicole was there when he walked into Karen's room. "How's it going?" he asked.

He stopped two steps inside the room, not prepared for what he saw.

Karen was sitting up in bed.

Upon hearing his voice, she turned to see him. "Hey, brat," she said, smiling. Her voice seemed stronger.

Justin shook his head, amazed. And speechless.

"She seems to be doing better today," Nicole said. "Eating a little, even."

Karen nodded. "More energy."

Justin fingered the syringe in his pocket.

"You okay?" Karen asked him.

A nervous laugh escaped his lips. "Fine, just surprised. You *are* doing better."

He turned to Nicole. "Has Dr. Stewart come by yet?"

"Earlier," Nicole said. "He wanted you to give him a call when you got here."

Staring at Karen, Justin pulled out his phone and called Dr. Stewart's number. He asked Stewart's office to page the doctor as requested and left his cell number.

A few minutes later, Dr. Stewart called and asked Justin to meet him downstairs in the coffee shop. Justin got there first and stood to shake Stewart's hand when the doctor walked in.

"Thanks for calling," Stewart said. "Have you been up to see Karen yet?"

Justin nodded. "I have. And I can't believe it. What's going on, doc?"

Stewart shook his head. "I wish I could give you an answer. The truth is, I don't know. I've got her scheduled for another PET scan and MRI this morning. We're also running some more blood work. My best guess right now is that it's a delayed response to the HDMTX regimen."

"Is that possible?"

Stewart shrugged. "Anything's possible. But no one else has seen this long of an interval between the last dose and some indication of improvement. Not only was there no improvement with your sister, but her condition had also deteriorated. I've been on the computer this morning, chatting with colleagues using this same protocol. They're as puzzled as I am. We should know more this afternoon."

"Are you going to resume the methotrexate?"

Stewart shook his head. "I want to see the test results first, but I doubt it. I think she had as much as she could tolerate."

Justin wanted to hang around for the MRI and blood work results, but he was due back at the lab to meet with Dr. Hadley at five.

"I wish I could stay, but I've got to get back to work," Justin said. "Will you call me as soon as you get the results?"

"Certainly. I should have them by mid-afternoon."

"Thanks," Justin said and went back upstairs to visit with Karen. He still couldn't believe the change. While she certainly was in no shape to go home yet, her improvement was pronounced.

He observed her closely as they chatted. She seemed more alert, her color was good, and her breathing didn't seem to be as laborious. She was talking more.

They chatted for a while, and then she seemed to tire. He told her goodbye and asked Nicole to call him later. He was anxious for the results.

Later that afternoon, he was at his desk back at the lab when Dr. Stewart called.

"Justin, Elliott Stewart here. Got a few minutes?"

"Certainly. You have the results already?"

Justin knew it could take 24-hours or more to get radiology results. As head of oncology, though, Stewart had the clout to push it through quicker.

"I do." Stewart summarized the results of the PET scan and blood work. "And, before you ask, yes, I did rerun the blood tests. Same results."

Justin let the comment about rerunning blood tests slide. He couldn't believe what he was hearing.

"Let me get this straight. You're saying that Karen's cancer is in full retreat?"

"Full retreat is overly optimistic at this point, but yes, all of her numbers are headed in the right direction. The scans show that the number and size of the hot spots have markedly decreased. Her methotrexate levels are down. Her body is beating back the cancer. She's not out of the woods yet, but everything looks positive at this point."

"So, are you planning on resuming the methotrexate?"

"No. I don't think that's necessary at this point."

Justin hung up the phone and just sat there for a few minutes. He didn't think it was the methotrexate. Even Dr. Stewart was skeptical. It was the healing tree, but Stewart didn't know about that. Now, what?

The good news was that it worked, but that raised more questions. Will Karen need more? What strength? Will it last? Stewart said the number and size of the cancer spots had decreased, not disappeared. Her body was defeating the cancer, but she wasn't out of the woods yet. Would something unique show up in her blood work based on the extract? Stewart had already discussed Karen's case with colleagues around the world. Sooner or later, this was going to break wide open.

Damn, Justin thought. He was overwhelmed. Nobody knew about the extract, including Tsula and her mother. Alice didn't know. The Cherokee didn't realize there was a potential shitstorm on the horizon.

But Karen was doing better. He practically floated over to Dr. Hadley's office for his meeting.

Dr. Hadley was sitting at his desk with his back to the door. Justin raised his hand to knock, then remembered his previous admonishment.

"Professor. You wanted to see me," Justin said as he walked in and sat next to his mentor's desk.

Hadley forbade anyone to call him "doctor," maintaining that title was strictly for practicing medical doctors. While he preferred everybody to use his first name, he acquiesced to being called professor. Technically, he still was that, as a tenured professor at University of Oxford.

Hadley turned to Justin. "Close the door, please."

Surprised, Justin closed the door and returned to his seat, nervous. The only time he'd ever known Hadley to close his office door for a conference was to fire someone.

Hadley finished reading the document in front of him, then steepled his hands and swiveled in his chair to face his pupil. His grey eyes bore into Justin.

"Mr. Reeve, would you mind sharing with me exactly what you've been up to this past week?"

Justin swallowed, the lump in his throat growing uncomfortable. *What the hell was he talking about?* Deciding he must be referring to his excessive absences, Justin began, "I know I've been out a lot. You know my sister Karen has—"

"Please don't insult my intelligence by babbling on about your sister as if I were senile. You told me that she has advanced metastatic breast cancer, that she's in Wake Forest Baptist Hospital, enrolled in the HDMTX protocol. I know you've been visiting her daily since last Thursday. Coming in late in the afternoon and staying half the night."

He paused to give Justin a chance to process what he'd said and then continued.

"I *am* getting up in years, and my time on this planet is limited. Please don't waste any more of it."

Justin tried to meet the professor's stare but was unsuccessful. He almost said that this would take a while but knew that comment would incur further wrath. He took a deep breath, struggling to decide how much he could tell without compromising his promise to the Cherokee.

"Remember when I came to you and asked about Taxol? I told you that Alice and I had found an unfamiliar tree while we were hiking."

"Yes, yes," Hadley said, impatient, his grey eyes never leaving Justin.

"Well, I decided to run some experiments on the material I collected. Basic toxicity—"

"Was it successful?" Hadley asked.

"Was what successful?" Justin said, repeating the question and stalling for time.

Exasperated, Hadley shook his head. "What is it that you Yanks say? Cut to the chase? You've been working on something in the lab. I have my speculations, but I'd rather you tell me why you chose that tree and what exactly you've been doing."

Justin stared at the man, wondering if he was psychic. *He knows. Somehow, Hadley knows.* This time, he held Hadley's stare for what seemed like an eternity, trying to decipher how much Hadley knew. He became acutely aware of the clock on the bookcase ticking.

Sacrificing himself for Karen's life was easy. But disclosing the story of the tea was betraying Mary and the Cherokee. He'd trusted Hadley when he first told him about the tree, and he still didn't have to disclose the location.

Taking another deep breath, Justin started into his story. He kept the details about the Cherokee relationship to a bare minimum, emphasizing that the tree was sacred and a closely guarded secret. He spelled out everything he'd been doing, right up to the phone call from Karen's doctor minutes ago.

When he finished, he sat there, wondering what he'd just done. Buoyed by his sister's miraculous improvement, he was prepared to accept the consequences, however severe. Even if he got fired, it was worth it. At the same time, he felt guilty for betraying the Cherokee. He needed to talk to Tsula and her mother and confess. That would be tougher. So far, Hadley had said nothing.

"I'm sorry," Justin said. "I know what I did was wrong, and—"

The professor held up his hand. "You broke every rule in the book. And probably some that haven't occurred to me yet. Not to mention a few laws as well."

Justin lowered his head. "I'll get my resignation to you as soon as I get back to my desk."

The professor moved closer with a single shake of his head.

"No, you won't. Early in my career, when I was about your age, I was in a similar position. Reggie, my only sibling, was dying. I spent every waking moment in the lab, trying to divine a cure. By sheer chance, I stumbled across something, something I was convinced would save him."

Hadley paused, then slowly shook his head. The professor seemed to age in front of him as he continued.

"I couldn't do it. I'd taken too many shortcuts, skipped too many steps. I was afraid. I didn't give it to my brother, and he died. I never knew if it could've saved him."

He stared at Justin. "Your discovery saved a life. There's no putting the genie back in the lamp. The question is how we proceed."

Shaking his head, Justin thought, *What have I done? I've created a monster.*

13

Rhonda tapped on Alice's open office door. "Ms. Foster is here to see you."

Alice had seen Debra Foster come in and walk over to Rhonda's desk in the lobby. Pretending she hadn't noticed the woman, Alice peered around Rhonda to see Debra sitting in the waiting area and nodded.

"Thanks. Please tell her I'll be right out."

Alice picked up Debra's folder from the stack on the corner of her desk. Discreetly, she eyed Rhonda speaking with Debra. Alice opened the file and acted as if familiarizing herself with the information. In reality, she was composing herself for the performance about to begin.

After a few deep breaths, she stood and walked out to greet the tall, slender blonde. As she approached, Alice extended her hand.

"Ms. Foster? Hi, I'm Alice. Why don't you come on back?"

Debra looked up and cocked her head. For a brief moment, Alice thought she'd recognized her. Debra stood and shook Alice's hand.

"Debra, please."

Alice turned and extended her hand, pointing to her office a few yards away.

"Please. Have a seat," she said after following Debra into the office.

Inside, Alice shut the door and walked around behind her desk, all business. She sat, folding her hands on the desk in front of her.

"I understand you and your husband are looking to buy a vacation home in the area?"

"Yes, we are. We've been looking in east Tennessee and Western North Carolina for a mountain house and have decided on this area." Debra stared at her. "Forgive me, but you remind me of someone I knew. Are you by chance from the Indianapolis area?"

Alice smiled politely and shook her head. "No, afraid not. I'm originally from Colorado and moved to North Carolina years ago." She held Debra's gaze. "In fact, I've never been to Indianapolis. I hear it's a nice area, though."

Debra nodded. "It is. I grew up there. Brad—my husband—is from Michigan. We met in college."

To change the subject, Alice picked up the cover sheet from the folder and asked, "I see in your application that you haven't decided on a place yet. You simply want to pre-qualify, is that correct?"

Again, Debra nodded. "We're working with Lisa at Hilltop Realty. She's been showing us properties, but we haven't made a decision yet. We wanted to make sure we could get a loan first."

"I see. Lisa's a good realtor. I'm sure she'll help you find something suitable. I'm happy to tell you that you're pre-approved for the $300,000 requested."

Alice pulled a sheet out of the file and slid it over to Debra. "Of course, the final loan approval is subject to income verification, property appraisal, and a few other items listed here."

Debra scanned the page and nodded. "Great. We're looking forward to spending more time here, especially in the summers."

"It's a lovely area. As soon as you decide on something, give me a call, and we can get started. Any other questions?"

"Uh, no. Thank you."

Alice stood. "We appreciate your business, Debra, and look forward to working with you and your husband." She handed Debra a business card. "Here's my information. If you think of anything later, or Lisa has any questions, please call."

Alice walked her to the front door and watched, curious as to what Debra drove. She got into a white, late-model BMW sedan.

Alice nodded. That was a car to avoid. She went back to her office, convinced Debra didn't recognize her old classmate.

14

Hadley leaned back in his chair and stared at Justin. "Why do you believe it's the extract and not the MTX? You said that Stewart attributed it to a delayed reaction."

"He doesn't know about the extract. A delayed reaction was the only conclusion he could reach, regardless of how far-fetched. He acknowledged that no one else using the HDMTX protocol had seen anything close to Karen's response.

"My sister was dying, professor. Her last PET scan before I gave her the extract showed cancer everywhere. Her blood work was dismal. Dr. Stewart had thrown in the towel and asked me to move her to hospice. His exact words were, 'we're out of options.'"

"Can you get me a copy of your sister's medical record? I want to review it."

Justin nodded. "I've got healthcare power of attorney for her, and I know Dr. Stewart has a copy. I'd love to get your opinion. You'll have it before I leave this afternoon."

"Good. Moving along, we have a significant issue we have to address right away. Legally, the extract is the property of Nuran Labs."

"I have the formula for compounding the tea into an injectable, but I didn't make the tea. The tree belongs to the

Cherokee, and a Cherokee healer brews the tea," Justin said. Mary always made the tea for him.

"Doesn't matter. Review your employment contract. It includes all notes, documentation, intermediate products—everything, electronic or hand-written, even if someone else did it at your direction," Hadley said. "If they could extract your brain cells, they would include those as well."

Justin shrugged. "Even if I had the formula for the tea—which I don't—the raw material is organic. Without the tree, there's no extract."

"Perhaps. Maybe it could be synthesized, maybe not. It doesn't matter. You told me the tree was in the National Park?"

"Possibly. There's reason to believe that it may be on Cherokee land." Alice, Tsula, and Atohi were the only ones besides himself who had seen the tree and knew where it was. At least he hadn't broken that promise.

"Was that the only one you found?"

Justin nodded.

Hadley stroked his beard, thinking. "We have to tell the company."

"What?" Justin asked. "We can't. I swore to the Cherokee I wouldn't tell anyone. I've already told you more than I should've." He could accept that the compounding formula belonged to the company, but to disclose everything he'd done? That would be ruinous. His Cherokee family would never forgive him for breaking their confidence and unleashing the corporate hounds.

"You—an employee—developed this here at the lab, using our equipment and materials. We're obligated to notify the company that you have identified an agent with potential anti-cancer properties. As required, you've notified me, the senior research scientist. Now, you have to turn over all legal documentation related to the extract."

"But that means the description and exact location of the tree?"

"I thought you said you hadn't identified the tree. Are the precise coordinates of the location in the company files? You haven't given them to me."

Justin stared at his mentor. "No, but—"

Hadley held up his hand. "I said all 'legal' documentation."

Justin cocked his head, not sure of exactly what the professor was saying. "So, with regards to Karen—"

"You don't know what the anti-cancer properties are, do you? How could you?"

"But—"

"Without rigorous clinical trials, there is no way you could know anything about the efficacy, correct?"

Justin stared at the bearded man, confused. Then, it dawned on him. Hadley was suggesting that they not disclose specifics about the tree or what Justin had done with his sister.

"Forgive me," Justin said, a smile creasing his face. "You're right. I don't know what kind of tree it is. And no determination of efficacy is possible at this juncture. How could it be?"

"My point precisely. Get everything to me this afternoon so that I can comply with company policy."

Justin grinned and nodded. "Certainly. I understand." He was a little slow, but now he was on the same page as the professor. Hadley was giving him an out.

Back at his desk, Justin called Tina and said that he wanted a copy of Karen's medical record.

"You should have a copy of the healthcare power of attorney naming me as her health care agent," he said.

"Yes, I remember you giving that to us. Her medical records are available on our health care portal. Do you still have the password?"

He'd forgotten about the patient portal. "Yes, I do. Will everything be on it?"

"It should, everything through midnight last night."

"Great. Thanks."

Justin hung up and turned his attention to his files on the company server. Although he'd been careful to put all information related to Karen and the extract on his personal laptop, he wanted to make sure there was nothing incriminating on the Nuran server.

Once satisfied, he booted up his personal laptop, which he never connected to the Nuran network, and inserted a thumb drive. He went through his files on the extract, careful to redact things that might point to the healing tree. He referred to it only as a new, unknown species in the GSMNP. With over a thousand new species discovered in the Park to date, it would buy him time should anyone go snooping around.

He transferred the bare minimum information that would satisfy the legal requirements. He didn't download files containing any reference to Karen and what he'd done. Once finished, he removed the thumb drive and downloaded the contents into his Nuran computer.

Still logged on to the company computer, he checked everything once more. Satisfied that he had cleansed and segregated the information, he shared the lawful files with Hadley through the company server. Now, Hadley had the information he needed to report the discovery but without revealing any detail.

Back on his personal laptop, he logged on to Karen's patient portal and downloaded her medical record. He transferred a copy to an empty thumb drive, removed it, and stuck it in his pocket for Hadley. Justin logged off, packed his laptop, and made ready to leave. He'd drop it off on the way out.

As he headed toward Hadley's office, Justin was still uneasy, concerned about the brewing storm. Another lie—this one of omission—but another strand in the web of deception. He had to come clean with his family. Now.

15

After stopping by Hadley's office to drop off the thumb drive, Justin drove home. Home was a log cabin that had belonged to Justin's grandmother. Near the Park boundary, it sat on several acres high up in the mountains.

It had been a shack when he acquired it, but he'd remodeled and expanded, adding modern conveniences. He kept the wood stove, moving it to his study to provide a cozy warmth during the cold mountain winters.

Justin pulled into the driveway and parked next to Alice's car. He'd called her on the way back from the hospital, describing Karen's miraculous recovery. After talking to Dr. Stewart, he'd called her again to tell her what Stewart had said. She had insisted on inviting Tsula and Atohi over for dinner to celebrate.

He switched the SUV off and sat there for a minute before going inside to face the music. A celebration and confession. Thankfully, Atohi and Tsula weren't due for another hour. That would give him a chance to tell Alice what he'd done before they arrived, then he'd have to repeat his story for them.

They all knew he was going to give Karen the tea, just not in injectable form. That was the easy part. Then, he had to admit that he'd told Hadley about the tree and what he'd done. Further, Hadley was going to tell Nuran. He didn't want to think about the response that would elicit.

Inside the house, Justin shut the door behind him and hung up his jacket. Alice walked out of the bedroom, clutching her bathrobe around her, her hair wet.

"I thought I heard you," she said. "You're early. I decided to take a quick shower before you got home."

She greeted him with an enthusiastic hug.

"We need to talk," he said, not in the mood.

She let go of the robe, and the lapels fell away, exposing her naked body underneath. He stared at her, tongue-tied. She took his hands and placed them on her breasts.

"I had something else in mind," she said.

Her nipples underneath his hands excited him despite his initial reluctance. Reflexively, he squeezed gently. Alice responded by lifting her head and kissing him. As she unfastened his belt, he lowered his hand between her legs. She was wet and not from the shower.

He pushed the robe off her shoulders, and as it dropped to the floor, he kissed her neck. She moaned and fumbled to unzip his pants, pulling them down.

"I want you," she said. "Now."

Afterward, they lay in bed, Alice in his arms. "We really need to get dressed before our company gets here," she said.

He nodded, his breathing finally returning to normal. He kissed the top of her head.

"You mentioned you wanted to talk?" she said.

He exhaled, jolted back to his original intention before Alice had distracted him. He looked over at the clock. Their company would be here any minute.

"Might as well wait till they get here." At least he wouldn't have to tell the story twice. He heard a car drive up.

He and Alice quickly dressed and met Tsula and Atohi at the front door.

Alice had prepared some snacks, and after they all got drinks, they settled comfortably in the living room.

Justin told them about his visit that morning with Karen.

"That is wonderful news," Atohi said.

"Amazing," Tsula said. "What did her doctor say?"

Justin hesitated and glanced over at Alice. "He thinks it's a delayed response to the methotrexate."

Tsula looked at him. "You don't sound convinced."

"I'm not." He took a swallow of his beer. "It wasn't the methotrexate. It was the healing tree."

He took a deep breath and continued. "I told you that I was going to give Karen the tea that Mary brewed, which I did. There's more to it."

He described making a concentrated form and drinking it himself. Alice stood, hands-on-hips, staring down at him when he got to the part about injecting it into Karen's IV line.

"You did what? You said you were going to give your sister the tea. Now, you're saying that you injected her with some untested concoction you cooked up in the lab."

"It *was* the tea. I just . . . I just reduced it, if you will, to make it stronger. Giving her tea to drink wasn't going to be enough. Karen was dying."

Tsula said, "You injected an experimental substance into her body. Multiple times. While she was in the hospital. That's a lot different than giving her a cup of tea. Do you realize how illegal that is? You could go to prison for that."

"Why didn't you tell me? We're getting married, and you're keeping secrets like that from me?" Alice said, shouting now.

"She was dying, and I had to move quickly. I figured that if none of you knew what I was doing, you couldn't be held responsible in any way. You have every right to be upset, but please, let me finish."

Shaking her head, Alice sat down in her chair and crossed her arms, eyes ablaze.

He told them about Karen's PET scan and lab results. "It's the healing tree. I know it."

Tsula shook her head. "According to you, Dr. Stewart said it was a delayed reaction to the HDMTX. What makes you so certain it's not?"

"He said no one else using the same regimen as Karen had seen that kind of response. She'd finished eight cycles, and there was no improvement. She was getting worse. He even told me that he had no explanation, but he didn't know about the tea. The only reason he could come up with was a delayed reaction. I know better. It had to be the healing tree extract."

"So, what if they find traces of the extract in her blood work? Have you thought about what that's going to mean? And, her doctor has already shared the results with others." Now, Tsula was getting louder.

Atohi spoke. "Don't get us wrong, brother. We're all glad that Karen's doing better. That's great news, but isn't this going to bring down all sorts of unwanted attention?"

Shit, Justin thought. *And this was the easy part.* He paused, then continued.

"I told Dr. Hadley."

Everyone's jaw dropped. Alice said, "Oh my God, you didn't? You told your boss what you did? Have you lost your mind?"

The looks on Tsula and Atohi's faces were like daggers in Justin's heart. Disappointment turned into anger as they processed the implications.

Tsula leaned forward in her chair and stared at Justin. In a measured tone, she said, "You promised. You promised my mother—all of us—that you wouldn't tell anyone."

"I had to. The work I've done belongs to the company. I'm required to disclose it. But all I've disclosed is that I've identified a compound with *potential* cancer-killing properties. Nothing about the tree or its location. And nothing about giving it to Karen."

"You've opened Pandora's box," Atohi said. "You can't un-open it. Anything else you've conveniently forgotten to tell us?"

His best friend's sarcasm cut Justin like a knife. He knew he deserved it, but it hurt just the same. He told them about the conversation with his boss earlier that afternoon.

"Hadley agreed to keep it under wraps as long as he can. He's the one who suggested only sharing the barest of information. He's reviewing Karen's medical record to confirm it was the extract."

"You should've had told me," Alice said, arms still crossed.

"I know, and I'm sorry," Justin said. He looked at Atohi and Tsula. "I know I've let you down, and I'm sorry. Please forgive me."

"I need to tell Mother," Tsula said, crossing her arms.

"I'm willing to go with you. I'm the one who screwed up," Justin said.

Tsula shook her head. "I'm not sure that's a good idea." She looked over at Atohi. "We can go there when we leave."

Atohi nodded. "You're convinced the healing tree has potential as a cancer drug?"

"I know it does," Justin said. "I wish you could have seen the difference in Karen. I expect Hadley will confirm it."

"And you're certain no one knows the location of the tree?" Tsula asked.

"Positive. I told you, we are the only ones who know. Dr. Hadley doesn't know. He doesn't even have a clue what the tree looks like."

"Sam Bear knows," Atohi said. "I took him out there while you were going to see Karen, remember?"

Justin had forgotten about the Cherokee surveyor. Atohi took him to the tree so he could determine if the tree was on the Qualla Boundary.

"Him, I'm not worried about," Tsula said in an agitated voice, still glaring at Justin. "How can you guarantee that no one else will find out? The first thing your company will want to know is what kind of plant and where it is. Then what?"

Justin didn't have a good answer. If Hadley confirmed the effectiveness, they'd have to cross that bridge when they came to it.

* * *

Wednesday afternoon, Hadley called Justin into his office.

"Close the door and have a seat," the professor said as Justin came in.

Justin sat as requested. His mentor's tone made him uncomfortable, and he wondered what Hadley wanted. The only thing he could think of was something in Karen's medical records.

With no preamble, Hadley said, "I've reviewed your sister's records. I've also shared her information— anonymously, of course—with several of my colleagues. The consensus is that your sister is in remission. No one had a reasonable explanation, other than the feeble attribution to a delayed response to HDMTX."

Justin breathed a sigh of relief. He'd worried that Hadley had found something otherwise or wouldn't accept an unconventional explanation.

Hadley continued. "Anecdotally, it would appear that your intervention was the reason. Although trained in Western medicine, I've never arbitrarily discounted indigenous remedies. Still, one case does not constitute a clinical trial. This leads to my quandary."

Justin wrinkled his brow, curious as to where the professor was going.

Hadley picked up a binder on his desk. "I'd like more data—official data. This is my report to Robert Kendall on HT67. I'm recommending that we designate it as our top research project."

"HT67?"

"Your extract."

Justin assumed that HT referred to the healing tree, but what was 67?

As if reading Justin's mind, Hadley said, "The year the Beatles released *Sgt. Pepper's*."

Justin suppressed a slight grin. He should've known. Hadley had initially named Tramorix as YS69 for *Yellow Submarine*, 1969.

"What's the dilemma, then?" Justin asked.

"If I give HT67 the attention it merits, there will be intense pressure to disclose the location and identity of the tree. But if I downplay the significance, we won't get the necessary resources I believe it deserves."

Justin panicked, realizing the implications of Hadley's recommendation. Suggesting Nuran make it a top research project would be disastrous. "You can't do that. I gave the Cherokee my word. I will not give up the location of the tree. Or it's value."

"You may have stumbled onto a revolutionary treatment for breast cancer. Think of the lives it could save. Morally, we have to pursue it."

Justin shook his head. While he was pleased with Hadley's endorsement, he would not break his vow to his Cherokee family again.

"I'm sorry, but I have to talk to the Cherokee first." He folded his arms across his chest. "Look at your files on

HT67, as you call it. I refuse to give a description of the tree and divulge where it is before getting their consent. Fire me if you want. There are over a half-million acres in the National Park. It's going to be tough to find a needle in that haystack."

Hadley stared at him, expressionless. After a minute, he said, "I have to tell Kendall something."

"I understand," Justin said. "Give him the bare bones, as you previously suggested. Enough to fulfill our obligation to disclose, but without any detail."

Hadley seemed to consider this, then said, "Fine. When can you talk to your friends?"

"I'll call as soon as I get back to my desk."

Hadley nodded. "I'm troubled by the fact that you've only seen the one tree. Basing a cancer treatment on one plant is pointless if we can't isolate the active agent to ensure a steady supply for testing and possible subsequent production."

"I agree. I'm working on it." That was all he intended to say at this point. He'd already considered enlisting the Cherokee to look for others, if they hadn't already, but wanted to see if it was on the Qualla first.

"When are you meeting with Kendall?" Justin asked.

"As soon as I can make a few revisions to this," he said, patting the binder in front of him.

16

R obert stood as his assistant ushered Dr. Hadley into his office for their monthly project status meeting.

"Gareth, how are you today?"

"I'd be better if I spent more time working and less time in bloody meetings," the gruff man said as he took a seat in front of Robert's desk.

Robert smiled as he sat. Gareth Hadley was never one to mince words.

"I understand. I won't keep you long."

Hadley placed the binder he held on Robert's desk. As usual, Robert didn't look at it, preferring to get a verbal summary from his chief scientist first.

"Only one small change from last month," Hadley said. Not waiting for Robert to ask, he continued. "We have a new project, dubbed HT67. It's a plant derivative. Initial tests indicate it may have anti-cancer potential."

Robert scowled. "This is the first I've heard of this."

Hadley shrugged. "I just found out about it a few days ago. Since I knew our status meeting was today, I felt like it could wait."

"A plant derivative?"

Hadley nodded. "Justin Reeve came across a new plant while hiking. Later, while trying to identify it, he did some preliminary tests. It might be promising, so he brought it to my attention."

"Anti-cancer potential? Can you be more specific?"

Hadley shifted in his chair. "It's in my report. Preliminary, but at first glance, a crude extract appears to exhibit cytotoxicity to human cancer cells."

"What kind of cancer cells?"

"Breast cancer."

"Are you kidding me? Breast cancer? You're talking about a possible competitor to Tramorix?"

Hadley shook his head and held up his hands. "I told you this is very early. All new theories are promising at this stage. You know most ideas—I hesitate even to call it a project at this point—do not amount to anything."

"Last week, I told you that Bearant was considering buying us out. Specifically for Tramorix. I asked you then if you were aware of anything out there that might even be remotely a threat to Tramorix. You said, and I quote, 'nothing.'"

"I told you, I just found out about this. At the time, I didn't know."

"What are you recommending?" Robert asked, tapping on the binder in front of him.

"I think HT67 merits further investigation. Based on my early review of Mr. Reeve's information, I'd like to devote more resources to it. Specifically, isolating the active agent so we can perform more detailed tests. It's all in there," he said, nodding toward the binder.

"Further research? More resources?" Robert shook his head. "No way. Bearant will go ballistic if they get wind of this."

"Why? They'll own it."

Robert snorted. "Gareth, they're talking about five fucking billion dollars. They'll want to know why this is just now surfacing, wondering if we knew about it all along. They'll view it as a potential threat to what they're buying."

Hadley shook his head. "Even *if* HT67 does prove effective, which is a long shot, it is different. HT67 is plant-based. Tramorix is synthesized. Your train of thought is pure conjecture."

"What kind of plant? You said he found it while hiking. Where?"

"I don't know. He didn't say."

"Well, find out. That is *our* information, Gareth—Nuran's. Reeve works for Nuran, so whatever he found belongs to us."

"Of course, HT67 belongs to us. I reminded Reeve of that very fact. But you are overreacting, Robert. This is a moonshot, at best."

"Bearant won't see it that way. Anything that smells the least bit off will make them nervous. They'll think that as soon as the deal closes—you, me, Reeve, whoever—will be setting up shop to compete. The whole world knows how difficult non-compete agreements are to enforce."

Robert pushed the unopened binder back across the desk to Hadley and then folded his hands together on the desk.

"I'm concerned you may have been a bit hasty in preparing this. I'd rather you take a little more time before formally submitting it."

Hadley stared at him.

"Gareth, you and I go back a long way. After Margaret passed, you took a huge risk by coming with Nuran. I'm grateful for that and what you've accomplished with Tramorix. It represents my life dream. The reality is Bearant can take it to the next level much quicker than we can, saving hundreds of thousands of lives in the process. I've spent every dollar I could get my hands on and years of my life. This acquisition represents our retirement—mine and yours. I want to make sure we don't do anything to jeopardize that."

Hadley stood, picking up the binder. "I understand." He turned and strode out.

Robert watched as Hadley left. He didn't like surprises, and alarm bells were sounding.

As currently structured, the deal would put five billion dollars in cash in Nuran stockholders' pockets, in addition to some Bearant stock options. Since Robert and his son owned seventy-five percent of the Nuran stock, this meant almost four billion dollars to the two of them. This was the kind of deal that Robert had worked for his entire life. No one was going to get in the way.

He picked up his phone and called his son.

"This is Bobby."

Robert still cringed whenever he heard his son's nickname out loud. He knew everybody referred to his son, Robert Kendall, III, as Bobby. Robert had quit fighting that battle years ago.

"I need to see you. Now."

"On my way."

Five minutes later, Bobby entered his office.

"What's up?"

"Have a seat. I just had an interesting meeting with Dr. Hadley. He told me about a new project he called 'HT67.' Some type of plant derivative that your friend Justin discovered."

Bobby nodded. "Justin mentioned it the other day. He was at his desk, looking up Cherokee medicinal plants or something like that. Said he found a new tree in the Park."

Robert was surprised. This was considerably more than Hadley had told him. Either he didn't know, or he was concealing information. "Hadley suggested it may have anti-cancer properties."

"Really? Justin didn't mention that. Maybe it could be the next Tramorix?"

Robert gazed out the window. He knew that Bobby and Justin were close friends, but damn, Bobby was slow. He took a deep breath then looked back at Bobby.

"Let me put this in context for you, son. Bearant's offer for Nuran is five billion dollars in cash. Since we own seventy-five percent of the stock, that means $3.75 billion goes to us."

"Five *billion* dollars—cash?" Bobby repeated, emphasizing the *b*. "And we'd get seventy-five percent? Jesus."

Robert nodded, happy that his son understood the importance. "We just have to make it to closing with no hiccups."

Bobby flipped his hands over, palms up. "No problem with that. I mean, we're clean."

"Good," Robert said. "Here's the thing. We don't need to confuse Bearant with a wild goose chase. It's unnecessary. Remember the old adage, 'never sell someone who's already sold?' Well, Bearant's sold. They can make Tramorix the next blockbuster cancer drug. We don't need another Tramorix. In fact, we don't want another Tramorix. Understand?"

Bobby nodded. "I get it."

"Good. Let me know if you hear any more about that damn tree extract."

"Justin and I are going out after work this afternoon. I'll find out what I can."

"Discreetly," Robert said.

Bobby rose to leave. "What's going to happen to this place?"

"DKDC. Don't know, don't care. Three-point seven five billion dollars—cash. That's all you need to focus on, son. Bearant can do whatever the hell they want to for that kind of money."

As soon as his son left, Robert took a cell phone out of his top desk drawer and punched CALL. He needed to know more about HT67.

"Hello," the voice answered.

The voice belonged to a man claiming to be Matt Farmer. Although he'd dealt with the man for over a decade, Robert doubted that was his real name.

Matt operated on a need-to-know basis, and Robert didn't need to know much. All he knew was that Matt took care of things for him, whatever involved.

Matt was a professional "fixer." He wasn't some heavy-handed goon who busted kneecaps. However, Robert suspected he was capable of that if the situation required it. He knew that Matt had always used the minimum effort necessary to achieve the desired results. He had faithfully and discreetly served Robert, never failing him.

"I need you to do a little research for me," Robert said.

17

That afternoon, Justin left the lab and went to Frog Level, meeting Bobby for a beer.

"Hey, stranger," Mary Ann said as she poured Justin his usual Nutty Brunette. "What's going on with you? I haven't seen you in a week."

"Work's been crazy. And I'm sure you've heard about my sister." There were no secrets in a small town like Waynesville.

Mary Ann nodded. "How's she doing?"

"Much better, thanks." He picked up his beer. "I'll settle up when we're done."

She laughed. "I'm not worried. I know where to find you and Bobby. He's out on the deck."

Justin walked out on the deck and spied his friend sitting at their usual table by the creek.

"It's been a busy week," he said, sitting opposite him.

"Yes, indeed. I hear you've been busy in the lab," Bobby said, winking. He held his glass up to Justin's. "Congratulations."

Justin touched glasses, then they both took a drink. "For what? What'd you hear?"

"Hadley told Dad about your discovery. HT67. Sounds like exciting stuff."

Wary of the direction the conversation had taken, Justin said, "What did Hadley tell him?"

"Pretty much what you'd told me. Some plant you found hiking in the Park. Hadley told Dad that it showed anti-cancer potential."

Justin nodded. "Promising, maybe, but a long way to go."

"Tell me about it," Bobby said. "Is it going to be our next blockbuster? Another Tramorix?"

Justin chuckled. "That's a giant leap. You know how long these things take. Taxol took thirty years. This is just something I've been messing around with in the lab. Who knows if it will amount to anything?"

"What made you decide it had any value?"

Justin shrugged, wondering why Bobby was so interested. "Luck. Alice and I were hiking and stumbled across a plant I'd not seen before. I was curious and wanted to identify it. I ran some basic tests, and it appears that it might have some anti-cancer potential."

"So that's why you were looking up Cherokee plants, huh? What kind of plant is it? Did you ask your Cherokee friends?"

Justin thought that Bobby seemed to be too interested in all of this, and he feigned disinterest. "Not sure. I haven't spent a lot of time on it. Probably some invasive plant. Who knows?"

"You said you and Alice found it in the Park. Where?"

Justin ignored the question, took a drink of his beer, and changed the subject.

"Karen's doctor thinks she may be able to go home soon."

"That's great news. How's she feeling?"

Justin wondered if Bobby suspected anything but decided he was only making conversation. "Much better, thanks. Getting her strength back and anxious to get out of the hospital."

"Awesome. I know how much you wanted to give her Tramorix. But it sounds like what they were doing at Wake Forest worked."

If you only knew, Justin thought. "Speaking of Tramorix, when is that going down?" With everything else going on, he had almost forgotten about the sale of Nuran.

"The banker from New York is coming down next week. Dad says they're close. If everything goes well, the sale will go through by this time next month."

"What is that going to mean to the lab?"

Bobby shrugged. "Don't know. Tramorix production will still probably move to Mexico—that's always been our plan, you know that. We're R&D here. That's why I was glad to hear about your discovery—more reason to keep the lab going if we have a new project. Nothing will change. You'll be fine, especially with that."

Bobby looked around, making sure no other ears were listening. One couple was on the upper deck but a safe distance away. He leaned over and whispered to Justin, "I probably shouldn't tell you this, but you need to understand what's at stake. The offer on the table is five billion dollars. Cash."

"Are you shitting me?" Justin said out loud. "Five billion dollars?"

Bobby held his finger up to his lips.

Justin didn't know how much of Nuran the Kendalls owned, but he figured most of it. That was insane money.

Bobby nodded. "I know. Crazy, huh? I can't even imagine that kind of money. We'd be billionaires. Overnight. With that in reach, the old man is obsessed with seeing this happen. He doesn't want to rock the boat."

Justin thought about HT67 and tried to figure out the impact. "Wouldn't a new drug sweeten the pot for Bearant?"

Bobby shook his head. "Not according to him. He's afraid it would confuse things and derail the offer."

Justin digested the news. This amount of money shed new light on everything. All he could think about was the Cherokee. Tsula was right—corporate America would do anything.

"Just sit on this HT67 thing until the deal closes," Bobby said. "Don't make waves."

They finished their drinks and rose to leave. Justin's head was still spinning. "Thanks for the beer. My turn next time."

"I'll hold you to it. Let me know when," Bobby said as they walked out the front door.

On the way home, Justin tried to call Atohi and Tsula, with no success. He wondered what would happen to the lab after the acquisition. He didn't buy the old "nothing will change" argument.

He who has the gold makes the rules. That was the golden rule in corporate America. He wondered if Hadley knew how fast the acquisition was moving?

When he got home, he opened the front door to the aroma of home cooking. Alice was in the kitchen, preparing dinner.

She had regular hours working at the bank, unlike him, so she was responsible for dinner during the week. He took the weekend shift.

He walked up behind her, put his arms around her waist, and kissed her neck. He peeked over her shoulder to see what was cooking. Fresh corn. Peas. Tomatoes.

"Looks good," he said. "I'm starving."

They ate dinner with little conversation. Justin worried about the future of the lab. He didn't know yet if Karen would need additional doses of the extract. Suspecting she might, he had to keep producing it. With the acquisition, would he be able to continue with his clandestine research and production?

When they finished eating, Alice said, "Go on. I'll clean up."

Justin didn't argue. He picked up his wine and went to the living room. Standing there, he eyed the television, then shifted his gaze to the piano. Opting for the latter, he walked over, found the music he wanted, and sat.

His father had been a musician. He was always on the road, touring, he called it. It wasn't until after a stroke claimed him that Justin realized "touring" meant a succession of small clubs and honky-tonks from Chicago to New York. His father was a talented musician, but like so many, he could never seem to catch a break. His entire life was a struggle, and Justin regretted not getting to know him better before he passed.

Justin warmed up with a few scales and then eased into a song. When he finished, he looked up to see Alice standing in the kitchen doorway with a glass of water, studying him.

"What's the matter?" she said.

He shrugged. "Nothing. Why?"

"You always play that when something's bothering you."

"It was one of my dad's favorites. *Hymn to Freedom* by Oscar Peterson. I wish I could play it like him. Did I ever tell you that he played with Peterson?"

She shook her head and walked over to take a seat on the stool beside him.

He turned to face her and said, "Oscar Peterson was one of the jazz greats. My father played a few gigs with him."

He shook his head, saying, "Dad always wanted me to play jazz. I tried. I can sight-read most anything, but improv . . . not me."

"You miss him, don't you?"

He nodded. "I wish you could've heard him play. He had a gift."

"I hear you play. You have a gift. And I know he's proud of you."

Justin exhaled and closed the piano. He never once recalled his father saying that he was proud of him—for any reason. His father kept his feelings to himself, and Justin always vowed he'd never do that. Looking at Alice, he realized he was doing the same thing.

"Bobby mentioned that his dad plans to sell Nuran," he said.

He didn't disclose that Bobby had first mentioned it several weeks ago. *No harm, no foul.* After their fight yesterday, he wasn't about to go there tonight.

"Really? Is it serious?"

Justin nodded. "He has a good offer from Bearant. Bobby swore me to secrecy."

"Well, he doesn't have anything to worry about with you," she said. She took a drink of her water. "Sorry. That was a cheap shot. I apologize."

"Deserved. Apology accepted." Justin was glad to see that she was softening. "I'm just wondering what that'll mean to the lab—my ability to continue to work on the extract. Karen's probably going to need more. What if I don't have a job?"

She reached out and put her hand on his shoulder.

"You'll be fine, don't you think? Especially with the new drug you're working on. Plus, Bobby has always looked out for you."

Justin nodded. "He has. But there is no formal new drug project. I asked Hadley not to push too hard on the extract until I can talk with Tsula and her mom. What if the Cherokee won't permit us to proceed with it? Plus, Bearant has a huge R&D group in Silicon Valley. Even with a new drug, I can't imagine why they'd keep the lab here."

"Maybe we'd have to move to California. That wouldn't be the end of the world."

Justin stiffened and shook his head. "I don't want to move to the West Coast. This is home."

"I know," Alice said. "But sometimes we have to do things we don't want to do. Be positive. You're jumping way ahead."

18

The next afternoon, Justin was at his desk on his personal computer, looking at Karen's most recent blood tests. Thankfully, Dr. Stewart was doing frequent testing. He wanted to ensure that the cancer was indeed in retreat.

Justin wanted to correlate the efficacy of the various doses he'd given Karen with changes in her test results. He didn't doubt that HT67 was the reason for her recovery but wanted to determine if she needed additional therapy and he should tweak the dosage.

"Mr. Reeve."

Justin recognized his mentor's voice. He turned, surprised to see the heavyset man standing there. "Sir?"

"I've taken another look at your sister's records, and I've revised my opinion. After further study, I agree with Elliott's assessment. Her recovery seems to be a delayed reaction to the methotrexate."

Justin was stunned. "That's impossible," he stammered.

"Not only possible but probable." His stare warned Justin to back off.

"Based on that, I went back through your work on HT67. I tried to duplicate your preliminary tests here in the lab." Hadley shook his head. "My results did not match yours."

"That can't be," Justin said. He felt like he was being ambushed.

"Perhaps your samples were contaminated, or you were in a hurry. At any rate, I think I was premature in my conclusion that HT67 has anti-cancer potential. I've revised my official report to Robert Kendall. I'm recommending that we discontinue any further work on it. You need to shift your attention back to the production standards for Tramorix."

"But—"

"Sometimes, when one is emotionally involved, one tends to see what they wish to see. As scientists, we must let the facts dictate the proper path. In this case, the evidence does not justify the further expenditure of resources."

Justin was angry now. "How can you do that? Yesterday, you were going in to ask Kendall for more resources. Did he talk you out of it? Now, you've completely reversed yourself. What happened?"

"I understand you're disappointed, but I think you may be letting your sentiments overrule your judgment. On more than one occasion in my career, I've had to abandon my efforts. On many of those projects, I spent considerably more time than you have on this one. It's time to let it go."

Justin shook his head. "I don't believe this. You've turned 180 degrees in less than twenty-four hours. Why?"

Ignoring the question, Hadley said, "Tramorix standards. I'll expect a draft by Monday morning." His tone left no room for misinterpretation. He turned and shuffled away.

Justin was in shock. He couldn't believe Hadley was shutting down research on the healing tree. There had to be more to this.

He picked up his phone and called Bobby. "I need a beer this afternoon," he said when Bobby answered.

Later, when Justin met him at Frog Level, Bobby had two beers in front of him, one for each of them.

"Three times in one week. Man, this is like the old days," Bobby said. He took a swallow of beer and stared at his friend. "What's up? You look like someone stole your dog."

Justin sat and took a long drink from his glass, then said, "You haven't heard?"

Bobby shook his head. "Heard what?"

"Hadley pulled the plug on HT67."

"Pulled the plug?"

"The son-of-a-bitch told me that he sent his report to your father this morning recommending that we drop it. 'Not worth pursuing,' he said."

"That's news to me. Obviously, you disagree."

"Hell yes. He's wrong."

"No offense, buddy, but Hadley is one of the top cancer scientists in the world. Without him, Tramorix wouldn't be where it is today."

"He may be, but he's dead wrong on this."

Bobby shook his head. "I don't understand. How can you be so sure?"

Justin debated on what to tell his friend. He needed to continue his work on the extract and wanted Bobby to get his dad to overrule Hadley. How could he convince Bobby without breaking his word to the Cherokee?

He looked around to make sure no one was listening. Lowering his voice, he said, "Because I know firsthand it works."

Bobby stared at him. "How could you possibly know that?"

Justin shook his head. "You can't repeat this. Remember what you said about giving me inside information on the Bearant acquisition?"

"Hell, yes. I could go to jail."

"Well, what I'm about to tell you is in the same category. It could land me in jail." Justin hesitated, then said, "I gave HT67 to Karen. That's why she's alive today."

"You did what? Are you crazy?"

"Keep it down," Justin said, looking around again to see if anyone heard.

Bobby said, "You told me it was a delayed reaction to the methotrexate."

Justin nodded. "That's what her doctor thinks. He doesn't know anything about the HT67."

"I can't believe you did—"

"I didn't have a choice, Bobby. The methotrexate wasn't working. She'd had eight treatments and was getting worse. She was dying, and we were out of options."

Bobby shook his head. "Jesus Christ. You need to go to Hadley and tell him."

"I already did. I told him that I gave it to her."

"He knew? Dad didn't mention—"

"He couldn't tell him. He can't. He could go to jail, too."

"Does Hadley think it works?"

Justin nodded. "He reviewed Karen's medical record, and when I talked to him Wednesday morning, he believed HT67 was responsible for her getting better. He had discussed her results—anonymously, of course—with other scientists. They all agreed the patient was in remission and that it couldn't have been the methotrexate. Then this morning he kills it?"

"Man, this is all fucked up. I need to talk to Dad. Maybe I can make him understand."

Justin put his hand on his friend's arm. "See if you can persuade him to overrule Hadley. But you can't tell him any of this. You promised, remember?"

Bobby shook his head. "Then, how am I going to convince him? What are you going to do?"

"Maybe we can get someone else to look at it. Let me talk to Hadley first. Just don't tell your dad about any of this."

"Okay. Keep me posted."

It was dark when they settled their tab with Mary Ann and walked out the front door. Justin noticed the glow of a cigarette to his left. A man was standing in the shadows next door, smoking a cigarette.

Bobby put his arm on Justin's shoulder as they turned in the opposite direction, and headed to Justin's vehicle, parked two cars away.

"Everything's going to work out. Don't worry," Bobby said.

Justin fumbled for his keys as he opened the unlocked door. "Thanks for listening."

"Hey, what are friends for? You've always been there for me."

Justin got in and started his SUV. He watched as Bobby crossed the street and got into his Corvette. At the traffic light, his phone buzzed. He picked it up and looked to see who was calling. Tsula.

"Hey," he said.

"I called the house, and Alice said you were out with Bobby."

"Yeah, I'm on my way home. We need to talk."

"Yes, we do. Sam Bear called. He's certain that the tree is within the Qualla Boundary and not in the Great Smoky Mountains National Park."

"Really?"

"He's been surveying in this area for thirty years. He double-checked his calculations, and he's positive. What did you want?"

Justin thought about Tsula's news. This was getting more complicated by the minute.

"Are you guys busy?" Justin asked. "I'd rather talk in person."

"Okay. Why don't you pick up Alice and come over?"

"You think you could get your mom to come?"

Tsula hesitated. "Probably. Why?"

"We've got a lot to talk about."

* * *

Justin picked up Alice and headed over to their friends' house. Atohi and Tsula were waiting on the porch, along with Mary.

"Mary, good to see you. Thanks for coming." As always, she hugged Alice and him.

"How was your hunting trip?" Justin asked Atohi as the women led the way inside.

Archery season for deer had opened in North Carolina the day before, a full two months earlier than firearms season. Atohi liked not having to worry about "idiots" in the woods with guns for that period. He preferred hunting with a bow, considering it more sporting. To him, hunting with a scoped, high-powered rifle was cheating.

"Successful. I'll bring you some venison when we get it from the processor."

Everyone gathered around the dining room table, where Tsula had laid the surveyor's report. A blue X marked the location of the tree, clearly just inside the Qualla boundary.

"Did you have any trouble finding the tree?" Justin asked Atohi, forgetting his friend was more comfortable in the woods than even he.

Atohi laughed. "I took Sam Bear straight to it. Man, he's got some fancy gadgets. The fieldwork didn't take him long."

"What did you want to talk about?" Tsula asked.

Justin shrugged. "I guess it doesn't matter now."

He told them about his initial discussion with Hadley regarding the extract, now called HT67.

"With his report to Robert Kendall, Hadley wanted to make it a priority research project."

"But if he does that—"

Justin silenced Tsula with a raised hand. "Then, they'll want to know what the tree is and its location. I told Hadley that I wouldn't disclose anything else without the Cherokee's permission. And, by the way, he doesn't know anything about your involvement in this."

"Why did you say it doesn't matter?" Mary asked.

Justin dropped his eyes. "I just found out this morning that Hadley changed his mind. He's officially dropping the project. That was his recommendation to Kendall."

"I can't say as I'm disappointed," Tsula said, taking a sip of her wine.

Justin bristled. "The problem is that he's forbidden me to work on it."

"Why's that a problem? I thought Karen was well?" Atohi said.

"Karen's doing better and is on the mend. But I've been looking at her latest test results, and she's not out of danger yet. I'm pretty sure she's going to need additional doses of the extract."

"Can't you work on it on your own?" Atohi asked.

Justin shook his head. "No. I don't have the equipment. I have to use the lab's facilities."

He looked at Mary. "I'm going to need more material and more tea. I want to go back Saturday and get more samples from the tree."

Alice raised her eyebrows. "Why? I thought you said Hadley forbade you to work on it?"

"He did. But he can't be there around the clock." Justin realized he was skating on thin ice with the professor, but he couldn't afford to put everything on hold. What if Karen needed more of the extract?

"I can't go Saturday. I've got to work," Atohi said.

"We've got a book club meeting and lunch," Alice said, nodding toward Tsula.

Still looking at Mary, Justin said, "I can go alone. But I need your permission."

Mary nodded. "Get more material, and I'll make more tea for you."

"You need to be careful going against Dr. Hadley," Alice said. "You could lose your job, which would also mean no access."

"I know. I will," Justin said.

19

When he woke up Saturday morning, Justin was still thinking about how to confront Dr. Hadley. He had to be careful. As Bobby had pointed out, Hadley was not someone you wanted as an enemy.

Alice had already left for her book club meeting in town. She and Tsula were meeting for lunch later, so Justin was on his own for most of the day.

His phone vibrated as he sat at the bar drinking his coffee. Bobby.

"What's up?" Justin asked when he answered.

Bobby told him that he'd asked his dad about revisiting HT67, not mentioning anything about Karen.

"What was his response?"

"It's not going to happen," Bobby said. "The only thing the old man's interested in is closing this Bearant deal. He also said Hadley owns five percent of Nuran and doesn't want to 'muddle the deal' either."

"Maybe I could run it by someone else?"

"Whoa. What are you talking about?" Bobby asked.

"Just thinking out loud. Maybe talk to some other scientists. I could mention it to Karen's doctor over at Wake. He might know—"

"Hold on a minute, buddy. Think this through, okay? What exactly are you going to tell anyone else? You can't disclose that you gave it to Karen, not unless you want to bring a shitstorm down on you. Plus, you don't want to cross Hadley. I mean, he's an 800-pound gorilla in cancer research."

Bobby hesitated before continuing. "Going public with this would also screw up the Bearant deal. For something this big, buyers want known quantities—no surprises. It could delay or even cancel the closing.

"Just chill out about this, okay? At least until we sign the deal. Once it's closed, you can bring it up with Bearant and be a hero. That'll give them an incentive to keep the lab open. Plus, they'll probably throw a bunch of stock options at you."

Something clicked in Justin's head. He'd blown off Bobby's earlier comment about Hadley owning a small piece of Nuran. But five percent of five billion dollars was a lot of money. At the time, he'd not thought about how much. He quickly did the math. Now, he knew what was gnawing at him about Hadley.

"Wait a minute. Earlier, you said Hadley owns five percent of Nuran? That would mean his stock is worth 250 million dollars."

Bobby chuckled. "That's what I'm saying, buddy. You don't want this to come out now. Better to keep this card in your back pocket. Bring it out when Bearant takes over, and you'll be rich. Just like old Hadley."

Justin hung up and got on the computer to look up the ownership of Nuran Labs. He wanted to confirm what Bobby had told him.

Since Nuran was privately owned, he had to dig a bit to find what he was looking for. But that was the great thing about the internet. You could find out almost anything if you dug deep enough and long enough. He found what he was looking for in an earnings announcement about Nuran.

As the senior researcher for Tramorix, Dr. Gareth Hadley owned stock options equaling five percent of Nuran's stock. Bobby was right.

Justin sat back in his chair. Two hundred fifty million dollars was more money than he could imagine. No wonder Hadley shut down HT67.

He could care less about Hadley's financial stake, but he didn't want to screw up the Bearant deal for the Kendalls. Justin's only goal was to continue his research and acquire more HT67 for Karen.

He needed to think this through, and the Park was the place to go. The woods were where he did his most productive thinking. After packing a lunch, he headed out.

Hadley had made his decision and was unlikely to change his mind. Justin would have to bypass him somehow. By the time he got to the Hyatt Ridge trailhead, Justin had decided to give the HT67 data on toxicity to cancer cells to Dr. Stewart.

As usual, no one else was there. Justin parked and stepped outside. It was a beautiful fall morning, with temps in the mid-fifties and a Carolina-blue sky. He strapped on his pack, grabbed his hiking stick, and shut the door.

He seldom bothered with locking it. It was an older model with over two hundred thousand miles, easy enough to break into. There was nothing of value in it, and he didn't worry about anyone stealing a ten-year-old truck with that many miles.

Justin hiked in at a fast pace, thinking about how best to approach Dr. Stewart. The trick would be how to disclose enough meaningful data about HT67 to pique Stewart's interest without divulging Justin's earlier intervention with Karen.

He began to craft a story about researching a Cherokee medicinal plant for friends who believed the plant had healing abilities. After further thought, he decided to leave the Cherokee out of the story. He'd just say that he was researching a purported medicinal plant for friends.

He'd have to share some of the lab data on HT67 and its supposed anti-cancer properties. Since Stewart knew Hadley, Justin would have to come up with a plausible explanation for why he was asking him instead of Hadley.

When he got to the point where he usually left Enloe Creek Trail, he was surprised to see a piece of fluorescent orange tape on a rhododendron limb. He shook his head. Sam Bear, the surveyor, must have left it. Justin didn't want a marker of any kind drawing attention to the area. He removed the tape and stuffed it in his pocket.

He glanced around to see if there was any other indication. He noticed some trampled underbrush and a few broken limbs on low shrubs. *Damn.* Might as well have a neon sign pointing the way.

Justin tried to repair the damage as much as he could. He deliberately went ten yards farther before he left the trail. It meant more bushwhacking and some backtracking, but he didn't want to leave any more telltale marks hinting at the tree's location.

Before long, Justin had arrived at the healing tree. He took a break, gathered his samples, and started back toward the SUV.

At the Hyatt Ridge Trail intersection, he stopped for lunch. Sitting on a tree trunk, he wolfed down his peanut butter and jelly sandwich and washed it down with water.

As he was finishing, a stranger approached from downhill, coming from the trailhead. The man appeared to be about Justin's age. Taller, with short blond hair, and in excellent condition. His gear looked to be new.

"Morning," the man said.

"Morning," Justin replied.

"Where you headed?"

"Back to the trailhead. You?"

The man shrugged. "Just exploring. I've never been over in this area. Anything in particular worth seeing?"

A little odd, Justin thought. Not many tourists used this trail. It was tough, all uphill with no real views, and not easy to get to. When he did see other hikers, they were always backpacking, with large, stuffed packs containing enough gear and food for several days in the backcountry. He noticed the man had a small brand-new daypack, which indicated he wasn't planning on an overnight trip.

"Depends on what you find interesting," Justin said. "Not a lot to see in this area unless you plan on spending the night."

The man shook his head. "Not this trip. Just thought I'd scope it out first, then maybe come back and camp next time."

The man pointed at the trail signs. "Which way did you come from?"

Justin capped his water bottle and stuck it in his pack. "Just made a loop on the Hyatt Ridge."

He wasn't about to tell the stranger that he came from the Enloe Creek Trail and have the man stumble upon the tree. He stood to put the pack back on his shoulders.

"Nice talking to you. Enjoy your hike," Justin said.

"Thanks. You, too."

When Justin got back to his SUV, a new, silver 4-door Nissan Altima was parked next to him. He figured it belonged to the man he'd met on the trail.

It looked like a rental car, Justin thought. He scrutinized it and saw bar code stickers on the windshield and rear window. No dealer stickers on the trunk, either. All signs of a rental.

Why would a tourist renting a sedan drive out to this remote trailhead?

Justin decided he was getting paranoid. Still, he could only hope this trailhead hadn't recently gained attention on some hiking blog. Thank goodness he'd removed that survey tape.

20

After their book club meeting, Alice and Tsula headed to the Sweet Onion in downtown Waynesville for lunch. The hostess seated them in a booth in the rear of the popular restaurant.

"Any idea as to your pick next month?" Alice asked. Members of their book club took turns selecting the monthly read for the group. The next month was Tsula's choice.

Tsula shrugged. "Not sure. We've had 'chick' reads the last couple of months. I'm ready for something a little more exciting, someone new."

Alice laughed. "You're going to rock the boat, in other words?"

She was facing the restaurant's corner and saw the hostess leading two men to the lone booth behind her and Tsula. She recognized the first man. It was Robert Kendall, Jr.

He was a distinguished-looking older man, dressed in slacks and a golf shirt. She'd never met him, but the entire town knew who he was. He was followed by a heavyset stranger, out of place in a coat and tie. The hostess seated them in the last booth, which was directly behind Alice.

She pointed over her shoulder and mouthed, "Robert Kendall," to Tsula.

Raising her eyebrows, Tsula nodded. "Any suggestions?" she asked, returning to their conversation about book club picks.

"What about Greg Iles? He's got a new one out. *Cemetery Road*." Iles was one of Alice's favorite authors.

"He's good, but we've done a couple of his. We need someone new."

"Jo at Blue Ridge Books mentioned a new book by an author I've never heard of. Robert Pobi? *City of Windows* is the title."

They got their order in for lunch and continued talking about different authors and books. Alice overheard Kendall and his companion order lunch. Even though they didn't seem to be talking particularly loud, their voices carried in the back of the room. She tilted her head to the side to hear better.

"Crab cakes," she whispered to Tsula. The other one ordered the trout. She repeated that order to Tsula. They both giggled like schoolgirls, amused at eavesdropping.

Losing interest, they went back to their conversation about books and Tsula's upcoming choice.

"What's the Pobi book about?" Tsula asked.

"A thriller set in Manhattan is all I know."

The word *Tramorix* caught Alice's attention. She tuned Tsula's reply out and cocked her ear to the conversation behind her.

". . . fucking Indian tree . . . too much invested in Tramorix . . ."

"Are you paying attention to me?" Tsula asked.

Alice nodded and made a circle with her forefinger to indicate that she should continue talking.

Puzzled, Tsula fell silent.

Crap, Alice thought. She made another circle with her forefinger, but too late. The men behind also fell silent, probably from the sudden quiet coming from Alice and Tsula's booth.

"Jo thought it was excellent. Sounds like something you're looking for," Alice said, intentionally loud. She pointed over her shoulder at the men, then twirled her finger again.

Tsula nodded, this time understanding Alice's hand signal.

"I'm not sure," Tsula said, her voice also a notch louder. "You know how the group is. Maybe we should just go with another Nicolas Sparks' book."

"Oh, please," Alice said. "I don't think I can take another one of those. I thought you wanted something different?"

She heard the men resume their conversation. She smiled and nodded to Tsula.

They both continued to babble nonsense about the book club while Alice strained to hear more. The men had lowered their voices, making it harder for her to understand what they were saying, but she heard, ". . . going to muddle the deal . . . shut it down."

Their food arrived, and they slowed their chatter as they ate. It didn't matter since she couldn't hear much anymore.

The men finished their lunch, and as they passed, Alice and Tsula pretended to ignore them as they left. In her peripheral vision, Alice could see Kendall eyeing them.

When she was sure they were gone, Tsula said, "What the hell was that all about?"

Alice shook her head. "I'll tell you when we're on our way home." She grinned. "You have to be careful talking out in public."

* * *

"How was book club?" Justin asked when he got home. Alice had made it to the house before him. He set his pack down and removed the contents.

"Good," Alice said. "Lunch was interesting. Guess who I saw?"

"No clue."

"Bobby's dad."

Justin nodded. "Yeah, Bobby mentioned yesterday that he was supposed to meet with some banker. Where'd you see him?"

"Sweet Onion. Tsula and I had lunch there. They sat right behind us."

"They? Was Bobby with him?"

"Nope. Some heavy-set stranger in a suit. I overheard some interesting conversation, though."

Justin laughed. "What, were you two eavesdropping on Mr. Kendall?"

She told him what she'd heard.

When she finished, he digested the information, trying to decipher what it meant. "You're sure he said, 'Indian tree?'"

"*Fucking* Indian tree, to be precise."

"Which one of them said it?"

"I don't know. I had my back to them. What difference does it make?"

He repeated the phrases Alice had heard.

She nodded. "What's that mean, Justin?"

"I'm not sure. The reference to the tree had to mean the healing tree. 'Muddle the deal' was the same phrase Bobby had used to describe his father's concern about the Bearant acquisition. That makes sense, coupled with the mention of Tramorix. The term 'shut it down,' did it sound like a question or more a statement?"

"More like a statement or an order," she said. "Whoever said it was emphatic, that was obvious."

Justin shook his head. "I wonder who was with Kendall? And what were they talking about shutting down?"

The bits and pieces of the conversation were disturbing. Kendall referred to the healing tree as the Indian tree. How much did he know? Also, Justin couldn't picture anyone bossing Robert Kendall around, which meant Robert was giving the order to shut it down. Robert had already killed the HT67 project, so what else could he want to shut down?

Looking at the bark and tree leaves Justin removed from his pack, Alice asked, "How was your hike?"

"In and out. Since I was by myself, I made good time."

She put her hands on her hips and gave him a fake pout. "Are you insinuating that I slow you down?"

He couldn't help but laugh. "No, not at all. Just saying that anyone hiking alone will be faster. I only ran into one person—a tourist—at the intersection."

"What, was he lost?"

He shrugged. "Don't think so. He said he'd never been in the area and was just checking the trail out, but he was in pretty good shape. He wasn't a hiker, and I don't think he's from around here."

"Why do you say that?"

"New gear, right off the shelf. Too light for backpacking. When I got back to the SUV, there was a car parked next to me. Since I didn't see anyone else on the trail, I assume it was his. The car was a rental." Coupled with the conversation Alice and Tsula had overheard, Justin wondered if he was paranoid about the stranger? What was that Joseph Heller said in *Catch-22?*

"Just because you're paranoid doesn't mean they aren't after you."

21

In his home study, Robert Kendall stood, looking out his window at the mountains. There was something peaceful about them, something eternal.

He knew that over a thousand new species had been discovered so far in the Great Smoky Mountains National Park. New to science, not to just this area. He wouldn't be surprised if there were a tree out there with anti-cancer properties.

After his lunch with Carter Knox, Robert had called Matt Farmer and summoned him to the house for an update. He turned back to his visitor, who sat silently, waiting for Robert's directive.

"Knox is worried that somehow this damn Indian tree is going to kill the Bearant deal. What have you found out?" Robert asked.

As usual, Matt had no notes. He delivered his reports verbally, in concise terms. If he ever wrote things down, Robert had never seen any evidence of it.

"Reeve found a tree in the Park, apparently somewhere not too far from the reservation. He doesn't know what it is—unusual for a plant guy who grew up in the area. It seems the Cherokee thought it was extinct. They believe it has powerful medicinal properties. Reeve has done some testing, and he convinced Hadley it merits investigation."

Robert leaned forward. "That's a little more than what Hadley told me Wednesday. He acted like it was not important, more a matter of scientific curiosity. He didn't mention anything about the Cherokee connection. I wonder why? I told Hadley to revise his report before he submitted it to me, which he did. He's killing the project. I told Carter that we'd shut it down, but he's still nervous."

Matt said, "There's more. Reeve's sister is in Wake Forest Hospital. Breast cancer. They were getting ready to move her to hospice. Reeve went over there five days in a row. The latest is she's doing better."

Robert scowled. "How?"

Matt shifted in his seat. "That's what I'm wondering. Reeve finds a tree that the Indians think has healing properties. He's been putting in a lot of time at the lab. Coincidence, maybe, but I'm not a big fan of coincidence. Plus, a couple of meetings with your son."

Robert nodded. "Yesterday, Bobby told me he met with Reeve Friday. Reeve told him that he didn't know what kind of tree it was, and he wouldn't tell Bobby where he found it. Reeve convinced him that there's something to this tree. Bobby then leaned on me to reverse Hadley. I told him 'no way,' and to tell Reeve to keep his mouth shut."

Now Robert was suspicious of Bobby trying to get him to take a second look at the tree drug. Was Reeve playing Bobby? Bobby wasn't the sharpest knife in the drawer, and Reeve was no dummy.

"Something doesn't feel right about all this," Matt said.

"What do you mean?"

"Can't put my finger on it, yet, but something smells. I'm pretty sure Reeve is still working on it."

"What do you suggest?"

"Give me another week. I've got tabs on Reeve and some other feelers out. I'll get to the bottom of it. Soon."

Maybe we should get rid of the tree? Robert thought. No tree, then no extract and no threat to the deal. But what if the tree does have anti-cancer properties? He couldn't help but think of his wife—may she rest in peace. But if there's one tree, there's bound to be others. All they needed to do now is eliminate the one so the acquisition can close. Then, we can look for others.

Robert cocked his head and said, "Maybe we should get rid of the tree—as a preemptive measure?"

"My thoughts exactly. But we don't know what we're looking for, and I don't have the location yet. I'm working on both of those, and we should have something soon. I'll get back to you in a couple of days."

22

H ey," Justin said, entering Karen's room. "I brought someone to see you."

Alice stepped from behind him, grinning. She rushed over to the bed to hug her future sister-in-law.

Karen took her earbuds out. "Oh my gosh, Alice. I'm so glad to see you," she said as she embraced her.

Alice stepped back, still holding Karen's hand. "You look great."

Justin ambled over, stopping short of her bedside. "Yes, I'm glad to see you, too," he said, with a measure of sarcasm and a fake pout. "I don't know why I even bothered to come."

Karen looked at Alice and rolled her eyes. "See? Now you know why I gave him the nickname 'Brat.'" They both cracked up, laughing at Justin's expense.

He picked up Karen's phone, looked at her playlist, and nodded. "John Prine. At least you got my good taste in music."

He leaned over and kissed the top of her head. "You're looking good. Glad to see you're feeling better."

Karen nodded. "Dr. Stewart said I might be able to go home this week if my numbers continue to improve."

"Awesome," Alice said. "You'll be back hiking with us before you know it."

"I'm looking forward to it," Karen said. "How are the wedding plans coming?"

"Good. I wanted to show you what I'm considering for the bridesmaids." Alice glanced over at Justin. "If we can get rid of him for a few minutes, I'll show you what I'm thinking about for my dress."

Justin shook his head. "Go for it. I'm going down to Starbucks," he said. "Do either of you want anything?"

"A macchiato for me, please," Karen said.

"Cappuccino with an extra shot, thank you," Alice said.

"Got it. I'll be back in a few."

Justin took the elevator down to the main floor and headed toward Starbucks. Just outside the entrance, he ran into Dr. Stewart and Tina, who were leaving.

"Hello, Justin," Stewart said.

"Dr. Stewart, Tina. I just left Alice with Karen to catch up. She said you told her she might be able to go home this week."

Stewart waved them to the side of the busy hallway. "She's continuing to improve. Her labs are looking better. I want to do another set of scans this week. If they look good, we'll move her to outpatient monitoring and treatment."

"That's great news. I appreciate all you both have done."

"Sometimes things work out," Tina said, looking at her watch. "It's great when they do. Sorry, Dr. Stewart, but we need to make rounds. Good to see you, Justin."

Before they walked away, Justin said, "Dr. Stewart. Is it okay if I call you sometime later this week? Nothing to do with Karen. I want to get your advice on a project I'm working on."

"Sure. Late mornings are usually best. Tell Karen we'll be up later," he said as they turned to leave.

Standing in line to get drinks, Justin was glad he ran into Dr. Stewart. More than ever, he was convinced the healing tree was the reason for Karen's sudden turnaround. Now, when he called Stewart, it wouldn't be a total surprise.

On his way back to Karen's room, he knew he needed to tell Karen what he'd done. He'd put it off long enough.

As he walked through Karen's door, he heard laughter.

"Should my ears be burning?" he asked as he sat the cardboard tray with three cups on the table by Karen's bed.

"Karen had started to tell me a story about your junior high recital," Alice said. "I'd asked her why she calls you brat."

"I forgot the name of it, but it wasn't an easy piece. They never had an eighth-grader play it before."

"*Cristofori's Dream* by David Lanz," Justin said. "Still one of my favorites. It's not that difficult."

Karen turned to Alice. "Anyway, he played it flawlessly until the very end. He missed one note. Pitched a fit. Right there on stage. Kicked the piano stool and stormed off stage."

Alice looked at him. "Justin. I can't believe you did that."

He shook his head. "I'm embarrassed. Missing that note was stupid. I was glad that Dad wasn't there to witness it."

"Now you know why I call him brat," Karen said, laughing.

"You never told me that story," Alice said to Justin.

"I was what, thirteen? Give me a break."

Karen reached out and put her hand on his arm. "He's a perfectionist, but I love him anyway. He just can't stand to make a mistake. In anything."

Justin nodded toward Alice. "I didn't make a mistake with her, did I?" The comment earned him two head shakes in agreement.

"I ran into Dr. Stewart and Tina downstairs. He's pleased with your progress."

"The methotrexate worked, didn't it?" Karen said.

Justin glanced at Alice then back at his sister. "It wasn't the methotrexate."

Karen shook her head. "What do you mean? What else could it have been?"

He looked over at Alice, and she nodded.

"There's something I need to tell you, sis." He told her the story about the healing tree, starting with Alice and him finding it. Mary Richardson recognizing it as a potent ancient Cherokee healing remedy. His discussions with Dr. Hadley about Taxol. When he got to the point where he gave her the medicine, he hesitated and took a deep breath.

"That day when you told me you were ready to give up?" Justin asked. "I gave you the first of five doses of an experimental extract called HT67, made from the tree. I injected it into your IV line. I'm convinced that was responsible for your miraculous recovery, not the methotrexate."

Karen was silent, processing. At last, she said, "You did that? How did you know . . ." Her voice trailed off.

Anticipating her question, Justin met her eyes and said, "I didn't know if it would work. I knew it killed cancer cells in the lab, but that was it. And I didn't know if it was safe. I ingested it twice with no apparent side effects. That was all I had time to do. Dr. Stewart was going to transfer you to hospice. It was a Hail Mary."

Again, Karen was quiet for a moment, then looked at Alice. "Did you know?"

Alice nodded. "He told Atohi, Tsula, and Tsula's mom that he was going to give you the tea that Mary made. We didn't know at the time he was going to inject it."

Karen shifted her eyes back to Justin.

"I distilled it down to a concentrated form," he said. "I didn't think drinking the tea would act fast enough to save you."

"Does Dr. Stewart know?"

Justin shook his head. "No. He still believes it was a delayed reaction to the methotrexate, although none of his colleagues had ever seen such. Dr. Hadley knows. I shared your medical record with him, and he agrees it was the extract that healed you, not the methotrexate."

Karen paused before speaking. "Wow. I don't know what to say. That's a lot to absorb."

"I know. I'm sorry, sis. It was a huge risk, but you were dying, and I was desperate. I wanted to talk with you about it before, but your condition worsened, and there wasn't time."

Karen extended her arms and hugged him. "Don't be sorry. You saved my life. You did what you thought was right. Had I known, I would've told you to do it."

She released him, and a worried look crossed her face. "Will I need more?"

Justin held his hands out, palms up. "I don't know. The main thing is you're doing well. Dr. Stewart is pleased with your progress, and he's going to discharge you. If you do need more, don't worry—I'll make it. We'll figure it out at that point."

He put his hand over hers. "I didn't let you down before, and I won't let you down now."

23

As requested Justin got the rough draft of the Tramorix production standards to Hadley by Monday morning. Barely. Hadley was leaving that afternoon for a conference in Washington, D.C. On his way out, he returned the draft to Justin.

"An acceptable first version," Hadley said when he handed it back to Justin. "I've made a few comments. I trust the next edition will be improved. I'll be back Wednesday evening. Have it waiting for me first thing Thursday morning, please."

Not waiting for a reply, he turned and walked away.

Justin casually gave him the finger. Childish, he knew, but he couldn't resist. Then he smiled. With Hadley out of town, Justin would have a chance to do some additional experiments with HT67 without the professor snooping around.

At his desk, Justin flipped through the document. Almost every page had comments in red ink. It looked like it had been through a slaughterhouse.

He threw it down on the desk and took a deep breath. The report could wait. He intended to take advantage of Hadley's absence to build a case for Dr. Stewart.

By Wednesday morning, he'd managed to conduct several more lab tests on HT67. Contrary to Hadley's statement, Justin was able to replicate his initial results.

Proof that Hadley was sabotaging HT67 so as not to interfere with the Bearant acquisition.

"Muddle the deal," Justin said out loud, recalling the phrase Alice had overheard.

He was ready to approach Dr. Stewart, but first, he wanted to run it by Bobby. Justin picked up his phone and texted his friend.

Beer. F L @ 6?

A few minutes later, Bobby replied.

No can do. How about Fri?

Shit, Justin thought. Hadley would be back tonight.

Lunch? My treat

A few minutes later, he got Bobby's reply.

Cafeteria. Noon.

Justin got there first. He went through the line and ordered a meatball sub and a small salad. As he pulled out a twenty to pay, Bobby walked up.

"Put his on my card," Bobby said to the clerk at the register. He turned to Justin and said, "Why don't you grab us a seat outside?"

A few minutes later, Bobby joined him. "I would've rather had a beer, but I've got a busy afternoon. Dad's got the banker honcho in, and we're going over to Asheville for dinner."

Justin shrugged. "I'll take a raincheck." He thought back to Alice's comments. "Alice said she saw your dad and some stranger at lunch the other day."

Bobby nodded. "Yeah, that was probably Carter Knox, the banker honcho. He's been here all week with Dad. He's head of the New York investment banking firm putting the deal together."

"The deal still looking good?" Justin asked.

"Yep. How's Karen?" Bobby asked.

"Alice and I drove over to see her yesterday. She continues to show improvement. I ran into Dr. Stewart, and he thinks she'll go home this week. Speaking of Dr. Stewart, I wanted to run something by you—as a friend."

"Sure."

"Hadley's gone this week, so I've had a chance to do a little more testing on HT67."

Bobby stiffened. His body language changed. "I thought Hadley told you to drop it?"

"He did. Don't worry. I'm careful. You gave me good advice on that. I'm doing this on my own time. Hadley's out of town till tonight. He'll never know, okay?"

Bobby nodded but didn't appear to be convinced.

"Anyway, one of the reasons Hadley said he was killing HT67 is that he couldn't duplicate my test results. But I did. This week. Twice." He paused to let that sink in. "That gives me something to discuss without mentioning Karen. I'd like to get a fresh set of eyes to review the test data, that's all."

"Justin, look, I told you—"

Justin held up his hand. "I get it, okay? I understand that nobody, including me, wants to screw up the Bearant acquisition. All I want to do is show the results of the tests to Karen's doctor. I'll tell him it's something I've been doing on my own—not affiliated in any way with Nuran. If he says it's bullshit, then I'll drop it. I promise. If he says it looks like it could be something, then I pass the ball back to you. Your call. Do whatever you want to with it."

Justin could see the wheels turning as Bobby weighed his proposal. He pleaded. "I just need to know if I'm crazy or not. I mean, is this stuff for real? It certainly seemed to work for Karen."

"You swear you'll drop it?"

Justin allowed a slight smile. Bobby was putting his money on Gareth Hadley. In his place, Justin would too.

"Absolutely. End of story. Just another myth that proved untrue. No harm to anyone."

As soon as Justin got back to his office, he called Dr. Stewart. Getting his voice mail, he left a message asking that Dr. Stewart call him at his earliest convenience to discuss something unrelated to Karen.

Earlier that morning, anticipating Bobby's consent at lunch, Justin had already packaged the data along with a written synopsis. He'd also crafted his cover story for Stewart.

Asked by a friend, Justin had agreed to investigate the properties of a medicinal plant used in rural Appalachia to ascertain if it had any value. The investigation was solely Justin's work, on his time. It had nothing to do with Nuran or the lab. He just wanted a professional unaffiliated with Nuran to review his work. Nothing more.

Stewart called back an hour later.

Justin took a deep breath and said, "Thank you for returning my call, Dr. Stewart. I need a cursory review of some outside work I've been doing and would like your opinion. Nothing formal. No obligation."

"What is it?"

Justin launched into his spiel, keeping it concise.

"Why aren't you asking Gareth? He's certainly eminently qualified to give you the kind of evaluation you're requesting."

"Absolutely. I think the world of Dr. Hadley. But, as I said, I've been doing this entirely on my own strictly as a favor to my friend, basically to debunk a myth. I don't want to put Dr. Hadley in an awkward position since he's my boss. All I want is a strictly off-the-record review as to the validity of my basic tests. Nothing more."

Stewart asked a few more questions about the type of tests and the supposed properties. Justin kept it short and sweet.

"Send it to me," Stewart said. "I'll give it a quick once over. Nothing formal, mind you. Just my thoughts."

"That's all I ask. Thank you so much, Dr. Stewart. I'll send it to you as soon as we hang up."

Later that afternoon, as Justin was wrapping up the next edition of production standards for Hadley, his cell phone vibrated, and he picked it up to see who was calling. Atohi.

"I'm ready for a beer this afternoon," Justin said.

Atohi laughed. "No, sorry, no can do this afternoon. That's not why I'm calling. I just talked to Sam."

"Sam?"

"Sam Bear, the surveyor? Someone broke into his office last night."

Before Justin could respond, Atohi continued.

"The only thing disturbed was his files. Specifically, the drawer with clients' last names beginning with R."

Mary Richardson was the first name Justin considered. *Damn.* The healing tree survey report. With the location.

"The only reason he noticed was that he took the report out of his briefcase to make a folder for it and put it in his file cabinet."

"You're telling me the survey on the healing tree wasn't in his file cabinet?"

"That's right. The only copy was in Sam's briefcase."

"Maybe he'd misfiled her folder?"

"Not a chance. Sam is OCD," Atohi said, using the acronym for obsessive-compulsive disorder. "I've known him for years, and he's always been that way. That's why he noticed someone had riffled the drawer."

"Somebody broke into his office to get the report on the healing tree?"

"That's what it looks like. Nothing was missing. I asked Sam to keep Mary's file with him and reminded him not to discuss it with anyone. Thought you'd want to know."

Justin nodded. "Thanks."

He disconnected and placed the phone on his desk. *Somebody was looking for the healing tree. Who, and why?*

He looked down at the report for Hadley. Maybe it was time he confronted the professor.

24

"Mr. Reeve, you appear to be distracted. Am I boring you?"

Justin shook his head and tried to focus. Dr. Hadley was reviewing Justin's final draft of the Tramorix production standards. This was the recipe for manufacturing the drug in commercial quantities, the last step before actual production began.

Right before his meeting, he'd gotten a call from Dr. Stewart.

Limited data and testing, as you know. But the test results are impressive and appear to warrant further investigation.

Now Justin was even more convinced that the healing tree had been responsible for Karen's improvement, not the methotrexate.

"Mr. Reeve? Your comments, please."

"I'm sorry," Justin said. "Where were you?"

"Hmpf. I was asking about the tolerance parameters on the last step. I think we should tighten them."

Justin flipped over to the last page and looked down at the specified range. He'd plugged in the active ingredient at eight percent of volume plus or minus .04 percent.

"I think that's within the limits on our Phase III trials," Justin said.

"Granted, but with the temperature range we're permitting, I'd like to see a little less discretion. I'm thinking .035 percent. Maybe less."

"Fine," Justin said, giving an indifferent shrug. "I'll change it."

Hadley dropped his copy on the table. "Is that the extent of your comments on the parameters?"

"I'll do whatever you want."

"What I want is for you to justify what you suggested. If I simply wanted someone to follow orders, I have a considerable number of candidates here to choose from," he said, sweeping his hand across in front of him.

"Tramorix is *your* drug," Justin said, answering the challenge. "You're the boss. Whatever you want."

Hadley studied him, fixing him with his penetrating stare. "Tramorix is *our* drug, *our* being Nuran, the company that pays *our* salary."

"Evidently, some of us stand to make more than salary from 'our' drug," Justin said, the sarcasm dripping from his voice.

A thin smile crossed Hadley's face. "Would you like to elaborate?"

Justin's face flushed. He was angry, and his emotions were taking over.

"There's a big payday for some people—stockholders, for example—with the sale of Nuran. But I guess you already know that."

"Your point?"

"My point is that you stand to get a big check from Bearant with the sale of Nuran and subsequent launch of Tramorix."

"And?" Hadley was leading him, and it was pissing Justin off.

"*And,* after talking with Kendall, you didn't want HT67 competing with Tramorix."

Hadley snorted. "Let me get this straight. You think that I killed HT67 because I was afraid it would jeopardize the Bearant deal and, by extension, the monies I'd get from my ownership?"

"Yes, I do," Justin said, now fully engaged, his eyes flashing. "Don't tell me you're going to deny it. I know you own five percent of Nuran."

"Do I deny that I'll receive a sizable check—in the neighborhood of two hundred million dollars—if the sale to Bearant goes through? Absolutely not."

Justin was surprised by Hadley's quick acknowledgment. He was glad he'd done his homework.

Wearing an amused look, Hadley leaned back in his chair. "Care to hear the rest of the story before you send me to the gallows?"

Justin forced the corners of his mouth down, trying to erase his smug look. Before he could comment, Hadley continued.

"I would suggest that in your youthful exuberance, you are jumping to conclusions without knowing all the facts."

Now it was Hadley's turn to exhibit a smug expression.

"Any money I make from Tramorix or the sale of Nuran goes to a foundation I set up in honor of my brother, Reggie. I don't see a penny of it, not one cent. You remember Reggie, the brother who died because I was unwilling to take a risk?"

Justin staggered at the revelation. Trying to recover, he lashed out.

"Why did you kill HT67 then? You know it works."

Hadley shook his head as if dealing with an immature six-year-old. "Yes, I do believe HT67 worked with your sister. It has enormous potential. And yes, I did deliberately kill the HT67 project. You are dead wrong about why and who receives the proceeds."

Justin was confused. All he could say was, "I don't understand."

"There are those who would go to any extreme to avoid doing anything that might jeopardize the sale of Nuran. Suppose they perceive that HT67 has the potential to challenge Tramorix? In that case, they will do whatever they have to in order to block it. What would be the easiest way to sabotage HT67?"

Justin shook his head.

"I'm disappointed. Put yourself in the shoes of the other side. What's the quickest way to stop HT67?"

Justin's mind raced as he considered the possibilities. *Discredit HT67? Stop work on it?*

Hadley sat there with his fingers steepled, silent, waiting for an answer.

Justin considered more nefarious ways. *Sabotage the tests? Kill him?* Then, it hit him. *Eliminate the source.* Of course. Right now, there was only one known source—the healing tree. As far as anyone knew, there was only one of them. Destroy the tree—problem solved.

Hadley smiled as if reading his mind.

"Destroy the tree," Justin said softly, the anger draining from him. It all came together. "You knew I'd keep working on it."

"I was counting on it. You didn't disappoint me, did you?"

Justin slapped his forehead with the heel of his hand. Dr. Hadley had been protecting him. And HT67.

"If you publicly killed the project, then whoever would lose interest in killing the tree?"

"Precisely. And you would continue to work on it in secret. So now, will you bring me up to date on what you've been doing?"

Justin told Hadley what he'd done since Hadley had taken his files. "Does that mean you'll give me back my notes?"

"Yes," Hadley said. He swiveled around to the file cabinet next to his desk, unlocked it, and opened the second drawer. He pulled out a file and froze.

"What is it?" Justin asked.

"Somebody's been in my file."

"Who?"

Hadley shook his head. "I don't know. But I'm the only one with a key to this cabinet. Not even the secretary has a key."

He looked up at Justin. "Somebody wanted to know about the healing tree."

"Shit," Justin said. "That's why someone broke into Sam Bear's office."

"What on earth are you talking about?"

"Tsula's mother—Mary—had a Cherokee surveyor go out to determine if the tree is in the Qualla Boundary. His name is Sam Bear. Atohi called me yesterday to tell me somebody had broken into his office. The only thing disturbed was the drawer that would normally contain Mary's file."

"Someone stole the survey?"

Justin shook his head. "No. Sam had it with him in his briefcase."

Hadley raised his bushy eyebrows. "Is the tree on Cherokee land?"

Justin hesitated before responding, then nodded.

"Who knows the location?" Hadley asked.

He told him that besides himself, Alice, Atohi, Tsula, Tsula's mother Mary, and Sam Bear were the only ones who knew the specific location.

"Anyone else?" Hadley asked.

Justin thought for a moment. "Not that I know. I told Bobby Kendall about the tree, but only that it was in the Park. I didn't mention where. I told Karen's doctor— Elliott Stewart—that I'd done some experiments with a plant extract, but nothing more specific about the plant."

Hadley raised his eyebrows as Justin explained why he told Dr. Stewart.

"I was angry with you, and I wanted another opinion. All I told him was that I was researching an Appalachian medicinal plant as a favor for a friend. He knows nothing about the tree or that I gave HT67 to Karen. You'll be pleased to know that he asked why I wasn't taking it to you."

Hadley chuckled. "I always thought Elliott was bright. What was your answer?"

"I told him this was a personal project, and I didn't want to involve you or the lab. I reran my tests while you were gone and sent him the most recent toxicity data."

"Has he reviewed it?"

Justin nodded. "He said, and I quote, 'Limited data and testing, as you know. But the test results are impressive and appear to warrant further investigation.'"

Hadley nodded. "I told you he was intelligent. So, only you and five others know the precise location. Anyone else?"

Justin thought. "No . . ."

"What?"

"I just remembered. Saturday, I went to the tree to get more material. I ran into a stranger at the trail intersection. At the time, I thought it was odd. It's a remote area, with only backpackers. This guy had a new daypack."

He recalled the silver car parked next to his SUV. "When I got back to the trailhead, there was a car that looked like a rental parked next to me. I don't know for sure that it was his, but I didn't see anyone else hiking and no other vehicles."

"Did he see you at the tree?"

Justin shook his head. "I'm pretty sure he didn't. The tree is off-trail, in a heavily wooded area. After I left my vehicle, I didn't see a soul until I saw him at a trail intersection on my way back. I was sitting there when he walked up, so he had no way of knowing which trail I had hiked."

"We have to be careful. We need to figure out who and why."

A chilling thought crossed Justin's mind.

"What if they manage to kill the tree?"

"We would have to find another one. Or synthesize the raw material. Our priority now is to protect the one we have. Otherwise, we lose everything."

"But I need more material. I don't have enough here to make another dose for Karen. I have to go back into the woods."

"You shouldn't go alone. Not only is the tree in danger, but you could also be as well. More than you realize."

"I'll take Atohi. He's an experienced woodsman. I trust him, and he already knows where the tree is."

"Be careful."

25

At breakfast Saturday morning, Justin asked Alice, "Where do you want to go hiking today?" They had decided to drive over and see Karen the next day, so today was theirs. The weather was perfect for a hike.

"What about Balsam Mountain?" she said.

He shrugged, his lack of enthusiasm evident. "I'm ready for a change in scenery. I was thinking about Low Gap and Snake Den Ridge. We haven't been over to that section of the Park in a while."

"Fine with me, as long as we're back by three," she said.

Tsula and Atohi were coming over for dinner at five, and Alice needed time to get ready for them after the hike. But the loop Justin suggested was a hard twelve-and-a-half-miles, which translated to a good six hours of hiking. They needed to start soon.

They packed lunch, loaded the 4Runner, and headed toward Cosby Campground and the trailhead. Traffic was light on I-40, and they arrived at the paved parking area shortly after 8 a.m. Several vehicles were already there.

"We're late," Justin said, parking. They put on their packs, grabbed their hiking sticks, and headed to the trailhead.

"I need to stop and pee first," Alice said. "Too much coffee."

Justin nodded. He really didn't feel the urge but thought, *never pass up a chance.* Alice complained that the boys had an unfair advantage when relieving themselves while out on the trail.

They walked over to the restrooms and parted. As usual, Justin finished first. He stepped out onto the sidewalk and waited for Alice.

A moment later, he watched as a nondescript white sedan pulled in and parked next to his SUV. The driver got out, took his backpack out of the rear seat, and looked over at Justin's vehicle. Then he looked around the parking lot. When he saw Justin, he walked around to the car's far side, out of sight.

"Ready?" Alice said, adjusting her pack as she walked up.

Justin nodded, but he was still watching for the guy. The break-ins at Sam Bear's and Hadley's offices had rattled him. He scolded himself for being paranoid. The healing tree was safe, far away from here. He scrunched up his shoulders to his neck and took a deep breath.

They headed up the path to the trailhead, starting slowly to loosen their muscles. The first hour, they didn't see another person on the trail. When they came to a stretch that offered some visibility in each direction, Alice stopped.

"I can't believe it, but I need to pee again. Next time don't let me have more than one cup of coffee."

Justin laughed. "I'll stand guard," he said. Alice walked ten or twelve feet off the trail to a small clearing. He saw her lower her shorts and squat. She was right. It was a lot of trouble for women.

Other than a few birds and squirrels, the forest was quiet. He looked up the trail, listening for anyone coming, and then turned toward Cosby. Again, he strained to hear anyone. Nothing.

He thought he saw movement farther down the trail but heard nothing. He stared, wondering if his eyes were tricking him, when he caught a glimpse of someone standing still alongside the trail, partially hidden by a tree. The person—he couldn't tell if it were male or female—stood there and appeared to be looking at Justin. They wore a ball cap and sunglasses, but that was about all Justin could make out.

"Sorry," Alice said, walking up next to him.

Still staring at the person, Justin offered her a water bottle.

Taking the bottle, she took a drink and handed it back to him. "What are you looking at? A bear?" she asked.

He chuckled. That was a standing joke between them. As much hiking as they'd done in the Park, they could count on one hand the number of bears they'd seen out on the trail. Black bears were generally shy around humans.

A bear was the least of his worries. He wondered if ball cap was following them. Justin thought about heading back to see if the person would confront them but decided to keep going and see if they followed. That would give him time to formulate a plan or perhaps see someone else on the trail.

"Nah. I thought I saw another hiker." He took a swig of water, then put the bottle back in the side pocket of his pack.

They continued up the trail, occasionally stopping for water. Every time they did, Justin looked behind them, hoping for another glimpse of the hiker he saw earlier. He never saw anyone behind them again the entire hike, even when they stopped for lunch.

When they got back to the parking lot, he looked over to where he'd seen the stranger earlier. The sedan was gone.

* * *

Sunday morning, Robert was waiting in his study for Matt. Matt had contacted him and said they needed to speak. Robert was anxious, as he hadn't heard anything from him since last Saturday.

Outside his study door came the sound of voices. Matt walked in, trailed by Belle, Robert's housekeeper. She stopped at the door, closing it behind Matt as she turned to leave.

"What's so urgent, Matt?" Robert said as soon as the door clicked shut. "I'm late for my tee time."

"We've got a problem," Matt said, crossing his legs as he sat. "The healing tree is the real deal."

"What? How do you know?"

Matt ignored the question. "HT67 exists. Reeve made it and gave it to his sister. She had one foot in the grave, and now she's in remission. Because of HT67."

Robert sat in his chair, putting his hands on the desk.

"He made it? And gave it to his sister? How the hell—"

"He did it without anyone's knowledge."

"Does Hadley know?"

Matt nodded. "He knew when you talked to him. He's reviewed her records and also discussed them with a few colleagues. He's convinced HT67 works."

Robert slammed his fist on the desk. "That lying son of a bitch."

He'd thought that Hadley's report had shut the door on HT67. Hadley had double-crossed him. If Bearant found out, he could kiss the four billion dollars goodbye.

Robert leaned forward. "I want you to destroy that fucking tree. Burn it, chop it down, poison it—whatever it takes to get rid of it."

Matt folded his hands in his lap. "I don't know where it is."

Robert exploded. "What do you mean, you don't know where it is? You said you were working on getting the location. That was a week ago."

"A Cherokee surveyor recently mapped the location of the tree to determine whether or not it is on Cherokee land. I thought I could get a copy but was unable to do so."

Robert shook his head. He was sure Matt explored every possible avenue, legal or not, but he didn't want to know any details.

Matt continued. "Hadley doesn't know where it is. Sooner or later, Reeve has to have more material. He'll eventually lead me to it."

"We don't have time to wait for him *to eventually lead you to it*. That could take weeks. Bearant is sniffing around. They saw Hadley's report, and they want assurance that this healing tree is not a threat before they close. Carter wants to close in thirty days."

Matt shrugged. "I can do it, but that's going to involve more pressure."

Robert didn't want to know what that meant. All he knew was that Matt needed to do whatever the hell it took to make sure this Bearant deal went through.

"You have a green light. As long as that tree is gone no later than thirty days from now."

Matt nodded. He got up and walked out.

26

Wednesday morning, when Alice got to her desk at the bank, there was a manila envelope with her name typed on the outside. Stamped below her name was PERSONAL AND CONFIDENTIAL in red ink.

She picked it up and studied it. No postage, no nothing. Just her name and the stamp. She flipped it over. The envelope was sealed. She shrugged and opened it.

There were two pieces of paper inside. The first was what appeared to be photographic paper, the blank side facing her. She flipped it over. It was a picture of a gravestone. Looking closer, she read the inscription.

Timothy Carver
Beloved Son
September 16, 1998 – April 9, 2009

The second page was a copy of a newspaper article from *The Indianapolis Star,* dated the same month and year as on the gravestone—April 2009. The headline read:

Carmel Child Killed by Hit-and-Run Driver

Slowly, she sat in her chair, trying to catch her breath. Her hand holding the picture was trembling.

"Are you okay?" Rhonda said, standing in Alice's doorway. "You look like you've seen a ghost."

Alice quickly flipped the picture over, covering the article, and lay both of them on her desk. She picked up the envelope and held it up, shaking it at Rhonda.

"Where did this come from?"

Rhonda shook her head and straightened at the accusation. "I don't know. It was in the night depository this morning. Your name was on it along with confidential, so I put it on your desk."

What the hell? Timothy Carver was a part of Alice's previous life, a life she'd thought was buried. Just like him. She tried to get her emotions in check before responding.

"I'm sorry, I didn't mean to snap at you. Probably some kind of prank from a former classmate. Don't worry about it," she said, dismissing Rhonda.

Alice leaned back in her chair. Memories of a night she'd tried to erase returned in vivid detail.

She'd grown up in the Indianapolis area. One of her high school classmates threw a senior party at his house since his parents were out of town. Passed out from partying, she woke up early the next morning, still drunk from the night before. She had to get home before daylight, so she drove home. It was before dawn and foggy, which made the winding road more treacherous than usual. She remembered being thankful there was no traffic.

Coming out of a curve, she miscalculated, and the right wheels went off the pavement. Suddenly, there was a shape directly in front of her. She jerked the wheel to the left as she braked, thinking she'd dodged whatever it was. She heard a thud indicating she was wrong. She stopped, collecting her thoughts. *Must have been a deer.* She looked up in the rearview mirror and saw something lying on the edge of the road. It didn't look like a deer.

Alice got out and looked at the right front fender of her car. A slight dent, but the lights were still shining and seemed to be intact. She guessed the bumper absorbed most of the impact, which minimized the damage.

Behind her, the taillights' red glow cast an eerie light on the object. It wasn't a deer. Maybe it was something on the side of the road, and it was a glancing blow. A dirt road intersected the paved road she was on and at the junction was a small shelter—a school bus stop.

A horrific thought entered her mind. *No,* she thought. *It couldn't be.* As she looked around, she couldn't' see any lights in any direction. Something forced her to walk toward the lump. As she got closer, she put her hand to her mouth, almost dropping her phone. It was a small boy, in a dark jacket, lying motionless on the shoulder.

Oh, my God. The child's eyes were open, blood pooling on the dirt beneath his head. He didn't look as if he were breathing. She touched her phone, illuminating the screen. She punched in 911 but froze before hitting Send.

She looked up and down the road. Still no lights, but she knew that wouldn't last. If she called 911, they would know it came from her phone. But he needed help. *Or did he?*

Slowly, she moved her hand toward his neck. Gingerly, she put her fingers against his neck, willing a pulse. Nothing. His skin was preternaturally cool. Holding her breath, she placed them against her neck to compare. Warmer, and she could feel her heart pounding.

She gasped, a squeak escaping her lips as reality flooded over her. He was dead. She had killed him. She caught a rank whiff of bourbon, lingering on her breath, and she almost puked.

Only eighteen, and her life was ruined. She would go to prison. Maybe for the rest of her life.

She looked at her phone, then looked down at the child. Nothing could help him now.

She erased the digits on her phone and walked back to her car, still idling on the side of the road. She got in, buckled her seat belt, and looked in the rearview mirror. The fog had moved in, covering up the product of her mistake.

Suddenly, she was exhausted. She'd go home, crawl under the covers, and close her eyes. When she awoke, she'd tell her parents what happened.

The next morning, when she awoke, the incident seemed no more than a bad dream. She showered, trying to wash away what happened.

She padded downstairs, where her parents were sitting at the breakfast table, having coffee.

"Good morning," her mom said.

With a disapproving look, her father said, "You must have been out late. I didn't hear you come in."

Alice started to tell them what time she got home but closed her mouth. She opened the refrigerator, got out the milk, and took her seat at the table. Her mom had left the box of Cheerios at her bowl.

After breakfast, she went out to the garage to get her backpack out of the backseat. She forced herself to examine the front of her car. Besides the slight dent, there were scuff marks on the bumper.

She took it to the car wash. Back home, her father was out washing his car when she drove in.

"Your car looks nice and clean," he said, looking disapprovingly at her car.

"I took it to the car wash."

"Must be nice," he said, grabbing the hose and squirting the soap off his car. As he looked at her car, he scrunched his eyes, staring at the front fender. He walked over and ran his finger over the dent. "Another one," he said. "That happen at the car wash?"

Alice nodded.

"I hope you reported it."

"I didn't see it until I stopped at the grocery store. I noticed it on my way out. I wasn't sure if it happened at the car wash or there."

He shook his head and walked back over to his car. "Well, it's going to have to last you for college."

That week, Alice dropped out of the local community college. She announced to her parents that she was now going by Alice, her middle name, and would no longer respond to Payten. She had discovered that in Indiana, a person seventeen or older could legally change their name.

Without telling her parents, she changed her name to Alice Miller, adopting her favorite aunt's last name. She informed her parents that she needed a change of scenery and enrolled at the University of North Carolina. She planned to move to Durham and live with her aunt until she could find a job. Shortly after she left Indiana, her parents and aunt were killed in an auto accident when traveling to the Outer Banks.

The beginning of her *never* life. She never used her first name—Payten—again. Never went back to Indianapolis. Never went back to Indiana, not even for her parents' funeral. Never had another drink. By the time she met Justin at UNC, she had thought that her secret was safe.

Her thoughts were interrupted by the buzzing of her cell phone. Rhonda was back at her desk. UNKNOWN, the display read. At home, she wouldn't have answered. At work, she usually did.

"Hello, Payten," the male voice said.

Alice's heart jumped. No one had called her by that name since she left Indianapolis.

"I'm sorry, you must have the wrong—"

"Don't fuck with me, Payten *Alice*. I know who you are and what you did. I'm the one who sent you the picture."

Alice froze. She tried to recover and asked, "Who are you?"

"Wrong question. It should be 'what do you want?'"

What kind of sick game was this person playing?

"What do you want?" she said quietly, trying to keep her voice from cracking.

"Don't worry. I don't want money or anything complicated. It's actually very easy."

She doubted that. "I'm listening."

"Good. I need to know where the healing tree is. That's it. Tell me where it is, I disappear. No one knows anything. No one gets hurt."

Who the hell was this? she thought. Questions flooded her brain. How did he know about the tree? What did he want with it?

"Why?" she asked, hoping he would give her a clue.

"Why is not important."

She hesitated, wondering what on earth he'd want with it.

"I don't know where it is."

"Don't lie to me, Payten. I don't like being lied to."

"Quit calling me that," Alice said, angry at hearing her old name again out loud. "My name is Alice." She took a deep breath, trying to get her bearings. "I'm not lying. It was in the Park, but I don't know exactly where the tree is. I've never been there by myself. How did you find out?"

"That's not important, either. If you don't remember where it is, then you'll have to get Justin to take you back."

She inhaled sharply. This must have something to do with Justin. She knew his work with the tree would cause problems.

"Get him to take you there. I'll give you a number to call. Leave a message the day before with the time you're leaving your house. Nothing else."

"I . . . but . . ."

"If you don't, that picture will show up on his desk at the lab. Along with the newspaper article. Understand?"

She was shaking her head. *He knew where Justin worked.*

"I didn't hear your answer. Do. You. Understand?"

"Yes," she whispered.

"And don't even think about reporting this call to anyone. Are we clear on that?"

"Yes," she repeated.

"No one will be hurt. All I want is the location. Once I've verified it, I'll be gone. You'll never hear from me again."

"How do I know that?"

"You have no choice. Get a pen, and I'll give you the number."

She grabbed a pen and the envelope to write on. "Okay."

He gave her the number, then said, "Repeat it to me."

She did as he asked.

"Good. It must be this weekend. No later."

"But—" She heard a click.

He'd hung up.

Alice went to the restroom and splashed cold water on her face. Staring in the mirror, she shook her head.

Ten years had passed. The nightmares and memories of that fateful night had finally begun to recede. However, she still had trouble sleeping without pills. She and Justin were getting married this spring, but not if he saw what was on her desk.

All she had to do was get Justin to take her to the tree and make a phone call. But what was the caller going to do with the knowledge? He said no one would be hurt. Still, she'd have to betray Justin, her friends, and the Cherokee.

How did she know if she could trust the stranger? She dried her face with a paper towel and turned to go back to her office. She didn't know, but it didn't matter. He was right—she had no choice.

27

Since the call Wednesday, Alice had worried about getting Justin to take her to the tree this weekend. She'd dropped hints about hiking, but Justin had been noncommittal. She waited until dinner Friday evening at home to push it further.

"Let's go hiking tomorrow," she said.

Justin wrinkled his forehead. "I'd love to, but not this weekend. I've got to work. Hadley is up my ass these days."

"What about Sunday? You could work tomorrow."

"I can't. Maybe next weekend. Why don't you call Tsula? Maybe she and Atohi can go."

Next weekend would be too late. The caller had only said that he needed to know the precise location. What difference would it make who led them to it? She knew Atohi could find the tree, so maybe she could get them to go.

After dinner, Justin got up from the table to work. Alice offered to clear the table, and after she finished, she called Tsula.

"Hey," Alice said.

"Hey, girl. What's up?"

"Not much. Trying to find hiking partners for tomorrow. Justin has to work, and I need some Park therapy."

Tsula laughed. "I can go. Atohi has a tribal council meeting tomorrow, so he's out."

Alice didn't feel comfortable going without Atohi, plus she couldn't bank on Tsula being able to find it.

"What about Sunday?" Alice said.

"That's possible, but the rain's coming in after midnight Saturday. Tomorrow would be a much better day. You and I could go. It'd be fun with just us girls anyway."

Now what? Alice thought. The idea of the stranger following her and Tsula in the woods bothered Alice. The tree was in a remote area with no cell service.

"Justin's motioning for me," Alice said. "Let me call you right back." She hung up, her mind racing. Somehow she'd have to convince Justin to go.

She found him sitting outside at the table on the porch, papers spread out in front of him. She walked over, put her arms around his neck, and kissed his ear.

"How am I supposed to concentrate on work with you doing that?" he said, moving his face closer to her lips.

"Take me hiking in the morning. I'll make it worth your while." She traced the outer edges of his ear with her tongue and drew her fingertips on his neck. His head leaned back closer to her.

"You don't play fair," he said, slowly pulling away. "I can't. Tsula and Atohi couldn't go?"

She couldn't use Atohi's meeting as an excuse since Tsula was available tomorrow.

"They can't go till Sunday, and it's supposed to rain Sunday."

She bent over and whispered in his ear. "We can get up early. We'll be back by lunch. You can work then."

He leaned his head toward her lips. The fact that he didn't refuse showed he was weakening. She nibbled on his earlobe to seal the deal.

"Please," she whispered.

He put his pencil down. "Okay. We'll go early. But I have to get some work done tonight and tomorrow afternoon."

She smiled, then kissed his neck. With her lips brushing his ear, she said, "I promise I'll make it worth it."

"I'm going to hold you to that. Now, scram."

She went back inside and called Tsula. Alice was relieved that it went straight to voice mail, and she left a message. "Hey. Justin changed his mind, so we're going early in the morning. I'll give you a call when we get back tomorrow."

Alice hated cutting her friend off like that, but she didn't want Tsula tagging along. Alice pulled out the number the caller had given her and dialed it. A mechanical voice answered, "Leave a message."

She did a quick calculation and said, "Seven o'clock tomorrow morning." When she hung up, she wondered how he would follow them. He had to be watching the house or the lone road down the mountain. Since he knew Justin's name, she assumed he also knew what kind of vehicles they drove. A shiver went down her spine as she wondered how he knew so much about them.

That night, she set the alarm for six. She figured it would take them no more than an hour to get dressed, have breakfast, and fix a snack. They should be leaving by seven, right on time.

The next morning, Justin was up before the alarm went off. Alice must have glanced at the clock a dozen times and deliberately dawdled.

"Geez, you are so slow this morning," he said. "We need to get going. I have got to get some work done this afternoon."

She kissed him, letting her lips linger. "I know you're in a hurry. Don't worry. I haven't forgotten my promise."

He shook his head and smiled. "You're bad."

Despite Alice taking as much time as she could, they were in the 4Runner at 6:45, ready to roll.

"Where to?" he asked as they pulled out of the drive.

"Let's do Hyatt Ridge."

"I'm tired of that one," he said, protesting. "I just did it last weekend. Let's go somewhere else."

She reached over and put her hand in his lap, giving him a gentle squeeze.

"You didn't do it with me. We'll be all alone. Perfect for what I had in mind."

He looked over at her and grinned, shaking his head.

"Hyatt Ridge, it is."

The entire trip, she kept looking in the outside mirror to see if someone was following them. A couple of times, a vehicle appeared behind them, and she thought it could've been him. But each time, the car turned off well before they left the Blue Ridge Parkway.

When they turned onto Heintoga Ridge Road, no one was behind them. She didn't see another car until they got to the picnic area at the end of the paved section. There, she noticed a white 4-door sedan parked. No one was in it, and there was no sign of anyone. From that point, Balsam Mountain Road was a narrow, twisting, one-way, gravel road for the next fourteen miles. There was still no glimpse of anyone behind them.

Alice began to worry. *What if he didn't get the message? How would she know?* She'd upheld her end of the bargain so far. How would she let him know where the tree was? They hadn't discussed that.

She thought back to her conversation with the anonymous caller. "Get Justin to take you to the tree. Call the day before with the time you'll be leaving the house," he'd said. She hadn't told him where they were going. He specifically said to leave only the time and nothing else, which meant that he would follow them.

Maybe that was his white car at the picnic area, but the car was there before them. How would he know where they were going?

They got to the Hyatt Ridge trailhead and parked. This location was also accessible from Cherokee, but no one else was there.

"7:30," Justin said, looking at his watch. He always marked the time they left to gauge distance on a trail. "Ready?"

They set off, Justin quickly establishing his usual pace. Behind him, Alice kept looking back over her shoulder, hoping to see someone. Nothing.

An hour and a half later, they got to the junction with the Enloe Creek Trail. They stopped for water, sitting on a fallen tree trunk by the trail. They had yet to see anyone.

Alice took another drink and put her water bottle back in the side pocket of her pack. Justin stood in front of her. "Pretty secluded, alright."

She nodded, looking around in every direction, straining her ears to hear. Nothing. *Where was he?*

Justin hadn't moved. She looked up at him, recognizing that silly grin on his face. Now she knew why he was just standing there.

She looked around and shook her head. It was too exposed here, and the stranger could be watching. She was not going to put on a show for the creep.

"Ready?" she asked.

"I guess," he said, the disappointment evident in his voice. "How much further are we going?"

"I told you, I want to see the tree," she said, pouting her lips. "Besides, this is a trail intersection. Someone might come by."

She nodded down the Enloe Creek Trail. "The tree's only what, thirty minutes away. Let's have lunch now. On the way back, before we get here, I can have dessert. It'll be more private down there." She forced a seductive grin.

He smiled. "Sounds good. Let's go."

She blushed at his reaction. They ate their lunch, and then Justin took her to the healing tree. Half an hour later, they stood facing the tree.

"Satisfied?" he asked.

"Yes. It's beautiful. Thank you. What happens when this one is gone?"

"I've been thinking about that. We need to figure out how to propagate it."

"Do you think there are others?"

He shrugged. "Probably. Who knows? There's so much in this park that we don't know."

"You don't need any more samples?"

"No. I got enough my last trip to hold me for a while. I can always come back if I need to."

She reached out for his hand and attempted a sexy grin. "Seems like I remember a fallen tree about ten minutes up the trail. Might be a good stop for dessert."

His face lit up at the recognition that she had not forgotten her promise.

They made their way back to the trail, and twenty minutes later, they came to the fallen tree. It was probably two feet or more in diameter. They still hadn't seen or heard anyone else.

"You were right. This is a good place for a break," Justin said, unable to conceal his anticipation.

Alice scanned the trail in both directions. Nothing. The only sounds were the occasional cries of a bird or the squeak of a squirrel.

She didn't know what had happened to the mystery man. For all she knew, he'd been following them silently and was watching even now, unseen. The thought gave her the creeps, but she couldn't stall any longer. She'd done her job and led him to the tree. There'd be no reason for him to follow them now.

She removed her pack and sat on the log, stealing one last glance around, convincing herself that he was not anywhere near. She felt cheap. Seducing Justin because a total stranger was blackmailing her, blackmailing her for a terrible mistake she'd made long ago. A mistake that Justin knew nothing about. The guilt had come back with a vengeance.

Trying to mask the sadness within, she looked up at an expectant Justin. She could delay no longer and reached out her hands.

He walked over and stood in front of her. She unzipped his fly and lowered his shorts. Seeing the bulge in his briefs, she struggled to focus.

"I think somebody's glad to see me," she said, feigning interest as she slowly pulled them down. As she took him in her mouth, he whimpered, and she felt his knees buckle.

Sex in the woods was nothing new to them, but today, with the disturbing thought of the stranger in the back of her mind, she wanted to get it over with as quickly as possible. It didn't take long.

"Oh my God," he said afterward, pulling up his shorts. "You are incredible."

She avoided meeting his gaze, thankful that he misinterpreted her hurried pace as desire. She glanced around the clearing. If the stranger had followed them, then he was a ghost.

She took a swallow of water and pasted on a smile before facing him. "Glad you enjoyed it."

He grinned as he took her hand. "Oh, yes. Your turn."

She blushed at his gesture and pulled her hand away, almost repulsed at the thought. "Let's wait until we get home."

They hiked back to the trailhead, still not seeing anyone else the entire time they were in the woods. As they rounded the corner down the last hill to the small parking area, she saw a car parked next to them. It was a white Ford sedan.

Alice panicked. It resembled the same car she saw up at the picnic area before they got on the one-way gravel road.

"Whose car is this? We didn't see anyone," she said. "Or hear anyone."

Justin laughed. "No, and hopefully, they didn't see us. If they did, they got a show."

Alice blushed, thinking back to the scene on the log. *Had the stranger been watching?* The thought made her ill. Her previous sense of relief turned to dread.

Seeing her embarrassment, Justin put his arm around her. "Don't worry. They had to have taken the Hyatt Ridge Trail past the junction. Otherwise, we would've passed them coming out." He kissed the top of her head. "Nothing to be ashamed of."

It took every bit of her willpower to keep from bursting into tears.

28

Back home, they showered. Afterward, Justin made good on his promise. Usually, Alice enjoyed it, but this afternoon she was preoccupied with the caller and why he didn't show.

Not wanting to disappoint Justin, she faked pleasure, something she seldom had to do. Soon after, Justin went out to the porch to work.

She started getting dressed. Before she finished, her phone buzzed. It was a number she didn't recognize. She ignored it and put the phone down while she finished dressing. It vibrated again, the same number. Curious, she answered.

"Hello, Payten."

A chill ran down her spine. It was the same male voice from before.

Keeping her voice down, she hissed, "What do you want? I did what you asked. I left you a message and got him to take me to the tree." she said, keeping her voice low.

"Your message said 7:00. I waited thirty minutes for you to leave, but you never showed."

Alice swore under her breath. She'd stalled Justin for as long as she could, but they'd left the house at 6:45.

"We left at a quarter till. I couldn't delay him until seven. There wasn't any way I could call."

"You'll have to get him to take you again. Or you can show me."

She couldn't ask Justin to take her back, not this soon. He'd be suspicious. But she also wasn't sure she could find it. She'd been so busy trying to find a spot for her and Justin to have sex that she hadn't paid attention once they left the trail. He'd even mentioned he took a slightly different path each time not to leave any signs.

Atohi or Tsula could find it. But how could she ask them without Justin finding out? Maybe Tsula could go with her.

"I need to find that tree, Payten."

She shivered. Every time he said her name, it was like running fingernails over a chalkboard.

"I can show you. But I can't go until next weekend."

"Not good enough. Tomorrow, Payten."

There was no way she could get away tomorrow. Maybe Monday.

"I can't. There's no way—"

"You will." The anger in his voice startled her. "Or the picture and newspaper article will be on your fiancé's *and* your boss's desk first thing Monday."

"Monday morning, I promise I'll take you as soon as he leaves for work. Please."

She hated begging him, but she was desperate. The thought of being in the woods alone with this creep frightened her. But even more terrifying was him exposing her past.

"Morning morning is your last chance. What time?" His voice was calm again, and the anger switched off as suddenly as it had switched on.

"Eight o'clock. He's gone by then. I'll call you to confirm," she said. Justin usually left for work before she did. Still, she didn't want to take any chances, so she added thirty minutes to his normal departure.

"Eight o'clock. I'll be waiting."

She hung up the phone, her hand shaking. She'd have to call in sick.

* * *

As predicted, it rained all day Sunday. It was forecast to last another day. Justin worked, holed up in his study. Knowing she would call in sick in the morning, Alice chose to work as well, trying to get ahead.

That evening, Alice started preparing dinner. Although Justin usually cooked on the weekend, she wanted something to occupy her mind.

"I was going to cook dinner," he said as he walked into the kitchen.

"You were working." A spoon slipped out of her hand and clanged to the floor. "Shit," she said, reaching for a clean one out of the silverware drawer.

"Everything okay?" he asked.

She shrugged. "Fine. Just work stuff. I'm behind and decided to get a head start on month-end. You were busy, and it was raining. Nothing else to do."

"What's for dinner?" he said as he poured himself a glass of wine.

"Trout. Fresh veggies, tomatoes."

"Good. I'm hungry."

For the first time in years, she eyed his wineglass and was tempted to pour herself one.

At dinner, he told her he'd talked to Karen's doctor that afternoon. "Stewart said her numbers have plateaued. I'm worried. I think she needs more of the HT67. I'm going to call Mary and discuss it with her."

"Makes sense," she mumbled. She was thinking about her conversation with the stranger.

"I may have to go back tomorrow. So I can get more material—"

"Back where?"

He wrinkled his brow. "Aren't you listening? I said I was going to call Mary. I think I may need to get more material from the tree. I don't have enough to make another batch."

"But . . . we just went yesterday."

"Yes, and I didn't get any material. Remember, I told you that I didn't need any? That was before I talked to Dr. Stewart. What's the problem? You've got to work."

She shook her head. "Nothing." She paused and then added, "Maybe I could go with you?"

"How? You're working. Besides, it's supposed to rain again tomorrow."

"I could take the day off," she said, reaching over and running her fingertips across his arm. She was desperate. "We could repeat yesterday."

He wore a puzzled expression. "That would be nice, but you just got through saying you were behind at work. And it's going to be miserable tomorrow. Heavy rain again all day." Exasperated, he said, "I'm going to call Mary."

Alice overheard bits and pieces of the phone conversation. When he hung up, he said, "Mary suggested giving Karen the tea first and see if that helps. All I have is the extract, and Mary thinks freshly brewed tea would be better. She said that if I'd get the material tomorrow, she'd brew a fresh batch. I've got to get up early."

Later that night, Justin's snoring didn't bother her in bed. She couldn't sleep anyway, trying to figure out what the hell she would do tomorrow. Not only was she feeling guilty about keeping secrets from Justin, but she was now worried about the stranger destroying the tree.

Justin believed that the healing tree was responsible for Karen's improvement, and he wanted to give her more. She couldn't let him down.

* * *

Monday morning, the rain drumming on their tin roof woke Alice before daylight. Justin wasn't in bed, and she could smell fresh coffee. She panicked, thinking she'd overslept, but when she looked at the clock, it was only 5:15.

She padded into the kitchen, where Justin handed her a steaming cup of coffee. "Geez, you're up early this morning." The coffee was hot and strong, just what she needed.

"I've got a long day ahead." He nodded toward the window. "See, I told you. It's nasty out there."

"You going to the lab first?" she asked.

He shook his head. "No. I doubt I'll make it in today. After Mary makes the tea, I'm going to take it over to Karen."

She nodded, relieved for the unexpected window of time. There's no way she'd let anyone destroy the healing tree, not when Karen needed it. Alice planned to take the stranger to another trail and show him a tree that could pass for the healing tree. Afterward, she'd come back to the house, shower, and change before Justin got home.

Justin finished his coffee and left after kissing her goodbye. She took her time, having a big breakfast and not putting her hiking clothes on until 7:40.

At 7:50, she called the number and left a message. "Leaving at 8 o'clock." She wasn't taking any chances.

She still wasn't sure which trail to go to. She wasn't sure how long it'd take but figured it didn't matter now that she had plenty of time to get home before Justin. Since the stranger wanted to know what time she was leaving, he must plan to intercept her and follow.

She put on her rain jacket and pants, then went out to the car at precisely 8:00 a.m. It was pouring. Justin was right—the weather was miserable.

As she drove down the mountain, she kept looking for a car behind her. At the crossroads, she noticed a silver sedan pull out of a side road behind her.

She didn't want to risk running into Justin, which ruled out any trail off Balsam Mountain Road. Since he would be coming from the lab, he'd probably use that route.

The next closest trail she could think of was the Cataloochee Divide Trail from Cove Creek Gap. It was the closest to her house, and the climb wasn't too difficult. She wasn't sure what kind of shape the mystery caller was in, and she wanted to ensure they could get in and out as quickly as possible. When she turned left off US 276, the silver sedan was still behind her.

She planned to take him far enough down the trail to be credible, take him off-trail, and show him a tree that could pass for the healing tree. She was betting that he didn't know what he was looking for.

The narrow, twisty unpaved road was treacherous in the rain, slippery with blind curves. Fortunately, she didn't meet any traffic. When she got to the trailhead, she pulled off and parked. The silver car pulled in next to her.

Alice waited for him to get out. After a few minutes, she figured he wanted her to get out first.

A flash of lightning startled her. The thunder rolled in seconds later. *Damn, that was close, within a mile,* she thought, with only a few seconds between the flash and the thunder. The Divide Trail was a ridge trail, not a good one to be on in a thunderstorm.

Alice zipped up her rain jacket and pulled the hood over her head. Out of habit, she checked the time on her phone. 8:50. She took a deep breath, put her phone in the side pocket of the jacket, and left the safety of her car.

Standing in the pouring rain, she didn't bother to lock the car door. She stared at the driver's side of the silver sedan, a Nissan, waiting for her caller to get out.

The door opened, and a man dressed in camouflage rain gear stepped out. He wore a wide-brimmed hat, water dripping off the edge. She was surprised that he was tall and appeared to be in excellent shape. Even more surprising, he was wearing a camouflage face shield that covered his mouth and nose. Only his eyes were showing.

He looked around, seeming to survey the area. He walked over to her and held out his hand, his eyes dark and alert.

"Your phone," he said. His tone implied an order, not a request.

She shrugged. There was no service in Cataloochee anyway. She reached into her pocket and handed him the phone.

He turned it off and handed it back to her.

"Turn around. I need to check you for weapons."

"You're kidding? I don't have any *weapons*," she said.

"That's what they all say. Turn around."

Disgusted, she turned around. Feeling his hands run down her body made her shiver, but he was quick and professional. She'd had more objectionable pat-downs at airport security.

"Okay," he said. He pointed down the road.

"Where does this go?" he asked.

"It dead-ends down in Cataloochee Valley."

"How far?"

She shrugged. "I don't know. Five, six miles."

"Good. We'll park your car there."

"What? No, I mean, why can't we go from here?" Alice panicked. She thought she'd just walk down the trail for a couple of miles, show him the tree, then leave.

"No. Get in, drive as far as you can. I'll be right behind you, so don't get any ideas. Park, then get in my car, and we'll come back up here."

"But—"

"Take me to the tree. Then I'll take you back to your car."

She drove to the end of the road and parked, as he ordered. She switched the car off and fingered the keys. *Take them with or leave them?* she asked herself. Afraid he'd ask for them, she put the keys under the seat.

She got out, walked over to his car, and slid into the passenger seat next to him.

Neither of them said a word on the way back up to Cove Creek Gap. He pulled in at the trailhead and switched off the car.

"Out," he said.

She got out and turned around. He was removing a small cylinder from the back seat of the sedan. She recognized it as a pump sprayer, the kind Justin used to spray weed killer around the house.

She noticed a bulge on his right hip. *A gun,* she thought. He strapped the sprayer on his back.

"What's in that?" she asked.

"Something to take care of the tree. Let's go," he said, nodding toward the trail.

29

With the heavy rain, Justin decided to take the Blue Ridge Parkway to Big Cove Road and go to the trailhead from Cherokee. That part of the road was in much better shape and shorter than coming in from Balsam Mountain. If he hadn't needed the raw materials for Karen, he wouldn't have bothered to go out on a day like this.

After he turned onto the gravel road from Big Cove Road, he didn't see another vehicle. He parked at the trailhead and switched the truck off. The rain was pounding on the roof and showed no signs of letting up. He put the rain cover over his backpack and zipped up his rain jacket. Twisting in the seat, he managed to get the pack over his shoulders. He tightened the drawstring on his hood and stepped outside into the pouring rain. *A good day for ducks,* he thought as he headed up the muddy trail.

It was tough slogging, but he made good time by himself. He got to the intersection at Enloe Creek Trail and continued straight, not bothering to stop. When he passed the log where he and Alice had sex, he smiled.

On the drive over, he'd thought about who could be behind an attempt to find the tree. Certainly, Nuran had a motive. Justin didn't want to believe that the Kendalls would consider destroying anything with the potential to help so many people. Still, five billion dollars was a lot of money. He wondered if Bobby knew anything about the search for the tree.

The thought crossed his mind that the Cherokee tribe also had an incentive—not to destroy the tree but to profit from it. Now that they knew it was on the Qualla Boundary, they stood to make a windfall profit from any drugs developed from the healing tree. He made a mental note to mention that to Atohi. Maybe Sam Bear had an ulterior motive?

When he got to the tree, he stood there taking it in, rain dripping from the brim of his hat. Surrounded by the much taller tulip poplars and pines, it looked small. He realized that it was probably thirty feet tall. Now that he knew its capabilities, he was worried. The tree represented a considerable step forward in cancer treatment, possibly equaling or even exceeding Taxol, but only if they could get to the next level.

Was this the only tree? He wanted to believe there were other ones, undiscovered. They needed to find others or quickly learn how to propagate it. They'd have to discover how to synthesize the active ingredient, but they had not isolated the active ingredient yet.

Although the tea didn't require a lot of raw material, it was still only one tree. Whatever the growth rate, he knew it couldn't regenerate fast enough to replace what he was taking.

He felt a sense of guilt as he went about collecting what he needed. He took as much as he dared, then took a different route back to the trail. As he went, he carefully covered his tracks, the heavy rain helping his efforts. Once back on the trail, he satisfied himself that his path was sufficiently hidden and started the trek back to his SUV.

* * *

Even though the Divide Trail wasn't that steep, it was narrow and slippery. With every thunderclap, Alice flinched. This wasn't a smart place to be for many reasons. After what she guessed to be an hour, she stopped and looked around as if trying to find something.

"How much further?" he asked.

She jumped, not realizing how close he was to her. He'd said nothing since they left the car, and she didn't bother with any small talk. "This looks familiar," she said.

He looked around, studying everything for clues. "What exactly are you looking for?" His eyes bore into hers.

"It's off-trail, downhill to the right of a large tulip poplar," she said, pointing to the large tree next to her.

He knelt, examining the trail and the underbrush. He reached out to inspect several low-hanging branches. He grunted and shifted his cold, dark eyes up to her. "When was the last time you were here?"

"I told you. Saturday."

He stood, facing her, rain dripping off his hat. He shook his head. "Nobody has been off-trail here that recently. Either you have the wrong tree, or you're lying."

Alice glanced away, thinking about what to do. He was not stupid. Now, she was worried whether she could sell another plant as the healing tree. She didn't think that he'd seen a picture, but she had to be careful. She hoped he didn't have a working knowledge of plants in this area.

"I've never been out here by myself. It's always been with Justin, and him leading the way."

She looked at the tree again, avoiding his glare. She shook her head.

"I know it was a tulip poplar about this size. There aren't many this big, but this may not be the one. How long have we been walking?"

He looked at his watch. "Sixty-five minutes."

She nodded. "It's a little slower today with the rain. I don't think we're there yet. It must be a little farther."

As they walked, he started peppering her with questions about the tree's location. She knew he was trying to pin her down and catch her in a lie. She willed herself to remain confident.

The rain finally stopped. They walked for another ten minutes, and as they rounded a curve in the trail, she spotted another large tulip poplar. As they got closer, she could see that something had slightly trampled the vegetation next to it. Probably a game trail, which would be convincing enough.

She stopped. "This is it. I'm sure." She watched as he examined the faint path next to it.

"How far off the trail?" he asked as he stood and stepped toward her.

Although he was invading her personal space to intimidate her, she tried not to flinch.

"I'm not sure," she said. "Maybe ten minutes?"

He cocked his head, staring at her, trying to decide if she was lying.

"It better be down there. If not, the package will be on Justin's desk first thing in the morning."

A cold chill ran down her spine. She had to find an uncommon shrub down there and convince him it was the healing tree. If not, for the second time, her life as she knew it would be over.

30

Leaving the Park, Justin considered going home first to shower and change, but Mary's house was on the way. On her porch, he removed his rain jacket, shaking the water off when she opened the door.

"A messy day to be out in the woods," she said. He removed his boots, and she ushered him into her small home.

"I know, but I wanted to get the tea over to Karen today." He handed her the leaves, along with a piece of bark and a flower. He'd never watched Mary make the tea and was unsure where he was supposed to wait.

"You can watch," she said. Justin followed her into the kitchen. "Agitsi's recipe stated to brew the tea from recently gathered ingredients for best results. Of course, that was in the day before refrigeration."

Justin didn't want to pry but was curious. "Have you given it to any of your . . . patients?"

She looked at him, seeming to determine how much she should say. "A few." She smiled. "All with good results."

After she'd brewed the tea, she poured it into a small glass jar and screwed a lid on it. "Get this to her as soon as you can. And make sure she drinks all of it."

"Thank you, I will," he said as he turned to leave.

At his house, he took off his boots and rain jacket before entering. A hot shower and dry clothes would feel good.

Once inside, on his way to the bedroom, he noticed a folder on the bar. Curious, he walked over and flipped it open, thinking maybe he'd left something.

It was Alice's. He recognized it as what she'd been working on last night. He shrugged and put his keys on top of her folder. He'd drop it by her office on his way over to Karen's.

Driving to the bank, Justin tried calling Alice's cell phone, but it went straight to voice mail. No answer. Once there, he parked and went inside. He turned right toward Alice's office and noticed her light was off.

Rhonda, the receptionist, was sitting at her desk. She looked up to see Justin and smiled.

"Hey, Justin."

"Hey, Rhonda." He held up the folder. "Alice left this at home, and I thought I'd drop it off in case she needed it today. I tried calling her cell, but it went to voice mail."

Rhonda had a puzzled look. "Alice called in sick first thing this morning."

Now Justin was confused. "She did?"

Rhonda nodded, wearing a sheepish grin. "I . . . she . . . I haven't talked to her since then."

He handed her the folder. "Hmm. Well, tell her to call me if you hear from her. I've got to run." He turned and walked out, wondering what was going on. Alice seemed fine when he left. Maybe she was playing hooky, and her phone died while running errands.

On the way to Winston-Salem, he tried calling her a couple of times, but with the same result. Voice mail. Alice knew that he was making a quick trip to check on Karen, so he wasn't too worried.

When he got to Karen's, he was relieved to see that she was in good spirits and feeling okay, though a little tired. He told her about his conversation with Mary and insisted that she drink the tea before he left.

"You sure you won't stay for dinner?" Karen asked.

"I can't, but thanks. I need to get back." He was starting to worry that he hadn't heard from Alice. He didn't mention it to Karen because he didn't want her to fret. When she finished the tea, he kissed her goodbye and left, promising to check on her in the morning.

* * *

Off the trail, Alice stopped. She'd spotted a longstalk holly, what Justin had seen that day he first discovered the healing tree. Perfect. It was not familiar enough that a casual observer would recognize it.

"There," she said, pointing to the tree in front of them. "That's it."

He cocked his head and stared at it for a moment, then looked at Alice. "You sure?"

She nodded. "Yes. Positive." She tried to sound confident.

He stepped over and broke off a low-hanging branch. He pulled out his cellphone to take pictures, first of the limb and then the tree.

"Damn," he said, looking down at his phone. "No service."

"That's pretty common out here," she said.

"As soon as we get to where I have service, I'll send the picture to my botanist friend."

Panic lodged in Alice's throat. Any botanist would verify that the tree was a longstalk holly. The stranger would know that she lied to him.

The other thing that struck fear in her heart was that he said *we*. He had no intention of letting her go until he knew it was the healing tree.

She watched as he took the sprayer off his back and set it down in front of him. He pulled the plunger out and started pumping, pressurizing the tank. Now was her only chance.

She looked to either side of her kidnapper, trying to determine which route offered the most cover. To his left, it was steeper, but the rhododendron thicket on his right provided more cover.

He finished pressurizing the tank and picked it up to start spraying the tree. He stopped and stared at her.

"What's in there?" she asked, trying to mask her intentions.

"Hexazinone. Highly effective. It'll kill anything growing within the area sprayed. Even with it wet."

Alice shuddered, glad she hadn't taken him to the healing tree. Her question seemed to cause him to relax his guard. He picked up the tank and headed to his right. "Won't take but a few minutes. Then we're out of here."

As soon as the tree was between him and her intended path, she bolted down the hill, half running, half falling.

"Hey. What the?" She heard him yell, but she didn't stop. She was hoping the head start would be enough.

The hill was steeper than she thought. Branches and briars scratched her arms and legs. Grateful for the protection of her rain jacket and pants, she prayed she wouldn't fall and break something.

She heard him yelling, "Stop, or I'll shoot." She didn't slow down, still scrambling down the hill as fast as she could. She wanted to put as much distance between them as quickly as possible.

A gunshot whizzed over her head to her right. She ducked before realizing it hadn't been as close as she thought. She was hoping he'd take a more cautious and slower path to look for her. Two more shots rang out, both farther away than the first. The sound was more muffled, which meant the gap between them was increasing.

She had no idea where she was going and didn't care. First things first. Get the hell away from him. If she managed to do that, then she'd be alive to think about the next steps.

Alice kept moving. Daylight was fading fast. After a while, she found a small stream and stopped for water. She knew drinking unfiltered water wasn't safe, but it was better than getting dehydrated. In the distance, she heard the stranger calling, but his voice was getting fainter and farther away.

On this side of the Divide Trail, the stream had to lead down into Cataloochee Valley. She patted her pocket for her car keys, then remembered she'd left them in the car. If she could get there, she'd have a way out.

She felt her cell phone. Excited, she pulled it out and switched it on. No service. She slammed it against her leg, then switched it off to save the battery. She rose and followed the stream downhill, wanting to put more distance between her and her kidnapper before dark.

Soon, she came across a rock outcropping, large enough to provide shelter. She scrambled underneath and sat with her knees drawn up. What she'd give for her daypack right now. In it were a water filter, matches, compass, and space blanket. Fumbling around in the pockets of her rain jacket, she found a cereal bar. She ate half of it, savoring every bite, saving the other half for later.

Alice strained to hear, but the only sound was rain falling. She knew she could survive for weeks without food as long as she had water. She cupped her hands and held them under the dripping edge of the rock, gathering water.

After drinking several handfuls, she looked around at her accommodations.

At least she was covered and well-hidden should her kidnapper make it that far, though she hadn't heard him in hours. In an unfamiliar area, with daylight waning, chances were he'd given up searching. The heavy rain dampened the sounds of her movement, which was to her advantage and muted any noise he might make. The adrenaline from the escape had faded, and she was exhausted. With no light or compass, she decided to stay put for the night.

She knew it was a long shot but switched on her phone anyway, hoping to get lucky. No surprise, there was still no service. The battery was down to ten percent, so she turned it off and shook her head. A cell phone was useless in the Park.

Scratched and bruised, she considered herself lucky she hadn't broken anything. Her right ankle was tender, but that was it. She thought about the 58-year-old man who'd wandered off on Purchase Knob recently. Wearing nothing but shorts, a t-shirt, and a ball cap, he spent five days in the wilderness before rescuers found him. She was younger, knew the area, and had a rain jacket and pants. If he could survive, so could she.

Alice wondered how long it would be before Justin started looking for her. And how long before he looked in this area. She had to get back to her car, but what if the kidnapper was there, waiting? There was a ranger station in Cataloochee. Maybe she could go there first. Either way, as soon as it was light, she'd have to leave this spot.

She closed her eyes, trying not to get ahead of herself.

31

When Justin got home that evening, he was surprised to see that Alice's car was not there. He went inside, expecting a note or explanation. Nothing. Her car keys and rain jacket were missing, as well as her red clutch that he knew contained her license, credit cards, and cash.

He called Tsula's phone.

"Hey, Justin," she said.

"Do you know where Alice might be?" he asked.

"Uh, no. I haven't talked to her today. Why?"

"I just got home, and she's not here. Not answering her phone, either."

"Probably working late," Tsula said.

"I don't think so. I went by the bank earlier today, and she wasn't there. Rhonda said she called in sick today. She was fine when I left the house early this morning."

"Odd. I'll check with the book club members, see if any of them have heard from her."

"Thanks. Talk to you later."

Justin pulled up the Find My app on his phone and signed on. The icon for Alice's phone was gray, indicating it was offline. Maybe the battery had died. Alice was notorious for letting it run down. The last location was Cove Creek Road, just off Jonathan Creek road. What was she doing over there?

It was still raining as he jumped in his truck and headed toward Cataloochee.

Fifteen minutes later, he turned off onto Cove Creek Road. He drove for another half hour to the end of Cataloochee valley before seeing another vehicle. There, at the end of the road, was Alice's blue Honda Civic.

The rain was coming down harder. He pulled the rain jacket hood over his head, got out, and walked around the car, peeking through the windows. No one was inside, and nothing seemed out of place.

He tried the driver's door. It was unlocked, so he got in, thankful to get out of the rain. He looked around inside. Again, nothing out of the ordinary.

He felt underneath the driver's seat and pulled out a candy bar wrapper. Snickers, Alice's favorite. He smiled and reached down again. This time, his fingers touched something metal, not part of the vehicle. He pulled out her car keys and held them up. *Odd.* He stuck them in his pocket and continued searching, not finding anything else.

Back in his vehicle, he tried to figure out where she could be. Something told him that she was in trouble. Four different trails led out of the valley, all in different directions. He had no idea where to start looking.

He drove back out to Jonathan Creek Road, where he had cell service, and called Atohi.

"I found Alice's car. At the end of the road in Cataloochee. No sign of Alice, but her keys were under the seat," Justin said.

"Where are you?" Atohi said.

"At the Exxon station by I-40."

"Stay put. I'll be there in thirty minutes."

Twenty-five minutes later, Atohi pulled in next to him.

"What's going on?" Atohi asked when he got into the truck, rain dripping off of his cap.

Justin told him everything he knew. He'd not seen or talked to Alice all day. She'd left her work folder at home, and he'd taken it by the bank. Rhonda, the receptionist, had not seen or talked to Alice since she'd called in sick that morning.

"She wasn't home when I got there. I checked the Find My app," Justin said. "Her phone was offline. The last location was just up Cove Creek Road. I drove as far as possible into Cataloochee Valley, and that's where I found her car."

Atohi looked outside and shook his head. "It's pouring rain and late. I'm not sure what we can do right now."

"Alice is missing. We need to call the sheriff's office or the Park Service or somebody."

"You don't know that," Atohi said. "There's probably a reasonable explanation. Maybe she had car trouble. You said her keys were under the seat. Did you try starting the car?"

Justin shook his head. "I didn't think to do that."

"No worries. Tsula's calling everyone to see if anyone knows anything."

"Why hasn't she called?"

"You know how cell service is in the mountains. Maybe her phone died. Who knows? I know you're upset, but there's nothing anybody can do right now anyway. This rain is supposed to move through later tonight. Let's go back to the house and see if Tsula's found out anything."

When they got to Atohi's, Tsula met them at the door, shaking her head.

"I've called everybody. No one's talked to her today."

"We need to call the sheriff's office," Justin said as they took off their jackets and went inside.

Tsula looked at Atohi, then back to Justin.

"Maybe we should try to find her first," Tsula said.

"What do you mean?" Justin asked.

Atohi spoke. "I can round up some help tonight so we can get a fresh start in the morning."

"Okay, but why wouldn't we call—"

"Justin, we don't know what is going on," Tsula said in a gentle tone. "Think about it. Alice called in sick today. You said she was fine this morning, so obviously, she'd planned something. Something that none of us know about."

Justin started to respond, then stopped. Tsula's comment stunned him. Alice had called in sick, so what was she doing?

He stared at Tsula, wondering what she was thinking. He sensed that she knew more than she was saying.

"I get that no one can do anything tonight, not with this weather, but I want to call the sheriff's office or the Park Service and at least report Alice missing. Tonight," Justin said.

Tsula looked at Atohi. He gave her a slight nod, and then he looked at Justin.

"You might want to wait till in the morning before you do that," Atohi said.

"But she might be hurt. Or worse. Someone might have—"

Atohi looked at Tsula and said, "You need to tell him."

"Tell me what?" Justin said, pleading.

"Rhonda—at the bank—thinks that Alice may be seeing somebody. Last week, she happened to overhear Alice on her cell phone saying something about meeting someone."

Justin felt like somebody had punched him in the gut. Now, he understood why Rhonda had acted so sheepishly when he stopped by the bank yesterday morning. *Was Alice having an affair?*

He stared at Tsula, then shifted his gaze to Atohi. "I don't believe it. For Christ's sake, we're getting married." He refused to believe that Alice was having an affair.

"Look, Justin. We don't know what Alice was doing, but there's no harm in waiting. Nobody can do anything tonight with this weather. Let me round up my crew tonight, and we'll get started first thing in the morning. We'll be in the Park before daylight. We'll be out there hours before the authorities can fill out the paperwork."

Justin shook his head. He was in shock but realized what Atohi said was true. They could be out looking for Alice instead of answering a bunch of stupid questions and filling out forms.

"Go home and try to get some sleep," Tsula said. "Alice may show up there."

After a long pause, Justin nodded. "Okay. Call me if you—"

"We will. And let us know if you hear anything," Atohi said. "Otherwise, we'll see you back here in the morning at five."

Tsula added, "I'll have coffee and breakfast waiting."

32

Before daylight, Justin awoke, his neck stiff from sleeping on the couch. Still wearing the clothes he wore last night, he had fallen asleep, waiting for Alice. He checked his phone. 4:37 a.m.—no missed calls and no Alice. He got up, splashed some water on his face, and headed out the door.

It was still dark when he got to Atohi's before five. A group of volunteers had surrounded Atohi's dining room table, studying a Park map. Justin poured himself a cup of coffee and joined them.

Four trails led out of Cataloochee Valley, all in different directions. Atohi drew a circle around the end of the road and another circle around the Cove Creek Gap trailhead. The rings represented the maximum estimated distance Alice could've traveled in the last twenty-four hours to establish an initial perimeter for the search. He assigned two-person teams to each trail.

"How do we know that's where she started from?" one of the volunteers asked.

"We don't," Justin said.

He explained that her last phone location was Cove Creek Road, just off of Jonathan Creek Road.

"But, I found her car here in Cataloochee," he said, pointing to the first circle on the map. "The keys were under the seat."

"Maybe it broke down," someone said.

"Somebody could have come along and given her a ride," someone else said.

The group got quiet, and the volunteers looked at each other.

Justin knew what they were thinking—there was another person—a likely scenario. *Was Alice a willing participant or not?* Regardless of what Tsula said last night, he still held onto the belief that something terrible had happened. In some ways, that was preferable to acknowledging that Alice was having an affair. And, he had still not notified the authorities.

"Possible. I don't know," he said. "But her phone's offline, and she hasn't called." He stared at Atohi. "We need to call—"

"Tsula's doing that as we speak." Atohi looked at his team. "Tsula is notifying the Park Service and the Sheriff's office, but let's don't jump to any conclusions. Cell service is practically non-existent over there, so that doesn't necessarily mean anything. We have to start with what we do know," Atohi said. "Let's go."

It was still dark when the first two teams pulled off at Cove Creek Gap and barely daylight when the others got to the Cataloochee Campground. Justin, Atohi, and another two-person team stopped there. The rest of the crew continued to the other trailheads farther into the valley.

The plan was for each team to work their way toward the end of the road where Justin had found Alice's car.

After quickly setting up camp, the four of them set out on the Caldwell Fork Trail. At the first intersection, Justin and Atohi stayed on Caldwell Fork. The other two searchers went left on the Boogerman Trail, which reconnected to the Caldwell Fork Trail four miles later.

After ten minutes of hiking in silence, Justin asked, "Do you think . . . she's seeing someone else?"

Atohi stopped and turned to face his friend.

"Look, I don't know anything more if that's what you're asking. And neither does Tsula. Is it possible?" Atohi shrugged, holding his hands out, palms up. "Do I think so? No. Right now, the priority is to find her and make sure she's okay."

Four hours later, they were almost to the junction where the trails rejoined. Atohi's radio crackled.

"We've got her," the voice said.

"What's your twenty?" Atohi asked.

"At the intersection."

"We'll be there in five, out."

They ran the last hundred yards. As they approached the junction where the trails rejoined, Justin saw three people up ahead. Two of them, Atohi's friends, were waving their arms.

"Alice," Justin said. He recognized Alice's rain jacket and ran faster, Atohi behind him.

As soon as Alice saw him, she ran toward him. Tears were streaming down her face as Alice threw her arms around his neck. His mixed feelings aside, he embraced her in a bear hug.

"Are you okay?" he asked. He separated and held her at arm's length so he could see for himself. Her jacket and pants were torn, but other than that, she appeared fine.

"Yes," she said, tears in her eyes. "I am now."

"Can you make it back to the campground? We're probably three to four hours out." Atohi said.

Alice nodded. "I may be a little slow. My ankle's bruised, but I'll be fine."

Justin reached out and hugged her again.

"I'm so glad to see you. I was worried sick."

"Not as glad as I am to see you."

Atohi called the others on the radio, telling them they'd found Alice and were headed back to the campground.

As they made their way back, Alice told them that she'd gotten lost off the Divide Trail and spent the night under a rock outcropping. At daylight, she followed a stream that led to a trail. It was the Boogerman, though she didn't know it at the time. With the sun up, she went west, figuring it would lead her into Cataloochee Valley. That was when the other team found her.

Back at the campground, Atohi asked Justin for the keys to Alice's car. He sent the other team to get it and then started a fire. Silently, Alice sat on a stool, warming herself. Justin made a pot of coffee while Atohi radioed the other teams.

"How did you end up on the Divide Trail?" Justin asked as he handed her a cup of coffee.

She took the coffee and, with both hands around the cup, sipped it.

"Thank you. Give me a few minutes, and I'll explain. It's complicated."

Before she could continue, Atohi walked over as the other two searchers drove up in Alice's car. He held out his hand to Justin.

"Give me the keys to the 4Runner," Atohi said. "You take her car and get her home. We'll clean up here, and I'll bring yours back later." He turned to join the others.

"Thanks," Justin said. He stood and held out his hand to Alice.

They got into Alice's car, and Justin drove. As they pulled out of the campground, she put her hand over his and kept it there.

"I was worried sick about you," he said.

Justin had held off asking as long as he could. "What happened, Alice?"

He glanced at her and saw a tear rolling down her cheek. He braced himself for what was coming.

"Someone blackmailed me. I thought I could handle it."

He turned his head toward her, almost running off the road. "Blackmailed you? What do you mean?"

Tears streaming down her face, Alice told him about the stranger contacting her. He knew about the healing tree and Justin giving the experimental medicine to his sister. If she didn't lead him to the tree, he threatened to expose Justin, which would mean the end of his career and possible jail time.

"He told me no one would be hurt. All I had to do was take him to the tree. If I told you or anybody else, he'd go public with what you'd done," she said.

She had agreed to meet him and take him to the tree. But then Justin told her about needing to give Karen more of the extract. Afraid the stranger intended to destroy the tree, Alice knew she couldn't take the stranger near it. She called in sick and decided to lead him to the Divide Trail instead.

He insisted on parking her car at the end of the road. He drove her back to the trailhead, where she took him to a holly and convinced him it was the healing tree. That was when she realized he had no intention of letting her go until he verified it was the healing tree.

While he sprayed the holly with poison, she escaped into the forest. She spent the night in the woods above Cataloochee, afraid for her life.

Justin pulled off on the shoulder of the road and took Alice in his arms. "Oh my God," he said. "Why didn't you tell me?"

She looked up at him. "I'm sorry. I was afraid. I did it to protect you and Karen."

"But you were kidnapped. And he's still out there. We have to call the cops."

Her eyes widened as she shook her head. "No. No, we can't. If we go to the authorities, he will ruin you. You'll go to jail. Worse, you wouldn't be able to continue giving the extract to Karen." She paused to calm down before continuing. "I'm okay. He didn't touch me. I'm here, and he doesn't know where the tree is. That's what counts."

Justin considered what she said. Alice was right. Exposing what he'd done would ruin him, but he was more worried about the extract for Karen. *Oh shit.* He had to call Tsula.

He picked up his phone and dialed Tsula's number.

Jolted by his actions, Alice started to speak, but Justin silenced her with an upheld finger.

"Tsula," he said when she answered. "Have you talked to Atohi?"

"No. I figured he was still in the Park—"

"Alice is fine. She's here. Did you report Alice missing?"

"Yes, right after you left the house. The ranger said—"

"Call them all back. Let them know Alice is fine and she's home. False alarm. Tell them to call me if they have any questions. I'll explain later." He hung up before Tsula could respond.

Justin pulled back onto the road. "Tsula called the National Park Service and the sheriff's office to report you missing."

Alice put her hand over her mouth.

"Don't worry. We'll just say it was a mistake."

He realized he didn't know how much Tsula had told them. He redialed Tsula's number, but it was busy.

They both jumped when his phone buzzed. It was Atohi.

"Hey," Justin said, answering the phone.

"Everything okay?" Atohi asked.

"Yeah, we're almost home. I just talked with Tsula. I told her Alice was okay and to call the authorities back to let them know it was a false alarm."

"I just got cell service a few minutes ago. That explains why her line was busy. I'm in the 4Runner, and I was going to bring it to your house."

"In the morning's fine. Call me as soon as you get home. I'll explain then."

Justin disconnected and put the phone down.

As they pulled into their driveway, Alice said, "Right now, I just want to take a hot shower and get something to eat." She looked over at him. "I know it's the middle of the afternoon, but would you make me breakfast? And call the bank?"

Once inside, Justin told her to shower while he cooked a big breakfast for them both. First, he called the bank and told Rhonda that Alice was fine. Her car died in an area where she had no cell service, and she'd call tomorrow.

After he hung up and was getting started with the meal prep, Atohi called.

"What did Tsula tell them? About Alice missing?" Justin asked as soon as he answered.

"Fortunately, she was pretty vague. She said that you and Alice had an argument and that you were worried about her when she didn't come home yesterday evening. When she called back after talking to you, she said that it had been a misunderstanding and that Alice had spent the night at a friend's house in Suttontown. Alice was home, and the two of you had made up."

Justin breathed a sigh of relief. "Great, thanks." As he finished cooking, Alice came out of the bedroom, her hair wrapped in a towel.

"Good timing. Sit," he said to Alice as he put the plates on the counter. He mouthed "Atohi," pointing to the phone.

To Atohi, he said, "We're about to sit down and eat. I'll explain in the morning when you bring the truck back."

Justin sat next to Alice. He recounted the conversation with Atohi, and she filled in the details about her harrowing experience as they ate. When they finished, Justin cleared the table and refilled their coffee mugs.

Alice said, "That was delicious. Thank you for cooking—and understanding. I'm exhausted."

He nodded. "Go to bed. Get some rest. I'll clean up." He watched as she padded out of the room.

Justin washed the dishes and put everything away. With a fresh cup of coffee, he went outside and sat on the porch, trying to clear his mind. He was thankful Alice was unhurt and relieved to know that she wasn't having an affair, but he didn't think either of them was safe.

He remembered he needed to check on Karen and called her.

"How are you feeling?" he asked when she answered.

"Better. Thanks for coming over. I'm on the other line. Can I call you back?"

"Sure. No rush. I was just checking on you."

He disconnected, his thoughts turning back to Alice's kidnapping. He sipped his coffee as he considered what had happened. He doubted the kidnapper was the blackmailer. More likely, the blackmailer had hired the kidnapper. *Who was the mastermind?* He went through the list of people who knew about the tree. Who had the most to gain or lose?

Robert Kendall, Jr. was a logical choice for who. He was about to cash a check for five billion dollars. If he thought the deal was somehow threatened, Kendall would do anything to make sure it was consummated. Five billion dollars was a big incentive.

The Cherokee had a lot to gain from knowing where the healing tree was located. Atohi, Tsula, and Mary knew. But they had nothing to gain from destroying it and everything to lose. The same for Sam Bear, the surveyor. Besides, he already knew exactly where the tree was.

Alice had no motive to kill it. By taking the kidnapper to a different location, she proved she was trying to prevent its destruction.

A few days ago, Hadley would've been a prime suspect. Since their confrontation, Justin now knew he was a trusted friend.

He kept coming back to the Kendalls and the conversation Alice and Tsula had overheard at lunch. Justin recalled the bits of dialogue. The derogatory description of the tree. Too much invested in Tramorix. Muddle the deal. And the order to "shut it down."

Justin could understand why they would want to know about the tree. But why would they want to kill it? Logically, it would seem that Robert Kendall, Jr., would wish to have another blockbuster drug. It had to be that somehow, the healing tree was a threat to the Bearant acquisition. All signs pointed to the Kendalls.

Justin didn't want to believe that Bobby was in on the plan, but five billion dollars was a lot of money. And Robert Kendall was an intimidating person.

Someone out there desperately wanted to find the healing tree. To destroy it.

Justin couldn't let that happen. Karen needed the extract and may need more. And he was the one who spilled the beans to those outside his Cherokee family. It was his duty to protect the tree.

33

Early the next morning, as daylight just started to stream through the window, Justin awoke. Alice was still asleep. Careful not to disturb her, he rose and tiptoed out of the bedroom.

As he made coffee, his phone chirped. It was a text from Atohi, wanting to know if he was up. Justin texted him back and told him to come on over. He'd have coffee waiting.

Thirty minutes later, Justin was glad to see his friend pull into the driveway.

When Atohi walked up on the porch, Justin said. "Alice is still asleep. Have a seat. Let me check on her, and I'll be right back."

Justin quietly opened the door to the house. Inside, he tiptoed back to the bedroom and looked in to check on Alice. She didn't stir and appeared asleep.

In the kitchen, he refilled his cup and poured a fresh one for Atohi. He went back out on the deck, leaving the door cracked so he could hear Alice if she awakened.

"She's still asleep," Justin said, handing Atohi a mug of steaming coffee. "Thanks for coming over."

"No problem. Is she doing okay?" Atohi asked.

"I think so." Justin took a sip of his coffee. "A stranger blackmailed her. He knew about the healing tree and me giving the compound to Karen. If she didn't take him to it, he threatened to expose everything. That's why she called in sick."

"Jesus. Who the hell was this guy?"

Justin shook his head. "Don't know. He wore one of those camo face masks, so she never got a good look at him. She said he was tall, thin, and in good shape."

"How did they end up in Cataloochee?"

"She suspected that he wanted to destroy the tree, and she was afraid to take him anywhere near it. Instead, she took him to the Divide Trail and convinced him another tree was it. The son of a bitch sprayed it with poison. While he was spraying, she ran off into the woods toward Cataloochee. She spent the night out there, hiding from him. At daylight, she made her way down to where your guys found her yesterday morning."

"I don't get it. Why would he want to destroy the tree?" Atohi asked.

"I'm not sure, but I guess that he's a contractor—a hired hand. I think Robert Kendall's behind it." Justin told him about the proposed buyout and his theory about the tree threatening the deal. "Somebody like Kendall isn't going to get his hands dirty. It's the only explanation that makes sense."

Atohi whistled when he heard the amount. "Five *billion* dollars?" He took another sip of coffee, seeming to compose his thoughts before continuing.

"I know he's your friend, but do you think Bobby's in on it?"

Justin shrugged. "I'd like to think not, but I honestly don't know. He did pressure me to back off."

"What now?"

"I don't know. We can't let them destroy the tree. My guess is whoever it was will contact Alice again," Justin said.

"Maybe I could contact him first?"

Justin and Atohi swiveled around to see Alice standing at the door in her robe. They hadn't heard her.

"I heard the two of you talking," she said, walking out on the porch with a cup of coffee. She took a sip and sat.

"By now, he probably knows that's not the tree and that I tricked him. Let me call him. Remember, he gave me a number to get in touch with him."

"No way," Justin said. "You are not calling the lunatic who kidnapped you."

"You said yourself, 'we can't let him destroy the tree.'"

"Why do we need to call him? He doesn't know where the tree is," Justin said.

"Precisely. He wouldn't have kidnapped me if he could've gotten the location elsewhere. He broke into the surveyor's office. And Hadley's. With no success. He knows that you and I know the location. And he knows all about Karen. If he exposes you, that will prevent you from continuing her treatments."

"And what could you say to keep him from doing that—aside from giving him the tree's location?"

"Convince him the tree is worth more alive than dead. He knows what the tree is capable of, right? So let me convince him that he can make a lot more than whatever Kendall is paying him by working *with* us, not *against* us."

"You're suggesting we try to turn Kendall's hired hand against him?" Atohi said.

"Exactly."

Justin shook his head. "Too dangerous. No way I'm letting you meet with him."

Alice crossed her arms and looked down, pouting. Then, with a smile, she looked up at Justin. "You could talk to him. You could convince him."

"And exactly why is he going to trust me?"

"Because he has a trump card. He can always turn you in if you don't deliver. The same leverage he had to blackmail me."

Justin frowned. "I don't know. This sounds risky to me."

"He won't harm you. As far as he knows, you and I are the only ones who can lead him to the tree. If he harms you, I go to the authorities. He loses both ways."

Atohi nodded. "It might work. And I can be there as a backup in case he tries anything."

Alice looked at Justin. "You know this tree has the potential to help millions of people. This is a way to keep him from trying to destroy it."

Justin tilted his head, warming to the idea.

They were working out the details of their plan when Alice's phone rang.

Puzzled, she reached into her pocket and pulled it out. She looked at the phone, then up at Justin.

"It's him," she whispered, a look of panic on her face.

Justin took the phone and answered it, putting it on Speaker.

"This is Justin. What do you want?"

"Well, well. The wonder boy himself. You've got me on speaker. Who else is there?"

Justin looked over at Atohi and put his finger across his lips. "Just me and Alice."

"Ah, the little angel. Then, you know what I want. Did she tell you what'll happen if I don't get it?"

Alice's face drained of all color.

Justin said, "She took you to the—"

"Bullshit. We both know it."

"We've got a proposition for you," Alice said, interrupting.

"Ah, she speaks. Go ahead, *Alice.*"

Alice looked as if she were about to throw up. "Just hear us out. Please."

Justin glared at her and made a slashing motion with his hand across his throat.

There was silence on the line. Justin thought the connection had been broken.

"Not on the phone. We need to meet."

"We can talk now," Justin said, still staring at Alice.

"No. In person. You and Alice."

Atohi was shaking his head.

Justin said, "Not Alice. I'll meet with you. Just the two of us."

There was another pause on the line.

Atohi was mouthing, *Spruce Mountain.*

"No more tricks. Last chance," the voice said.

"Spruce Mountain trailhead," Justin said. "It's on Balsam Mountain Road."

"How do I know you'll be alone?"

"It's on a remote one-way gravel road. I'll be in my red 4Runner."

"One hour. Don't be late." The call was disconnected.

"Shit," Justin said. He looked over at Alice, who was still pale. "Are you okay?"

She nodded. "Hearing his voice was upsetting, that's all."

"We need to be there first," Atohi said. "I need to stop by the house on the way."

Atohi turned to Alice. "Get dressed and come with us. You can stay with Tsula. You'll be safe there."

34

They loaded up and drove over to Atohi's house, where Justin explained to Tsula what was going on while Atohi changed.

Minutes later, Atohi came out dressed from head to toe in camouflage. Even his bow and quiver were camo. "Let's go."

"You look like you're going hunting," Justin said as Atohi put his bow and arrows in the back seat.

"That's the purpose. I don't want to be seen."

When they got to the Heintooga picnic area at the end of the paved road, there were no other cars around.

"Good," Atohi said. "About a half mile before the trailhead, let me out in case he's already there."

Justin passed through the open gate to the one-way gravel road, keeping his eye on the rearview mirror.

Fifteen minutes later, as they approached a sharp right-hand curve, Atohi said, "Stop. Let me out here. The trailhead is just ahead."

He got out and collected his gear. "It'll take me ten minutes to get to my spot. Going in, I'll be on the right-hand side of the trail. Take him ten yards from the trailhead and keep him on that side where I can see him."

"Okay." Justin knew better than to ask his friend where he'd be. He knew he'd never spot Atohi, which was good. Neither would the stranger.

When he got to the tight parking spot at the trailhead, no one was there. Justin pulled off the road on the left side of the space, forcing anyone else to park on the right side— the same side as Atohi.

He looked at his watch. Fifteen minutes early. He relieved himself and then stood with his back against the passenger side of his truck.

Five minutes later, Justin heard a vehicle approaching. A nondescript, white four-door car pulled in next to him. *Shit,* he thought. He hoped Atohi had enough time to get in place.

The door opened, and a tall, slender man climbed out, scanning the area surrounding them. He walked over to Justin and extended his hand, palm up.

"Phone."

Justin hesitated. Alice had said her kidnapper wore a mask. This man wasn't wearing a mask and looked vaguely familiar. Not good. He looked closer and thought he recognized him. He resembled the lone hiker Justin had seen at the trail intersection that day he hiked in alone.

He hoped Atohi was in place and watching as he handed him his phone.

The man turned the phone off and stuck it in his pocket. "Turn around. I need to frisk you."

Justin stretched his arms out. "For what?"

"Make sure you're not armed or wired."

Disgusted, Justin shook his head and complied. The man was quick and thorough. *Not his first time doing this,* Justin thought.

"Okay. What's your proposition?" the man asked.

Justin turned to face the man, who was now holding a pistol pointed at him.

"Hey, what the—"

"I underestimated your girlfriend. I won't make that mistake again."

Justin exhaled, not expecting this. He looked back toward the road and remembered Atohi's instructions.

"Can we walk down the trail a few yards? I mean, if someone happens to come by, I don't think you want to be standing there with a gun in your hand."

The man snorted, then nodded toward the trail.

Justin headed down the trail, not bothering to look for Atohi. He knew he'd never see him. Besides, he didn't want to alert the stranger.

Ten yards in, just out of sight of the vehicles, Justin stopped. He positioned himself on the left side of the trail and turned around to face the man.

"I'm listening," the man said, still pointing his gun at Justin.

Justin launched into his spiel, keeping it concise.

"I know Robert Kendall hired you. I don't know how much he's paying you, but it doesn't matter. I've got a better offer." Justin paused, but the man remained expressionless. "He's paying you to destroy this tree. And you already know what it's capable of, right?"

This time, the man nodded once, still not speaking.

Justin continued. "What you probably don't realize is how much it's worth. Kendall doesn't want this tree to become knowledge because it's threatening an offer to buy his company. You know how much he's getting?"

Again, no expression or acknowledgment.

"I didn't think so," Justin said, trying to gauge the man's reaction. "I've got a copy of the news release. It's in my left front pocket."

The man nodded. "Slowly. Don't even think about trying anything."

Carefully, Justin pulled out a copy he'd printed of the news release concerning the buyout. He handed it to the man with the gun. "Five billion dollars. Cash. Seventy-five percent of that goes to Kendall."

The man's eyes got wide, and his eyebrows rose. He glanced down at the paper where Justin had highlighted the amount and then looked back up at Justin.

Justin said, "I'm guessing that's a hell of a lot more than he's paying you to destroy it. I'm prepared to offer you considerably more for you to let it be."

The man's eyes narrowed as he processed what Justin was telling him. The wheels were turning, and Justin thought he was going to bite.

The kidnapper shook his head. "It doesn't matter. My job's to kill the tree. Your fucking girlfriend led me on a wild goose chase to kill a holly. Now, where is it?"

Justin shook his head. "I'm not going to tell you."

The man raised the pistol and pointed it at Justin's head. "This is my proposition."

Justin started sweating, wondering about this whole setup. "If you kill me, then you'll never find it."

The man snorted, a twisted grin on his face. "You think I'm stupid? Just because your little girl-toy got away from me? Where do you think she is right now?"

"What do you mean?"

He chuckled. It was an evil rattle. "You're not as smart as you think. I don't need you. I just wanted to find out how much you knew. My associate is on his way to give your little sweetie a ride. By the time we're finished with her, she'll tell us everything we want to know."

Justin gasped, his eyes wide in panic. This man was going to kill him. And Alice was going to be kidnapped again, this time with far worse consequences. He'd failed.

A yell came from his right, somewhere in the trees. The man reacted and, for a split second, shifted his eyes toward the sound. Without thinking, Justin lowered his head and charged toward the man who tried to recover and sidestep the maneuver. The combined distraction was just enough to cause the man's aim to be off when he pulled the trigger.

Justin heard the gun go off as he glanced off the gunman and hit the ground. His ears ringing, he closed his eyes, waiting for the next shot. It didn't come.

When he raised his head, he saw the stranger kneeling next to him, an arrow sticking out of the stranger's neck. He'd dropped the gun, and his hand was on the arrow's shaft. On the opposite side, the arrow's broad blade was poking out. He was making a gurgling sound, and blood was pouring out of his neck. As if in slow motion, the man crumpled on top of himself, unable to squeeze the trigger again. It was surreal.

It was then that Justin realized what had happened.

Atohi had killed the man.

35

Justin got up on his knees, staring at the dead man a few feet away. The only dead people he'd seen before were in a hospital bed or funeral home, not like this. He turned to the side and vomited, the bitter taste of bile in his mouth.

He wiped his mouth on his sleeve and caught movement in his peripheral vision. He turned to see Atohi materialize out of the woods with his bow and walk toward him. Justin's ears were still ringing.

Atohi looked down at the stranger. He knelt beside him and felt for a pulse. Atohi rose, looked down at Justin, and shook his head.

Justin tried to stand, his legs wobbly. Atohi reached over to steady him.

"Shit, " Justin said. "The son of a bitch was going to kill me. Thank God you were here."

Atohi nodded. "I know."

Justin reached for his phone and realized it was in the dead man's pocket. He looked over at Atohi. "You've got to call Tsula—"

"I heard. Don't worry. One of my brothers is watching our house. They'll be okay there." He nodded toward the body. "What are we going to do about this?"

Justin stared down at the dead man. "I suppose we should call it in." They were in the National Park, so he figured they should call the Park ranger.

"You sure?" Atohi asked.

Justin didn't answer. He was still thinking about it. Even though it was clearly in self-defense, it would be a significant hassle. What would happen to Atohi? And him? It would be messy. Everything about the healing tree would come out, which would mean the end of producing the extract for Karen. And for what? Doing the right thing wasn't always the best thing.

He looked over at Atohi. "Who do you think would be looking for him?"

Atohi shrugged. "Hard to say. His associate, for sure. A hired gun probably doesn't have a lot of people who know what he does and where he goes."

Justin looked around. They were in a remote area of the Park, off a rarely-used trail reached by a seldom-traveled dirt road. His gaze returned to his brother.

"It'd be hard to find anything out here," Justin said. "Maybe we should bury him?"

The words hung in the stillness. A bird chirped in the distance.

After what seemed like an eternity, Atohi looked at him and asked again, "You sure?"

Justin nodded. "I'm sure."

Atohi pulled gloves out of his pocket and slipped them on. He took out another pair and handed them to Justin. Atohi took Justin's phone out of the dead man's pocket and gave it to Justin, then removed the arrow from the dead man's neck.

Justin stared at the phone. No service. He wiped it off on his shirt before putting it in his pocket. He nodded at the gun, lying on the ground next to the man. "What about that?"

Atohi looked at the pistol, then picked it up and stuck it in his pocket.

Together, they managed to drag the body well off the trail down a steep incline.

"We need to cover him with enough brush to make him invisible in case someone happens to pass nearby," Atohi said.

Justin cocked his head and asked, "Don't we need to like, bury him or something?" It seemed disrespectful to leave him out there covered in leaves.

"No," Atohi said, shaking his head. "Better this way. The animals will come when we leave."

Justin shuddered as he stared at Atohi, surprised at the apparent lack of empathy in his eyes. True, the stranger tried to kill Justin, but still. Then Justin recalled that Atohi had done three combat tours in Force Recon with the Marines. Atohi had more experience in this than Justin wanted to acknowledge.

Atohi removed the dead man's pistol from his pocket and laid it on the ground. He and Justin then arranged brush naturally over the body and gun. Once finished, they made their way back to the trail as Atohi was careful to erase any signs of where they'd taken the body. Even there, Atohi was meticulous in hiding any indication of their presence.

When they got to the trailhead, Justin looked at the man's car. "What do we do about this?"

"We leave it," Atohi said. "He said he had an associate. My guess is his friend will find it before anyone else. Go back your truck out on the road."

Justin did as instructed. Parked in the middle of the road with the engine running, he watched as Atohi carefully covered the tracks and any evidence they'd been there.

"Rain's coming. That will help," Atohi said as he climbed in. "Let's go."

As soon as they left, heavy rain began to fall. Neither of them spoke until they were almost to Cherokee, ten minutes later.

As they passed another vehicle, Justin said, "First car we've seen."

On the way, they had rehearsed their story. They decided to keep it simple. When the kidnapper never showed, they left and came home. If anyone ever found the body, Justin and Atohi would claim that they went hiking on the Hyatt Ridge Trail and left early because of the rain. They never saw any sign of anyone.

Justin hated lying to Alice. He knew she'd worry about the stranger reappearing, although Justin knew that he would never bother her again. Over time, she'd recover.

It was still raining hard when they got to Atohi's. As they pulled into the driveway, Justin turned to Atohi and said, "Thank you."

Atohi nodded. "He left us no other choice."

Justin wanted to ask if Atohi knew that would happen before they left but decided it fell into the category of things he didn't want to know. Still, Justin felt guilty that he'd led the man to his death.

"Do you think he really had an associate?" Justin asked. If so, that meant another potential killer was still out there.

Atohi shrugged. "Hard to tell. I'll check with the guys watching your house, see if they noticed anything."

Justin looked around for Atohi's friends but saw no one. But he didn't expect that he would. He felt better knowing Atohi's brothers were watching. But the man who kidnapped Alice and tried to kill him didn't seem like one to bluff, particularly after Alice had escaped. *Would they ever feel safe again?* he thought.

When they walked inside, Alice ran over and hugged Justin. "I'm so glad you're back. How'd it go?"

"He never showed," Atohi said before Justin could answer.

"He didn't?" said Tsula in disbelief. She looked hard at Atohi. "Nobody came?"

Meeting her stare, Atohi said, "Nope."

Furrowing her brow, Alice gave Justin a worried look. "What do you mean he didn't show?"

Justin shook his head and held out both hands, palms up. "We waited at the trailhead for an hour, but no one showed. We didn't see anyone. The rain came in, and we left. Did he call back?"

"No, no calls," Tsula said.

"So, he's still out there?" Alice said, alarm in her voice.

"Maybe he changed his mind. He didn't show, and he didn't call," Justin said.

"What do we do if he calls again? He kidnapped me, for God's sake."

Justin tried to put his arm around her. "He won't hurt you. I promise." But his mind went back to the man's proclamation of an associate.

Alice refused to be consoled. "You don't know that. I spent the night in the woods. Alone, dammit. A kidnapper with a gun stalking me. And he's still out there. Somewhere."

"Maybe you both should stay here tonight," Tsula said. "You'd be safer."

Justin looked at Atohi, who gave him a slight nod. "That's probably a good idea. See if he calls—"

"You don't understand," Alice said, frantic. "We can't stay here forever. What if he tries to do it again?"

Alice was right, Justin thought. She was afraid of the kidnapper returning, even though Justin knew that was impossible. But the kidnapper's associate might still be out there wanting to finish the job. Atohi's friends were watching both places for now, but that couldn't last forever.

"I'm going to talk to Bobby," Justin said, picking up his phone.

36

It was evening when Bobby called him back. Justin told him that he needed to talk with him. When Bobby asked why all Justin said was that it was personal and urgent.

He told Bobby to meet him at the rest area on the bypass, just south of Waynesville. Justin wanted someplace public but where they could talk in private.

Atohi offered to go with him, but Justin wanted Atohi to stay at the house with Alice.

The rain had lifted, and fog had settled into the valleys when Justin drove to meet Bobby. Justin kept looking in his rearview mirror, trying to see if anyone was following him.

He pulled into the rest area, glad to see a vehicle parked in the security space. However, he didn't spot the nighttime guard anywhere. The streetlights cast an eerie glow over the few cars parked in front of the building. Bobby's Corvette was parked alone next to the picnic area.

Justin parked next to Bobby's car. He got out and surveyed the area for anything that looked suspicious. Nothing looked amiss. In the dim haze of the parking lot lights, he could see Bobby sitting at a picnic table, smoking a cigarette.

"Hey, bro," Bobby said, snuffing out his smoke as Justin approached. "You look like shit. Everything okay?"

218 · DARRYL BOLLINGER

"No, everything's not okay," he said as he sat across from his friend. "It's been a long day."

He paused for effect and to watch Bobby's reaction to what he was going to say next.

"Alice was kidnapped yesterday," Justin said.

"Kidnapped. What the hell? And you just now called me? Is she okay?"

"She's fine. She's home. Atohi and Tsula are with her." He wasn't giving Bobby anything else until he found out where his friend stood.

"Who? What happened?"

"That's what I'm trying to figure out. I thought maybe you could help me."

"Sure, you know I'll do anything. What can I do?"

"I need to know who hired the man who kidnapped Alice. He told Alice that if she didn't lead him to the healing tree, he'd ruin my career."

Bobby had a puzzled look. "Hired? How do you know—"

"Alice and Tsula overheard your father and a stranger at lunch the other day."

Bobby sat up straight. "Wait a minute. Are you saying my old man hired someone to kidnap and blackmail Alice?"

"I don't know. Did he?" Justin fixed his gaze on Bobby, looking for a tell.

Bobby started shaking his head. "That's crazy. He's an asshole, but he'd never do—"

"Five billion dollars is a lot of money. What was it you told me? 'Chill out about this until we sign the deal.'" Justin let the words hang, his eyes never leaving Bobby. He could see that his friend was processing everything, trying to connect the dots.

After a few moments, Bobby leaned forward and hissed, "Are you accusing me of having something to do with this?"

Justin waited for a few beats. "Like I said, I'm trying to find out who's responsible. The kidnapper told Alice that it was his job to kill the tree."

In the dim light, he could still see Bobby's face flush. "Jesus Christ, Justin. How long have we been friends? Do you honestly think I'd ever do anything to harm you or Alice?"

Justin stared at him. "Right now, I'm not sure what I think. All I know is someone hired this goon to blackmail my fiancée and destroy the healing tree."

"But you said she was home. And okay?"

"She took him to the tree. While he was spraying it with poison, she escaped. After spending the night in the Park, Atohi and I found her this morning. Scratched and bruised, but otherwise okay."

Shaking his head, Bobby said, "Jesus. And you're convinced Dad's behind this?"

"Think about it? Who else would want the tree destroyed bad enough to do something like that?"

Bobby sat there silently, head in his hands. After a minute, he looked up at Justin. He rose to leave. "There's one way to find out. I'm going to see him. Tonight."

"Take me with you."

Bobby cocked his head and thought about it. He shook his head. "No, I want to go alone. This is between him and me. I promise you I'll get to the bottom of it. I'll let you know."

* * *

Robert Kendall hung up his phone. He'd left yet another message for Matt to call him ASAP. The second message this evening.

Carter Knox was coming in tomorrow evening to finalize the deal with Bearant. His first question was sure to be about the Indian tree.

Robert wanted confirmation that Matt had taken care of it. He'd not heard from Matt, which was unusual.

The cell phone on his desk buzzed. This was a second phone with a number unknown to all but Matt. Robert picked up the phone and answered.

"It's about time. Where the hell have you been?"

A modified electronic voice answered.

"This is Tony, Matt's associate. He's unavailable."

Robert was puzzled. He'd never heard of Tony. In all the years he'd used Matt, he didn't know of any associates. Yet, "Tony" had called him on Matt's secure phone.

"Where the hell is he? And how do I know you're who you say you are?"

Tony recited specific details of a job that Matt had done for Robert two years ago, particulars that only Matt would've known.

Convinced that Tony did indeed work with Matt, Robert repeated his question. "Where's Matt?"

"He's not available. What do you need?"

Robert was losing his patience with the cloak and dagger routine. "I need to know if the Indian tree matter has been resolved."

"Not yet."

"What the fuck do you mean, *not yet?* I've got a dinner meeting tomorrow. Matt assured me it would be resolved before then."

"It will be. I'll call you on this number to confirm."

"Goddammit, it better—" Robert realized he was talking to a dead line. Tony had hung up.

37

B ack in his SUV, Justin headed to Atohi's house. He was still unsure of Bobby's loyalty. His phone buzzed, and he checked the caller ID before answering. Atohi.

"Hello," Justin said, putting the call on speaker. Although North Carolina didn't have a law against handheld cellphone use, he didn't want the distraction.

"You on your way?"

"Yeah, probably twenty minutes out. Why? You need something?"

"We've got a problem. Alice just got a call." Atohi paused. "From her kidnapper."

"Her *kidnapper?* How the hell?"

"I'm not sure what's going on. We'll be waiting." Atohi disconnected the call.

Justin shook his head. "What the fuck?" he said out loud. "That's impossible."

He recalled the confrontation with the kidnapper in the Park. The arrow through the kidnapper's neck. *No way,* he thought. That guy was stone-cold dead.

The sound of a car horn snapped him back to the present, and he jerked the wheel to the right. He'd drifted into the left lane on the four-lane divided highway. An angry driver, who had to swerve to the shoulder, gave him the middle finger as he passed.

Justin exhaled, urging himself to be more careful. The last thing he needed now was an accident.

The caller had to be the kidnapper's associate, but how to explain this to Alice.

Atohi met him outside the house as soon as Justin arrived. He looked as shaky as Justin felt.

"She's pretty shaken up," he said as Justin got out of his vehicle.

"It had to be the associate," Justin said.

Atohi nodded. "No shit. We know who it wasn't."

"What exactly did he say?"

"Let's go inside. I'll let her tell you."

Alice was a wreck. She was still shaking when Justin walked through the door. She was trying to hold a glass of water and started crying when she saw him.

He went over and took her into his arms. "It's okay. He's not going to hurt you."

After a few minutes, when her sobbing ceased, he asked, "What did he say?"

She tried to answer between sniffles. "He said . . . he said the plant . . . was a holly."

Tsula handed her another tissue. Alice wiped her nose and continued.

"He said he was going to make good on his threat if I didn't take him to the tree first thing in the morning. I asked him why he didn't meet you today."

Justin glanced at Atohi.

"He didn't answer. He just repeated that I'd taken him to a holly and that he wanted the real thing or else," she said.

He stroked her hair. "It doesn't matter anymore. You told me about it."

She started bawling again. Minutes later, she looked up at him. "It does matter. You could still go to jail. What are we going to do?"

* * *

Robert sat at his desk in his study. Bobby had called and was on his way over. He said he needed to talk to him immediately and hung up before Robert could ask him anything.

He heard his son's voice in the house, and then the door to his office flew open.

"We need to talk," Bobby said, striding into the room. He stopped just short of Robert's desk, his face angry.

Bobby never entered the study without knocking, and Robert wondered why he was upset. Without showing any emotion, he gestured to the empty chairs facing him. "Have a seat. Would you like something to drink?"

Still standing, Bobby attacked. "What are you doing, Dad?"

Robert turned and poured himself another whiskey, buying time for Bobby to calm down. Clutching the glass, he swiveled back to face his son. "What do you mean?"

"Justin's fiancée, Alice. Somebody kidnapped her yesterday."

"My goodness. What happened? Is she okay?"

Bobby stared at him, eyes blazing.

"The guy who did it blackmailed her into taking him to the healing tree. He said he was hired to poison it."

Trying to maintain his composure, Robert took a sip, the whiskey warming his throat. Matt was supposed to be taking care of the tree. Then he disappears, and Tony calls, saying they hadn't finished the job. But kidnapping?

He shook his head. "What on earth? Blackmailed? Healing tree?"

Bobby nodded. "The *Indian* tree, as you called it. The person threatened to ruin Justin's career if she didn't cooperate."

"Oh, yes. The one that Justin was researching. As I recall, Dr. Hadley killed that idea."

Bobby locked eyes with him. "Did you hire someone? Someone to kill the tree?"

Robert shook his head in disgust. "Of course not. Why would I hire someone to kidnap . . . Alice, is it?"

"That's not what I asked. Did you hire someone to poison the tree?"

Robert was beginning to lose his patience with Bobby. "Have you been drinking, son? Why on earth would I hire someone to kill a worthless tree? One of the foremost minds in cancer research said the idea had no merit. None."

"Alice and her friend overheard a conversation at lunch between you and Carter Knox."

Robert leaned forward, raising his voice. "You come into my house and accuse me of hiring a kidnapper? How dare you." He exhaled a sharp breath. "That's ridiculous. I'm appalled that you would even entertain such a thought."

Bobby sat in the chair after Robert challenged him. His anger seemed to dissipate as he appeared to weigh whether or not to believe his father.

"More importantly, is she okay?" Robert asked.

Bobby nodded. "Justin said she escaped when he was spraying the tree with poison."

Robert raised an eyebrow. "The kidnapper managed to kill the tree?" Tony had told him otherwise.

"According to Justin."

Robert shrugged and took another sip of whiskey. "I have no idea who was behind all of this. The main thing is that she's okay." He glared at Bobby. "For the record, I had *nothing* to do with it."

Bobby nodded and rose. In a quieter, less threatening tone, he said, "Somebody did. The question is who." He turned and left.

Robert watched Bobby leave, closing the door behind him. He wasn't sure that Bobby believed him.

What a cluster, he thought. Blackmail. Kidnapping. Matt disappears. Tony enters, taking over for Matt. Then, Bobby shows up with this story. Something didn't add up. Is the tree dead or not?

Robert reached into the drawer for his secure phone and called the only number stored on it. When he got no answer, he left a message.

"Call me ASAP."

38

Everyone was exhausted, especially Alice. Atohi had convinced them to stay there until they could figure out what to do. In the guest bedroom, she and Justin undressed and got in bed.

Justin turned out the lights, reached over, and pulled Alice next to him in a spoon embrace. "Try to get some sleep."

Alice nodded, but her eyes were wide open. She was trying to think of a way out of her dilemma.

She had counted on Justin negotiating an agreement with the kidnapper. When she saw Atohi with his bow when they left to meet with him, she secretly hoped that Atohi would kill the man. That would have been the best ending, but either way, she had been optimistic, thinking the nightmare was over.

Unfortunately, neither had happened. When Justin and Atohi returned and said the stranger didn't show, she panicked. Although Justin had tried to persuade her that maybe the kidnapper thought he'd poisoned the tree and moved on, she knew better. She shuddered as she recalled his voice.

It was a fucking holly, you bitch. If you don't lead me to the real thing by noon, those pictures and the article will be in Justin's hands before the end of the day.

Alice knew he wasn't bluffing. She couldn't let Justin find out about her past. It would destroy him, and things would never be the same.

She would have to take the kidnapper to the healing tree, but how?

* * *

"We need to meet," Tony said over the phone to Robert Kendall.

"You're goddam right. Meet me at my house in an hour. I assume you know where I live." He disconnected and slammed the phone down on his desk.

Forty-five minutes later, Robert heard voices outside his study. There was a light tap on his closed door.

"Come in."

His housekeeper, Belle, opened the door. A stocky man with close-cropped brown hair stood next to her. He was dressed in khakis and a gray polo shirt, looking like he'd just walked off the eighteenth green. He stepped inside, and she closed the door behind him. The man was shorter and older than Robert had pictured.

"Tony Lewis," he said, with a trace of a Brooklyn accent. He took a practiced glance around the room and then walked over.

Robert doubted Tony Lewis was the man's real name. He stood, extending his hand. Tony's grip was firm, belying his casual appearance. Robert nodded toward the single chair in front of his desk as he sat.

"Something to drink?" Robert said, holding up a decanter of bourbon.

"Your housekeeper kindly offered to bring me a cup of coffee, thank you," Tony said, making himself comfortable.

Robert added a finger of bourbon to the glass on his desk and set the bottle down. He took a sip, then asked,

"What in the hell is going on? Kidnapping? And where is Matt?"

"Matt's gone. I'm your contact now."

"Gone? What does that mean?"

"I found Matt's rental car at a trailhead in the Park. Unlocked, his phone in the console. No sign of Matt."

Robert sat back in his seat, stunned. "I don't understand."

There was another tap at the door.

"Come in, Belle," Robert said in a loud voice.

The door opened, and she entered, carrying a tray containing only a small stainless coffeepot and a single porcelain cup. No cream, no sugar. She sat it on the corner of the desk in front of Tony.

Silently, she poured the coffee, steam rising from the cup. She handed it to Tony and placed the carafe back on the tray.

"Thank you," he said. He sipped it while she shuffled out.

Once she closed the door, Tony continued. "I was in Asheville. Matt called and told me he was meeting Justin Reeve at a trailhead in the national park. He said that Reeve had a proposition for him. I asked him to wait until I could get there and provide backup, but he said it wasn't necessary. That was the last call on his phone at 9:10 this morning."

"What happened?"

Tony shrugged. "Don't know. I took care of the car. I didn't want some nosy park ranger asking questions. When I'm done with this job, I'll go back out to the Park for a hike. Look around."

"Reeve met with my son earlier this evening. Before I called you. He told Bobby that someone blackmailed his girlfriend the day before yesterday in order to find the Indian tree. He forced her to take him to it, but she escaped. According to Reeve, the man told her he had been hired to poison it."

Tony nodded and slid a plain manila envelope across the desk.

Robert opened it and pulled out an 8x10 photo along with a copy of a newspaper article about a hit-and-run accident that killed a young boy. He read the article and then looked at the photo. It was a picture of a small gravestone:

Timothy Carver
Beloved Son
September 16, 1998 – April 9, 2009

Robert held his hands out, palms up. "So?"

"The driver was Payten Thomas."

Robert wrinkled his brow and reread the newspaper article. He looked back up at Tony. "It says the driver was never found. Who is Payten Thomas?"

"Matt found out who the driver was. Payten *Alice* Thomas."

He stared at Tony with a blank look. "And?"

"Payten is Reeve's Alice. She changed her name to Alice Miller."

"You're sure?"

Tony nodded once.

Robert digested the information and then asked, "Does Reeve know about this?"

"Nothing, nothing about any of it. He only knows her as Alice Miller."

He nodded toward the article and picture in Robert's hand. "That was what Matt was using to get her to cooperate."

"Wait a minute. Bobby told me that the threat was to ruin Reeve's career."

Tony shook his head. "We considered that option. We knew that Reeve was working with something from the tree, and he gave it to his sister." He tapped his finger on the documents in front of Robert. "But this was the real leverage."

Robert considered this new information. Alice—Payten—told Reeve about the kidnapping but didn't disclose her secret.

"On the phone, you said the job wasn't finished. But Reeve told Bobby that Matt poisoned the tree. That was how she escaped."

Again, Tony shook his head. "She took him to a tree in the Park and said it was the healing tree. With no cell service, he couldn't confirm it at the time. He started spraying the tree, and she escaped. When he couldn't find her, he left and sent a pic to a plant guy. It was a damn holly."

Robert was curious. Did Reeve believe someone had destroyed the tree? Or did he deliberately mislead Bobby? Robert didn't think that Bobby had lied to him.

Tony said, "I called her an hour ago. I told her we knew the tree was a fake. If she didn't take me to the actual tree by noon tomorrow, Reeve would get the material that's in front of you. Based on her reaction, he still doesn't know."

"With Matt missing, I think that might be too risky," Robert said.

"That's not your concern. Our job was to eliminate the tree before your meeting tomorrow."

Robert looked out the window, drumming his fingers on the desk. He picked up the documents in front of him and studied them. "Can I keep these?"

Tony nodded. "Sure. One other thing."

"What?"

"The price of the job has gone up."

Robert glared at him. "Matt and I had a deal. He fucked up and let the girl escape. It seems to me that's your problem."

Tony leaned back in his chair and steepled his hands. "Matt was just a hired hand. Now that I know what this buyout is worth to you, I think a million would be a more appropriate amount."

"A million? You're fucking crazy. Matt and I agreed on the fee. Fifty thousand dollars for killing a tree is more than generous."

Tony leaned forward across the desk, and Robert drew back in his chair.

"Matt doesn't make the decisions for my company. He was just one of my employees. All these years, you've been dealing with my organization, but there's no link to me. It'd be a shame if the tree's information found its way to the right person at Bearant. Along with the information that you were behind the girl being kidnapped."

Tony leaned back in his chair.

"Now that I think about it, one million out of five *billion* is a bargain. I'll have the tree's location tomorrow. The price is now two million. Cash. End of day tomorrow."

"That's . . ." Tony's stare stopped Robert from continuing.

Tony rose and prepared to leave. "Get the money. I'll call you tomorrow afternoon with instructions. I'll let myself out."

Robert stared at the big man's back as he walked out.

39

I've got to go to work," Alice told Justin the next morning at breakfast.

"I don't think that's a good idea," Justin said, looking over to Atohi for support. Before he could respond, Alice continued.

"I thought about it all night. You're right. We can manage the situation now that everything's out in the open. He has no proof that you've done anything. And he doesn't know where the tree is, so it's safe."

Justin shook his head, surprised at her change of heart. "I don't know—"

"I can't curl up in the corner and hide for the rest of my life. Besides, the bank is probably one of the safest places to be. He'll suspect that someone will be watching me so that he won't try anything there."

Tsula nodded. "Good point. We can have somebody keep an eye on your place for a few evenings."

Atohi looked at Justin. "She makes a good argument. No one will try anything at the bank." He turned to Alice. "I know Walter, the president. I'll call and give him a heads up."

Her heart started racing. "No, I don't want anyone to know what happened."

Atohi shrugged. "No worry. I'll tell him that you've gotten a couple of crank calls, and we don't want to take any chances. Nothing more."

Relieved, Alice nodded. "Thank you—for everything. No offense, but I'd like to go home and get ready for work."

As Justin drove to their house, Alice glanced in the vehicle's side mirror. Atohi was still behind them. He had suggested following them home to make sure everything was okay. Justin would follow her to the bank on his way to the lab.

"I'll be fine," Alice said to Justin, putting on a brave face. "Whoever it is is just pissed because we outsmarted them. You're right. They're probably long gone by now."

When they got to their house, Atohi went in first to make sure nothing had been disturbed. In a few minutes, he came back out on the porch holding a cup of coffee and motioned them inside.

"Everything looks good." He held up the cup. "I hope you don't mind. I helped myself to your Keurig. I'll just sit out here with my coffee while you two get ready."

In their bedroom, Justin said to Alice, "Go ahead and take your shower. It takes you longer to get ready than me."

As she showered, Alice tried to figure out how she would get away to lead the caller to the tree. She'd somehow have to take hiking clothes with her to work without arousing Justin's suspicion. Then, she'd have to find a way to leave without being followed.

She got out of the shower, dried off, and wrapped the towel around her. Maybe she could stuff everything in her purse.

She opened the bathroom door, and Justin was sitting on the bed, reading.

"Your turn," she said.

He got up and started into the bathroom. "I won't be long."

As soon as he shut the bathroom door behind him, she walked over to the closet. She looked in at her hiking clothes and then down at her purse. It was big, but even if she dumped everything out, there was no way she was going to get it all in there.

She walked back over to the dresser and spotted Justin's phone next to hers. She cocked an ear toward the bathroom. The shower was running, and she had another idea. She picked up Justin's phone and opened the GPS app he used when they took Tsula and Atohi to the tree.

She'd never used it before, so it took her a few minutes to navigate. She found the map of the area where the tree was located and pulled up the coordinates. Perfect. It showed the trail as well as the coordinates. The shower had stopped.

She looked around for a pen and paper. No time. She grabbed her phone and opened the camera. Zooming in, she took several pictures of Justin's screen.

Quickly, she reviewed the photos she'd taken to confirm the latitude and longitude numbers were legible. She started to set his phone down, then realized she hadn't shut down the app.

Just as she closed it, Justin opened the door. "You're not even dressed yet." When he saw her holding both phones, a puzzled look crossed his face.

Alice held up his phone and then set it down on the dresser. "A phone buzzed, and I thought it was yours. It was mine. Becky, at work, texting me."

Thirty minutes later, they were ready to leave and walked back out on the porch.

"Thanks again, Atohi," Alice said. "We appreciate the hospitality, but it's great to be home."

He laughed. "I understand." He looked at Justin. "Everything looks good here. Give me a call when you head home this evening, and I'll have the house covered."

Justin nodded. "Thanks."

Driving her car to the bank, Alice kept waiting for her phone to ring. Glancing in the rearview mirror, she saw Justin close behind.

She shook her head. There was no way she was going to be able to leave without being followed. Justin wouldn't leave until she'd gone inside. She'd have to convince the kidnapper to accept the coordinates she'd copied from Justin's phone.

Her phone rang, and she jumped. Unavailable, the screen read. Her hand shaking, she pressed the answer button on her steering wheel.

"Hello," she said.

"Hello, Alice." It was the same voice as yesterday. "Alone?"

"I'm in my car, headed to work."

"Good. How long before you get there?"

"I should be there in fifteen minutes. I'll need a little time after I get there to take care of some things at work."

"I'll call you in forty-five minutes. Be ready to walk out the door. No surprises, this time, *Payten.*"

Precisely thirty minutes after she got to the bank, her phone buzzed. She took a deep breath and answered.

"This is Alice," she said as she closed her office door.

"Here's where we're going to meet," the voice said.

"I can't leave."

"Unacceptable. I told you, Payten, no more—"

"Look, I have the exact coordinates of the tree and pictures. Justin followed me to work, and his friends are watching the bank and my house. I can hardly go to the bathroom alone. I swear the information is good. I'll send you pictures of the trail map and the tree."

"Why didn't you give that to me before?"

"I didn't have it. He got it only a few days ago. I was with him, so I know it's right."

There was a slight pause, then the voice continued. "I won't make the same mistake again. This time, I will confirm that it's the right tree. If you're jerking me around, *Payten,* or if anything happens to me, I promise you will regret it."

"I'm not, I swear," she said. "Give me a number, and I'll text you the information as soon as we hang up."

"It better be right."

She started to reply and realized he'd disconnected. A minute later, her phone vibrated. It was a text from an unknown party, containing a phone number and nothing more.

She texted the pictures and coordinates to the number he'd sent her.

By mid-afternoon, Alice had not heard back from him. She had been too nervous to eat lunch and was beginning to worry. *What if he couldn't find it?* She didn't let her phone out of her sight and jumped every time it rang.

It was almost four when her phone buzzed. Number unavailable. She took a deep breath and answered. "This is Alice."

"Your information was good," the robotic voice said.

She exhaled, both relieved and sad. "I told you. When do I get my information back?"

The mechanical laugh sent chills down her spine. "It's my insurance policy. To make sure you never go public. As long as you keep your mouth shut, you're safe."

"But how do I know—" She heard a click, and the voice was gone.

She put the phone down and looked out the window. She thought she'd be able to identify him, so she didn't think he would ever publish the information. The more she thought about it, the more she convinced herself that he had as much to lose as she did.

She'd dodged a bullet.

40

That afternoon, Robert was in his study as instructed, waiting for Tony to call. The secure phone on his desk vibrated, indicating an incoming call. He picked it up and answered.

"Is it done?" Robert asked, tapping his finger on the desktop.

"I have the exact location of the tree, and I've confirmed it," Tony said.

"That wasn't what I asked. How do I know—"

"The only thing you need to know is to be at milepost 422 on the Blue Ridge Parkway tonight at eight with two million dollars in cash. Devil's Courthouse. Appropriate place, don't you think?"

"But you were supposed to destroy—"

Tony chuckled. "Did you really think I was going to kill the tree before I got the money? Get your dipshit son to do it. Maybe he can manage that. When I get the money, you'll get the coordinates and a picture."

"But that wasn't the deal," Robert said. When he got no response, he realized that he was talking into a dead phone. Tony had already hung up.

"Son of a bitch," he said, slamming the phone down. He had to destroy that damn Indian tree, but he didn't even know where it was. Damned if he would pay two million dollars for a location that might or might not be the right one.

Fuck Tony Lewis or whoever he was. Robert was tired of relying on others to take care of business. He'd handle this himself.

He picked up the phone to call Bobby.

"What's so important, Dad?" Bobby said as he walked into his dad's library thirty minutes later.

"Have a seat, son." Robert was seated in front of his desk, where he had positioned a second chair. He wanted this to be an intimate father-son conversation.

After Bobby was seated, Robert said, "Mark your calendar. We're set to close the deal with Bearant a week from Monday. That's the day that we become billionaires."

"Awesome. See, I told you it was going to work out."

Robert leaned over and held his thumb and forefinger in front of Bobby's face. "We're this close, son." He paused and then continued. "But we're not there yet."

Bobby shook his head. "Not there? What do you mean?"

"There's one critical task left." He paused for a moment to make sure he had Bobby's undivided attention. "We need to know the location of that Indian tree."

Bobby shook his head. "I don't understand. What's that got to do—"

"The closing is contingent on the tree being eliminated as a potential threat to Tramorix. That makes the location worth five billion dollars. We will be signing documents stating that we are unaware of anything that would be a potential competitor to Tramorix. If news of that tree gets out and Bearant finds out that we knew about it, then they're coming back to us for that money. Every last cent."

"What are you saying?"

Robert reached over and grabbed his son's collar. "Dammit, boy, what don't you understand? We've got to destroy that tree."

"But, Dad, what about—"

Robert slapped him, hard, with an open palm. "I've worked my entire life for this. For us. For your damn future. Do you want to be slinging burgers in a fast food joint? This is our big chance."

Stunned by the blow, Bobby rubbed the side of his face. "But I don't know where it is. How are we—"

"Goddammit, son, use your brain. Two people know where it is. Justin and Alice."

"But Justin will never—" Bobby stopped mid-sentence when he saw his father clench his fist.

"Forget him. Call Alice. Get her to meet you at your house. Alone."

Bobby shook his head, confused. "How will I do that? She won't give me the information without his okay."

Robert took a deep breath and exhaled, trying to keep his emotions in check. "She will. Tell her it's urgent and that you need to talk with her about 'Timmy Carver' and hang up. She'll come, trust me. When she shows up, tell her that I've discovered that someone is trying to kill the tree. I need the location so that I can protect it. It's the only way."

"But that's a lie. You just said—"

In a measured voice, Robert leaned forward and said, "Wake up and smell the coffee, son. We are broke, tapped out. I've borrowed money against everything we own—this house, your house—everything. Tramorix is the payoff. If the Bearant acquisition doesn't close, we don't get our piece of the pie, which is almost four billion dollars. We lose it all."

He paused, letting Bobby absorb the gravity of the situation, before continuing.

"Bearant will not close unless that tree is gone. We have to do whatever it takes to make it disappear. I understand you're worried about your friend, but think about it. If there's one tree in that vast park, then there's bound to be more. He and his Indian friends will find it eventually, and they can do whatever they want to with it. We get our money, and Bearant can't do anything about it. Everyone wins."

Bobby nodded. "Okay. I understand. I'll get the location."

Robert stood. "Good. I knew you would. We need it tonight. Call me as soon as you have it."

After Bobby left, Robert began to prepare for his meeting with Tony. Now that they would soon be getting the tree's location, he had no further need for Mr. Lewis.

Driving to meet Lewis that evening, Robert had forgotten how dark it was up on the Blue Ridge Parkway at night. An overcast sky made it even more foreboding. He occasionally passed another vehicle and hoped no one would be at the Devil's Courthouse when he got there.

When Tony had revised the terms of the agreement to kill the tree, he knew Tony had to go. How quickly the price had doubled was an indication of where the relationship was headed. The extortion would never stop. Two million would become three million, which would become four million, and so on. Robert knew it would never end.

With Bobby getting the location from Alice, Robert no longer needed Tony. He knew Tony was a professional—armed and physically superior. But Robert had the element of surprise. He was counting on Tony underestimating him.

Robert arrived at the agreed-upon location early. A nondescript sedan sat alone in the parking lot. He killed his lights and parked next to it.

Tony leaned against the hood, the glow of his cigarette silhouetted against the dark sky. Scattered clouds slid across the half-moon.

Robert stuck the loaded pistol in his jacket pocket and grabbed the duffel in the passenger seat. He'd turned off the interior light in the car before he'd left the house. He opened the door, picked up the bag with his left hand, and glanced around the dark, vacant parking lot. Lightning flashed in the distance.

"You're here early," Robert said. He stopped a few feet away, clutching the duffel with his left hand. "Have you got the information?"

Tony dropped the cigarette on the sidewalk and ground it out with his foot. "You have the money?"

Robert held up the bag. "It's all here. As soon as I get the location."

Tony snickered and pointed a gun toward Robert. "Throw the bag over here."

Robert didn't move. "What, you don't trust me? Are you going to stand here and count it?"

Tony laughed. "I don't trust anyone. I'll count it later. I just want to make sure the bag contains cash and nothing else. Toss it over here."

Robert tossed the bag, and it landed at Tony's feet.

"Keep your hands out where I can see them," Tony said. Slowly, he knelt, keeping a wary eye, and his gun trained on Robert. Tony unzipped the bag and stuck his free hand inside. He rummaged around and suddenly frowned.

"A tracking device, I presume," Tony said as he pulled a small, rectangular-shaped black plastic box out of the bag. He held it up and stared at it. "You're dumber than I thought, Kendall."

Robert slowly inched his hand closer to the jacket pocket.

Tony laid his pistol down, grabbed the duffel, and turned it upside down, releasing the contents. Neatly wrapped stacks of hundred-dollar bills tumbled out.

At that exact moment, Robert shifted his eyes above Tony's left shoulder and gave a slight nod, as if signaling someone. Tony caught the gesture and turned his head to see who was there.

At that precise moment, Robert pulled out the 9mm, aimed it at Tony's chest, and pulled the trigger. Too late, Tony realized the older man had tricked him. Robert's first shot caught him center mass, the sound echoing off the rock formation. A split second later, the next bullet was lower and just to the left, anticipating Tony's move to reach for his pistol.

Tony fell backward, laying on his back and clutching his gut. Blood began to gurgle out between his lips. Disbelief was written on his face.

Grinning and keeping his weapon trained on Tony, Robert stepped over and knelt. He looked down at the dying man. "I was right," he said. "You underestimated me."

"Fuck you," Tony whispered.

A light rain began. The lightning moved closer. The temperature dropped, and the wind picked up. The following clap of thunder indicated the storm was less than a mile away.

"Goodbye, Tony," Robert said. He stood, backed up a couple of steps to avoid any splatter, and took aim at Tony's head. He pulled the trigger a third time, and Tony's face disappeared.

After donning gloves, Robert rifled through Tony's pockets to remove any potentially incriminating evidence. He found a slim wallet containing a single credit card, a few hundred dollars, and a Virginia driver's license issued to a Carl Vincent. Robert returned it to the place where he found it. In another pocket, he was surprised to discover a sheet of paper with latitude and longitude, clipped to a picture of a tree.

"Well, I'll be damned," he said. He guessed it was the Indian tree. He put those in his own pocket.

Pushing Tony's body over the cliff proved more difficult than he figured. At last, he managed to give it a final shove. A moment later, he heard brush crashing as the corpse gained momentum going down the steep incline.

As the rain started to increase, Robert got in his car. He left the bag and money where it lay. Only the top ten bills in each bundle were real, so there was maybe $30,000 in the bag. Far less than the two million Tony expected, but enough to convince anyone that it was a drug deal gone awry. The black box "tracking device" was a fake, planted to further cement the charade.

Robert started the car and drove toward Asheville. He'd take the long way home to cover his tracks, but what did an extra hour matter? He had the tree's location and plenty of time to get someone to take care of it.

41

Are you alright?" Justin asked Alice as they were finishing dinner at home. "You seem preoccupied."

"I'm fine. Just thinking about work. Things I need to do tomorrow."

He pushed away from the table to take their dishes to the sink. "Speaking of work, I need to finalize a report for Hadley tonight."

"Go ahead. I'll finish up in here."

Justin went over to his chair in the living room and sat. He grabbed the folder he'd left on the table beside him. Reading through it for the umpteenth time, he was interrupted by Alice's phone ringing.

He heard her answer it and didn't bother to turn around. But when he didn't hear Alice say anything else, he turned around to see what was going on.

She had a frown as she stood in the kitchen with the phone to her ear. When she saw him staring at her, she mumbled an "uh-huh" and nodded, then shrugged.

He turned his attention back to his reading and overheard her say, "Okay, I'm on my way."

"Everything okay?" Justin asked.

"Yeah. Work drama. That was Becky, who works at the bank. Her boyfriend left her, and she's hysterical. I need to go over and check on her."

She wiped her hands on the dishtowel and started toward the bedroom.

"I'll go with you," Justin said. "I can finish this later."

"No," Alice said. "No need. You stay here."

Justin stood and walked over to her. "I don't want you going out alone. It's late. I'll go with—"

"I'll be fine." She held up her phone. "I have my phone with me. And she lives in Hazelwood with lots of neighbors. I'll text when I get there and again when I leave. Stay here and finish what you're working on."

She marched into the bedroom to change.

Justin went back to his chair and sat down. He wasn't keen on Alice being out alone. He knew Matt was no longer a threat, but he was concerned about Matt's associate. They still had not heard anything more from him.

A few minutes later, Alice emerged with her jacket and grabbed her car keys and purse.

"I'll text when I get there," she said as she hurriedly walked out the door.

As the front door shut, Justin put his report down, unable to concentrate. He slipped his shoes on and grabbed his keys as he heard Alice's car pull away from the house.

He caught up with her halfway down the mountain. He didn't want her to think he didn't trust her, so he slowed down a comfortable distance behind her.

As they approached the traffic light at SOCO road, he slowed and moved over to the left lane, anticipating her turning in that direction. She remained in the right lane, and when she got to the light, she turned right.

What the hell? Where was she going? Alice said that Becky lived in Hazelwood, which was the opposite direction. He waited to clear a car behind her, and then he switched lanes. He turned right, a vehicle now between them. At the entrance to Hawks Nest, Alice slowed and turned left.

Justin shook his head, more confused. Hawks Nest was an exclusive, gated community. He couldn't picture Becky living there. In fact, the only person he knew who lived there was Bobby Kendall.

He slowed as he watched Alice pull up to the keypad in front of the gate. She reached out and punched in a code, and the gate opened.

Damn, he thought as he watched Alice drive through the open gate. He turned and pulled off to the side. There was no way to get up there and through the gate before it closed. Bobby had given him the code, but he didn't remember it.

Justin pulled out his phone and quickly scrolled to Bobby's name. He had stored the four-digit number there, and he hoped it was still the correct code.

He pulled up to the keypad and quickly entered the code, barely able to see the taillights on Alice's car, disappearing ahead. When he pressed enter, the gate didn't open.

Shit. He re-entered the code, slower this time, careful to punch in the number stored on his phone. He held his breath, and this time, the gate opened.

He drove through, but Alice had vanished. He had no way of knowing where she'd gone. The good news was that Hawks Nest was not that large, and there was only one road in. Farther up the mountain, several other streets branched off like the limbs of a tree.

When he got to the first intersection, he stopped, straining his eyes to catch a glimpse of Alice's car in both directions. He tapped his fingers on the steering wheel. Left. Right. Straight.

He turned the wheel right and gunned the 4Runner. Slowing as he passed each house, he searched for Alice's car. After reaching the cul-de-sac and not seeing it, he sped back toward the intersection and roared straight across, not bothering to stop.

Again, nothing. He drove back to the intersection and turned uphill, toward the top of the neighborhood. At the next corner, he repeated his search pattern, again coming up empty-handed.

He recognized the third junction. To the right was Bobby's house, close to the end of the street. He turned that direction, looking at each home as he drove past.

As he approached Bobby's house, he was surprised to see a car that looked like Alice's parked in the driveway. It couldn't be. He knew Bobby owned several luxury cars, but there was no blue Honda Civic in his stable. As he slowed, he recognized the tag on the Honda. A *Friends of the Smokies* tag. It was Alice's car.

Justin's phone buzzed. A text from Alice.

At Becky's

Becky's my ass, Justin thought, feeling his face flush in anger. He drove to the cul-de-sac, made a partial loop, and stopped, facing his friend's house. He switched the engine off and killed the lights, sliding down into his seat.

* * *

Bobby closed the door behind Alice after she stepped inside. He held up his glass, half full of an amber liquid. "Hey, Alice. Can I get you a drink?"

She stood just inside the foyer of Bobby's house, arms crossed. "This isn't a social call, Bobby. I'm fine right here."

Alice had never trusted Bobby. When she and Justin first started dating in college, Bobby had hit on her one night when she was with a group out at a bar. Justin was working, and she never told him what had happened. She chalked it up to the alcohol but made sure Bobby understood never to do it again, or she'd tell Justin. For some reason, Bobby was afraid of Justin, and he never came on to her after that.

Bobby's call tonight, more of a summons, had made her uneasy. But given the bait he used, she was glad that Justin wasn't with her.

"Where did you get that name—Timmy Carver?" she asked.

"Look, I know you're upset, but let me—"

"Where did you get the name?"

He hesitated and then said, "The old man gave it to me. He told me to mention it, and that would get you to come over." Bobby grinned. "He was right."

Alice scowled. "What else did he tell you about it?"

"Nothing, I swear. That's all. Who is Timmy Carver?"

"None of your business. What do you want?"

"I—he—needs the location of the tree. Location and description."

"What makes you think I have it?"

Bobby shrugged. "He said you and Justin have it. I'm just doing what he asked, okay?"

"Why didn't you ask Justin?"

"He wouldn't give it to me. You know that."

"What makes you think that I will?" Alice asked.

"Look, Daddy asked me to get the information from you. Tonight. He told me to use the name."

"Why does he want it?"

"He found out that someone wants to destroy the tree, and he wants to protect it."

"Jesus, Bobby. *He's* the one that wants to destroy it."

Bobby looked at the floor, refusing to meet her stare.

"Oh my God, you know that, don't you?" Alice said.

Sheepishly, Bobby nodded and met her eyes. "If Bearant finds out about the tree, they won't close on the purchase of the lab. If that doesn't close, we're bankrupt. Broke. Daddy told me that he'd put every penny he has into Nuran and mortgaged everything he owns—his house, this house. C'mon, Alice. One tree is not a big deal. There's got to be more. Justin and Atohi will find them."

Alice shook her head. "Unbelievable. It was your father. He's the one who hired the man who kidnapped me."

Bobby shook his head. "No, he wouldn't do that. He told me. He'd never do anything to hurt you."

"Are you that gullible? Timmy Carver was the name the kidnapper used to blackmail me. It came from your father."

Bobby hesitated for a moment, wheels turning. "Does Justin know about Timmy Carver?"

Alice glared at him. Bobby had leverage and knew it. She didn't think Bobby had more than a name, but she knew his father had additional knowledge. Dangerous knowledge.

She was tired of all the lies. It was an addiction. Just one more, and then she'd quit except one more led to another. It never ended. Maybe she should go to Justin and come clean, take her chances.

Alice shook her head, knowing she couldn't do that. But she convinced herself that once she got out of this jam, no more. She'd already given the tree's information to the kidnapper, so what was the harm in giving it to Bobby? Justin hopefully had enough of the extract to continue Karen's treatment until he and Atohi could find more trees. Maybe this was her way out.

"I'll give you the information, but I want something in return. If I give it to you, Justin must never know about Timmy Carver." Alice cocked her head, waiting for Bobby's answer.

Bobby's slight hesitation before nodding in agreement bothered her.

Alice stared him down. "If he does, I'll assume it came from you. And I will go to Justin and tell him everything plus. Including that night in Chapel Hill. And I'll swear that you tried to repeat that tonight. Do I make myself clear?"

Bobby's red face confirmed that he got the message. "Agreed," he said. The swagger was gone.

"Good. I'm glad we understand each other. Get a pen and paper." She pulled up the tree coordinates on her phone. When Bobby returned, she held out her phone for him to see.

Bobby looked down at her phone, then up at her with a frown. "I could've just taken a picture of that with my phone," he said.

Alice shook her head. "Oh, no. And if it ever comes up, I'll deny I gave them to you. You asked, but I said I'd have to talk to Justin." Another lie, but she wasn't giving Bobby any more than she had to.

"But what do I tell the old man?"

"Tell him you stole them—I don't care what kind of lie you make up. But I didn't give them to you."

He copied the numbers down, then asked, "What are we looking for?"

"It looks like a rhododendron with blue flowers. It's in a small clearing by itself, so it's hard to miss." She didn't give him a copy of the picture. She could deny giving him the coordinates, but not the photo.

She put her phone in her pocket. "Now go call Daddy and tell him what you have. And don't ever call me again."

With that, she turned and walked out.

42

Justin's initial reaction was to confront the two of them together, but he knew he needed to calm down first. *Alice and Bobby?* He had doubts about Bobby's loyalty, but not Alice's.

He tried to think about any signs he might have missed. Nothing, but he recalled the adage about the partner being the last one to see the writing on the wall. He didn't want to believe there was something between them, but why would she lie about where she was going? The fact that she knew the gate code and went straight to his house was troublesome.

The longer he sat and thought about it, the angrier he became. He had decided to confront them when twenty minutes later, Bobby's front door opened. Alice stepped out and waved over her shoulder toward Bobby Kendall as she went to her car.

He saw her lights come on, but she sat there. He gritted his teeth and waited for her to leave.

Justin's phone buzzed again. He looked down to see another text from Alice.

On my way home

She backed out and drove toward the main street leading to the exit. Justin gave her a few minutes lead, and then he started his truck and pulled into Bobby's drive.

At his friend's door, he banged on it with his fists, ignoring the doorbell.

"What, did you forget something?" Bobby said as he opened the door.

Justin hit him with a right fist, knocking his friend flat on the floor of the foyer. Bobby lay there, rubbing his jaw, shocked to see Justin.

Justin glared down at him, massaging his right hand. "Yeah, I forgot something, alright. I forgot who my friend was."

Holding his hands up to protect his face, Bobby said, "Hey, it's not what you think it is."

"Yeah, well, why don't you explain exactly what it is, then. All I know is what I see. What I see is my fiancée lying to me about where she's going, and she comes to your fucking house."

He reached down to pull Bobby up to hit him again, and Bobby scrambled away.

"Let me explain, Justin. I swear it's not what you think. My dad wanted me to talk to Alice about the tree. That's all."

Justin straightened up. "What are you talking about?"

Careful to keep his distance from Justin, Bobby explained that his Dad wanted the tree location so he could protect it.

"Protect it? The son of a bitch wanted to destroy it."

Bobby shook his head. "No, really. He told me he wanted to protect it. He knew you wouldn't believe him, so he told me to go to Alice."

"Bullshit. Why would Alice give it to you?"

"I'm just telling you what Dad said. I swear."

"Did she give it to you?"

Bobby shook his head. "I told her what Dad said, but she wouldn't give it up. She said she'd have to talk to you first."

Justin, his fists still clenched, stood over his friend.

"Get up."

Bobby scooted farther away, then got to his feet, keeping a close eye on Justin.

"Let's go," Justin said. "We're going to see your dad. I want answers, truthful answers."

Still rubbing his chin, Bobby said, "I need to get my phone and let him know we're—"

Justin took a step toward him. "You don't need it. We're going unannounced, and I'm driving."

Questions flooded Justin's head on the way over to Robert Kendall's house, only fifteen minutes away. He looked over at Bobby, who was leaning against the side window.

Justin believed that Robert wanted the location of the tree to kill it, not protect it. But he wasn't sure if Bobby was that naïve or was in on the conspiracy. What puzzled him more was Alice. Why would she lie about going to see Bobby?

"How did you convince Alice to come to your house?" Justin asked, breaking the silence.

Bobby jumped at the intrusion.

"What?"

"I said, how did you persuade Alice to come over to your place?"

"Uh, I told her that my father had important information about the tree and that he told me to talk only to her. Not you."

"That's bullshit. I'd already told her my suspicions that your father wanted to kill the tree. How did you get her to drop what she was doing and come to your house? Alone. At night."

Bobby's eyes darted around as he seemed to search for an answer.

"Dad told me that he'd found out that Bearant was trying to kill the tree. He wanted to protect it and needed the information ASAP so that he could. He knew you wouldn't believe him and asked me to contact Alice. I asked her to come over so I could persuade her in person. Without you around."

Justin shook his head, not sure he trusted Bobby's explanation. He wanted to hear the elder Kendall's story.

They pulled into the long, winding driveway of Robert's mansion and made their way to the house. Justin parked in front, and they walked up the steps to the door. He was careful to stay behind Bobby, who rang the doorbell.

After a few minutes, when no one answered, Bobby turned around and said, "Maybe he left the house. We should've called first."

Before Justin could respond, they heard a rustling behind the door as someone unlocked it and opened it.

Robert Kendall stood there with a pistol in his hand, pointed down but at the ready. The top two buttons of his shirt were undone, and his hair was unkempt.

"Hey, Daddy," Bobby said. He looked down at the gun and then back up at his father. "What's with the pistol? Where's Belle?" Bobby asked.

Ignoring the question about the gun, Robert said, "I sinner her home. What are you doing here?"

Robert's speech was slurred, and "sent her" came out sounding like one word. Even behind Bobby, Justin could smell the alcohol on Robert.

Bobby glanced at Justin, then turned back to his father. "Are you okay?"

"I'm fine." Robert stared at Justin and asked, "Why are you here?"

"I wanted to talk to both of you," Justin said.

Robert looked confused. "'bout what?" he asked, looking from his son to Justin and back. He stood in the middle of the doorway, making no effort to invite them in.

"The healing tree," Justin said, pushing Bobby forward into his dad.

Robert stumbled backward, almost falling. He motioned them inside with the gun. He looked outside in all directions, then closed the door behind them, locking the deadbolt.

"What's so 'portant that you barge into my house unannounced?"

Bobby said, "I told him—"

"Shut up, Bobby." Justin held up his hand to silence his friend. Staring at Kendall, he said, "Bobby told me that you wanted the location of the healing tree. Why?"

Robert shrugged. "I had information that people wanted to destroy it. I wanted to protect it."

"That's a lie. *You* were the one who wanted to destroy it. You hired the thug who blackmailed and kidnapped Alice."

Justin looked at Bobby and then Robert. Alice seemed to be the common dominator. "Why did you tell him to call Alice?" he asked Robert.

"Knew you wouldn't believe me. Figured she'd be more open-minded."

Bobby shuffled his feet and looked at Justin. "I told you. He convinced me that he wanted to save—"

"Bullshit," Justin said, staring at Bobby. "You're part of it, aren't you?"

A smirk crossed Kendall's face, and he snickered. "It doesn't matter. It's too late, Reeve. The wheels are already in motion."

"That's not true," Justin said. "You don't have the location." The doubt was evident in his tone. He turned to

Bobby. "You told me that Alice didn't give you the location?"

"She didn't," Bobby said.

"Why would I lie now?" Robert asked, letting the question hang. His laugh came out as a cackle. "You're not as smart as you think. You don't know who she is. You'd be surprised at what she'd do. Ask her about 'Timmy Carver.'"

At the disparaging reference to Alice, Justin bristled and took a step toward Robert Kendall.

"What are you talking about?" he asked.

"I'm not letting you fuck this up, Reeve." Kendall unsteadily moved his gun hand up toward Justin.

"Daddy. Put the gun down," Bobby said, pleading.

Justin started to take another step as Kendall raised the pistol and fired.

The shot hit Justin's left leg, taking it out from under him and sending him to the floor. It stung as though someone had stuck a knife in it. Stunned, he grabbed his leg. It felt wet. He looked down to see blood covering his hand. His ears ringing, he looked up to see Bobby wrestling with his father, trying to take the gun away.

As Justin tried to get to his feet, a second shot rang out. A surprised look crossed Kendall's face. He collapsed back against the wall, clutching his chest, and slid to the floor. A red splotch spread across the front of his shirt.

The last thing Justin saw was Bobby, standing there in shock, holding the gun.

43

The next morning, Justin awoke in the hospital. Alice was sitting beside him in a chair, her head tilted back and mouth open. She was asleep. He tried to move, and pain shot through his left leg, stopping any movement. He took a breath and looked down at his heavily bandaged leg.

Alice stirred, sensing that he was awake. She blinked and looked at him. Leaning over, she placed her hand on his arm.

"How are you feeling?" she asked.

"My leg hurts." He shook his head. "So tired. What happened?"

"You don't remember?"

"Some of it. I remember getting shot. Bobby and I were at his dad's."

Alice nodded. "They had to do surgery on your leg because of the bleeding. The surgeon said fortunately, the bullet missed the bone, nothing serious. Expanding hematoma, she called it. You'll probably limp for a while, but you'll be good as new. She thinks you'll be able to go home tomorrow, but you need to take it easy for a few days."

"Bobby?"

"Physically, he's fine."

"Physically?"

Alice hesitated, trying to find the words. "Robert Kendall's dead."

"What? How?" His voice trailed off as he tried to remember. He and Bobby had gone to see Robert. About the healing tree. He started to ask if she was sure, but her look confirmed it. Bobby's father was dead. As much as he despised Robert, Justin felt sorry for Bobby. His dad was the only family he had left.

Justin closed his eyes as if that would help him recall. Why were they at Robert's house? Then, he remembered. He'd seen Alice at Bobby's.

"Why were you at Bobby's house?" he asked, opening his eyes and looking at Alice. "You told me you were going somewhere, but I don't think it was Bobby's."

Alice nodded. "I'm sorry. I didn't know what to do. Bobby called and wanted to meet with me. He didn't want me to tell you because he knew you'd talk me out of it."

"Talk you out of what?"

Alice avoided meeting his eyes. "He told me that he had information to protect the tree, but he wouldn't tell me anything over the phone. I was afraid that the kidnapper would find the tree and destroy it, so I used Becky as an excuse to leave. When I got to his house, he told me that his dad needed the location so he could safeguard the tree."

"You gave Bobby the location of the healing tree?"

She shook her head. "No. I didn't trust Bobby or his father. I told him I'd have to talk to you." She squeezed his arm. "I went because I wanted to help you. And Karen. Speaking of Karen, I talked with her earlier, and she sends her love. Obviously, with her immune system compromised, she can't visit, but said she'd call later."

His mind still muddled, Justin thought about what Alice said. "Kendall wanted to destroy the tree, not protect it. He's the one who hired the thug who kidnapped you," he said.

She stared at him, then shook her head. "Bobby swore he didn't. Robert told him he didn't have anything to do with it. Anyway, when I got home, you weren't there. Next thing I know, Bobby called and told me you'd been shot and were in the hospital."

Justin closed his eyes tight and tried to remember. He and Robert got into a heated discussion about the tree. It's too late, Robert had said.

Justin's eyes flashed open wide, startling Alice. "Give me my phone. I've got to call Atohi."

"I . . . I think—"

"Give me yours."

Alice handed him her phone. He snatched it out of her hand and called Atohi.

"You've got to get someone out to the tree," Justin said when Atohi answered.

"What? Are you okay? Alice said—"

"You've got to get someone out there, now."

"Calm down," Atohi said. "What are you talking about?"

"The tree. Make sure it's okay. Someone's trying to destroy it." He hung up.

His thoughts were interrupted when he heard Bobby's voice.

"Hey. Can I come in?" Bobby asked.

Justin looked over to see the haggard face of his friend, who was standing in the doorway. Bobby looked like he hadn't slept in days. "Hey. Come in."

"How are you feeling," Bobby said as he came over to the bed.

"Okay," Justin said. "I'm sorry, Bobby."

Alice said, "He just woke up. He's having trouble recalling what happened. I told him about your father."

Bobby nodded and sat on Justin's bed. "How's the leg?"

"Sore. I'm still a little foggy. How are you?"

Bobby shrugged. After a long pause, he said, "Kinda sleepwalking right now. It doesn't seem real."

He looked down at Justin's bandaged leg. "I'm sorry about that. After Momma passed, he was never the same. He never used to drink like that."

Justin put his hand on Bobby's arm. "It wasn't your fault."

Bobby had a faraway look in his eyes as he tried to keep it together. "I was afraid he was going to kill you." He shook his head. "I tried to get the gun away from him. It went off, and Daddy collapsed on the floor."

"I'm so sorry, Bobby," Justin said. "It wasn't your fault."

The ensuing silence turned awkward, then Bobby said, "I should probably let you get some rest. You need anything?"

Justin shook his head. "Thanks for coming by. Take care of yourself, okay?"

"Thanks, Bobby. Let us know if you need anything," Alice said.

Bobby nodded, turned, and walked out. Seconds later, a woman in blue scrubs with a stethoscope slung around her neck walked in.

"Good morning. I'm Rebecca, your nurse today. How are you feeling, Mr. Reeve?"

"Groggy. My leg hurts."

"On a scale of 1 to 10, how would you rate it?"

"Uncomfortable. Three, maybe."

She smiled and nodded. "Not unusual. I'll make a note of it. Any other issues?"

He shook his head.

"Let's take a look at you."

She checked him over, pausing to make a few adjustments to his IV. She entered a few notes into the bedside computer. "Everything looks good."

"Let me know if you need anything," she said and then turned to leave.

"Thanks."

Alice stood and stretched. "I think I'm going to go down and get a cup of coffee. Want anything?"

Justin shook his head, looking at his fiancée. What was that Robert Kendall had said? *You don't know who she is.*

"Who's Timmy Carver?" Justin said, suddenly remembering the name.

Alice flinched, then recovered. "Who?" she asked, shaking her head.

"Timmy Carver. I just remembered Bobby's dad telling me to ask you about Timmy Carver."

Alice shrugged. "Are you sure? I don't know anybody by that name."

Justin shook his head, confused. "I could swear that's what he said. Maybe not. I'll ask Bobby when he comes back."

Alice's lips tightened. "You get some sleep. Rest for now, and I'll be back in a bit."

* * *

She caught up with Bobby downstairs in the coffee shop as he was leaving.

"Hey. I'm glad I caught you before you left," she said.

He nodded, holding up his cup. "Thought I'd get one for the road."

Alice shifted and glanced around, then asked, "After you left, Justin asked me about Timmy Carver. He thought he remembered your dad mentioning the name last night."

Bobby cocked his head and then nodded. "He did. Right before the chaos started and all hell broke loose. But that was it." He took a sip and asked, "So, who is Timmy Carver?"

"Someone from my past. I told you last night—Justin doesn't need to know."

"He won't—not from me. Sorry I asked. It's none of my business."

"How did your dad get the name?" Alice asked.

"I told you I have no idea. When he told me to get the tree's location from you, all he said was to mention the name and you'd come. That was it."

"Justin said he was going to ask you if you remembered the name coming up last night."

"I don't know anything about that name." His expression was stoic.

Her eyes pleaded with Bobby. "I know you're hurting, and I'm sorry about your dad. But it wasn't your fault. Telling Justin won't bring your father back, and it would only hurt Justin." Alice shook her head, looked away, and then back at Bobby. "We all have mistakes in our past. Mistakes we regret. You know how Justin is. He never forgets, and he has a hard time forgiving."

Bobby nodded and said, "What am I supposed to say when he asks?"

"You don't know the name. That's the truth. Let your dad rest in peace and leave it at that."

Bobby thought for a minute, then nodded. He held up his cup. "I need to run. I'll come back later."

Alice went back upstairs to Justin's room. She peeked inside and found him asleep. Quietly, she eased the door shut and decided to go for a walk outside.

She was thankful she caught Bobby downstairs. She felt sorry for him but was relieved to find out he didn't seem to know anything more about Timmy Carver and glad that he was inclined to deny even knowing the name.

Alice had felt guilty about giving the kidnapper the tree's location yesterday morning. When he called later and confirmed the information was correct, she assumed he had poisoned the tree.

Last night, when Bobby had invoked Timmy Carver's name, she knew that it was Robert Kendall who'd hired the kidnapper. But if Robert was still trying to get the location, then the tree may be safe. Now, Robert Kendall was dead, and she'd received no further calls from the kidnapper. And, so far, her secret was still safe.

Alice allowed herself a slight smile and crossed her fingers. Maybe things were working out. She was anxious to hear what Atohi had found out.

44

The day after the funeral, Bobby was in his father's study, going through his things. The room was Robert Kendall's inner sanctum, and his presence still filled the space. Bobby could detect the scent of cigars and whiskey.

He felt like an intruder. His father never allowed anyone in there without him. It was surreal. He half expected his father to walk in, even though Bobby saw him laid to rest the day before.

He was curious to see what secrets awaited him in the room. Since he was the only heir and Robert's will left everything to him, there was no concern about the inheritance or who got what. No relatives—at least any Bobby knew of—would be seeking their piece of the family fortune.

Bobby walked around the perimeter of the room, browsing the books lining the shelves. An eclectic collection. Several of the titles surprised him, and he wondered if his dad read them or they were mere decoration.

Behind the massive desk, he stopped and stared at the wall of fame, photos of his father with various celebrities. One picture caught his attention. Robert Kendall and Carter Knox were posing with Lee Iacocca in front of a classic 1965 Ford Mustang convertible.

He smiled, recognizing the gold car. It was in Robert's garage.

Bobby turned around and considered the elegant cherry desk. The top was uncluttered, covered with a leather-edged blotter. A desk phone sat on one side, a lone framed photograph on the other.

He picked up the frame and stared at his parents' wedding picture. His mom was an attractive young woman, and they made a handsome couple. They looked happy. He replaced the picture and opened the top drawer.

Bobby studied the meager contents, all orderly. He was surprised to see a flip phone, one he'd never seen his father use. He guessed it must have been his father's old one.

He picked it up and opened it. The screen was blank, so he turned it on. Surprisingly, the screen lit up, and the battery was half-charged. Bobby chuckled. He pressed the CONTACTS button. Only one number was listed, shown as Private.

He pushed the arrow keys. A list of entries he assumed were recent calls popped up. Every single one was the number listed in contacts, but with various dates and times.

"What the hell?" Bobby said. His dad had a burner phone? For what? He scrolled to the last number and pressed SEND. A robotic voice answered with simply "leave a number." Bobby ended the call. He powered the phone off and placed it back in the drawer.

In the same drawer, he saw a checkbook, pens, and various business cards. Conspicuous was a manila envelope with a picture of a tree clipped to the outside. He'd never seen the picture before. In an unfamiliar hand, somebody had written 35°36'41" N and 83°14'56" W across the bottom.

Bobby lifted the photo. Underneath, the name Timmy Carver was handwritten on the envelope along with the same numbers. He recognized the elegant writing as his father's. The coordinates were the ones Alice had given him for the tree. Bobby had called as soon as she'd left, and his father must have written them down here.

He flipped the envelope over. It wasn't sealed. After opening the metal clasp, he looked inside and removed the two pages.

The top one was a photograph of a gravestone. It read:

Timothy Carver
Beloved son
September 16, 1998 – April 9, 2009

That was the name his father had given him to lure Alice to his house that night. He started to put it down and looked again at the dates. *What the hell?* Timothy Carver was not even eleven years old.

When Alice had told him Timmy Carver was a name from her past, he'd assumed he was someone with whom she'd had some sort of a relationship. Not a ten-year-old kid.

He set the photograph on the desk and studied the second page. It was a photocopy of a newspaper clipping from *The Indianapolis Star.* Bobby looked closer at the date. The year was the same as the year on the gravestone— 2009.

Carmel Child Killed by Hit-and-Run Driver

The article described a ten-year-old local boy, Timothy Carver, who was killed by a hit-and-run driver. They never found the driver.

Bobby laid the article on the desk and swiveled around to his dad's computer on the credenza. He went online and searched for *The Indianapolis Star* website.

Gannett had acquired the newspaper, and it was now called the *IndyStar*. On the newspaper website, he queried the online archives for the name and date. Several entries popped up, all relating to Timothy Carver. The most recent, dated a year after he was buried, said the driver had not been found, and they had no leads.

Puzzled, Bobby turned back to look at the picture and article on the desk. Locking his hands together behind his head, he sat back and thought about Alice.

He remembered Justin meeting her when they were at UNC in Chapel Hill. It was the fall of 2009. Justin had told him that Alice had moved to the area from Colorado. Her parents had been killed in a small plane crash. She wanted a fresh start and chose North Carolina. Bobby couldn't remember her ever saying where in Colorado she was from.

The gravestone haunted Bobby. He couldn't get it out of his head. Was Alice the driver? That would explain her sharp reaction to the name. It was apparently a name that his father used to blackmail her, and a name powerful enough to get her to meet him with a phone call.

How did his father find out? Too many unanswered questions and no one around to answer them. Except for maybe Alice. He thought about how he could approach her without alerting Justin, who knew nothing about Timothy Carver.

A knock on the open study door interrupted his train of thought. He turned around to see Justin come in, limping.

Bobby placed the picture and article back in the envelope as Justin flopped down in the chair across from him.

"Belle let me in. You doing okay?" Justin said.

"I guess. Glad yesterday's over. Sorry I didn't get much of a chance to talk with you at the funeral."

"I understand. It was a nice service. Your dad had lots of friends. Karen sends her love. She was sorry to miss it, but she's still avoiding crowds."

Bobby nodded and said, "Tell her, thanks, I understand. It feels strange in here without him. I'm just going through some of his things." He glanced down and added, "How's the leg?"

"Good. I'm supposed to take it easy for a few weeks. Keep it elevated when I can. The physical therapist gave me some exercises. I have to get it checked this week. If I'm compliant, it'll heal sooner, and I won't have to go back. Physical therapists are all sadists, so I'm going to do everything I can to avoid that."

Bobby chuckled. "Are you supposed to be driving?"

Justin shrugged and said, "Doctor said not to for a few days, and then only if I felt like it. I feel fine. It's my left leg, so driving isn't too bad. Just a little stiff getting in and out."

"When are you going back to work?"

"When I leave here, I'm going by the lab to talk with Hadley. I'm going to take it easy for a few days."

"You should. Thanks for being there yesterday. Glad you stopped by today. I wanted to talk to you about the tree. Is it alright?"

Justin stiffened, then nodded. "It's still there."

"That's good." Bobby hesitated, then added, "Maybe he *was* trying to protect it."

After an awkward silence, Justin said, "It's fine. Atohi's keeping close tabs on it. Since it's on the Qualla, the tribe is helping him."

"Look, I've been thinking about it. The tree belongs to them. It's caused enough problems. All I want is that the lab officially has nothing more to do with it. Hadley is on record with his report saying it has no potential. What happens later is not my concern. I don't want to know."

"I'm sure the Cherokee will be happy to hear that."

"One more thing," Bobby said.

"What?"

"I'd like to request that no one, you or anybody from the tribe, make public anything about the tree until well after the closing. I'm meeting with Carter Knox later today, the investment banker. He said that the closing is still on, and I want to assure him the tree is no longer an issue."

"Knox is the heavyset guy? I met him yesterday at the funeral."

Bobby nodded.

Justin shrugged. "I don't see that being a problem. The Cherokee don't want anyone outside the tribe to know about it. Never did."

"You say that now, but it's potentially worth a lot of money to them if they commercialize it. Eventually, they may."

"Possibly, but not anytime soon. I'll pass it along and let you know what they say."

"Thanks. How's Alice?"

Justin nodded. "She seems fine. No more calls from the kidnapper. I'm glad things are settling down."

"That's good to hear. One of Dad's friends at the funeral said he was from Colorado. I told them that she was from there, but I wasn't sure where."

"Montrose, a little town in western Colorado. Near Telluride."

"Was she born there?" Bobby asked.

"Not sure. She doesn't talk much about it. You remember what happened to her parents?"

"They were killed in a private plane crash, right?"

"Yeah. She's never said much about it. I don't push."

"That reminds me," Justin said. "Do you remember your dad mentioning the name 'Timmy Carver' that night? I vaguely remember him saying something about me not knowing my girlfriend and telling me to ask her about a Timmy Carver."

Bobby looked up at the ceiling as if he were trying to remember. He shook his head, avoiding his friend's eyes.

"He may have, but no, I don't recall that name coming up. That night is a blur. Everything happened so fast."

"I know. I asked Alice, and she didn't recognize the name, either," Justin said. "Maybe it was Jimmy Carver. Oh, and Detective Cullen came by and chatted with me. I doubt I was much help. I told him what I could remember, which wasn't a lot. Since I'm not sure about the name, I didn't mention it. I wanted to ask you first."

"Sorry, I don't remember him mentioning it."

Justin stood. "I better go and let you get back to it. I wanted to go by the lab and see Hadley. Let me know when you want to grab a beer."

"Will do. Thanks."

Bobby sat back in his chair after Justin left. He hated lying to his friend, especially now that he knew who Timmy Carver was. He was certain Justin knew nothing about him. Bobby recalled his promise to Alice, but after finding out the truth, he wondered if he should tell Justin.

Bobby believed that Alice was the driver in the Indiana hit-and-run fatality. Why else would the name have such power over her? Indiana was a long way from Colorado, and he didn't know what she'd be doing halfway across the country from her home. If Colorado was her home. Based on what Justin said, she was pretty vague about her supposed upbringing in Colorado.

He pulled the contents of the envelope back out, staring at the gravestone. Bobby had made plenty of mistakes in his life and didn't claim to be an angel. He blamed himself for his father's death, even though it was an accident. But he took responsibility for it and would have to live with the consequences for the rest of his life. He didn't run away and lie about it, like a hit-and-run driver. A driver who killed a child.

45

Bobby felt strange, holding court behind his father's desk. Carter Knox had stopped by on his way out that afternoon and was seated across from him. He looked down at the picture of his dad, Carter Knox, and Lee Iacocca that lay on the desk.

"You doing okay?" Carter asked.

Bobby nodded. Carter had come down for the funeral and was leaving to fly back to New York. Bobby picked up the picture and handed it to the stocky man seated opposite him.

"I thought you might like to have this. He would've wanted you to have it."

Knox took the picture and stared at it, then chuckled. "I remember that day well. After all these years, your dad kept the car, didn't he?"

Bobby laughed. "The only one he did keep. He traded cars like baseball cards. It's in the garage and still runs great. He took good care of it."

"Thank you, Bobby. I appreciate this. A great keepsake." Carter nodded. "I'm sorry to bring up business at a time like this, but we need to talk."

He shrugged. "I understand. Life goes on."

Carter shifted his heavy frame in the chair.

"Bearant still wants to close Monday, as we originally planned. I think we should proceed. Things move fast in this business, and I'd hate to see them change their mind."

Bobby nodded. "I agree. I don't see any reason why we can't."

"Good. Monday morning after the closing they want to have an employee meeting at the lab."

"It'll be their company. They can do what they want."

"They'd like you to be there. It's important to communicate that it's a friendly transition and you're onboard. With closing the lab here, they're concerned about mass defections. Most of the employees will be offered positions in Cupertino."

"The least I can do. Assure them that I won't be a problem."

"Good." Carter shifted in his seat and cleared his throat. "I know your father talked to you about the Indian tree, as he called it. What's going on with that?"

Bobby shrugged. "It's not an issue. Hadley said the project didn't have merit, and he killed it. His report is on record. I talked with Justin Reeve earlier today, and according to him, the tree is on Cherokee land. I don't want anything else to do with it, and Nuran has no interest whatsoever. What the Cherokee do is up to them. I don't care."

Carter grimaced. "Hmm. So, the tree is still alive?"

"According to Justin. Why? What difference does that make?"

Carter shifted again in his chair.

"Your father and I discussed . . . eliminating the tree as a threat."

"Eliminating? Are you trying to tell me that my father was going to have the tree killed?"

Carter shook his head. "No. If he was, I'm not aware of it. But Bearant is worried about it being a potential threat.

All I did was pass along their requirement that we guarantee the tree would not be a problem. He assured me and them that it wouldn't be. That's all I know."

Bobby put his hand on the desk, thinking about the phone in the top drawer. "The day he died, he told me that was a condition. Why would they insist on that? Hadley's formal report said that it had no merit. Even if it did, a potential cure would be years away. It would be no immediate threat to Tramorix. Why should Bearant care?"

"Bearant doesn't want a cure. No pharmaceutical company does. They want a cash machine, which Tramorix is. Twenty-five thousand a pop, and patients take it for life. That's what Bearant's buying. A cash cow, not a cure. Five billion dollars is a lot to you and me, but that's chump change for a blockbuster drug. Lipitor has generated over $150 billion in sales since its debut. Rituxan, another cancer drug, $82 billion."

"Jesus Christ. I had no idea."

"Bobby, when I get back to New York, the first thing Bearant is going to do is ask me if the tree has been eliminated."

"Tell them it's *not* a threat. Besides, I have no control over the tree. It's on the Qualla."

Carter shook his head, his jowls flopping.

"I don't think that's going to be sufficient. You want me to tell Bearant it's not a threat, but the tree is still alive *and* that the Cherokee Indian tribe has ownership? They are not going to hand over five billion dollars in cash with that news."

Carter leaned over the desk. "Be smart here, Bobby. The tree has to go. Or this deal will not close. Have you looked at the financials? You are up to your eyeballs in debt if you don't already know it."

Bobby nodded. "Dad told me. Why couldn't we sell Tramorix to someone else or market it ourselves?"

Carter threw back his head and roared with laughter.

"Do you really believe that Bearant, the largest pharmaceutical firm on the planet, is going to let that happen? You don't realize who you are screwing with here. If they can't have it, no one else will."

Bobby shook his head. He was cornered, and he knew it.

"But I told Justin that I wanted nothing further to do with the tree. It belongs to the Cherokee."

"It's just one tree, a tree that happens to be worth five billion dollars. If there's one tree out there, there's probably more of them. Later, if the Cherokee find another one, then so what? Bearant can't hold us responsible."

Carter looked at his watch and stood.

"I've got to be back in New York to meet with Bearant first thing in the morning. I can take care of this if I know the location. You don't have to do anything. That way, you can honestly say you didn't know what happened."

Bobby looked up at the man and shook his head. He knew now that his father had hired someone to poison the tree. That someone was probably the person on the other end of the burner phone in the desk drawer.

It was the same person who blackmailed and kidnapped Alice. Now his father was dead. To collect the four billion dollars, Bobby would have to finish what his father had started.

All for one stupid tree.

Bobby removed the manila envelope from the top drawer and set it on the desk, the tree's picture clipped to the outside. Looking up at Knox, he slid the envelope across the desk.

Carter picked up the envelope and studied the picture. He removed it and held it up. "Is this the tree? And the location?"

"I assume it's the tree, but I've never seen it or the picture. The coordinates match what Daddy wrote on the envelope."

Carter looked down at the handwriting on the outside of the envelope and then at Bobby. "Robert's handwriting, alright. What's in the envelope?"

Bobby held his hand out, palm up, indicating for Carter to look for himself.

Carter looked down at the envelope he was holding, and for a minute, seemed to consider the invitation. Then, he shook his head. "Nothing I need to know."

He unclipped the picture, turned it over, and copied the coordinates down on the back. He stuck the picture in his pocket, placed the envelope back on the desk, and slid it over to Bobby.

"I'll see you Monday," Carter said as he turned and walked out.

46

As he drove to the lab, Justin couldn't get the name out of his head. Timmy Carver. He knew he'd never heard the name before. Alice didn't know it, and neither did Bobby. But it was like an earworm, nagging at him.

His conversation with Bobby got him thinking about Alice's parents. All he knew was what she'd told him when they'd first started dating.

According to her, they'd both died in a small plane crash in Colorado in 2009, the year he met her. He didn't recall what kind of plane, if she'd ever mentioned it, but he was sure of the year and the state.

Justin understood what it was like to lose both parents. His father's life ended early, but mercifully, when he died of a stroke on the road in a dingy nightclub outside of Cleveland, Ohio, with a glass of whiskey in one hand and a cigarette in the other. Three years later, he buried his mother, who lost her fight with breast cancer.

When he got to his desk, he opened up the browser on his computer and searched for general aviation accidents.

The first hit was AOPA, the Aircraft Owners and Pilots Association website. It listed a searchable accident database. He clicked on it and plugged in the parameters for fatal private plane crashes in Colorado in 2009. Only ten were listed.

Justin read each of the reports. None met the criteria for Alice's parents, such as names, ages, number of people on board, etc.

He sat back in his chair, tapping his pencil on the desk. He checked the year before and the year after. Similar results—nothing that fit. Alice's parents didn't die in a plane crash in Colorado.

Justin called Hadley to make sure he was in his office. The professor answered and told him he'd be there until four.

"How's the leg?" Hadley asked when Justin limped in and collapsed in the chair in front of his desk.

"Good, thanks. Trying to stay off of it as much as I can for a few days."

"Quite a turnout at the funeral. Bobby seems to be doing well, considering."

Justin nodded. "I stopped by the house on my way here. He's okay."

"That was quite a balls-up last week. What happened?"

Justin told him about the events leading up to Robert's death, including Robert's comment that it was too late to save the tree.

"It's still unscathed, I trust?"

"Yes, it's fine. The Cherokee are keeping a close eye on it. Robert tried to convince Bobby and Alice that he wanted to protect the tree."

"What do you think?"

"The same that I always have—Robert Kendall wanted to destroy the tree."

"And Bobby?"

Justin exhaled. "He swears his father wanted to protect it. I'm not sure, though. I don't trust him. He told me he agrees the tree belongs to the Cherokee, and he wants nothing further to do with it. All he asks is that the lab not be involved and that no one goes public with any information about it before the Bearant acquisition closes."

"Reasonable enough."

"Maybe, but I won't relax until after the deal is complete."

"I agree, but I'm not sure what else we can do at this point. You said the Cherokee are watching it."

Justin nodded.

"Let's keep our fingers crossed."

That evening, at home, Justin sat at the kitchen table as Alice cleaned up after dinner.

"I feel bad about not helping," he said.

Alice shook her head and chuckled. "You need to take it easy on your leg. I know you're not doing that at work."

"That's for sure. I saw Bobby today. I stopped by his father's house. He was going through his dad's things."

"How's he doing?"

"Okay. It felt strange being back there. Bobby told me one of the guests at the funeral was from Colorado. In chatting with them, he told them you were from Colorado also, but he couldn't remember where."

Alice dropped a glass on the floor. "Dammit. Clumsy me."

She went to the pantry and got the broom and dustpan. As she was sweeping, Justin continued.

"I told him, Montrose, out in the western part of the state. He asked if you still had relatives there."

She shook her head. "No. You know I was an only child, as were both my parents."

"I remember. I've never been to Colorado. One day, I'd like for us to go out there. I'd like to see where you grew up."

"After what happened, I wanted to get as far from there as possible. A fresh start."

"I understand. I remember you told me it was a private plane, but you never said exactly what happened."

Dropping her head, she said, "It's still hard to talk about it. They were flying back from Durango, where they'd spent the weekend. I was supposed to go, but I had a school play rehearsal."

"Your father was a pilot?"

She nodded. "Experienced and careful. He was a part-owner of the plane. The weather was iffy. The official explanation was they got disoriented and flew into a mountain." Her eyes became moist.

Thinking she was going to cry, Justin reached over and took her hand, pulling her close to him.

"I'm sorry," he said. "I didn't mean to resurrect unpleasant memories."

"I've never gone back there. I never want to, either," she said, hugging him.

"Forget it," he said. "I shouldn't have said anything." He felt terrible for bringing it up.

They moved to the living room, where Alice sat in her chair and picked up the book she was reading.

"Will it bother you if I put on some music?" he asked, nodding toward the turntable.

She shook her head. "No. I want to read a while before I turn in. Go ahead."

In Justin's mind, there was nothing like the sound of vinyl for recorded music. He could care less about cars and other toys. Music was his priority. He'd spent more on his Yamaha piano than some people spend on a car, and his stereo system had set him back thousands of dollars.

He switched on the amplifier and turntable, then thumbed through his selection of vinyl. He was searching for Oscar Peterson's *Night Train,* one of his favorites. As he placed the album on the turntable and gently lowered the cartridge, he wondered why Alice was lying about her parents.

What else was she hiding?

47

At work the next morning, Justin's phone buzzed. It was Atohi. "What's up?" Justin said when he answered.

"Where are you?" Atohi asked.

"At the lab. Why?"

"I'm sending you some pics. Call me back when you've seen them," Atohi said, then disconnected.

A few minutes later, Justin's phone dinged. He pulled up the message from Atohi and scrolled through the pictures.

At first, he wasn't sure what he was seeing. It was a tree lying on its side. He zoomed in to get a closer look. In disbelief, he recognized it as the healing tree.

The tree had been chopped down, severed at the base, apparently with an ax. In shock, he scrolled through the photos again, shaking his head.

His hand trembling, he called Atohi.

When his friend answered, Justin said, "What happened?"

"One of my guys was camped out at campsite 47. He checked on the tree yesterday afternoon, and it was fine. No sign of anyone being there. This morning, he went to check, and that's what he found. As soon as he got out to where he had cell service, he texted me the pictures."

Justin got up and started toward Hadley's office, still talking as he walked.

"How soon can you get people out there? We need to retrieve as much of it as we can as quickly as possible."

"I can probably round up two or three people in an hour. It'll take another hour for us to get to the site. What do you want us to do?"

"Get as many volunteers as you can. I'm on my way to Hadley's office. Call me as soon as you leave, and I'll let you know."

When he got to Hadley's office, the professor was at his computer, his back to the door. For once, Justin didn't even consider knocking.

"We've got a problem," he said when he walked in, startling the professor.

Hadley turned around in his chair.

"Someone cut the tree down," Justin said.

A look of alarm spread across Hadley's face.

"When?"

"This morning." He showed Hadley the pictures and relayed what Atohi had told him.

"I've got a crew on their way to salvage as much as we can get out."

"We need to keep the branches—"

"Cool and damp, out of direct sunlight," Justin said, finishing Hadley's sentence. He looked out Hadley's window. At least it was overcast today. That would help.

"Keeping it in as few pieces as possible will reduce the trauma," Hadley said.

"Damn. It's a hard, hour-long hike on steep terrain from the nearest road, just to get to it. We won't be able to bring out large pieces. Too heavy and too unwieldy."

"In that case, I'd suggest cutting as many three or four-foot-long pieces of the younger branches as they can carry out. Wrapping the cut ends to keep them damp would help. We've got to try to root as many branches as we can."

While Justin was glad it was late fall, that also posed another problem. Winter was coming.

"We need a greenhouse," Justin said.

"I know, but we can't bring it here."

Justin nodded, understanding. He thought back to his conversation with Bobby. For a variety of reasons, this had to be entirely off the books, unrelated to Nuran in any way.

Back at his desk, he called Atohi.

Atohi answered on the first ring. "I was just about to call you. I'm picking up three guys, and we're heading to the trailhead. What's the plan?"

Justin told him they needed to root as many branches as possible to start new trees.

"Keep the cut ends moist if you can. We need a greenhouse. You don't happen to know where we can find one we can use, do you?"

"Maybe. I'll check."

"Remember, as much as you can carry out. No shorter than three to four-foot pieces. I'd just slow you down with my leg, so I'll go round up some supplies. We're going to need pots, plant hormone, and seedling mix."

Justin wrapped up things at the lab, then went by the garden center. He picked up as much as he could stuff into the 4Runner. He was on his way home when Atohi called.

"We just got back to the trailhead. I found a small greenhouse. It's in the Qualla, down near the hatchery. We're on our way," Atohi said.

"Perfect. I've got a truck full of supplies. I'll meet you there."

Justin called Alice but got her voicemail. He left a message, telling her he was meeting Atohi and would be late getting home. He'd explain later.

When he got to the greenhouse, there were probably a dozen people there, including Tsula and her mother. He recognized many of the same faces that had helped him look for Alice in Cataloochee.

The tribe had once used the greenhouse for plants in the Qualla parks and roadways. Since they built a larger one a few miles away last year, this one was vacant. A stroke of luck, Justin thought. They needed every break they could get.

He tried to pick up a bag of plant mix, but his leg almost gave way. He still couldn't put any extra weight on it, so he resigned himself to ferrying empty trays and pots, a few at a time.

He felt helpless as he watched Mary take charge, direct traffic, and set up an assembly line to process the cuttings. Not only did he feel responsible for the tree's destruction, but he was unable to contribute in a meaningful way to the rescue effort.

Two people combined seedling mix and potting soil and filled garden trays with the mixture. The second team clipped off the end of each cutting, brushing plant hormone on the wound and then inserting it into the container. When a tray was full, someone else would take it over to the stands. Another person followed behind, watering them.

Even though he couldn't help with the manual labor, Justin felt compelled to stay, tallying the results. They finished around midnight, having prepared a total of forty-eight plants. Everyone was exhausted. Mary thanked everyone and told them to go home and get some sleep.

"We've done all we can, Justin," she said after all the workers had left.

He shook his head. "I've let you down."

Justin thought about his encounter with Robert Kendall. Since nothing had happened in the days following, and Atohi's brothers were watching the tree, he'd become complacent. He should've known better. He'd been right—Robert Kendall had intended to destroy the healing tree, and he succeeded.

"Don't be silly. It wasn't your fault," Mary said.

He shook his head, angry at himself. "It is. I let my guard down. I should've done something."

"Nonsense," Mary said. "Stop it."

"Come by the house and have a beer," Atohi said.

"I don't know," Justin said, looking at his watch. "It's late."

"Alice is probably asleep," Tsula said. "We could all use one."

A cold beer would be good, Justin thought. "Maybe one."

They all met up at Atohi and Tsula's. One beer turned into two. Even though he hadn't done much manual labor, Justin was mentally exhausted.

"So how did they find it?" Atohi said. "Do you still think it was Robert Kendall?"

Justin nodded. "Oh, yeah. The night . . . the night he got shot. Right before it happened, he said it was too late. How he got the location, I don't know yet."

"At least we were lucky to discover it as soon as we did," Mary said. "Another few days, and it would've been too late. We've done everything we can. All we can do is take care of the little ones and hope for the best."

"How many trees do you think will make it?" Justin asked.

Mary shrugged. "Not having rooted the healing tree before, I don't know what to expect. Typically, a high percentage of fresh cuttings, properly prepared, will grow roots. We'll know in 3-4 weeks."

"Then what?" Atohi asked.

"Then we plant them outside, in the ground as soon as the danger of frost is past. That's probably when we'll lose some, maybe thirty percent or so. The last step is to plant them in their native environment. That's when we'll lose the most. If we're lucky, maybe twenty percent of those seedlings will make it to maturity."

Justin's tired brain did the math. The result was a number he could count on his two hands with fingers left over. His stomach churned, and he felt sick. "I need to go. I wish I could've done more."

When he got home, he was surprised to see the lights on in the living room. Alice's car was in its usual spot.

The front door was unlocked. He opened it and saw Alice, asleep on the sofa.

She stirred, hearing his footsteps.

"Hey," she said, stretching. "What time is it?"

"After midnight."

"Where have you been? Is everything okay?" she said, sitting.

He shook his head. "No, it's not. Someone chopped down the healing tree."

"Justin, no. What happened?" she said, suddenly awake.

"Kendall succeeded. Someone knew where to find it and deliberately destroyed it," he said in an accusatory tone.

"Damn." She looked down, shaking her head. She looked back up at him. "I'm sorry. You were right."

He wanted to shout at her that yes, he was. But it was pointless. The damage was done.

He told her about Atohi's call that morning and their frantic effort to save as many cuttings from the tree as possible.

Alice cocked her head. "It happened last night?"

Justin nodded. "Atohi's had people watching it since last week. It was fine last night, but when his guy checked this morning, it was down. Atohi found a greenhouse on the Qualla. That's where we've been, planting cuttings, hoping they'll root."

"I wish you would've called me to come help."

He stared at her with no response. "Mary thinks we've got a good chance to save half of them since we recovered them so soon. I hope she's right."

"Can I get you anything? Did you eat?"

"I had a sandwich at the greenhouse. Tsula arranged for several of the women to bring some. I stopped at their house on the way home and had a beer. I was too keyed up to sleep."

"What can I do?"

"Nothing. I'm exhausted." He turned and went into the bedroom.

48

The next day at work, Alice was still fuzzy. Unable to sleep last night after Justin came home, she'd taken an Ambien. Taking it so late had been a mistake.

She felt guilty about the healing tree. Justin was devastated. He'd already left by the time she woke up and didn't bother to tell her goodbye.

He believed the Kendalls were the blame, but she knew better. She's the one who gave them the location, and now it was gone. Because of her.

She'd also been thinking about Justin's comments the night before. That was the first time he'd ever asked her anything about her parents.

Before she started seeing Justin, she'd met a girl who inadvertently planted the seed of a plane crash tragedy. The girl, an only child, had lost both of her parents the year before in a private plane crash in New Orleans.

It was the perfect solution to Alice's dilemma of explaining why she wasn't communicating with her parents. New Orleans was too close and too populated. She needed somewhere far from North Carolina and more remote. She'd once skied in Telluride and flown into Montrose, so she chose western Colorado.

Rhonda stuck her head inside the door, interrupting Alice's thoughts.

"You okay this morning? You look like you're half asleep."

Alice held up her coffee.

"Didn't sleep well last night. I just need to get the caffeine flowing."

"Debra Foster called. She's in town and wanted to come by and touch base with you about the closing. You didn't have anything on your calendar, so I told her to stop by this morning."

Alice nodded. "That's fine. Thanks." How fitting. Debra from Indianapolis was back.

An hour later, Alice saw Debra walk into the lobby toward Rhonda's desk. She wore a short, lowcut sundress as though she'd just come from a garden party. Through her open door, Alice could hear Debra's heels clicking on the tile floor. She took a deep breath and waved Debra back.

The blonde strode confidently into Alice's office, wearing a big grin and carrying a large dark blue book of some sort.

"Hi, Debra."

"Good morning, Alice," she said, emphasizing *Alice*. She closed the door as she sat, the book face down in her lap.

Alice looked at her, wondering what that was about.

"Well, thanks for stopping by," Alice said. "Everything is in order. We received the appraisal and the inspection report. Both looked good. You'll get copies at the closing. Based on the appraisal, I'd say you got a great deal on the house. I'll get everything over to the attorney's office this afternoon. I understand the closing is set for the day after tomorrow?"

Debra nodded. "That's correct. We are so excited. Brad is driving down for the closing. We plan on spending the weekend in our new house. Of course, it needs quite a bit of renovation, and we'll have to do some furniture shopping, but it'll suffice for now."

Alice smiled. She'd seen the house pictures in the appraisal and knew they were purchasing it fully furnished. Contrary to Debra's intimation, the house had been professionally decorated and was immaculate in every way.

"That's great. You're going to love this area. I'm so glad we could help you with the mortgage. We certainly appreciate your business." Alice made a point of looking at the clock on her desk. "Do you have any other questions?"

"Just one."

Debra flipped the book over and set it on Alice's desk with the cover facing up.

Alice was horrified when she saw what it was. It was a high school yearbook. 2009. The year Alice graduated, as Payten Thomas. From Carmel High School in Carmel, Indiana. She looked up at Debra, who was sporting that same obnoxious grin she had when she walked in.

"I knew I recognized you, although you do look a lot different. All for the better, I might add, *Payten.* Not sure why you changed your name. But I don't care. None of my business. We all have skeletons."

Debra picked up the yearbook and stood.

"I just wanted you to know that I knew. But not to worry. Your secret's safe with me."

With that, Debra wheeled and walked out.

Damn, Alice thought, her hand shaking as she picked up her coffee. First, Justin, now this. What the hell was going on? Was her karma catching up?

She took a deep breath, trying not to be paranoid. Just coincidence, nothing more. Debra was just being herself— an arrogant bitch.

Alice had never liked her much in high school. Debra was the debutante, blonde cheerleader. Miss Popularity. Alice never understood why Debra had befriended her all those years ago. Alice—Payten at the time—hadn't posed any competition.

Debra calling her out was unnerving. What could Debra have to gain by exposing her? Like she said, *we all have skeletons.* Alice guessed that Debra probably had plenty of her own, but would that keep her from making trouble?

Alice had her doubts.

49

At the lab, Justin went straight to Hadley's office after getting his morning coffee.

"Morning," Justin said as he limped in and plopped in the chair in front of Hadley's desk.

"You look like you didn't get much sleep," the professor said. "What's going on?"

"We spent yesterday evening planting cuttings in a greenhouse. In the Qualla. We finished after midnight. Thanks to Atohi and his friends, we ended up with forty-eight cuttings."

"Excellent."

"Mary thinks we'll be lucky if ten of them make it in the wild."

Hadley nodded. "Sounds about right. Maybe a little better since they were fresh and properly prepared. A greenhouse is also in our favor. Better environmental control and monitoring."

"I screwed up," Justin said, his head hanging low. He blamed himself. Trusting Bobby had been a mistake. "I'm going to talk to Bobby," he said, looking up. "I want to find out how they knew where it was."

Hadley shook his head. "I don't think that's a good idea. The damage is done, and we did what we could. Let me talk to Bobby first. I'll tell him that the tree is gone. Since there are eyes everywhere, we need to let the world know the tree is gone, but we need to keep the greenhouse under wraps."

Justin nodded. "You're right. The fact that the greenhouse is in the Qualla is good. Atohi plans to have eyes on it 24/7."

"Tell no one about the cuttings. Especially Bobby Kendall."

"I told Alice last night. I was tired and not thinking."

Hadley stroked his beard. "Forgive me for asking, but can you trust her?"

Justin considered the question, the same one he'd been pondering. It dawned on him. Both Alice and Bobby had denied Alice gave up the location. The problem was, how did Alice know? She'd been there, but giving directions to the tree versus taking someone to it were very different things. He remembered the second time he went, Alice had to remind him where they left the trail.

"Something doesn't add up," Justin said.

Hadley wrinkled his brow. "What?"

"How did Alice know the exact location? Think about it. The tree was off-trail in a remote area of the Park. I couldn't even find it myself the second time I went out there. How would you describe how to find it? I couldn't. Not without—"

Justin pulled out his phone and pulled up his hiking app where he'd saved the tree's location and picture. He looked up at Hadley and smiled. "Not without precise coordinates." He held his phone out so the professor could see the screen.

The professor's eyes lit up. "Simple latitude and longitude. Who else has the coordinates?"

Justin thought. "Besides me, Sam Bear. The surveyor. That's why someone broke into his office for a copy of the survey, but they didn't get it." He pointed to the professor's file cabinet. "And you never had the location. The Kendalls were pursuing Alice for the location. Why?"

"The current risk is the greenhouse. We want everyone to believe the tree is history. Call Alice and remind her not to mention it to anyone. I meant to ask yesterday, do we have any samples here at the lab?"

"A small batch I made up with the last material I had. That's it. It's labeled HT67 and in the back of the refrigerator."

"Replace the label with something different, something that doesn't indicate what it is. I'll talk with Bobby."

Justin rose to leave. "I'm on it."

Back at his desk, Justin changed the label on the last sample of HT67. He held it up and stared at it. This was the last for a while unless someone could find another tree. With everything going on, he realized he needed to check on Karen.

"Hey, how are you feeling?" he asked when she answered.

"Good. I had my appointment with Dr. Stewart yesterday. All my test results look good. If he's happy, I'm happy."

Thank God, he thought. He wasn't going to tell her about the tree. "Great news. A lot going on at the lab, so I'm not sure if we'll be able to make it over this weekend. I'll call."

Later that afternoon, Justin was working at his desk when Hadley stopped by.

"I met with Bobby," Hadley said. "When I told him someone had destroyed the tree, he reacted with genuine surprise. I don't think he knew, but at this point, we shouldn't trust him."

Justin nodded. "I'll try to meet him for a beer later and see what he tells me."

An hour later, Justin hobbled into Frog Level and made his way to the bar, looking for Bobby. He'd called Bobby and asked to meet him there.

"Good to see you," Mary Ann said from behind the bar. "You doing okay?"

"Alright. I'll be glad when I get rid of the limp and can go hiking."

"Are you supposed to be driving? Putting weight on it?" she asked.

He shook his head. "You're the third person today to ask me that. It's my left leg—I can drive an automatic."

She laughed. "Bobby's outside. Go on out and sit. I'll bring your beer."

"Thanks."

His leg was sore, and he was thankful that there were only a couple of steps up to the back deck. He was glad to see Bobby sitting to his left just outside the door.

"I sat up here so you wouldn't have to negotiate all the steps down to the creek," Bobby said.

"Thanks. Stairs are a pain in the ass." Justin sat on the bench across from him.

"Your leg doing okay?" Bobby asked.

"A little sore. I probably didn't rest it enough yesterday."

Mary Ann appeared with two beers and set them on the table. "I'll check on you in a bit."

"I wasn't expecting to have a beer with you this soon," Bobby said. "Hadley told me the bad news. What happened?"

Justin pulled up the pictures on his phone and slid it over to Bobby.

Bobby scrolled through the pictures, then looked up. "What's this?"

Justin glared at him. "It's what's left of the healing tree. Someone cut it down. Sometime between late Wednesday afternoon and early yesterday morning."

Bobby looked down at the pictures again, then shook his head. "Jesus. Sorry, I didn't know what it was. I've never seen it."

Justin stared at his friend. "You sure?"

Bobby narrowed his eyes at the accusation. "What are you saying?"

"Somebody knew what it was. And, where it was."

"Are you saying it was my father?" Bobby bristled.

"You were there when I confronted him. He practically admitted it. You asked Alice."

"I told you. Before you came over that night, he told me he wanted to protect—"

"Bullshit," Justin said. "His intention all along was to destroy the tree. He gave the location to someone who killed it."

"If he did, I don't know anything about it. What are you going to do?"

Justin shook his head. "Look at the pictures. Nothing to do. The tree's gone. And with it, any chance of finding out what secrets it contained."

"Don't you have some samples or stuff at the lab?"

"Nothing. I used everything with Karen."

Justin didn't tell him that about the single vial secreted in the lab. As Hadley had requested, he'd changed the label to MN21, for *means nothing* and his lucky number. Only Hadley knew.

"What can I do?"

"Help me find another tree."

"I wish I could."

"Do you?" Justin stared at him, waiting for a response.

When none was forthcoming, Justin said, "That tree saved Karen's life—for now. And, it could've saved many others. But Bearant should be happy. When's the closing?"

Bobby shifted in his seat and took a drink. "Monday morning. We have a company meeting scheduled afterward to announce it." He exhaled and said, "You might as well know. Bearant's consolidating everything at their main campus in Cupertino. But you don't have anything to worry about. They've agreed to retain you and Hadley."

"In California. How nice. What about the others?"

"Most everybody will be offered jobs."

"*Most* everybody. But not here in North Carolina. And, you?"

Bobby shook his head. "They don't need me. I don't know anything about running a research lab. That was Daddy's dream, not mine. Bearant got what they wanted."

"And so did you, right?"

He shrugged. "I suppose. I get money, but that won't bring him back. Damn, Justin. I didn't want this."

"Yeah, well, a few billion dollars should ease your pain."

Justin finished his beer and stood. "I'm outta here. You can settle with Mary Ann. The least you can do is buy me a beer."

50

Saturday morning, Justin woke up to the smell of breakfast cooking. He looked to his side, and Alice was missing. After his customary morning bathroom stop, he went into the kitchen. Alice had her back to him, cooking.

"Smells good," he said.

Turning, Alice said, "Almost done. Have a seat, and I'll get you some coffee."

She poured him a cup, then plated their food. She set the plates on the bar and joined him.

"Thanks for cooking," he said as they ate, breaking the silence.

"I was exhausted last night. I took an Ambien and was out before you got home."

"I had a couple of beers with Bobby."

"I'm sorry about the tree," she said, setting her fork down. "At least you've got the greenhouse."

Justin stared at her. Hard, looking for some indication of duplicity. "It is what it is." He finished his last bite and moved the plate aside. "I want to see the tree. What's left of it."

She looked at him questioningly. "I'd like to go with you. If you don't mind."

He shrugged. "If you want." They cleaned up the kitchen and then drove out to the Park.

When Justin and Alice got to the trailhead, no one else was there. It was evident that there had been recent traffic, though. Fresh tracks and ruts crisscrossed the tiny parking area.

They put their daypacks on and started up the trail. Justin's leg felt good, and he was faster than he anticipated. They stopped for a break at the junction before heading down the Enloe Creek Trail toward the tree.

"You've been quiet this morning," Alice said.

"A lot on my mind. Just trying to figure out how." He took another swallow of water, then stood.

"How what?"

He turned and looked into her eyes, trying to discern what lay behind them. "Think about it. Robert Kendall was the who, but how? How would you tell somebody how to find this place?"

Alice pondered his question, appearing confused as to what Justin was getting at.

"Ready?" he said, heading down the trail.

As soon as they rounded the last bend before the spot where they'd leave the trail, Justin stopped and shook his head. Atohi's crew had trampled the underbrush leading from the healing tree, carrying out the pieces. The sight broke his heart.

Alice said, "This was such a pretty area. And now, look."

Justin's eyes watered, and his throat caught. He wasn't sure he could trust himself to speak. "I want to see it," he said in a hoarse whisper, starting down the hill following the path of destruction.

When they got to the healing tree, he froze and gasped. The dismembered tree lay in the clearing like a mutilated body, stripped of its branches and foliage, discarded like yesterday's rubbish. The cathedral in the woods had been desecrated.

A bluish flower alongside the tree had somehow survived the carnage. He stooped to pick it up and gently held it in his hand, tears sliding down his cheeks. He understood why the Cherokee had named it the healing tree. It represented more than just his sister's cure. Who knew how many lives it had saved for the Cherokee? How many future lives could it have saved? He was responsible for its murder. The thought punched a gaping hole in his heart.

"This is depressing," Alice finally said.

Justin nodded. "I had to see it for myself."

"Do you think there are others?"

"I want to believe there are. This tree represents all the things out there that we don't know or understand. But will anyone ever find them? I can only hope. Seeing this makes me more determined to unlock the secrets of the healing tree, but I don't know how."

"Don't you have more of the extract in the lab?" Alice asked.

Justin shook his head. "No. Besides, Bobby told me they're going to announce the Bearant deal Monday morning at the lab. They're moving everything to California."

"Oh, my God. They're closing the lab?"

"Not surprising. Bearant didn't want the lab. They wanted Tramorix. Bobby said that Hadley and I have a job. In California."

"California? We'd have to move to California?"

Justin nodded. "If I want to keep working for Bearant— which I doubt." He turned around to leave.

On the way home, Tsula called Alice and invited them to dinner. When they got to Atohi and Tsula's, they were surprised to see Mary Richardson's car.

"This is a nice surprise," Justin said when they walked in.

"I hope you don't mind me crashing the party," Mary said as she walked over to hug them.

"Always good to see you," Justin said.

"Your timing was perfect. We've got a salad, roast venison, and corn. I hope you're hungry," Tsula said as they sat at the dining room table.

"How was your hike?" Atohi asked.

Justin shook his head, unable to speak for a moment as he recalled seeing the tree. "It was good to be back out in the woods. The leg did better than I expected, although I'll probably be stiff tomorrow."

He choked up as he continued. "The sight of the tree—what was left—was depressing. It made me realize what it represented—for all of us," Justin said, looking at Mary. "I'm sorry. It gives me a small bitter taste of the pain that your people have experienced. I'm sorry I didn't keep this from happening."

"You did what you needed to—you needed to save your sister," Mary said. "And, thanks to your discovery of its properties, we have a greenhouse full of hope."

"Maybe," Justin said. He looked at each of them before continuing. "Bearant's closing the lab."

"Why?" Atohi asked, stunned. "I thought they wanted Nuran."

"They wanted Tramorix. They're closing the lab and moving everything to Silicon Valley."

"Oh my God," Tsula said, looking at Alice. "Does everything mean you, too?"

Alice shook her head. "He just told me this while we were hiking. I haven't had a chance to digest it yet."

"I just found out from Bobby," Justin said. "According to him, Hadley and I have jobs—in California."

"California. What do you think about that?" Atohi asked.

"I don't know, other than I don't want to move, and I don't want to work for Bearant."

"When?" Mary asked.

"Not sure. They're making the announcement Monday morning."

51

C lose to noon on Monday, Bobby Kendall stopped by the bank where Alice worked. Inside, he stopped at Rhonda's desk. Over her shoulder, he could see Alice on the phone in her office, her back to the door.

"Hey, Rhonda. How are you?"

"I'm good, thanks. What are you doing here, Bobby?"

"I was out this way and thought I'd stop by to say hi. I see she's on the phone. I'll just stick my head in the door."

As he walked over, Alice was hanging up. She turned around, surprised to see him.

"What are you doing here?" she said, her face flushed in anger. "Looking for someplace to stash all your money?"

"I guess Justin told you the news. Is he okay?"

Alice crossed her arms, her eyes ablaze. "Yeah, he's fine. The tree's gone, the lab's closing, and he's out of a job. What could be better?"

"He's not out of a job."

"Right. He has one. With Bearant. In California. Where neither of us wants to go. Excuse me, but I've got work to do."

Alice reached for her phone, then Bobby leaned over and whispered, "We need to talk. Alone. Now." When she hesitated, he repeated his demand and added, "I'm going to ask you to lunch, and you're going to accept."

He straightened and said, loud enough for Rhonda to hear, "It's almost lunchtime. Want to get a quick bite? My treat?"

Alice glared at him, not answering. He set his jaw and cocked his head, returning the look.

"Uh, yeah, sure," Alice said, also loud enough for Rhonda to hear. "I need to make a stop first."

Bobby turned and walked out to Rhonda's desk while Alice went to the restroom.

"I didn't realize it was so close to noon. I offered to take your boss to lunch, so we're going to grab something quick."

Alice reappeared, and as they walked outside, Bobby pointed to his car and said, "I'll drive."

When she hesitated, Bobby held his hands out, palms up. "Just a quick bite at Ammons. We'll stay in the car and come straight back. That's it." Ammons was a locally owned drive-in restaurant that had been a Waynesville hangout for years, still offering curb service.

"What do you want?" Alice said as she got in his car, sitting as close to the door as she could get.

He retrieved a manila envelope from next to his seat and handed it to Alice while he drove.

The name Timmy Carver and map coordinates had been written on the outside. Alice recognized the location as the one she'd given Bobby for the tree. She opened the envelope and removed the contents. She was surprised to see the same picture and article the kidnapper had sent her.

She stared at the picture, then pretended to read the article. When she finished, she said in a measured voice, "I don't understand."

"I think you do, *Alice,*" he said as they pulled into Ammons and parked. He turned to face her.

"I found it in Daddy's desk. You were the hit-and-run driver, weren't you?"

Alice's eyes widened. "What makes you think—"

"I know you were. But Justin doesn't know, does he?"

She couldn't hold his gaze. "I don't know what you're talking about."

She looked back down at the newspaper article, picked it up, and waved it at Bobby.

"This is something that happened in Indianapolis ten years ago. I've never been there. I was in Colorado then. Take me back to the bank. Now, please."

Bobby shook his head. "Who said anything about Indianapolis?"

"The article said . . ." Her voice trailed off as she looked back at it.

"The article mentioned Carmel but nothing about Indianapolis. I blacked out the name of the newspaper. Only somebody familiar with the area would know that Carmel is a suburb north of Indianapolis."

Alice tried to speak, but only a pitiful squeak emerged.

"You didn't grow up in Colorado, did you?" he said. He pointed to the newspaper article. "We both know who Timmy Carver is. You were the driver. And Justin doesn't know, does he?"

Alice's mouth opened, but no words came out. Tears started to roll down her cheek.

"Bobby . . . you can't tell him. It'll destroy him." Alice sat back in her seat, staring out the windshield. "What are you going to do?"

After a few minutes of silence, he reached over and placed his hand on her bare leg, just below the hem of her skirt.

Alice flinched and turned to face him.

"It depends," he said.

She looked down at his hand on her leg and placed hers over his. She picked up his hand and dropped it back in his lap.

"I'll tell him myself first. Everything."

He snickered. "Go ahead. We'll see how that goes. Like you said, Justin has a hard time forgiving."

"He does, but he deserves better than you. Or me."

"Suit yourself." He looked down at the papers in her lap. "You can keep those. I have copies. Except for mine has the name of the newspaper."

Calmly, she put the papers back inside the envelope.

"Fuck you, Bobby. And, I don't mean literally."

"I'll give you a few days to think about it," he said as he started the car and drove away.

Alice couldn't stay focused back in her office, looking at the envelope Bobby had given her. Her world was crumbling around her. Justin suspected that her parents didn't die in a plane crash in Colorado. Why else would he be asking questions the other night?

Then, that bitch Debra Hunt Foster showed up with the high school yearbook from Carmel High School. She knew who Alice was. Debra's words echoed in her head.

We all have skeletons. Your secret's safe with me.

Alice didn't trust Debra then, and she surely didn't trust her now.

Wednesday night, someone killed the healing tree. Justin was devastated. And now the lab was closing, and he didn't have a job unless he wanted to move to California and work for Bearant.

The tree coordinates written on Bobby's envelope made her think. She gave the kidnapper the location last Thursday, and he confirmed it was accurate. Yet, the tree wasn't destroyed until a week later, *after* she'd given Bobby the location. Why didn't the kidnapper kill it when he was there? Something didn't make sense.

A shiver went down her spine when she thought of that creep Bobby's hand on her leg. He had the same information that his father had used to blackmail her. Now he was blackmailing her, wanting her to sleep with him.

Her past was catching up. For the first time since the accident, she didn't see a way out. Her skeletons were going to come crashing out of the closet for everyone to see.

When she got home, she found a message from Justin. He was going to work at the greenhouse with Atohi and would be home later.

She set the note down on the bar. She briefly considered calling and asking if she could help but decided she couldn't face him.

All afternoon, she'd tried to craft different scenarios for telling him. She was unable to come up with words she believed would work. How long did she have before her lies would bury her? Maybe she should do nothing and wait for the first brick to fall?

She opened the cabinet to get a glass and saw Justin's bourbon on the top shelf. Blanton's. She always liked the cute stopper.

In high school, bourbon had been her drink of choice. Nothing as fancy as Blanton's. Back then, it was Evan Williams. Her crowd mixed it with Coke. That's what she'd been drinking the night of the accident.

She reached up and gently took the half-full bottle off the shelf, caressing it before setting it on the counter in front of her.

Open me, it called.

What could smelling it hurt, she thought. She hesitated, then took the stopper out. As soon as she did, she caught a whiff of the unmistakable aroma of bourbon.

Slowly, she leaned over and closed her eyes, inhaling the intoxicating perfume. Vanilla and oak, she detected, surrounded by citrus and spices. Maybe that's what she needed to confront Justin. Liquid courage.

She took out a rocks glass and poured two fingers' worth. She added a couple of ice cubes, the way she'd seen Justin drink it. Bringing the glass up to her nose, she shut her eyes and inhaled. Sweetness. Smiling, she took a sip.

Alice winced and opened her eyes. It was the first alcohol she had tasted in ten years, and it was harsh. Then, the slow burn down her throat turned into a caressing warmth.

An hour later, she could barely walk. She'd lost count of how many drinks she'd had, but the bottle was almost empty. After the first drink, she was fortified and ready to talk with Justin. As time wore on, and he hadn't shown, she began to get weepy.

That asshole Bobby was right. Justin would never understand. While he might forgive her mistake, he'd never forgive her lying to him. Her web of lies was going to strangle her.

Maybe she should take Bobby up on his offer. But the thought of sleeping with him repulsed her. She wasn't sure which was worse—confronting Justin about her past or screwing his best friend. Both horrified her.

She made her way into the bathroom to find some aspirin. She recalled taking a couple on nights when she was drinking as an old standby to prevent hangovers.

When she opened the medicine cabinet, the small, orange plastic bottle of Ambien stared at her. Just like the bourbon, it beckoned.

Her hand felt like it belonged to someone else as it reached up for the pills. She watched, detached, as her fingers wrapped around the container and removed it from the shelf.

The name on the label mocked her. Payten Thomas. *Impossible,* she thought. She closed her eyes, shook her head, and reopened them. Alice Miller, the label read.

She struggled with the childproof cap and finally prevailed. Tossing it aside, she examined the contents.

Staring up at her, the dozen or so orange, round tablets inside looked like candy.

Alice downed the rest of her whiskey and filled the glass with water. Sleep was now calling. Things would be better in the morning, and she would have answers. She emptied the pill bottle into her hand. Two at a time, she swallowed every one of them, chasing them with water.

She'd nap until Justin got home. She staggered back out into the living room and collapsed onto the couch. Knowing things would work out, she lay back and closed her eyes.

52

Two funerals in as many weeks. Justin's mother always said bad things came in threes. He hoped to hell she was wrong. He wasn't sure he could handle a third.

Karen sat next to him, holding his hand. He'd tried to dissuade her from coming, but she insisted, even though her immune system was still not fully recovered.

Atohi and Tsula sat on his other side, Atohi's arm around him. Mary sat next to her daughter. Dr. Hadley and Bobby sat behind him.

Almost a week later, Justin was still numb. When he'd got home last Monday night, Alice was asleep on the couch. Or so he thought. When he tried to wake her, she was cold and not breathing. He called 911 and then started to administer CPR before he realized it was too late. She was already gone.

Alice's death had been ruled a suicide after the sheriff's office had found the empty pill bottle and the medical examiner had gotten the toxicology results back.

Feeling Karen's hand squeeze his brought him back to the present. The service was over, and they were leaving to go to the cemetery. Everyone was waiting for the family to go out first. She stood, still holding his hand, and in a daze, he rose.

The next thing he knew, he was sitting under the tent at the gravesite, staring at a coffin covered with flowers.

Alice's coffin. The priest had just finished his final remarks, and people were lining up to shake his hand and offer condolences.

He felt like a robot. Each person offered some variation of *we're so sorry for your loss*. He would respond with a nod and thank them for coming, then turn his attention to the next in line. It didn't matter how long the line was. He could've gone on forever—one after another.

A striking blonde, accompanied by a tall, sandy-haired man, stopped and extended her hand. "I'm so sorry for your loss," she said.

Justin looked at her but didn't recognize the face.

Sensing the confusion, the woman said, "I'm Debra Foster. This is my husband, Brad. We just bought a second home here in Maggie Valley. Alice helped us with the loan."

"So sorry," Brad said, shaking Justin's hand. "I didn't know her, but Debra and Alice went to the same high school."

"Thank you for coming," Justin said. As they started to walk away, Justin realized what Brad had said. The next person in line had already stepped forward.

Justin swiveled his head to see the couple walking away. "You went to high school with Alice?"

The blonde stopped, turned to face him, and nodded. Glancing beyond him at the line of people waiting to speak to him, she said, "Give me a call. Maybe we could have a cup of coffee sometime." With that, she turned and left.

"I'm so sorry," the woman standing in front of him said, leaning over to hug him. He recognized her as Rhonda, the receptionist from Alice's bank.

"Thank you, Rhonda. I know she thought a lot of you. Thank you so much for coming."

Rhonda separated from him, tears running down her cheeks. She nodded. "We're going to miss her. Let me know if we can do anything for you."

Justin turned his head to see Debra Foster fading in the distance and then looked back at Rhonda.

"That woman—Debra Foster. She said Alice helped her with a loan."

Rhonda nodded. "She did. I remember her. She stopped by the bank last week to see Alice."

"Can you get me her contact information? I wanted to thank her for the flowers. With everything going on, I neglected to get her phone number."

"I've got it at work. I'll call you in a few days."

"Thank you, Rhonda."

* * *

That evening at home, Justin reached out and took Karen's hand. "I keep thinking there was something I could've done. I should've known." A tear slid down his cheek.

Karen reached up and wiped it away. "It's not your fault. Nobody ever understands why something like this happens. But don't blame yourself."

He nodded. "Thanks for coming over this week. I don't know how I would've made it without you. I'm glad you're here, even though it probably wasn't a good idea."

Karen was seeing Dr. Stewart every two weeks. Her latest test results appeared to have leveled out. He was running more tests and another scan this week.

She squeezed his hand. "I'm feeling fine. You know how cautious Dr. Stewart is. He said my numbers weren't getting worse. They just weren't where he wanted them to be. He thinks it's a temporary plateau."

Justin thought about the only remaining vial of the extract and hoped Stewart was right. Karen was all he had left now. "You do need to be careful. Your immune system isn't a hundred percent yet, and won't be for some time."

"I am. He told me to avoid air travel and crowds for a while. I assured him neither was on my agenda."

He told her about Bearant buying Nuran and Alice's blackmail and kidnapping.

"Jesus, you didn't tell me any of this," she said.

"You were recuperating, and I didn't want you worried. I figured we'd catch up one day." He looked out the window. "I just didn't think it would be at Alice's funeral."

53

Monday morning, a week after Alice's funeral, Justin woke up and decided to go to the lab. He and Karen had spent the week around the house. She'd cooked for him and taken care of him while he grieved. But it would take longer than a week, and he needed to regain some sense of normalcy. Being at the lab might help him clear his head.

It didn't work. At his desk, Justin stared at the computer screen, thinking there was something he could've done to prevent Alice from killing herself. Some sign he missed, some action he could've taken.

A familiar voice interrupted his thoughts. "Hey, got a minute?"

Justin turned around to see Bobby Kendall standing in the doorway. "Come in."

Bobby came over and sat. "Good to see you. I heard you were in the building. How are you doing?"

"The truth? Shitty," Justin said. "My fiancée killed herself, and I keep thinking there was something I could've done to prevent it."

"There was nothing you could've done."

Justin snorted. "Yeah, keep telling me that. Congratulations, by the way. What's it like to be a billionaire?"

Bobby shrugged. "With everything going on, it hasn't sunk in yet."

"What are you going to do? Bearant talk you into staying with them?"

"No. I told you, it wasn't me they wanted. I'm thinking about buying Frog Level. You and I always talked about opening a brewery."

Justin nodded, disinterested.

Bobby continued. "I'm selling Daddy's house. His place is too big and too cold, much like him."

After another long pause, Bobby said, "Look, Justin, I want to try to make things right. I know I can't bring Alice back. Or the tree. That day when you told me the tree had been destroyed, I asked what I could do. You told me to help you find another tree. That's what I intend to do."

Expressionless, Justin looked at him without saying a word.

"I've set up a non-profit foundation to study traditional Cherokee medicine. It'll be managed and run by them," Bobby said.

The ensuing silence was awkward as Justin stared out the window.

Bobby stood. "I just wanted to check on you. Maybe we can get a beer sometime."

"Sure. Thanks."

Bobby turned and left. Justin's thoughts returned to Alice. In a fog, he heard his cell phone buzz. Without bothering to see who was calling, he answered.

"Hey, Justin. It's Rhonda—at the bank. How are you?"

"Managing, thank you. I came into the office for a bit." He started to add, *thinking it would help* but didn't bother.

"I was calling with that phone number you wanted. Debra Foster."

It took him a minute for the name to register, then he remembered. Rhonda recited the number, and he wrote it down.

"Thanks," he said, and before he could say goodbye, Rhonda added, "Also, I've boxed up Alice's office for you. I hope you don't mind."

Justin shook his head. "No, I appreciate it. With everything going on, I didn't even think about that. Maybe I'll stop by on my way home."

"I'll be here. Take care."

"Thanks, Rhonda."

He hung up and looked at the phone number Rhonda had given him. He didn't recognize the area code and dialed the number.

"This is Debra."

He recognized the voice from the funeral. "Hi, Debra. This is Justin Reeve. We met at the funeral."

"Of course. Again, I'm so sorry."

"Thank you. I appreciate you and your husband coming to the service. If you're still in town, I'd like to buy you a coffee sometime this week if it's convenient."

"Unfortunately, we're heading home after lunch. If you have time this morning, maybe?"

He wasn't getting anything done at the lab. "Yes, that's fine. Do you know where Panacea Coffee is?"

"No, I don't think so."

"It's in Waynesville, next to Frog Level Brewing."

She laughed. "Brad and I know where that is. Frog Level is one of our favorite spots."

"Great." He looked at the clock. 9:35. "Will ten o'clock work?"

"That's good. We'll see you there."

A few minutes before ten, Justin walked in and spotted Debra sitting alone at a corner table. She had a blue book in front of her. He walked over and leaned across the table, shaking her proffered hand.

"Hello, Debra. I appreciate you meeting me on such short notice."

"My pleasure. Brad needed to run by the attorney's office, so he just dropped me off."

"What would you like to drink?" he asked, still standing.

"A cappuccino, please," she said, reaching for her clutch.

"I've got," he said. He went up to the counter and ordered. A few minutes later, he returned with a cappuccino for Debra and a latte for himself.

"Thank you," she said as he put the drinks on the table and sat.

Unsure of where to start, he asked, "How did you end up buying a house here?"

Debra told him the story of her and Brad vacationing in the area and deciding to buy a second home here since they liked it so much.

"Where's home?"

"Indianapolis area, which is where I grew up. Brad is from Michigan, but we've lived in Indy every since we got married."

Indianapolis? He thought Brad had said that Debra and Alice had gone to high school together.

Debra seemed to sense his bewilderment. She opened the book she had brought and flipped to a marker. Justin noticed it was a yearbook.

"I apologize for Brad's comment about Alice and I going to the same high school," she said. "I didn't mean for that to come out, especially under the circumstances. But I brought this to explain."

She turned the book around and slid it over to Justin. She pointed to a picture of Debra Hunt.

"This is a much younger and less wrinkled me," she said.

Justin looked at the picture and then back up at Debra. "Younger, maybe, but you're still just as attractive, if I may say so."

"Thank you," Debra said, blushing. She flipped the page and moved her finger to a photo of Payten Thomas.

He studied the picture, not recognizing the young girl at first, though something about her looked vaguely familiar. Before Debra could say anything, he looked up and said, "Alice?"

Justin's heart skipped a beat. The eyes were what did it. The face was rounder and with glasses. The hair was long and blonde. But there was no mistaking her. It was the girl he knew as Alice Miller. His Alice.

He stared out the window to the back deck out by Richland Creek. A few months ago, he and Alice had sat out there eating lunch. Laughing, talking about the wedding.

He rubbed the tears out of his eyes and turned back to the yearbook, flipping to the cover. *The Pinnacle.* Carmel High School. He looked up at Debra for an answer.

"Carmel, Indiana. Right outside Indianapolis."

Justin's head was spinning. "I don't understand."

Debra shook her head and exhaled. "When I first met Alice at the bank, I thought I recognized her. I even asked if she was from Indianapolis. She told me no that she was from Colorado and had never even been to Indianapolis."

Justin looked back down at Alice's picture, staring at him. Then it dawned on him why it looked familiar. It was the picture that Alice carried in her wallet. She had told him it was her deceased cousin.

"I went home," Debra said, "and looked in the yearbook. When I went back to the bank last week, I showed it to Alice. I told her I didn't know why she changed her name, but it wasn't any of my business and that I wouldn't spill the secret. Then, yesterday, Brad blurted out that we went to high school together. I could tell that you were surprised. I apologize if all this disturbs you."

Justin shook his head, trying to comprehend. "This is news to me. She told me that she grew up in Colorado."

"That day in the bank was the first time I'd seen her since high school."

"Are her parents still alive?"

"I don't know. It was a large school. Alice and I weren't that close. After graduation, we went our separate ways. I went to college at IU—Indiana University—in Bloomington. Last I'd heard, she went to school out of state somewhere."

"She did. I met her at the University of North Carolina. She told me that both of her parents died in a plane crash. In Colorado."

"I'm so sorry. I wish I could tell you more, but that's all I know."

Justin was still in a daze as he left Panacea Coffee to go home. At the last minute, he remembered to go by the bank and pick up Alice's things.

He walked in, and Rhonda greeted him with a hug.

"Are you doing okay?" she asked.

He nodded but thought, *not really.* Like most people who asked that, Rhonda was just being polite. She didn't want to know how he tossed and turned at night, unable to shut his thoughts down about Alice. It felt strange being here where she worked.

"Getting by, thanks. I was in town and thought I'd stop by and pick up Alice's things."

"Yes, of course." She led him to Alice's office. All traces of Alice were gone. Two unmarked boxes sat on her desk. He hesitated for a second before entering as if he were intruding somehow.

He stepped over and picked up a box.

"Let me help you," Rhonda said as she grabbed the other one.

They took them out, and he put them in the back seat of the 4Runner.

"Thank you for taking care of this," he said.

"Glad to help," she said, hugging him again. "Let me know if you need anything."

He nodded, got in, and drove away.

At home, Justin took the two boxes inside and sat them on the dining room table.

"What are these?" Karen asked. Seeing the look of confusion on her brother's face, she said, "Are you okay?"

"Alice's things from her office. Rhonda from the bank boxed them up for me." He shook his head. "Remember the tall blonde from the funeral? Debra Foster?"

"Not really. Why?"

"At the funeral, her husband mentioned something about Debra and Alice going to high school together. I met her in town for a cup of coffee."

"So they were high school friends in Colorado?" Karen asked.

"Classmates, but not in Colorado. Not even close. Try Indiana."

"Indiana? I'm confused."

"You're not the only one. Alice Miller didn't grow up in Colorado. She grew up as Payten Thomas, outside of Indianapolis."

"What?"

"My reaction." He showed her the picture he took of Debra's yearbook page showing Alice's picture. Karen studied it and then looked up.

"That's Alice, alright. Why did she change her name?"

"I don't know. When we met, Alice told me her parents had died in a private plane crash in Colorado. She didn't talk about it, and I didn't pursue it. A few weeks ago, I brought it up, and she told me what happened. When I suggested wanting to visit where she grew up, she clammed up and said she never wanted to go back. I snooped around on the internet but couldn't find anything."

Karen shook her head. "Strange. Maybe there's something in the stuff from her office."

They sifted through the first box, finding the usual detritus—pencils, pens, business cards, rubber stamps, paper clips, etc. Nothing personal and nothing that offered any clues.

The second box contained pictures and a variety of documents. There were a couple of photos of him alone. The other images were of him and Alice hiking in various spots. Fond memories of the Alice he knew. He had to stop to brush the tears away.

There was a small stack of papers and folders underneath the picture frames. Karen took half of the stack, and Justin took the rest.

Sandwiched in between two folders, Justin found a manila envelope with Alice's name typed on the front. Stamped below her name was PERSONAL AND CONFIDENTIAL in red ink. Curious, he opened it and removed the two pages. The first item was a copy of a newspaper article, accompanied by what appeared to be a photograph, face down. He turned it over and recognized it as a picture of a gravestone. He looked closer to read the inscription.

Timothy Carver
Beloved Son
September 16, 1998 – April 9, 2009

"Timothy Carver. I know that name," Justin said.

Karen looked up, then back down at the folder she was examining.

Justin picked up the newspaper article. It was from the *Indianapolis Star*. The title read:

Carmel Child Killed by Hit-and-Run Driver

He read it and looked back at the photo, shaking his head. He studied the dates. Payten Thomas, aka Alice Miller, would have been a senior in high school the year Timmy Carver was killed. Could the driver have been Alice?

Karen put down the folder she'd been holding and asked, "Are you okay?"

He passed the photo and article over to her. Not speaking, he waited for her to finish reading.

When she finished, Karen looked at him, wearing a puzzled expression.

Justin held out his hands, palms up. "I don't know." He wanted to finish going through everything and put the boxes out of sight.

Karen read his mind. "You sure you want to do this tonight?"

He nodded. "There's not much left. I want to put the boxes up, clean off the table."

All that remained were the small stack that Karen had been working on and the similar size pile where Justin found the Timothy Carver materials. He looked back at his stack, and near the top, he found another manila envelope. Handwritten on this one was the name Timmy Carver along with what appeared to be map coordinates. He opened it and found a duplicate of the first envelope's contents.

Showing it to Karen, he asked, "Why would she have two copies?"

She shook her head. He set it aside, and they soon finished going through everything. Except for a few pictures and the two manila envelopes, they put everything back in the boxes. He picked up the two envelopes and stared at them.

The only markings on one were Timmy Carver and coordinates—both handwritten. He didn't recognize the handwriting but knew it wasn't Alice's. On the other, Alice was typed. Stamped in red ink below her name was PERSONAL AND CONFIDENTIAL.

It was maddening trying to figure out what was in Alice's mind. He felt like the answer was so close.

"Why? What would make her do it?" he said, trying to choke back the tears. "I don't understand."

Karen shook her head and put her hand over his as he sobbed. "I'm sorry. I will never pretend to understand how someone could end up in so a dark place they can no longer see the light of living. I'm a teacher, not a psychologist, although I'm not sure they have the answer either."

"Why didn't she tell me what was bothering her? She didn't have to do that."

54

The next day, Karen had to go to Asheville. When she left that morning, she told Justin she'd be back before dark. Restless at home alone, he looked again at the two envelopes, trying to put it all together. He had some of the pieces, but a few things were missing. Why two envelopes with the same contents?

Justin went into the bedroom to get a box that contained Alice's personal belongings. He took her phone out and turned it on. He entered her passcode and scrolled to pictures. When he found what he was looking for, he went back out to the dining room. He compared her phone to the envelope with the coordinates written on the outside. The numbers were the same. Latitude and longitude. Degrees, minutes, and seconds. He swiped to the next photo and saw a picture of the healing tree.

He picked up his phone and opened his hiking app. He pulled up what he'd stored for the hike to the healing tree and compared the information to Alice's phone. Same numbers, same picture.

He shook his head. Impossible. Two people, each with a GPS, could stand in the same spot and still get slightly different readings. Looking closer at Alice's phone, he could see that her pictures were photos of a phone. His phone. It was the only way the coordinates could be the same down to the seconds. The coordinates were for the healing tree.

Alice was the driver. That's what she was hiding. It all made sense, now. But somehow, Robert Kendall found out. That's what he used to blackmail Alice. But how?

Justin picked up his phone and called Rhonda at the bank.

"Hey, Justin," Rhonda said when she answered. "What can I do for you?"

"I had a question about Alice's things in the boxes you packed for me."

"Sure. What?"

"I wanted to ask about the two manilla envelopes."

There was a pause, then Rhonda said, "We had to go through everything to remove anything confidential or that related to customer privacy."

"I understand, Rhonda. You were just doing your job. I just wanted to clarify something. You saw what was in them. Both envelopes contained the same thing, right?"

"They did. I remember thinking the contents were kinda . . . odd."

"They were." Justin looked down at the two envelopes. "One envelope had her name typed on the outside, with PERSONAL AND CONFIDENTIAL stamped underneath in red ink. The other had the name 'Timmy Carver' and some numbers handwritten on it," he said.

"The one marked personal and confidential had been placed in the night depository, a month or so ago," Rhonda said.

Justin mentally scrolled through his calendar. That would have been about when somebody had blackmailed Alice.

Rhonda continued. "I remember it was the Wednesday before the Monday when she called in sick. It was the first time she'd ever called in sick."

He nodded, even though he was on the phone. "And the other one?"

Rhonda hesitated so long, Justin thought the call had dropped. "The day she . . . her last day, when she came back from lunch with Bobby Kendall, she had an envelope just like it with her. They didn't have it when they left. I didn't see it again until I was packing up her things. I'm pretty sure it was the same one. I remember she was upset when she got back."

Alice had lunch with Bobby the day she died? That was news. "What was she upset about?"

"I don't know. She wouldn't say," Rhonda said.

"Okay, thanks." He disconnected and sat back. Did Bobby give her the envelope with the coordinates written on it? If so, why?

He called Bobby, but it went straight to voice mail. Justin didn't bother to leave a message.

He picked up the *Indianapolis Star* article and re-read it. The detective's name was Frank Murphy with the Hamilton County Sheriff's Office. Justin wondered if the detective was still with the sheriff's office. He looked up the telephone number and called.

"Hamilton County Sheriff's office, Sargeant Tarrant speaking. May I help you?" the authoritative voice answered.

"I'm trying to get in touch with Detective Frank Murphy," Justin said.

"He's not in. Could I take a message?"

"Yes, please. This is Justin Reeve. I was calling about a hit-and-run case that Detective Murphy handled some years ago. I may have some relevant information." He explained that he was in North Carolina and left his number.

He hung up and called Atohi. "Where are you?"

"At work. Big meeting this morning. We just took a short break before we wrap up, then I'm headed home. Why?"

"Come by the house on your way home. I need to run some things by you."

"Sure. Should be mid-afternoon."

The more Justin thought about everything, the angrier he got. Alice had lied to him, but that he could understand. Somebody had blackmailed her with her past. Bobby had also lied to him and that he couldn't forgive.

He thought about driving to the lab to see Bobby, but he wasn't sure he'd be there. Besides, Justin wanted to talk to Atohi first. He was eating a bite of lunch when his phone buzzed. A 317 area code. Indianapolis.

"Hello," he answered.

"This is Detective Murphy with the Hamilton County Sheriff's Office in Indiana. I was calling for Justin Reeve?"

"This is Justin Reeve. Thanks for getting back to me. I may have information relating to an old case of yours. A hit-and-run fatality. Timothy Carver?"

"I'm listening," Murphy said.

Justin summarized the highlights, skimming over much of the background and ending with Alice's suicide. He gave Debra Foster's name to Murphy.

"I found the picture of Timothy's gravestone and a copy of the newspaper article in Alice's things from her office. This is what prompted my call."

"I have copies in front of me in the case file," Murphy said. He went on to explain that this case had haunted him for the past ten years. "I always thought that the answer was right in front of me, but I just couldn't see it. We had no witnesses, no body shop reports, nothing."

"Are Alice—Payten—are her parents still alive?"

"No. They died in an auto accident less than a year after Timothy died."

"I'm glad," Justin said. "I mean, I'm not glad they're dead but glad they don't have to find out about their daughter."

"I'm curious. When your fiancée was kidnapped, why didn't you call the authorities?"

Justin took a deep breath. "We didn't realize she was missing until late that night. We found her the next morning. It all happened so fast."

"But you said she told you about the blackmail and the subsequent kidnapping."

"She was unharmed and safe. She begged not to get the authorities involved. We didn't hear anything further, so we dropped it. I didn't know anything about this until I saw her classmate at the funeral."

Another lie, Justin thought. He was glad to be on the phone with the detective instead of in person.

"So, no idea of who the kidnapper was?"

"No. When Alice met him, she said he was wearing a mask." Justin shook his head. He didn't know who the kidnapper was. All he knew was that he was dead.

"Interesting, but somebody else's problem. I appreciate your calling. I want to call Ms. Foster and speak to her, but I think we may have enough to close the case and give Timothy's parents closure. I'd figured I was going to carry this one to my grave. If I have any more questions, I'll give you a call."

Justin was sitting on the porch drinking a beer when Atohi drove up. He held up an unopened bottle for Atohi as he walked up the steps.

Atohi took the beer, opened it, and sat. "Where's Karen?"

"She had to go to Asheville. She'll be back later. What was your meeting about this morning?"

"Interesting. Bobby Kendall's starting a foundation to study traditional Cherokee medicine," Atohi said. "We had a tribal council meeting to discuss it."

Justin wrinkled his brow. "Yeah, he came by at the lab yesterday and mentioned something about it. I honestly didn't pay much attention."

"What did you want to discuss?"

"I need to show you something." He went inside to get the envelopes. Back outside, he handed them to Atohi. He sat and watched his friend.

Atohi studied the outside of each envelope, comparing the two. He removed the contents of each, then looked at the photo and read the article. When he finished, he looked up at Justin with a puzzled expression.

Justin said, "You won't believe it. This is going to take a while. I'll get us another beer and explain."

He returned with two beers, handing one to Atohi as he sat. He took a long drink before he launched into the story.

"Alice grew up in Carmel, Indiana, not Colorado. She grew up as Payten Thomas. Sometime after graduating from high school and Timothy Carver's death, she changed her name to Alice Miller and moved to North Carolina, where I met her. To my knowledge, her parents didn't die in a plane crash in Colorado."

"Jesus. How long have you known this?"

"Just recently. The week the tree got cut down, I figured out that her parents didn't die in a plane crash in Colorado. There was no record of it anywhere. The rest surfaced only yesterday."

He shared the story about Debra Foster and how he came to find out about Alice's name change. He nodded toward the material Atohi had.

"After meeting Debra, I picked up Alice's things from the bank. Karen and I went through everything. That's when I found the article and photo."

Atohi looked down at the article and then back up at Justin. "You think that Alice was the driver?"

"I'm afraid so. Look at the dates. Why else would she change her name and moved to North Carolina? And the story about her parents?"

He told Atohi about talking to the detective in Indiana. "The case had never been closed. Her parents are dead, but they died in a car wreck a year after she moved. He's going to check the records on her name change and interview some of her classmates, but he seems to agree that Alice was the driver."

"Why was this in her desk?" Atohi asked.

"I think it's what the Kendalls were using to blackmail her." Justin told him what he'd learned about the two envelopes and his theory.

"Have you talked to Bobby?"

Justin shook his head. "Not yet. I wanted to talk to you first." An idea occurred to him.

"Tell me more about his foundation."

"He's offered to fund a foundation for the study of traditional Cherokee medicine. The tribe would run it, and they want Mary to head it up."

"What do you mean, fund it?"

"Bearant's donating the lab building as a gift to the community since they're closing the facility. Bobby's donating a generous endowment to sustain it in perpetuity."

Justin cocked his head. Blood money. Three people were dead, along with the healing tree. Bobby was trying to ease his guilty conscience. Maybe the Cherokee could turn it to their advantage.

"What's Bobby's involvement?"

Atohi shook his head. "None. Upon signing the papers Thursday, the assets would be transferred to the Cherokee tribe. He doesn't even have a seat on the board. Our attorneys are reviewing the draft of the agreement."

"Can we talk to Mary? Before they sign?"

55

Later that evening, when they got to Atohi's, Mary's car was in the drive. Everyone was sitting on the porch.

"Looks like a party," Justin said as he and Karen walked up.

They exchanged hugs, and Tsula asked what they were drinking. She left to get drinks, and as soon as she returned, they sat.

Over drinks and snacks, Mary described the flurry of events over the past few days. Last week, Bobby Kendall had asked to meet, surprising her with the idea of establishing a foundation for the study of traditional Cherokee medicine. He wanted her to act as liaison with the tribe to get approval for the plan.

She was shocked to learn that he had negotiated the lab building's gift for the foundation. He was also willing to fund the operations with a generous endowment.

The culmination was establishing the Kendall Institute for Cherokee Medicine, owned and operated by the Eastern Band of Cherokee Indians. Their charter is to study ancient and contemporary Cherokee healing remedies and search for new ones such as the healing tree.

"I hope you didn't tell him about the greenhouse," Justin said.

"Absolutely not. That is, and will continue to be, a closely held secret."

"What about the management structure? What's Bobby's involvement? Is the funding adequate, and what strings are attached?"

"Our attorney reviewed the agreement carefully. It is funded with a generous endowment, sufficient to maintain operation in perpetuity. Bobby Kendall has nothing to do with the Institute, not even a board position. The only stipulation is that it be named the Kendall Institute and be operated by the Eastern Band of Cherokee Indians, with a board appointed by the tribe. The principal chief asked me to be the executive director. As you know from Atohi, we presented this at a tribal council meeting yesterday, where it was unanimously approved."

Justin turned to Tsula, who had been quiet to this point. "What do you think?"

Tsula laughed. "You know me. I was initially suspicious. But after talking with Mother, she convinced me that it's legit. I think it's a great thing for our people."

Atohi said, "I had my doubts too, considering the source. But I trust Mary. The fact that the council unanimously approved it says a lot. As she can tell you, they seldom agree on anything."

Justin turned back to Mary. "Does the agreement specifically address any future royalties that might result from any of the Institute's work?"

"Interesting that you should ask. The initial draft gave Bearant the right of first refusal to acquire anything developed by the Institute. Our attorney caught that and changed it to give ownership to the Institute specifically. With the lab closing, what are your plans?" she asked Justin.

He shook his head. "I haven't had a chance to think about it. I don't want to move to California. But I'll probably stay with Bearant until I can find a position elsewhere."

Mary said, "What if there was something here?"

"Like what?"

"Come to work at the Institute. As a scientist. You could help me build the staff."

Justin looked over at Karen, who was grinning from ear to ear.

"Oh my gosh, that's great," she said. "You wouldn't have to leave."

"And I'd still have someone to go hiking and drink beer with," Atohi said, smiling.

"Mom," Tsula said. "That's awesome. You'll be perfect for the job."

Justin looked at everyone, speechless. He was overwhelmed.

"I don't know what to say. Of course, I'd love to be a part of it." He could continue his research on the healing tree. And other plants. Unencumbered by corporate greed. He wondered. Who would be the principal scientist? Certainly not him—he didn't have the experience—but who.

"Have you thought about who would oversee the research?" he asked.

"We didn't get that far. I want to get a world-class scientist with the requisite credentials and reputation. Someone like a Dr. Hadley, but I don't think we could afford him."

Justin grinned. "You may be surprised. Let me talk to him."

"Seriously?"

He nodded. "I think there's a good chance he might be interested."

"Of course," Mary said. "He'd be ideal. But let me know what his salary requirements are. I'm worried that he's out of our price range."

"I'll talk to him in the morning."

Karen talked the entire way home, thrilled that Justin would be staying in the area.

"Things worked out," she said. "I was worried about what you were going to do, and I certainly wasn't looking forward to you moving to California. The Smokies are your home, always have been. You belong here. You could do a lot of good, and I'm excited that you'll have that opportunity."

He chuckled. "It is home. I wasn't excited about moving, either. Now, if I can persuade Dr. Hadley."

When they got home, Justin saw the two envelopes sitting on the dining room table. His buoyant mood darkened.

He picked up the two envelopes and stared at them. So much heartache represented inside. He'd never understand why Alice wouldn't come to him. And why she'd take her own life. He put them back in the box and moved it to a hall closet with her things.

Justin went over to the piano, lifted the bench seat, and rummaged through the contents to find a particular piece of music.

When he found what he was looking for, he placed it above the keyboard and went through a few scales to loosen up. Karen came over and sat next to him on the bench. When she saw what he was going to play, she smiled.

"I haven't heard you play this in a long time," she said.

"I haven't played it in a long time," he said. "I'm probably rusty."

He launched into *Cristofori's Dream* by David Lanz. It was a beautiful piece, with a haunting melody, perfect for his mood. Midway through, he stole a glance at Karen. Her eyes were shut, consumed by the song.

When he precisely played the last notes, he closed his eyes while they sat, not wanting to break the spell.

"That was beautiful," Karen said at last. "I'd forgotten how well you play. Dad would be proud."

Justin teared up. "It is a beautiful song. You'd think I wouldn't need the music after all the times I've played it."

56

Wednesday morning, Justin awoke, thinking about his upcoming conversation with the professor. He'd tossed and turned all night, thinking about the conversation with Mary Richardson.

He drove to the lab, rehearsing his pitch to the professor. When he got to the lab, he was relieved to see that Bobby's Corvette wasn't in its parking spot. Justin parked and went straight to Hadley's office.

The professor had his back to the door, staring at his computer screen.

"Got a minute?" Justin said, tapping on the open door. Not waiting for an answer, he walked in and sat.

Hadley looked up from his computer. "Yes?"

"I'm sure you've heard about the foundation that Bobby Kendall is starting."

"I may be old and forgetful, but I do try to keep up with what is going on relative to the lab."

Justin chuckled. His mentor didn't miss a thing. "Then I'm sure you know the Kendall Institute for Cherokee Medicine's mission is to study ancient and contemporary Cherokee healing remedies. To confirm their efficacy or debunk the myths."

Hadley nodded.

"Are you aware that Mary Richardson is going to be the executive director?"

Hadley was surprised and shook his head.

Justin smiled, amused to be the one to tell him. "I had dinner with her last night. She offered me a job."

Hadley leaned back in his chair. "Excellent. I'm glad for you."

"Thank you, but I'm here to talk you into coming to the Institute." Justin proceeded to give his concise pitch.

After he finished, Hadley stroked his beard. "Do you trust Bobby Kendall?"

Justin laughed. "Of course not. But as far as the Institute is concerned, trusting him isn't a requirement. The tribe's attorney has reviewed the agreement thoroughly. The Institute is adequately funded—in perpetuity, operated and managed by the Cherokee tribe. Bobby doesn't have a seat on the board, and he can't control funding. He will transfer the assets upon closing, which is scheduled for tomorrow morning. Oh, and did I mention, the Institute retains all rights and ownership to anything developed by them?"

Hadley chuckled. "How clever. Good for them. By the way, I respect what you did with Karen and HT67. And I do trust you." He paused and shifted in his seat.

Justin panicked at the hesitation and started to open his mouth to speak.

"Count me in," Hadley said, grinning.

Justin exhaled, realizing the professor had done that deliberately. "You had me going for a minute," he said as he rose to leave. "I'll call Mary on my way out and let her know."

As he turned, he realized that he'd forgotten to ask Hadley's salary requirements. He took a deep breath and faced Hadley. "I almost forgot. She'll want to know what kind of salary you're expecting. She's concerned—"

Hadley held up his hand, interrupting Justin. "Not an issue. Tell her I will be content with whatever they have budgeted."

Justin's mouth dropped open. The man standing in front of him could waltz into any pharmaceutical firm in the world, and they'd be happy to pay him any amount he named.

The professor raised his bushy eyebrows and asked, "Is there anything else? If not, I have work to do."

57

Thursday morning, Justin waited anxiously for Mary's call. She said she'd call as soon as they signed the agreement and confirmed the transfer of assets.

"Will you quit pacing?" Karen said, watching Justin go back and forth in the living room. "Play the piano. Put some music on. Anything but what you're doing."

"Sorry," he said. "I keep thinking something's going to happen to derail it."

He jumped when his phone rang. He looked at Karen, then picked it up. He was afraid to see who was calling. Mary Richardson.

"Hello?" he said, holding his breath.

"It's done," Mary said. "Signed, sealed, and delivered."

"Thanks, Mary." He started to disconnect, but Mary continued.

"There's something else I need to tell you. I wanted to wait until after we transferred the funds."

Justin was curious. "What?"

Mary cleared her throat. "We've found another tree."

"What?" Justin couldn't believe what he was hearing. "Another healing tree?"

"Several. All on the Boundary. Not that far from the one you found."

"But . . . when?"

"We've been looking ever since you first found it, but with no success. We didn't find it until last week."

She didn't tell him. Neither did Atohi and Tsula. They all knew. And they didn't trust him.

"Please understand. I was afraid to take a chance on word getting out before Bobby signed the papers for the Institute."

Justin was wounded. The Cherokee didn't trust him, even though Mary herself had told him and Alice they were family. Then, he remembered Alice's words from that night on Atohi's porch.

> *The Cherokee have suffered greatly. Their lack of trust isn't personal. Surely, you can understand their reluctance? Any secrets would eventually be leaked to other whites who would then find ways to exploit them.*

Alice was right. Justin thought about John Ross, the blue-eyed son of a Scottish father and a mother who was only one-fourth Cherokee. Yet, he was beloved and the longest-serving principal chief.

The Institute was for the Cherokee. And for Alice.

"I understand, Mary. You did what you needed to do. Thank you."

"And you have done great things for us, for which we will be forever grateful. I'm sorry that we didn't find out before Alice's passing. If we had, I would've told you, and maybe things would've been different."

After he disconnected, Karen came over. "Everything okay?"

He nodded. "The agreement's been signed."

Karen hugged him. "Congratulations. But why so glum. What was that about another healing tree?"

He looked at his sister, also his family. Then, he shook his head. "She said she hoped to find another healing tree. We all do."

Karen smiled. "Hopefully, you will."

"Thanks, sis."

Karen sighed. "I wish we could celebrate, but I need to head on out. Next time—my treat. I'll call you as soon as I get home."

Justin hated to see her go. "Be careful. Love you."

"Love you, too. Call me if you need me."

He walked her out to her car and watched as she drove away. One final piece of business remaining. Justin went back inside to call Bobby.

That afternoon, he drove to meet Bobby at Frog Level. Mary Ann was at the bar when he walked in, carrying a thin manilla envelope.

"Hey," she said, already pouring him a Nutty Brunette. "Bobby's outside. Work?" she said, looking at the envelope.

He put the envelope on the bar. "Yeah. Would you mind hanging on to this? It's a surprise for Bobby, and I don't want him to see it just yet."

"Sure," she said, sliding the beer over to him and putting the envelope underneath the bar.

He took a sip of his beer and headed outside.

Bobby was sitting down by the creek, with his back to the door.

"Hey," Justin asked as he walked up behind him.

Bobby turned to see him. "Hey. I was surprised you called."

Justin sat. "I still like the beer. Regardless of who owns the place," he said with a thin smile.

Bobby returned the smile. "I don't own it yet. End of the month. I hope you keep coming in. How are you doing?"

"Struggling. Day by day."

"It's going to take time." Bobby held up his glass. "Congratulations. Mary Richardson told me you're coming to work with her."

Justin tipped his glass. "Thanks."

"You don't sound happy. What's bothering you?"

"It's been a long two weeks. I keep thinking there's something I could've done."

Bobby shook his head. "You've got to quit beating up on yourself. There's no way you could've known."

"I should've known something wasn't right. The signs were there." Justin took a long drink of his beer. "I found out that her parents didn't die in a plane crash in Colorado."

"Really?"

"She didn't even grow up in Colorado. I found out afterward that she changed her name. She grew up as Payten Thomas. In Carmel, a suburb of Indianapolis."

They both were quiet for a long time.

"How did you find out?" Bobby asked in a quiet tone.

"A woman at the funeral. Alice had helped her and her husband with a mortgage on a second home here. Her husband let it slip that she and Alice had gone to high school together. I met with her Monday, and she showed me their yearbook. She'd recognized Alice, but Alice denied knowing her, denied ever having been to Indianapolis. The woman looked her up in the yearbook and confronted her. She told Alice that her secret was safe, which it was until her husband stepped into a pile of crap."

Bobby chugged the rest of his beer, set the glass on the table, and stood. "I need to piss."

Justin gave Bobby a head start, then went inside to retrieve the envelope and order another round. He went back outside, and as Bobby returned to the table, Mary Ann appeared with two fresh beers.

"Justin told me you needed another round," she said as she sat the full glasses on the table and picked up the empties.

"Thanks," Justin said.

Bobby noticed the manila envelope on the table, the handwriting facing up. "What's that?" he asked.

Justin slid the envelope over to him. "I was hoping you could tell me."

Bobby studied the handwriting, then opened the envelope, never raising his eyes to Justin. He pulled out the gravestone photo and newspaper article. After staring at them, he looked up at Justin.

"Where'd you get this?"

Justin glared at him hard. "It was in Alice's desk." He paused to let the words register, then continued. "You didn't tell me you had lunch with her. Rhonda said she had this with her when she came back."

Bobby's eyes shifted away as he took a long drink from his glass. "I found it in my father's desk after the funeral. I gave it to Alice. She made me promise not to tell you."

His eyes still fixed on Bobby, Justin tapped on the gravestone photo.

"Timmy Carver. The name that I asked you about. You denied knowing anything about it."

Bobby didn't answer.

"You knew who it was, didn't you?" asked Justin

"Yeah, but she begged me not to—"

Justin slammed his fist on the table hard enough to slosh beer out of both glasses.

"You sorry piece of shit. Don't you dare blame Alice. You found it in your father's desk because that's what he used to blackmail her. And then you used it to get her over to your house that night."

Bobby opened his mouth to speak but shut it just as quickly when he saw Justin rise.

"Be glad that I wanted to meet you here instead of somewhere in a dark alley," Justin said, then spun and walked away.

* * *

That afternoon, Justin and Atohi sat on Justin's porch, each of them with a beer. Justin had told him about his encounter with Bobby.

"I'm sorry," Atohi said. "I know he'd been a friend of yours for a long time."

"I just wish I'd picked up on it sooner. Maybe I could've done something, stopped her."

After a long period of silence, Atohi said, "I'm sorry about Alice. The whole thing is pretty bizarre."

"The Indianapolis detective called back. He'd finished his investigation. The official conclusion is that Alice was the driver. Carver's parents were relieved to get closure. He's closing the case."

"We did the right thing, then."

"In more ways than one. You know, the thing is, I forgive her for Timothy Carver. We all make mistakes, and we all have secrets."

"Alice taking her own life is not your fault. You have to forgive yourself, brother. Sometimes, that's the hardest person to forgive."

They sat in comfortable silence, as only two good friends can do.

Atohi nodded, then took a swallow. "What now?"

"Looks like I'll be staying around here, which is a good thing. Hadley's coming on board with the Institute. I'm anxious to get back on track with the healing tree extract. I guess we'll have to come up with a new name since HT67 is part of Nuran's records."

Atohi finished his beer and stood. "I need to get home."

Justin rose, and they embraced. "Thanks. For everything."

"We'll have you over soon," Atohi said. "Take it easy."

After Atohi drove away, Justin went inside. The emptiness was overwhelming. He looked over at the new couch, thinking about Alice, then walked over to the piano and sat.

He opened the fallboard and stared at the keys, his hands in his lap. He started to get the sheet music out and decided he didn't want it. Without even warming up, he launched directly into Oscar Robertson's *Hymn to Freedom,* letting his fingers find the keys and playing from the heart. It sounded different than any other time he'd ever played it.

When he finished, he smiled. It sounded the way his dad would have played it.

Acknowledgments

As always, I remain indebted to many others for their support in my writing journey.

Special thanks to Chuck Dietrich—friend, neighbor, and hiking buddy. One day while hiking in the Great Smoky Mountains National Park, he suggested the premise. By the end of our hike, I'd fleshed out the entire novel.

Thanks to the following people for taking the time to read my manuscript and offer much-appreciated advice: Otis Scarbary, Mary Jo Burkhalter Persons, Cindy Deane, Donna Jennings, Diann Schindler, Jo Gilley, Linda Whitaker, and Kim DeWitt.

I am grateful for Heather Whitaker as an editor and good friend. Her tutelage continues to be priceless.

Thanks to Kieran Sultan, M.D., for help with pathology questions.

Carl Graves has done all of my covers and continues to amaze me.

Last, thanks to my wife, June, for continuing to support my writing habit. I couldn't do it without you.

Any mistakes that remain are mine.

Made in the USA
Monee, IL
18 January 2022